GW00500032

HEAR MY TRAIN A COMIN'

Popular Music History

Series Editor: Alyn Shipton, Royal Academy of Music, London.

This series publishes books that challenge established orthodoxies in popular music studies, examine the formation and dissolution of canons, interrogate histories of genres, focus on previously neglected forms, or engage in archaeologies of popular music.

Published

An Unholy Row: Jazz in Britain and its Audience, 1945–1960
Dave Gelly

Being Prez: The Life and Music of Lester Young
Dave Gelly

Bill Russell and the New Orleans Jazz Revival
Ray Smith and Mike Pointon

Chasin' the Bird: The Life and Legacy of Charlie Parker
Brian Priestley

Handful of Keys: Conversations with Thirty Jazz Pianists
Alyn Shipton

Jazz Me Blues: The Autobiography of Chris Barber
Chris Barber with Alyn Shipton

Jazz Visions: Lennie Tristano and His Legacy
Peter Ind

Lee Morgan: His Life, Music and Culture
Tom Perchard

Lionel Richie: Hello
Sharon Davis

Mosaics: The Life and Works of Graham Collier
Duncan Heining

Mr P.C.: The Life and Music of Paul Chambers
Rob Palmer

Out of the Long Dark: The Life of Ian Carr
Alyn Shipton

Rufus Wainwright
Katherine Williams

Scouse Pop
Paul Skillen

Soul Unsung: Reflections on the Band in Black Popular Music
Kevin Le Gendre

The Godfather of British Jazz: The Life and Music of Stan Tracey
Clark Tracey

The History of European Jazz: The Music, Musicians and Audience in Context
Edited by Francesco Martinelli

The Last Miles: The Music of Miles Davis, 1980–1991
George Cole

The Long Shadow of the Little Giant (second edition): The Life, Work and Legacy of Tubby Hayes
Simon Spillett

The Ultimate Guide to Great Reggae: The Complete Story of Reggae Told through its Greatest Songs, Famous and Forgotten
Michael Garnice

This is Hip: The Life of Mark Murphy
Peter Jones

Trad Dads, Dirty Boppers and Free Fusioneers: A History of British Jazz, 1960–1975
Duncan Heining

Hear My Train A Comin'

The Songs of Jimi Hendrix

Kevin Le Gendre

SHEFFIELD UK BRISTOL CT

Published by Equinox Publishing Ltd

UK: Office 415, The Workstation, 15 Paternoster Row, Sheffield, South Yorkshire, S1 2BX
USA: ISD, 70 Enterprise Drive, Bristol, CT 06010

www.equinoxpub.com

First published 2020

British Library Cataloguing-in-Publication Data
A catalogue record for this book is available from the British Library.

ISBN-13 978 1 80050 013 6 (hardback)
978 1 80050 014 3 (ePDF)

Library of Congress Cataloging-in-Publication Data
Names: Le Gendre, Kevin, author.
Title: Hear my train a comin' : the songs of Jimi Hendrix / Kevin Le Gendre.
Description: Bristol : Equinox Publishing Ltd, 2020. | Series: Popular music history | Includes bibliographical references and index. | Summary: "This book investigates the artist's immense creativity, and the intriguing relationship he had with the art of song, a platform for a multitude of ideas and improvisation"-- Provided by publisher.
Identifiers: LCCN 2020022215 (print) | LCCN 2020022216 (ebook) | ISBN 9781800500136 (hardback) | ISBN 9781800500143 (ebook)
Subjects: LCSH: Hendrix, Jimi--Criticism and interpretation. | Rock music--1961-1970--History and criticism. | African Americans--Music--History and criticism.
Classification: LCC ML410.H476 L45 2020 (print) | LCC ML410.H476 (ebook) | DDC 782.42166092--dc23
LC record available at https://lccn.loc.gov/2020022215
LC ebook record available at https://lccn.loc.gov/2020022216

Typeset by S.J.I. Services, New Delhi, India

For whoever plays and feels the freakish blues.

Contents

Introduction 1

Part 1: The Song and Jimi Hendrix 9

Part 2: The Songs of Jimi Hendrix 39

Part 3: The Songs from Jimi Hendrix 187

Notes 215

Bibliography 219

Index 220

Introduction

More than a bird on a wire

Competition between artists appeals greatly to both punters and arbiters of good taste. One act has to be better than the other so that fans and media alike can justify their allegiances and judgments, respectively, whether the choice is Duke or Count, Beatles or Stones, Wiley or Dizzee. Polls and award shows underpin the partisan parade with substantial fringe benefits. Grammys and Mercurys are supposed to boost the career of highly talented individuals who should be remunerated as well as celebrated.

Several statuettes were given to Jimi Hendrix in his lifetime. In 1967 he was voted Pop Musician of The Year by the readers of *Melody Maker*, one of Britain's key cultural barometers of the post-war era, while the influential American magazine *Rolling Stone*, which would be decisive in both reflecting and shaping tastes of a new generation of listeners who lived through the important phenomena of the hippie, the acid trip, and other rituals of the burgeoning counter culture, named him Performer of The Year in 1968, no doubt on account of the formidable reputation he carved out on stage following massive bouts of touring in America and Europe. The following year lesser-known publications such as *Disc & Music Echo* declared him to be World Top Musician, while in 1970 *Guitar Player* crowned him Rock Guitarist of The Year.

Having said that, since Hendrix's death the trophies have turned from a stream to a raging torrent. Inductions into the Rock & Roll Hall of Fame and the UK Music Hall of Fame dovetail with inclusion on numerous lists of Greatest Albums of All Time and singles, as well as commemorations that place Hendrix in the rarefied company of social activists and political leaders. There is a Jimi Hendrix Day in his hometown of Seattle, Washington and there was a United States Postal Service stamp in his honour.

All of which means Hendrix has come to represent a kind of ineffable force beyond his stature as a musician. Although the word is so overused it has seen its currency severely fall over the years, *cool* is still greatly synonymous with Hendrix insofar as the very mention of his name evokes much more than music. First and foremost there is colour, or rather a broad spectrum of hues, the brilliant dazzle of the trademark flamboyant stage outfits that made it impossible not to notice him amid the maelstrom of unprecedented sounds he was able to draw from a guitar and assortment of state-of-the-art accessories. But there is also Hendrix the sex symbol, the embodiment of erotic energy if not crude provocation that makes him worthy of a seat at the same table, or place in the bedroom, or jail cell if certain moral custodians have their way, as his predecessor and successor, Little Richard and Prince, respectively.

Hendrix was very much an audio-visual phenomenon. Creator of extraordinary music, he also had an image and performance skills that made him the epitome of the artist whose charisma took him into the realm of the otherworldly super-being liable to inspire a degree of hero worship that endures beyond any earthly existence, so that they eventually become an avatar on to which fantasies as well as devotion can be lavished. The idea of Hendrix, as *something* unique as well as somebody special who appears infrequently in the history of art, has simply grown over time, certainly as his music has been more widely used in mass media, from adverts to films, and even recruitment ads for physics teachers in secondary schools, to convey the sense of a preternatural entity standing at the crossroads of science and technology as well as poetry and music. If legendary black bluesmen sold their souls for the best tunes then Hendrix seems to have traded his for a supply of ageless weird and wonderful sounds.

Never mind The Experience; Jimi Hendrix has become *an experience*, a virtual rolling theme park in cyber space, as well as the leader of a defining act in pop history. The abundance of clips and articles online strengthen the presence of Hendrix on land, for you can admire his monochrome portrait on a shop shutter in Deptford high street, south London and spot an abbreviation of one of his great quotables in the neon-lit name of a bar in Crouch End at the other end of town. It is called Kiss The Sky.

Drop into the basement of a café in Helsinki run by the lauded Finnish filmmakers the Karismaki brothers and you'll see a starry photo of Hendrix, while a noble statue of the guitarist stands on the Isle of Wight, scene of one of his I-was-there concerts.

In September 1997 I attended the unveiling of the blue plaque in Hendrix's name at 23 Brook Street, Mayfair, central London, the top-floor flat he shared with his then girlfriend Kathy Etchingham in 1968, and found it impossible not to be buoyed by the waves of excitement that coursed through a fairly sizeable crowd assembled in front of rock dignitaries such as Noel Redding, his former bandmate, and Pete Townshend, his famous peer, as well as

Etchingham. The magnitude of the occasion was not lost on Hendrix's loyal fanbase, for his was now dubbed the first ever *rock & roll plaque*.

An exponent of the kind of popular culture that was once not readily accepted by members of the British establishment who were particularly averse to the sturm and drang of electric guitars being granted a seat at the table of respectability was indeed newsworthy, above all because that resistance to high decibel concerts has still not entirely died down. Even more so if one frames Hendrix as an African-American who declared that his religion was electric. On the wall of the adjoining building is a blue plaque for German-British composer George Frideric Handel. Both names are thus brought to the attention of any curious passerby who may be on their way to enjoy some high-end retail therapy in one of London's most chic quarters. Hendrix's plaque stands above the awning for posh perfumier Jo Malone, supplier of pomegranate noir cologne *entre autres*, and Handel's looks down on Aspinal, the emporium where upscale denizens splash out on luxury jewellery and men's and women's accessories made of soft Italian calf leather, for those who insist on refinement at all costs.

That Hendrix's name now nestles in the heart of grand exclusivity is ironic, given that he was born into modest circumstances, and that the early part of his life as a musician was precarious rather than stable. In the worst-case scenario there was exploitation by promoters or club owners which led to unedifying experiences on the road that would have appalled some of the well-to-do Londoners and tourists who breeze past his former residence on a daily basis, maybe not realizing that the name for an Aspinal bag, the "hobo", also means a homeless wayfarer. This was an apt description for a young Hendrix, and many of his predecessors, peers and successors who have had to (and continue) to struggle to make their commercial breakthrough.

With its neat circular design and clear lettering, the accolade to Hendrix in Mayfair is discreet rather than dazzling. No picture or sculpture of the incumbent accompanies the succinct occupation "Guitarist and songwriter". The blue plaque does not show a black man. Given the worldwide pervasion of his distinctive image on a plethora of merchandising, from posters and dolls to mugs and T-shirts, chances are that Hendrix's ethnicity does not need to be spelled out, as can also be said of The Beatles.

However, the Hendrix blue plaque does serve as a reminder of the complex web of relationships that Britain has long had with people of colour from around the world, particularly its former colonies such as America, the West Indies, India and Africa. If Hendrix and Handel, whose legacies are further enjoined and consolidated in the museum, Handel & Hendrix in London, form an inspiring blue plaque odd couple then a few miles away at 18 Melbury Road, Kensington there is another to cast one's eye upon: Cetshwayo, king of the Zulus (c. 1832–1884) and pre-Raphaelite painter William Holman Hunt (1827–1910). Their lives are linked through each having lived in the aforesaid property at different times. Cetsh famously defeated the British army at the battle of Isandlwana in South Africa. Hendrix, a former member of the U.S. Airborne division who sometimes matched his vibrant colours and non-regulation Afro with a hussar's jacket purchased from a shop called I Was Lord Kitchener's Valet, conquered British hearts and minds by way of the guitar rather than the gun. He also made a number of provocative musical statements on the ghastly horrors of war.

Much as Hendrix remains connected in varying degrees to identity politics, he is still defined first and foremost by rock. Millions of people across several generations already have a strong, if not intense relationship with his recordings and – for those lucky enough to be born at the right time – the many concerts he performed. Fandom was already prevalent in his day yet the idea of artist as super-being has scaled new heights since, facilitated firstly by the video age and then YouTube and the tools of social media, which make it possible to engage in depth with any designated hero.

Many know something about Jimi. The mere mention of his first name, that two-syllable handle with the unconventional orthography, is liable to bring forth a great flood of adulation if not devotion. To feed all hungry souls there are countless hours of audio and video of Hendrix floating in the digital ocean on which the bulk of us surf in our daily lives. From concert footage, to commentary on guitars and equipment, to tutorials that enable you to play just about every identifiable lick in his songbook, to testimonies of bandmates, lovers and fans, there is no end of material to satisfy the curiosity of both casual observer coming to his music for the first time and the paid-up fan who wishes to supplement what is probably already considerable knowledge.

For all the expansion of Jimidata, a contracted definition of Hendrix often still takes precedence. Like many complex characters he can be reduced to a simplified version of himself, which is an irksome possibility in a time-poor, fast-moving modern world. One of the more 'out there' stories that emerged on the BBC news website, uploaded on 12 December 2019,[1] the day the UK girded its loins for a long day's journey into night known as a general election, concerned Hendrix and British avian history.

Jimi Hendrix cleared of blame for UK parakeet release. Next to a colour photograph of the species in question, resplendent in lime-green plumage and crimson beak there is a monochrome still of Hendrix, abundant black afro like a crest against the sky, white Strat held aloft as he looks moodily out to what one imagines is a rapturous festival crowd. Despite the stark difference in brightness between the two images there is an implied affinity between man and beast insofar as both are exotic birds of paradise, the latter forever associated with the flourish in fashion of the swinging 60s. The piece states that Hendrix freed a pair of the winged wonders in Carnaby Street, Soho, central London, erstwhile summit of global hipness. In many ways the article is a perfect illustration of celebrity as curiosity fodder.

Attach a "name" to a story and the currency instantly increases, even if the premise of the reporting is woefully flimsy. Here the melodramatic headline posits that the event was significant in some way, especially as Hendrix is absolved of guilt, as if he had been formally charged with a crime, presumably that of endangering the great British public by exposing it to airborne diseases or blinding hues to match his own array of dazzling fabrics and the technicolour fantasia evoked in several of his songs.

Even more interesting is the description of Hendrix. He is seen playing guitar but he is not described as a musician in the single line of the text devoted to him. He is a *rock star* rather than a rock artist – which is deeply allegorical. As much as the core meaning of the term is a musician, a singer or player, in a specific genre, the overriding connotation is vividly behavioural. What immediately springs to mind is outrageous hedonism, a rollercoaster lifestyle in which the peaks are usually provided by substance abuse and an abundance of groupies, something that is not so casually consigned to high jinks in a post-MeToo world where the age of the girl in question is an issue, and the extremes of self-indulgence that materialize in the debris of wrecked hotel rooms and the not-so-cool misery of drying out after raising hell. There was a time when unchecked sexual conquest – for male superstars, obviously – as well as a run-in with the law, complete with grim mug shot after a bust, only strengthened the credentials needed to be taken seriously as a pop bad boy. All of which sells records.

Hendrix did not choose abstinence. The deep sorrow with which Etchingham recalled seeing a bag of white powder and a handgun in his suite during their very last meeting makes it clear that there were destructive forces in the artist's life, as well as manipulative individuals around him, from whom he really should have been shielded. However, skirting on the edge of illegal activity, if not associating with shadowy figures of the underworld, simply adds to the intoxicating mystique that some devotees and authors, as many a Sinatraphile will attest, tend to find irresistible.

Hagiography can soon turn into mythology from which it can become easy to lose sight of the most enduring creative achievements of the subject in question. The life of Jimi Hendrix is nothing if not enthralling, and it makes a whole lot of sense for biographies that distil truths from hearsay to be written. Yet there is still a real danger that the artistry can end up being sacrificed on the altar of sensationalism, or, as the parakeet dispatch demonstrates, puerile trivia probably best left blowin' in the wind.

Hear My Train A Comin': The Songs of Jimi Hendrix is an earnest attempt to shine a light on the musical achievements of Jimi Hendrix. It is not a comprehensive exploration of his childhood, formative years and *heure de gloire* following his journey from America to Britain, and back again in triumph, then back yet again in tragedy. That has already been done several times, providing a wealth of factual information that has proved essential for our understanding of who Hendrix was and how he negotiated the slings and arrows of both his outrageous talent and a world of fame that could take as much as it gave, perhaps more of the former than the latter.

Because of the generous and illuminating recollections of Hendrix's gifted former collaborators such as drummer Mitch Mitchell, bass guitarist Billy Cox and engineer Eddie Kramer, many of whose insights have been made available on the official reissues of *Are You Experienced?*, *Axis: Bold As Love*, *Electric Ladyland* and *Band of Gypsys*, the four albums recorded between 1967 and 1969 that constitute the spine of Hendrix's discography, the interested if not committed listener can now get close enough to the music in question to feel that they have a handle on the making of it. This is a reason to be cheerful.

My primary goal is to explore Hendrix as a creative phenomenon by placing his key songs under the microscope in order to elucidate his methodology and pinpoint his craftsmanship, rather than providing a blow-by-blow account of every studio date and stage show. I trawl liberally through his output. The artist was able to produce a cornucopia of fine songs in an action-packed 18-month period to the extent that his repertoire stands as a whole entity rather than a string of statements spread out over a longer period. Pieces such as 'Purple Haze', 'Crosstown Traffic', 'Little Wing', 'All Along The Watchtower' and 'Machine Gun' reflect a brilliant mind working at full capacity.

There are recurrent patterns and continuities in his creative process that are best decoded across *groupings* of songs. He also had range, and excelled on the 3-minute radio-friendly piece as well as the extended suite that could run to some 15 minutes. The spectrum is very wide. There is Hendrix reining in and Hendrix stretching out.

Why his compositions have endured is of the greatest interest to me because they have enormous richness in both form and content. Hendrix also provides a priceless opportunity to discuss the history of black music, and how he carved his own unique place within it. Indeed the relationship that he had with deeply rooted traditions such as the blues, as well as the more existential notion of what constitutes old and new music, is an intriguing aspect of Hendrix's aesthetic insofar as it questions our own understanding of the provenance of originality and its subsequent evolution.

When appropriate I supplement analysis of Hendrix's music with biographical detail, above all quotes from the artist himself, who consented to give many interviews in which he shared opinions on his work and a wide range of other subjects. He was a strong, bold personality whose many statements were pithy and thought provoking, often with a mischievous sense of humour, which surfaced in a number of his texts as well as the ear-catching comments he would make both on and off stage.

Hear My Train A Comin' comprises three sections in order to provide the relevant background and analysis for the task. *Part I: The Song and Jimi Hendrix* considers the artist in his pre-fame years in order to drill down into his own feelings of playing the music of others, for the most part in a tightly regimented framework that also involved stagecraft and performance. One of the central themes here is song as a vehicle for visual flair as well as aural richness, and how Hendrix managed to take a personal approach to cultural norms that he eventually found to be too restrictive. Racial politics is also an attendant topic that surfaces at many junctures in the text.

Part II: The Songs of Jimi Hendrix looks at his output in depth, focusing on a range of pivotal elements such as song structure, range of historic references, stylistic quirks, use of the guitar and voice, deployment of technology, and lyric writing, all the while seeking to contextualize the artist within the work of his instructive predecessors.

There is also the central question of the circumstances in which he made music, and I discuss Hendrix's absolute commitment to the culture of jamming as well as the impact upon him of being a transatlantic artist born in the USA and made in the UK.

Each one of the aforementioned themes could well be a thesis in its own right. My intention is not to be definitive on the given subject but to bring together disparate aspects of the Hendrix aesthetic in order to show his multifaceted nature, especially as he is so often profiled as the number one Greatest Of All Time rock guitarist, which has the unfortunate side effect of casting the songwriter, singer and lyricist into shadow, and consequently depriving us of as complete a portrait of Hendrix the artist as possible.

Part III: The Songs from Jimi Hendrix considers his legacy. The impact he has had on generations of musicians for the best part of five decades is substantial, and it would be remiss to complete a study of Hendrix's music without acknowledgement of how he facilitated the work of others after his death, just as others did his during his life.

No greater indication of the importance of an artist can be found than in the echo of their music far beyond their time on earth, and the spirit of Jimi Hendrix has pervaded some of the most progressive musicians active on a number of different scenes today.

As new Hendrix product arrives at regular intervals, some of which, such as re-mastered tapes of previously unavailable material, is fascinating, he seems more alive, in sound, than ever before. What he gave the world of creativity in the broadest sense is immense. The artist himself may have been happy to plug in to an electric discussion of the music he made as well as the life he lived.

Seven Sisters, London
January 2020

Part 1: The Song and Jimi Hendrix

In the aisles and in the streets trying to copy his steps

In post-war black popular music the dance routine was an integral part of show time. Singers and bands learned moves that synchronized with the heavenly sound of voices and instruments. Unlike the orchestras of the 1930s, as epitomized by swing-era stars such as Duke Ellington, Count Basie and Fletcher Henderson, many groups in the mid-1950s did not have members sat still behind music stands. Horn players and guitarists were thus mobile and carefully schooled to stride back and forth, lean from side to side, raise up, dip low, spin fast and hold their instruments aloft as trophies under the light. Dancing, singing and playing synthesized in one deft audio-visual spectacle.

Buddy Travis and Stacy Johnson cut the kind of eye-popping pomp-stomps audiences would have come to expect in the mid-1960s. Lesser known than other male duos who had found success on the soul scene such as Bob & Earl and above all Sam & Dave, Travis and Johnson nonetheless had a solid fan-base in northern California where they were able to tour extensively under the name of the Soul Deuce. As was often the case at the time they performed as part of a revue, a multi-artist bill in which there was a clear hierarchy between the opening act of little renown and headliners with pulling power.

Although a relative footnote in the history of modern music, the Soul Deuce has its place in the pantheon by way of association. They toured with one of the progenitors of rock 'n' roll, Little Richard, and it was the singer who brought them into contact with a young guitarist who would eventually exert an arguably greater influence on popular culture than the formidable stage diva whose energy levels were so hysterically high that more perceptive pundits dubbed him "the human atom bomb".

Richard's decision to hire Jimi Hendrix at the start of his career, when he was one of countless itinerant session players in R&B trying to make their way, as well as the inclusion of the Soul Deuce, who he deigned to rename

Buddy & Stacy for his revue, conspired to create a notable cultural time capsule: one of the first known televised appearances of Hendrix. The footage is much more than a must-see moment for fans.

Filmed in 1965 for a programme called "Night Train" on the CBS-affiliated WLAC, Buddy & Stacy are seen performing 'Shotgun' by Junior Walker, a saxophonist and occasional singer who had a knack of making the kind of irresistibly catchy, bluesy, groove-based records that brought him the enviable hit-maker status that proved there was a definite appetite for skilled instrumentalists as well as vocalists in that era.

Buddy & Stacy are at the front of the stage with Richard's band in the back. There is a three-piece horn section, drums, bass and two guitars, one of which is played by Hendrix. Except for the drummer, everybody is dancing. Dressed in the flamboyant outfits favoured by many African-American and Afro-Cuban artists of the day – high-waisted Sta-Prest trousers; open-neck shirts with billowing sleeves; fluttering bandanas – the singers have the most intricate routine, and their dynamism is sustained right through their performance, as if they were determined to boldly grab the chance of exposure on what was still a relatively new medium – the small screen had only been a standard household item for just over a decade – by the hips as well as the hands.

The duo shimmies and shuffles aplenty. Constantly on the move, with a kind of bouncing-ball energy to them, Buddy & Stacy are an obvious draw as entertainers, because they have a natural stage presence and joie de vivre that is impossible to ignore. They carry out moves that are relatively simple, such as a coordinated hand clap and foot stomp, the kind of action that audiences would be able to replicate, and ones that are more challenging, such as a fast spin and hop sideways. Among the highlights of their routine is a turn-to-the-side bend-the-knee-low jut-the-pelvis-forward-on-the-way-up, and a slow slide with a slanting shoulder, which has the effect of emphasizing the graceful elegance of both men, for all the effervescence they manage to stoke up.

Tucked away as he is in the background, Hendrix is clearly recognizable, his left-handed grip of the guitar making the instrument point in the opposite direction to that of his two right-handed colleagues stood next to him, so that the tableau acquires a certain non-linearity that becomes more apparent when all the players execute their moves. When Hendrix sways in time with the band his guitar is forcibly sticking out at an angle while the others form a parallel. At the start of the performance his stance is fairly rigid but he loosens up considerably as the group runs through the choruses and by the halfway mark he is dropping his shoulder much lower than those next to him, suggesting that he has fully absorbed the energy of both the song, a fantastically rousing ride on a bumping backbeat, and the singers spinning in front of him. Ain't no half steppin'. Hendrix throws himself full tilt into the allocated task.[1]

Here then is a snapshot, or rather a show reel, of an icon long before he achieved icon status. The footage is invaluable for the insights it provides on the formative years of the man formally christened James Marshall Hendrix (or Johnny Allen according to some sources) who became the musician known as Jimi Hendrix. Born in 1942 he came of age at a time of major evolution in black popular music in America, and the music to which he was exposed both as a music lover and musician was multi-faceted. In 1965, the year that the guitarist dutifully followed the formation moves mapped out for 'Shotgun', Motown, the Detroit-based imprint which had signed Junior Walker, the artist who originally enjoyed a hit with that song, and with whom Buddy & Stacy also worked, become a considerable force in popular music by way of a series of releases that balanced the brilliance of a house band that had funk as well as finesse with a coterie of supremely gifted writers, arrangers and singers.

Playing a substantial part in the appeal of the artists was the slickness of their choreography. Watch classic footage of the label's flagship artists such as The Temptations, The Supremes, The Four Tops and Martha Reeves & The Vandellas, and the dance moves, which vary from sassy twirls to easygoing feints, are impossible to ignore. In the years that followed, the Jackson 5 would enjoy runaway success because of the stratospheric dance skills of the child stars, particularly its lead vocalist Michael, who would further develop as a demon mover when he reached adulthood.

Consider several pictures of a black group that was clearly on the rise in the early 1960s: Smokey Robinson & The Miracles, a legendary ensemble with expertly crafted tales of anything from the pain of not being loved, to the need to get some good lovin' – think 'The Tracks of My Tears' and 'Let Me Have Some'. There is a palpable tension between polished, kempt appearance and lively, engaging gesture, each element presented in counterpoint to the other without lessening the market appeal of the artist.

The Miracles always looked fabulous. They had immaculate tailoring and grooming, and sported matching outfits with neatly processed hair. Some pictures have a bland composition with band members placed side by side looking straight to camera. Yet their arms are extended, fingers curling or clicking, while in other shots, they are seen swaying and thrusting their bodies from side to side, as if they are about to slope off in unison. If these publicity shots clearly imply that the band has energy, then stills of their live gigs at the time show that they were anything but sedate when the time came to "show 'n' prove" in performance. They lift their voices and move their bodies.

Even more interesting was the existence of song titles that *designated* dances, from the Cool Jerk to the Popcorn to the Mashed Potato. Delights for eyes and ears such as these led some record company marketing departments to enclose instruction booklets on how the listener, in the privacy of their own home, could also get lifted by the surge of excitement generated by these limb-loosening tunes. Of course seeing the likes of James Brown display his mastery of new steps was second to none, but what was more important was that he was sold as the man who was able to brilliantly translate dance into song. The sleeve notes of Brown's *It's A Mother* state: "There are those who claim he dances as well as he sings ... He soon noticed that at concerts the kids were dancing in the aisles and in the streets trying to copy his steps ... so he wrote a melody and rhythmic pattern for the dance and went into the studio and put it on a tape. MOTHER POPCORN is the biggest thing to hit since The Twist."[2]

Rewatch that historic clip of Buddy & Stacy's rendition of 'Shotgun' again, and what stands out is not just the exuberance of the dancing but the *large* amount of dances the duo performs. While short of Wilson Pickett's fabled 'Land of A Thousand Dances', there is more than enough variety to give credence to that claim, underlining the primacy of one of the most basic of human impulses, movement, in a musical setting, which is communicative and disciplined in concept and execution. The whole band is well rehearsed. They were obviously very aware of the expectation for choreography.

Seeing a young Jimi Hendrix in this setting is something of a shock. So anchored in popular consciousness is the image of him grandly taking centre stage, in front of a microphone, for the most part flanked by no more than two musicians who all have ample room to drift around the stage, that the sight of him behind leaders is somewhat disconcerting. Yet here he is as a young man engaged in the exercise of performance, which in the black popular music of the time meant learning how to *move* as well as how to play. He was doing an apprenticeship. He was learning all about stagecraft.

Artists such as Buddy & Stacy were consummate showmen who all upheld and extended the relationship between song and dance in black music that reached right back to the days of nineteenth-century minstrels, when fiddlers, banjo players and percussionists using tambo 'n' bones accompanied "hoofers", or in some cases, were proficient when it came to dance, too.

R&B musicians who moved while they sang or played string instruments, horns and drums were part of a lineage of entertainers for whom the line between disciplines that are now more separate, such as music, dance and comedy, were not set in stone.

Of the musicians whom Hendrix took a keen interest in during his youth who put a personal slant on that tradition, it is Chuck Berry who is the most conspicuous. The gifted guitarist-vocalist, who along with Little Richard and Bo Diddley was one of the main architects of rock 'n' roll, also sealed his place in history by way of the *duck walk*. He had an iconic dance that was a complement to his musicianship, to the extent that Berry is immortalized with the idiosyncratic stance that arose from the conflation of these skills. Mention his name, and the picture that pops into your head is that of his knees bent sharp, back held straight, chin thrust high and guitar pushed out, gun-like.

Needless to say the cultural impact of such a tableau was absolutely enormous. And when Berry is rightly held up as a founding father of both modern pop guitar licks and inventive, perceptive lyrics, a commentator astute enough to frame an apparently prosaic event such as a car journey with the energy rush of teenage sexuality – "Ridin' along in my automobile/My baby beside me at the wheel" – his lasting contribution to stagecraft is substantial. He played the guitar and used it as a prop while he danced. Holding the instrument did not suffice. There had to be some doing amid the playing.

Cast your eye on one of the earliest known pictures of Hendrix. His hair short and neatly hot-combed, he is wearing a bright red box jacket and light brown trousers, the standard attire of a young post-war black either kitted out by a fashion-conscious father or an older sibling wise enough to make astute wardrobe choices of his own. He is smiling as broadly as one might expect of one who can barely contain their excitement upon the discovery of something that to all intents and purposes is a new toy, though the device would become much less disposable in the hands of its owner over time.

What is striking is Hendrix's posture. He is leaning sharply to the side, legs at an angle, which imbues the image with a subtle but nonetheless discernible sense of swagger. He is posing with confidence and is very possibly just a swivel of the hips away from a shuffle, a twist or one of the many dances of the day he'd have known.

A similar choreography defines another photograph of one of the bands that Hendrix joined, the King Casuals. Hendrix, clad in a black suit and tie, leans back to dip his shoulder into that of Leonard Moses. Both have their knees bent and guitars tilted upwards at an angle, forming a kind of inverted triangle. Kneeling between them with his bass guitar held upright is Billy Cox. The tableau is highly stylized. It has dynamic rather than static figures. Movement is at a premium. Dance is in the air. Moses is almost teetering right up on his toes, a clear forerunner to Michael Jackson.

While this kind of presentation ran across the colour line – there are numerous white groups from the early and mid-1960s that also upheld the convention of pointing their instruments skywards in publicity shots – there is a notable sense of Hendrix and bandmates lending a decidedly more gymnastic flourish to the portrait, making sure that the pose they adopt makes them musicians who are to be seen as well as heard.

Claiming that the blacks had more sass, more flavour, more *soul* than their white counterparts entails the inherent danger of a racial stereotype that chimes with the destructive notion that all blacks have innate musical gifts. Yet there is such an abundance of material that shows Negro artists, as they would have been referred to in the era in which Hendrix came of age, displaying marked choreographic verve that the observation stands as a statement of fact rather than a purely fanciful notion.

Though the styling of an artist – which became a key part of Hendrix's identity – is one of the central components in the persona perceived and, hopefully, retained by an audience, dance, the inventive volleys of physical movement, of the impulse to visually underscore verse and chorus, both off and on stage, in front of an audience of hyped-up fans as well as a clear-eyed photographer in a studio, is also at a premium.

Hendrix's awareness of the on-stage actions of musicians is borne out by some of the sketches he did in his childhood, a time when he displayed a keen interest in visual art, particularly painting and drawing. In one work there is a band with a vocalist, his arms outstretched very dramatically in front of a freestanding microphone, flanked by trumpeters, saxophonists, pianist and double bassist. It is a jazz or R&B singer, with his accompanying horn players, who took solos, one assumes. There is no doubt who the star of the show is: the man who strikes a pose, as a prelude to more moves.

In another there is a three-piece group with a drummer, guitarist and lead guitarist who are very much in a "showtime" pose. The front man cocks his leg to the side in a manner that might have amused Berry. The duck walk has birthed duckling steps.

As a leitmotiv of the racial dualities of the music industry in 1950s America, the picture is priceless. As much as the stance of the figures is black, their faces are not. They are white. Chances are that Hendrix modelled the doodle on Elvis Presley, who made the headlines with a concert in Jimi's hometown of Seattle in 1957 and whose music the teenager was exposed to via local radio. The repackaging of rhythm and blues as rock 'n' roll, and styling of Presley as the King of the latter genre, with all of the attendant scandal and gargantuan financial rewards, only served to enshrine the image of an all-action singer with a guitar in the popular imagination and affect a generation of teenage boys as well as girls. Youth was having its day. Keeping up to date with new sounds was of paramount importance and in the 1950s Hendrix and his pals became diehard fans who tuned their transistors to small FM radio shows in Bremerton and Tacoma that broadcast specialty shows hosted by local pioneering African American DJs such as Bob Summerise (1925–2010) and Fitzgerald "Eager" Beaver (1922–1992). However, by the mid-1950s the musical revolution underway was too exciting for the mainstream to ignore and Presley's covers of songs by black artists were playlisted by top 40 stations who had to play the early big hits of the king – and subsequent legions of other Southern rockabillies and Hollywood-based wannabes that duly emerged.

If a picture can be worth a thousand words then these images are invaluable stories that take us informatively close to the mindset of Hendrix the child who is switching on to the power of music for the first time. They convey a sense of excitement, if not imagination, about the artist as performer, a being who is dynamic rather than static on stage, and who is seen to be clearly underlining his technical action with bold gesture.

To interpret these pieces of memorabilia, over which his father pored lovingly when reminiscing about his son, as a sign that Hendrix somehow telegraphed his own destiny at that point in his life would be unwise. He was known to enjoy American football and there are photos of him with the distinctive round helmet and chin guard worn by those practising what can be a very physically punishing sport. However, there were no drawings of any

MVP – most valuable player – of the NFL that he may have hero worshipped, as is so often the case of boys in their formative years.

There is a stock narrative of the legendary musician as a preternaturally gifted being or child prodigy who acknowledges and embraces his calling from the earliest juncture of awareness. Such is the extent of Hendrix's talent and the enduring impact of his body of work it is tempting to think that he became instantly wedded to the guitar. Yet there were difficulties to be overcome on account of Hendrix having a physical idiosyncrasy that in times past inspired fear, contempt and even censure.

Indeed Hendrix himself said that when he was first getting to grips with the guitar as a boy he encountered difficulties on account of him being left-handed. The strings were not set up to accommodate his ilk, and he lost interest, as one might expect of an eager adolescent yet to learn adult patience. However, a rock 'n' roll star had an entirely galvanizing effect on him. "I got tired of the guitar and put it aside. But when I heard Chuck Berry it revived my interest. I learned all the riffs I could."[3]

Hendrix would have heard the man who enjoyed hits with 'Maybellene', 'Johnny B. Goode' and 'No Particular Place To Go' and had seen him on television, and according to Hendrix's father Al, his son would have the small screen on in the background when he was nestled on the couch in the front room in the Rainier Vista housing project of Seattle, Washington to practise his guitar, "plunking away" for hours on end. Dedication to the instrument appeared to be unbroken from that point on.

Hendrix's debut gigs were with teenage R&B combos that he formed with school friends, the most notable of which was The Velvetones (later The Rocking Teens), who, being under age had to play gigs in a community centre, hoping to carve themselves the same reputation as that enjoyed by popular local band such as Tacoma's Wailers.

More steps were taken on the developmental ladder when Hendrix fell in with an older experienced Seattle bandleader by the name of James Thomas, who, although now a footnote in Hendrix history would nonetheless have the distinction of being one of the pallbearers at Hendrix's funeral in Seattle in October 1970. Thomas's band The Tomcats was a springboard for budding local musicians. Al Hendrix said of Thomas, "[He] kind of acted as an agent for the kids. He'd do different gigs for them maybe at parties, weddings, pick nicks or dances. He'd pay for maybe four or five guys ... Jimi got his early start playing with them."[4]

Thomas also used his connections to secure gigs at officers' clubs on air force bases, but the defining feature of this first phase of Hendrix's career is that he was involved in the entertainment business, playing music as part of a function band, thus fulfilling the expectations of audiences of both school kids and airmen who attended. This meant making sure that the punters had a rockin' good time in the company of a rockin' good band. By and large people came to hear the hits of the day rather than original compositions, a state of affairs that can be ascribed to the primacy of artists that had enjoyed the honour of having a hit record in an age when jukeboxes and radio and television shows that broadcast popular music had enormous cultural currency. Being able to play what the audience knew rather than what they didn't was sacrosanct in an age when choice of music was by no means infinite. Hearing live what had been heard on the airwaves or small screen was a visceral thrill for a teenager whose importance in the youth consumer market would grow exponentially in the coming decade. The onus on the familiar was a central tenet of an industry that put a premium on the communal experience created through the far-reaching tradition of vociferous audience participation in musical theatre, vaudeville and variety scenes.

Artists who didn't have all-important contracts, gold dust to those aspiring to make it at a time when record labels that had access to studios and extensive and effective channels of distribution wielded a great deal of power, were minded to play the songs of those who had the good fortune to be signed up and afforded a degree of profile.

R&B's shuffling, punchy beat, strong, emotionally charged singers and lyrics that could be both suggestive and romantic, captured the imagination of a new generation of listeners who wanted to hear something altogether more contemporary than Broadway show tunes; however there was still a series of constraints placed on the exponents of the new genre. As exciting as this world was, it could also prove to be highly precarious.

Financial rewards for Hendrix's initial foray in the field were scant. He earned the princely sum of 35 cents for one of his first gigs and stated that the setlist included music by The Coasters. The Los Angeles vocal quartet had become one of the prime movers of the R&B sub-genre of close harmony vocal singing known as doo wop and had gold records with mellow, affecting songs such as 'Searchin'' and 'Young Blood' as well as the raucous, madcap 'Yakety Yak' and the ribald, innuendo-laden 'Poison Ivy'.

Although there is no footage of Hendrix on stage with The Velvetones or the other bands he joined as a teenager, it is entirely likely that he was required to execute choreographed steps when playing material by the above and others just as had been the case when he became a professional musician a few years later after dropping out of high school. Chances are that the spectacle of Hendrix dancing and playing behind Buddy & Stacy in 1965 had precedents reaching back to his youth in the late 1950s.

Song and dance, or rather song with dance, song *tied* to dance, was an integral part of the musical awakening and development of Jimi Hendrix. It was a cultural reality, anchored in the deeply rooted, symbiotic relationship of the two forms in the African-American creative mindset, and it was also a professional necessity, an almost universally held requirement for musicians who plied their trade with the R&B and rock 'n' roll bands who vied for a foothold in what was a fiercely competitive market.

In addition to playing with Buddy & Stacy, Hendrix had some impressive credits as a sideman in the early 1960s. He gigged with bands that were led by charismatic singers such as Curtis Knight, Wilson Pickett, Ike & Tina Turner, and the aforementioned Little Richard, and also saxophonists such as King Curtis jnr. As an itinerant musician Hendrix clocked up a lot of miles, scooting around America's feted musical hubs such as Kansas, Atlanta and Nashville with the above in a variety of circumstances, from short tenures to six-month engagements, as with Little Richard. Hendrix also did the notoriously punishing nationwide "chitlin' circuit", namely, venues for mostly working-class black communities that were known to be rough and ready and audiences infamously unforgiving if they were not served up the bluesy fare they demanded.

Stage presence, a good sense of humour … respectful, polite

Our relationship with music is complex to say the least. Numerous are the advanced academic studies carried out on the effect of sound, and its main organizing principles rhythm, melody and harmony on the psyche. But the physical engagement, the phenomenon of movement, be it entirely ex-tempo or pre-conceived, practised and rehearsed, that accompanies sound, is also a fascinating phenomenon to bear in mind.

The first songs one recalls dancing to, regardless of the lyric, or indeed absence thereof, are important because they mark a moment of freedom of expression, regardless of how well or badly the incumbent can get down once they get up. The first songs one recalls dancing to with a romantic partner are important insofar as they also represent some kind of emotional growth. The first songs that a musician dances to on stage are important because they consolidate their relationship with the artform of music, and underscore sound with a concrete not abstract physical input – pinpointing what might have been going through Hendrix's heart and mind.

How did Hendrix feel about doing a half-spin and turning to the side with Buddy & Stacy? How did he feel watching Little Richard leap wildly about the piano as he backed him? How did he feel about watching the Ikettes do their "pony ride" when he was a member of Ike Turner's band? How did he feel about watching Ronald Isley of the Isley Brothers do the showstopper splits just a few feet away from him on stage?

Did those elaborate twists and turns resonate with him in any way? Did he himself like to dance as well as listen to and play music? In the acres of press coverage – Hendrix granted many interviews in his lifetime – the subject is not discussed in any detail. There are frequent references to his formative years but no comments on the specific subject of dance and the dances that he was asked to do as a musician.

One musician who played with Hendrix a lot in his formative years is the late drummer Paul Caruso. He argued that the guitarist's subversive creativity was a natural reaction against the micro-managed order of the bandleaders. "I guess out of boredom more than anything. There was a lot of routine in those soul bands, the steps and everything. The guitarist is a sort of sly prankster; they play behind their backs and with their teeth. This is a way of breaking the pattern, breaking the law."[5] Hendrix didn't like being told when to dance, and how to dance, or how to play or dress.

Regulation riffs, regulation steps, regulation threads. Each reinforced the other. As much as Hendrix was interested in music as a career, there was already at an early age a clear desire to lead rather than follow. The guitar for hire scenario was not compatible with a personality such as his own that had distinct ideas on his approach to song as well as the way he came across on stage, right down to his style of dress.

Interestingly he recalled a major clash with Little Richard on that very issue. "I wanted my own scene, making my music. Like once me and another guy got fancy shirts 'cause we were tired of wearing the uniform. Richard called a meeting. I am Little Richard, Little Richard, he said, the King of Rock and Rhythm. I'm the only one allowed to be pretty. Take off those shirts, man, it was all like that. Bad pay, lousy living and getting burned."[6] No deviant ways. No thinking for yourself.

In other words there was an uncompromising individuality in Hendrix that was diametrically opposed to the regimentation to which he was subjected as sideman in the world of R&B, playing songs that were not his own, executing dance moves that were not of his making and wearing clothes that were not to his liking, as he was at pains to make clear later in his career when he looked back on the early days.

> I had to conform when I was playing in other groups too. The so-called grooming bit. You know mohair suits, how I hate mohair suits! I was playing with The Isley Brothers and we had white mohair suits, patent leather shoes and patent leather hair-do's. We weren't allowed to go on stage looking casual. If our shoelaces were two different types we'd get fined five dollars. Oh, man did I get tired of that.[7]

Given the explosion of colour that would define his sartorial style when he began to lead his own bands, the monochrome impositions he describes above would indeed have been nothing less than a red rag to a bull. He was subjected to the weight of a hierarchy, which struck parallels with his brief time in the armed services. The rulebook was everything Hendrix was against as a person. His dissent appears inevitable. Hence, in that early part of his career song and dance were akin to formula, just as a suit and haircut represented a uniform that divested him of his true sense of self.

However, the Isley Brothers' own recollections offer another perspective on the issue of Hendrix as a free spirit chained down by conformist thinking of slick professionals. When asked to recall how they met the guitarist, Ernie and Ronald Isley maintained that he was down on his luck in the mid-1960s, having lived a precarious life as a sideman and attempted to graduate as a bandleader. While he was busy carving out a reputation in New York by appearing at venues like Café Wha?, his financial situation was so unstable that Hendrix had to suffer the indignity of pawning his guitar.

There followed an informal patronage from a future employer. In their version of events the Isleys went so far as to take in the destitute young Hendrix, generously securing accommodation for him, with the few worldly goods he lugged around, at their mother's house in New Jersey, and also replaced his tatty guitar with a brand new axe, another incidental but nonetheless meaningful indication of the need for polished presentation in the finest detail. The "beaten 'n' bashed, road-worn chic" of instruments that were damaged, discoloured or covered with stickers would not do.

So when Hendrix later bemoaned the sharply cut suits and conked hairstyle he was forced to sport, it is worth bearing in mind that the counterweight to that stricture was the gift of a gleaming white Fender Stratocaster, the kind of guitar that the bulk of young players would have been more than proud to own. He had the grade A gear.

More interesting though is the status that he was afforded. Because his impact was instant he was upgraded. "When we had our first gig ... he changed the whole band", Ronald Isley says. "He stood out in front of them, man, and people went crazy over him, you know." His brother Ernie gives an insight into both Hendrix's character and the rapid progress he made. "He had stage presence, he had a good sense of humour ... respectful, polite, he learned very fast, he was star of the band before the first rehearsal was over. And you know, like from the jump, he was given preferential treatment, which for some of the guys in the band it rubbed them up the wrong way."[8]

This makes the whole question of Hendrix's formative years an altogether more intriguing and complex issue. To argue that he was completely denied the latitude for any self-expression when he was a sideman doesn't entirely ring true because the Isley Brothers were a group of skilled musicians and songwriters who were forward thinking rather than backward looking, as can be heard in the important, very stylistically diverse body of work they created between the late 1950s and mid-1980s.

They clearly spotted and made space for his ability. In any case Hendrix readily corroborated the claim made by the Isleys. "They used to make me do my thing then, because it made them more bucks or something. But I used to like to do it then but most of the groups I was with then they didn't let me do my own thing."[9]

In other words there was a general resistance to the incipient unorthodoxy that Hendrix displayed at a time when the markets and image of exponents of black popular music such as R&B were, for the most part, tightly formatted. Although it was a generic term, Rhythm & Blues had several manifestations that ran from the song featuring the single commanding voice to vocal groups to instrumentals, often where saxophones (King Curtis or Junior Walker), or guitars (Freddie King, T-Bone Walker) took pride of place. Each sub-genre was clearly identifiable within the framework of the genre.

The central quandary for Jimi Hendrix as a sideman with aspirations to be a bandleader in his own right was how his creative mojo could go to work in any of the aforesaid formats, how a musician interested in the broadest sonic canvas imaginable might develop his own kind of song that wasn't an obvious prospect or readily understood commodity for the available markets of the day. Again the interviews that Hendrix granted later in his career attest to the friction he was causing several years before. He was already experimenting with feedback in the early 1960s but for bandleaders and players intent on finding success with a more palatable sound, that was beyond the pale. The tradition of hard honkin' reed players – some of Junior Walker's upper register screams and squeals are actually close to developments of the avant-garde in jazz – had proved to be commercially viable, as the chart hits of the above showed, but the manipulation of an amplifier to produce maelstroms of noise was still off the menu. There was no, or little, space for Hendrix to be Hendrix at that time.

"Just another Negro artist"

Such dilemmas should be cast against the wider backdrop of an American music industry that was by no means immune to the central pathology that had come to define the country since its birth: racial politics, and more specifically the enduring inequality between blacks and whites. The differing perceptions, expectations, and most importantly treatment of artists who fell on either side of the colour line was entirely logical, given the all-consuming struggle that unfolded for the full enfranchisement of people of colour, an endeavour carried out at the cost of the loss of inspirational black leaders as well as dozens of less heralded lieutenants.

Race music was a term that was openly applied to songs produced by black artists up until the late 1940s and this crude, guileless epithet, which vividly reflected the place of ethnicity at the forefront of the American establishment, essentially amounted to a kind of commercial quarantining. Black music for black audiences that, so the sub-text held, did not have the same refinement and good taste as their white counterparts.

The coining of the term Rhythm & Blues in 1949 may have been a specific de-racialization of black popular music but that by no means led to an instant redressing of the balance when it came to opportunities afforded black artists to reach the widest possible audiences. Because an artist had success in the R&B chart that did not mean that they could automatically crack the pop hit parade, or all-important Hot 100 compiled by the highly influential music industry trade magazine *Billboard*. Any black artist who could cross over, or *get over*, had hit the holiest of holy grails.

Seeing Elvis Presley become a phenomenon as a white singer who sounded black, and more to the point, covered songs by black artists, would have been a bitter pill to swallow for a black artist insofar as his breakthrough stood to underline the glass ceiling, which showed little sign of shattering. No greater sign of the resentment came than in the title of an album by the singer and composer Otis Blackwell, who is a relative footnote in the history of pop though he wrote some of its central chapters while in the wings.

These Are My Songs! by Otis Blackwell features several of the anthems that made Elvis, namely 'Don't Be Cruel', 'All Shook Up' and 'Return To Sender'. The admission that Presley was the more marketable face for his work would have been cold comfort to Blackwell, who was known to R&B fans for his song 'Daddy Rollin' Stone' in the 1950s, for the most important part of the story is the fact that when his talent was recognized by impresarios he did not have the leverage to see that he was paid in full.

Herb Abramson, co-founder of the Atlantic label that brought many black artists to prominence in the 1960s, takes up the story: "When Otis brought *Don't Be Cruel* to Goldy Goldmark of Shalimar Music Co in 1955 he was persuaded to give up 50% of his copyright to Elvis Presley, who, according to the publisher, was going to 'turn the music business around'".[10] Presley was given writing credits for what he didn't write.

Having said that, the phenomenon of song authorship being shared between those who did and those who did not take part in the composing process was not done purely on racial lines. It is a box rather than a can of worms that reflects the age-old iniquities of the music industry, as numerous cases of band members, black and white, ending up in court over disputed rights, attest. A parallel to the Blackwell/Presley case is that of the prolific composer Jimmy McHugh, who wrote 'When My Sugar Walks Down The Street' only to find that Gene Autry took half of the credit and royalties.[11]

Image was inevitably an integral part of the formula for success in a music industry where executive control was mostly in the hands of white rather than black men who were all too aware of the sense of unease that certainly middle America still had with the artistic output of the descendants of slaves, and the option of a white singer as a mouthpiece for a black artist was a policy that had great currency in the post-war years.

Artists such as the Isley Brothers were wise to the fact that greater challenges to black musicians were on the horizon – or rather, beyond America's borders. The "British invasion" of the early 1960s, an interesting moniker for the wave of young English groups spearheaded by The Beatles, which was kickstarted by the appearance of the "Fab Four" on the Ed Sullivan show, had not escaped the attention of anybody who could see that the combination of cute, stylish white boys who had the wherewithal to cover the Isleys' songs such as 'Twist And Shout' as well as material by other black R&B and rock 'n' roll artists such as Chuck Berry was a formula that had limitless commercial appeal. Ironically it also made the Isleys assess the value of the prize asset in their own band. Ernie recalls: "Kelly [Isley, singer and eldest of the brothers who co-founded the group in the mid-1950s] said this young English band has changed everything. They got two guitar players ... but we got Jimi! And when he said 'but we got Jimi', I looked over at Jimi and Jimi was grinning from ear to ear at that remark."[12]

Amidst this bonhomie one can only imagine how this significant new development in popular music was playing out in the minds of those who knew full well that what they created, their original contributions to the repository of songs that had already been proven to be able to capture hearts and minds around the world, could just as quickly become the basis for a new product that was considered more palatable.

The Beatles would evolve into one of the most imaginative and original forces in the history of pop but their formative years were characterized by adaptations of templates established in R&B. Concise, hook-laden tunes with catchy choruses were the order of the day. Covering a piece such as the Isleys' 'Twist And Shout' was a perfect career move because the rhythmic foundation of the music had joyously sensual, wrangling inflections that would dazzle British or American teenagers who had not been readily exposed to music that had such an irresistibly strong, insistent beat.

Although the young Merseysiders, with their two guitarists, could hold down the groove, vocally they were clearly no match for their sources of inspiration. Their attempt at the all-important "whooh" paled into insignificance compared to the performance by the men from New Jersey on their version. That blackness did not cross the Atlantic even as the dollars started to flow into pounds, shillings and pence.

While The Beatles and other members of the British invasion were vocally inferior to the likes of the Isley Brothers they were also a different kind of stage act. In essence, they didn't dance. They were relatively static under the lights. One of the key aspects of the stage performances of black R&B artists – choreography – was absent. The Beatles' all-important rendition of 'Twist And Shout' on the Sullivan show is actually notable for the considerable physical constraint of the musicians on stage, and this creates a discrepancy with what is the central mission statement of the song. Their stance is actually at variance with the meaning of the music they are playing.

It could be argued that a key factor in the Beatles vs Stones face-off was neither the oft-cited sweet boy–bad boy dichotomy nor the fact that the former remained pop while the latter were rock (which is itself a questionable notion), but something else. Mick Jagger danced with great abandon, sexualizing song in the process, though how *well* he could bust a move, when he was put up against a number of black artists – a Ronald Isley, a Tina Turner or above all a James Brown – is another matter entirely.

Yet what is no less significant is that The Beatles unleashed mass hysteria as they eschewed the paradigm readily applied by black groups of the time. What this might say about popular music seen through the prism of race in post-war times is open to interpretation. On one hand the Fab Four can be applauded for breaking with the norm, adopting their own approach to stagecraft, possibly because they knew that trying to rival the aforementioned black performers was a task that was more than river deep and mountain high. They covered black music but chose not to play black artists at a crucial aspect of their own game, namely the ability to embellish song with dance.

How the success of the British artists affected black artists in America is worth considering, for no other reason that the immense commitment to standards of excellence comes at a price that should not be underestimated. When the likes of Brown declared themselves to be performers who had to be seen as well as heard it was no idle boast or empty hyperbole intended to generate additional buzz in the market place. One of his other monikers, Mr Dynamite, was entirely apposite because of the irrepressibly explosive nature of his stage show. While that is not in doubt the more thorny issue is whether there was any real appreciation of how much work went into the development and perfection of his artistry, just how hard the "hardest working man in show business" actually had to work to make his appearances so unforgettable, not to mention how much painstaking rehearsal time was needed for his musicians to learn a series of steps as well as riffs, and co-ordinate their movements with his.

Assumptions about what black artists were capable of could easily lead to complacent views on the extent to which they pushed themselves to fulfil any talent they had. Seeing a white artist hit an unimaginable commercial jackpot without so much as a slide, shuffle or spin in between a chorus was arguably a bitter pill to swallow. In the R&B mindset that places value on dance the absence of it was an anomaly, which would simply compound the perceived inferiority of the interlopers as vocalists.

What complicates matters further is the fact that there was love for the white boys in black America, even though there is a received and somewhat reductive wisdom that black consumers couldn't identify with them. The Brits did find favour with many people of colour, especially when the Beatles and Stones proved that they had undeniable skill as tunesmiths by way of songs such as 'Daytripper' and 'Satisfaction' that had precisely the kind of spell-bound riffs that could charm both listeners and players, including Hendrix, who did live versions of the former with The Experience.

And yet the song – as a source of both financial gain and a paragon of artistic excellence – was still a contentious issue for black musicians who had to live through the British invasion because of the way both royalties, sales and media attention could be diverted from one artist to another. As the composer of 'It's All Over Now', Bobby Womack, one of the definitive figures of the history of soul music, had no reason to bear malice towards the Rolling Stones as their chart-topping cover of the song earned him a substantial payday. Yet any gratitude he may have felt has to be cast against the experience of Irma Thomas, the New Orleans singer who achieved legend status in R&B, who, like many female artists was not encouraged to write her own material, and was beholden to male composers and producers. She told me in 2007: "When the Rolling Stones covered 'Time Is On My Side' it wasn't great for me on a couple of levels. I mean firstly it actually *stopped* my record from selling; that's one thing people don't realize, once a 'hot' artist puts their name to a song the original artist gets forgotten. The other problem was I didn't think Mick Jagger could sing."[13]

In other words it simply wasn't enough to possess self-belief, conviction, confident sexuality and vanity, the cosmetic qualities that are traditionally assigned to exponents of pop music, who, so the wisdom holds, are at the lower end of a hierarchy that places classical music at the top. However it is a truism that Thomas and countless black performers in New Orleans R&B had very high standards of musicianship that stemmed from rigorous application as well as god-given talent.

One of her most simpatico collaborators, the composer and producer Allen Toussaint, may have been lauded for his ability to pen dozens of tunes that were irresistibly catchy but he had great knowledge of "serious" music upon which to draw. Anybody lucky enough to see him perform solo piano would have understood that, from the seamless transition he made between the music of Fats Domino, Thelonious Monk and Rachmaninoff. Thomas worked with players who did much more than play licks.

The cynical or perhaps realistic view is that the Brits didn't need to, according to Thomas's appraisal, sing that well, or dance, because they had the one thing Thomas and co. could never have, regardless of their talent: whiteness. Those iconic shots of teens hollering to the heavens in the throes of delirium at the sight of the Fab Four, marble-like under the lights, could also be equated with a more ready embrace of what passes as the acceptable face of popular culture in a racially divided society, an irony that would not have been lost on those on the frontline.

When Ronald Isley evoked the game-changing power of the "young English band" he could have just as easily said "the young white boys", though those words may have been precluded by the fact that the power he correctly afforded them was such an arch statement of the obvious for any cultural critics with a modicum of good sense.

Hendrix had sufficient powers of perception to comprehend the realities of race relations in the music industry. In the early 1960s he played a gig at the Arena in Cleveland, Ohio, as a member of Joey Dee & The Starliters who were part of a multi-artist bill that included Chubby Checker, the singer who enjoyed major success with 'The Twist', the song and dance whose phenomenal success sparked variations such as 'Twist And Shout'. Years later, when interviewed in Stockholm with The Experience, Hendrix reflected soberly: "Nobody talked to me. I was just another Negro artist".[14]

Observant and sensitive, he already had a clear awareness of a two-tier system for black and white musicians in an America that is anything but egalitarian in conception and discriminatory in terms of the roles that should be assigned to a so-called ethnic minority in an industry whose primary decision makers are white.

It is worth remembering that like many who came of age through the 1950s, he would have seen up close and personal exactly what a racially divided America meant, not just in terms of segregated lunch counters and washrooms, but also in the Spartan living conditions for "just another Negro artist", which included the prize luxury of sleeping in a housing estate under construction in Nashville whose floors and roof had yet to be installed, and being short-changed by promoters who would make a point of handing over lower fees than what was agreed while the musicians were on stage and quickly slipping away into the night, leaving the players to finish their set, unable to duck the sucker punch. Performing "just another Negro song" came with an inherent amount of risk in a world where exploitative behaviour and shady business dealings adjoined lack of equality for blacks in wider society. That Hendrix grasped the cynicism towards as well as contempt for musicians of colour in an entertainment industry that was more than happy to take an interest in their abilities without necessarily wanting to grant them equal status to whites shows that he was wise to the prevalence of rigid market segmentation and reductive racial categorization.

Little wonder he was absolutely intent on not being just *another* anything. Beyond the question of race there is the matter of the artistic coherence of the songs that became essential lightning rods at the time in pop. 'Twist And Shout' is interesting because of its common bond between icons – The Beatles, the Isley Brothers and Jimi Hendrix. Ronald vividly recalls his very first meeting with the young player in need of a gig: "He said 'Man, I heard all about you guys', as he was putting the strings on the guitar ... He said I like this song ya'll had called 'Twist And Shout'. And he started playing. I said 'Oh my!' We hired him right away, right away." The track's element of sociocultural power should not be masked by its enduring appeal. The reason why 'Twist And Shout' is so affecting is because it is actually a rip-roar call to arms of sorts.

Remember that the lyric of 'Twist And Shout' is an imperative. It demands physical action not a lack thereof. The song heralds one of the most popular dance crazes in 1950s pop, the twist, but it is actually much more than an invitation to loosen limbs. Sexuality and flirtation are foregrounded in the lyrics – "you know you look so good", "you know you twist so fine", "come and twist a little closer now and let me know that you're mine" – but the conjunction of actions in the title is of no less importance.

To twist and shout is to dance and express oneself, to release energy, to let go, to flout any demand for decorum. The joyous hands in the air or fingers flicked in the face of convention echoes down through the years. If 1960s R&B beckons us to twist and shout then 1990s R&B and hip-hop puts an erotic spin on that by way of the notion of "bump and grind" (which, ironically, is a shibboleth that had actually been in black culture for decades), and the decidedly more militant summons of "make some noise".

In any case Ronald Isley makes it clear that there is absolutely nothing timid in the underlying meaning of 'Twist And Shout', and his group's enactment of its content.

> Shake it up, we talking about shake your fanny, shake it up, baby, twist and shout, mix it up ... we were like wild in them days, man. We were like jumping off the stage and swinging off the ropes and curtains. I mean we were wild and people would go wild, you know you make me wanna shout ... people would jump up and lose it.[15]

Stomp your feet, jump up and down and do anything that you wanna do

The example of the Isley Brothers' electrifying performance of 'Twist And Shout' places the phenomenon of dance for black artists at the time of Hendrix's formative years in another perspective. While the large number of songs dedicated to steps that were fun – the twist, the shake, the shuffle, the slide, the hook and sling, the tighten up, the bump – all denote physicality that would also be expressed in a verb such as swing, there was stagecraft that chimes with the energetic moves and a substantial psychological dynamic of self-determination. To sing the Twist and Shout and dance the Twist and Shout will not suffice: one has to *do* the Twist and Shout in such a way that all possible anchors of restraint are duly cast off.

This idea that song and dance in the realm of R&B could foster such *extremes* of behaviour is also demonstrated by another composition from one of the Isley Brothers' peers, Little Stevie Wonder, the child prodigy who emerged from under the wing of his mentor, the "genius" Ray Charles, in the early 1960s to push soul to new heights of sophistication in the 1970s. Here is how he introduces 'Fingertips', one of his most celebrated breakout hits: "Now I want you to clap your hands, come on come on, yeah, stomp your feet, jump up and down and do anything that you wanna do."[16]

Because dance, especially when it appears in the arena of popular culture, is generally perceived as something whimsical, light-hearted and recreational there is a tendency to dismiss its possible political magnitude. Yet the very language that Wonder uses in the introduction of 'Fingertips' imparts to the act of dance a distinct sense of enfranchisement. On one hand the mandate to "do anything you wanna do" lights the touch paper of hedonism. On the other hand it creates an explosion of personal power, which can be nothing less than political in the context of America, a country with such a deeply rooted history of comprehensive oppression of people of colour, the nadir of which is the particularly brutal policing of the black male. A degree of physical release and mental liberation can be achieved through the act of dance.

Furthermore, there is a corollary of danger in the outright demand Wonder makes for each and every member of his audience to free up. He is not telling them *what* course of action to pursue but rather enjoining them to make a decision under their own steam. This makes the apparently perfunctory prelude of the song notable. What happens if patrons, instead of doing the twist to 'Fingertips', shout a little more loudly, scream a little more raucously, writhe a little more lasciviously, go a little more crazy?

In Wonder's urge to do anything, there is the possibility that a hardy soul could do something extraordinary, and such heightened intensity resonates with the gospel roots of black pop, the influence of preachers who were performers capable of leading churchgoers to explode all inhibitions. "They would have you screaming," recalled a musician who grew up in a black community in Los Angeles in the 1950s. "The whole thing was just so wild. It wasn't only about singing along to some Negro spirituals, which was important, sure. But people, they just went into another state entirely."[17]

An artist who fully understands the experience described above, the subversive dynamics of black experience, in which song and dance are self-fulfilment and self-assertion as well as self-expression, will make his work something never before heard as he proceeds to alchemize into something never before seen.

Isn't that the shorthand version of the story of Jimi Hendrix in concert? Such was the erotic charge of his showmanship that some venues were reluctant to book The Experience as the group started to gather some momentum on the touring circuit. While the eye-catching nature of his antics – the squatting down and holding the guitar between the legs in an undeniably phallic way; the lewd tongue strokes to conjure up cunnilingus; the playing of the guitar with the teeth or while holding the instrument behind his back – reflects a desire to affect audiences as well as give vent to the extravert on stage counterweighted by the much reported introvert off it, it is important to realize that Hendrix defines himself as an individual in the process.

It is fair comment that the artist who emerges as a bandleader in his own right after leaving America and launching his group The Experience in Britain in 1967 is making a decisive break with the praxis of strictly drilled choreography, sharply pressed suits and processed hair that was largely the remit handed to him as a sideman in the years prior to his transatlantic rebirth. Like little Stevie says, he *do anything he wanna do.*

Yet the primary pillars of the apprenticeship are not entirely removed for the plain and simple reason that Hendrix never actually stopped dancing.

Look at any amount of footage from his heyday as a leader and his rhythmic strutting, shoulder jabbing and hip thrusting are well to the fore. One of the most startling images of Hendrix in concert is of him on his knees with one raised arm as he leans so far back he almost skims the floor and then sways from side to side. Even more mind-boggling is this testimony from a fan, Tony Parry, who saw the artist at Sophia Gardens, Cardiff in 1967: "My enduring memory is of him rolling head over heels across the stage while continuing to play the guitar."[18] In other words Hendrix's athleticism and dynamism were prevalent, complementing his sexual charge. His moves were spontaneously executed rather than tightly mapped in unison with bandmates as was previously the case when he was under orders from another leader. In many performances he stands still at the mike as if he is summoning maximum concentration to sing, yet he then breaks into action as the moment takes him.

Studying Hendrix's movement in the crucible of a stage show is fascinating because of the immense variety he presents. He actually establishes poles of behaviour. At one end there is the undaunted steadiness. At the other there is the whirlwind turbulence. While it can be argued that the first option equates to a desire to be taken seriously as an artist in face of an expectation for excess that could be debilitating, he displayed an unfettered energy for dance throughout his career that suggests that shaking his body – as he saw fit – was integral to his conception of the performance of a song.

What emerges from the bulk of the first-hand testimonies of Hendrix on stage is the mercurial, attention-seeking nature of his performance, to the extent that a song is framed by an act where a number of elements, from sexual provocation to feats of virtuosity on the guitar to sculptural manipulations of noise to ecstatic dance, can be implemented at any given moment. There were many buttons Hendrix could push.

Contrast these two accounts of his concerts. When Eric Clapton, the primary British guitar hero of the mid-1960s, who Hendrix respected, saw the newly arrived American in London, he was totally knocked out by the no-holds-barred nature of what he witnessed. "I think he did a Howlin' Wolf number. He did this whole routine, playing the guitar with his teeth, laying it on the floor, playing it behind his head, doing the splits, the whole thing."[19] Several years later the bag of tricks was still used when Hendrix's second group Band of Gypsys played a historic engagement at the Filmore East but, crucially, there was also a tranquil force of Hendrix that came into play, as bassist Billy Cox recalls: "There was one show where Jimi just stood there and put all the fire he could under the band."[20]

It is entirely logical that Hendrix grew tired of all the stagecraft, the pyrotechnics and the pyromania, knowing full well that it was fast becoming a cliché that could undermine his status as a serious musician, and the perception of the media surely didn't help in this instance. The extreme irony of him being dubbed 'The Black Elvis' would not have been lost on him and chances are that he would have detected the racist subtext of a term such as "Wild

Man of Borneo" and realized that a black musician being a *Wild Thing* on stage as well as singing of the girl who "makes everything groovy", inevitably exacerbated deep-seated prejudices about the primitive ways of people of colour and the attendant threat that they posed to polite society.

In 1967 *The Observer* magazine ran a piece on Hendrix with the opening salvo: "This man is dangerous. He makes an indecent assault on his loudspeakers and has been accused of obscene exposure of an electric guitar. If he's been through your town recently things won't be the same again. Would you let your daughter undergo the Jimi Hendrix experience?"[21] And are we also to believe that your own wife will survive it? Or perhaps, with her precious virtue in peril, she would be coaxed into hitching her skirts to his gypsy caravan when it cleared the city limits after spreading wanton moral decay. The undercurrent of sexual deviancy running through the text is so strong as to criminalize Hendrix by the same token with which it immortalizes him as an agent of irrevocable change.

Yet Hendrix, as dedicated as he was to his music, came from a complex multi-layered black culture where the art–entertainment divide was by no means a clear one, and the use of gesture could be met with a range of responses. A bar-walking saxophonist sliding up the counter of a venue on his back could result in both admiration and derision but what is perhaps more important is that he may well have inspired a duckwalking guitarist who in turn would be a game changer in popular culture.

Such behaviour could be perceived as demeaning gimmickry but it also presents a lightheartedness that is not necessarily incompatible with artistic integrity. One thing that all of Hendrix's friends, acquaintances and casual observers agree on is that he had a sense of humour, a quick wit and gift for a pithy one-liner on stage. To all intents and purposes his desire to be taken seriously as an artist did not lessen his awareness of a bigger history of entertainment, vaudeville and variety in which any number of acts of differing degrees of quirkiness could be lumped together.

When The Experience found themselves on the same bill as a troupe of performing seals in Sweden there was a telling reaction from the star of the show. The band's tour manager Gerry Stickells recalls: "The show took place at a fairground and I said to the promoter who's going on first? He couldn't even explain. Then I went out and saw this ramp and the performing seals went on. They weren't even any good. They couldn't keep the balls on their noses! Hendrix thought it was hilarious."[22]

Rather than stiffening his spine at the affront to his dignity, he let his rib be tickled. If we put the incident into a wider context it is less of a surprise. In the early 1970s Miles Davis shared a bill with the popular black stand-up comedian Moms Mabley and in the 1990s James Brown had a magician accompany him on some of his last gigs. The serious and the frivolous often rubbed shoulders.

This is not at all to say that Hendrix, or any of the above for that matter, should be tagged as a novelty act. Indeed the very question of superficiality and cheap sensationalism was one that dogged him for much of his career even though he was able to exert an appeal on an audience that was more mature than the teenage constituency that had been instrumental in the growth of pop as a market force in the late 1960s. Bringing a new gravitas to the 3-minute song or the hour-long stage show was a primary goal Hendrix pursued in his lifetime but it is debatable that such a mission totally consumed the lighter side of his personality in the process. Dance as an expression of spontaneity, joy and freedom mark so many of his gigs.

Footage of what is largely acknowledged as the last major event he played, the Love and Peace festival at Fehmarn in Germany in 1970, makes for instructive viewing in this sense. For the most part he is moving very little around the stage and his gestures are sober but there is a fleeting moment where he rapidly rotates his arms to create an image of sidewinding snakes that is quite startling. It is a glimpse of the kind of move that became widespread in clubs in the age of disco, which is not a word readily associated with Hendrix, but is nonetheless apposite when one considers the primacy of flamboyance, sartorially and choreographically, in the genre, and the big influence on its development of the aforesaid Brown, an artist whom the guitarist much admired and whose 1964 album *Showtime* he was known to have bought and enjoyed.

Were they ever questioned on the content of Hendrix's stage show then anybody from Little Richard to Buddy & Stacy to the Isley Brothers might have had good cause to say that they taught him everything he knew, but they would not be entitled to claim credit for the breadth of imagination in the way the dispensed knowledge was so dramatically rechannelled and brought into thrilling collision with a world where state-of-the-art sounds are much more than an incidental backdrop to song and dance.

Of all the things Hendrix did on stage the enactment of simulated sex with the amplifier is the most meaningful, not for its eccentricity but for its conceptual and theatrical logic. The gesture symbolizes transformation as well as transgression because the man-made technological device, the machine, becomes part of a mating ritual, an agent of carnal provocation that lifts man beyond the confines of the flesh.

This electro-shocking spectacle upholds and daringly extends the core culture of song and dance in R&B. When performers launched into the Turkey Trot and Buzzard Lope in the 1920s, the Snakehips in the 1930s, the Camel Walk in the 1940s, the Penguin in the 1950s and the Funky Chicken in the 1960s they were acknowledging the infinite riches of the animal kingdom as a metaphorical basis for their choreographic imagination, and thus mimicked the creatures in question in order to push the artistic envelope. That wasn't enough, though. They had to go and invent the Robot and present themselves as automated beings whose crisp, curt, staccato shifts through the air enlarged the vocabulary of dance. Imitation of inanimate objects opened minds. There was recognition of the swish geometry of mechanization, the grand energy of electricity, the fact that the voltage brings heat, light and the intense thrill of shocks. Being a super dooper loverman was cool. Being a *sex machine* plugged into a funky new energy. It was part of a lineage. Pre-James Brown, R&B produced the risqué metaphor of *laundromat blues*, where "my baby has the best machine, the very best equipment in town", and post-Brown funk hailed the arrival of *techno freqs* and *computer love*.

From the declaration by Hendrix "My religion is electric" comes the nominal sub-text that his crucifix is the Stratocaster. But the credo does not preclude his sexuality and in the black pop of his youth the sacred was by no means divorced from the profane.

Because the amplifier is such a central emblem of the mythology of rock as it crystallized as a genre in the late 1960s away from R&B, because the amplifier is the hallowed source of power that enables an artist to crank up volume levels to unprecedented heights, and because the amplifier affects thousands of faithful followers in the new cathedral of a stadium, it is not readily associated with the old testament of the blues. But in the church of Showtime, as defined by those who shared Hendrix's otherworldly extremities of eroticism, any kind of paraphernalia is fair game. This means that there is really no difference between Hendrix in sexual congress with an amp and Tina Turner stroking a mike stand as if it were a penis.

Both of these examples are a logical progression from both the lyrical and choreographic bedrock of African-American popular culture that can be traced right back to the megawatt charisma that lit up the imagination of audiences who saw sexuality as a subject for celebration and torched the sensibilities of would-be arbiters of good taste.

In the 1920s there is the sound of Clara Smith bemoaning the absence of an able-bodied "daddy" to "grind her coffee" and serve her breakfast in bed, not the kitchen, with all the imperious energy of a woman who has no qualms in demanding the pleasures of the flesh. In the 1950s there is the sight of Little Richard cocking his leg over the frame of a piano and thrusting his pelvis as if he were asserting conjugal rights over the instrument. These are solid foundations for any artist who is minded to deploy artful lyric and sensational theatricality in order to enhance song in the heat of performance. As somebody who saw Richard pull off that very move during his formative years as a sideman, it was more or less inevitable that a highly ambitious individual such as Hendrix would undertake to uphold and adapt the wily ways of his former employer.

Today the sight of a musician stood in front of, rather than seated at the piano has absolutely no shock value whatsoever. The stance is part of the standard vocabulary of performance in popular music that would not be greeted with any fanfare by the bulk of audiences. Yet Richard on his feet in front of one of the largest, most cumbersome of instruments is nothing less than a revolutionary act. The object is too heavy to move but the artist still creates dynamism not stasis. The convention of being seated is cast aside as he asserts nothing less than his own freedom of movement. This fosters a much greater spectacle on stage. Richard is able to do *his* dance.

He opened doors for his successors. Hendrix grinding a guitar against his crotch or playing it behind his neck is right in the slipstream of Richard, who, after his saxophonist had jumped onto the body of the piano, would stand with his back to the keyboard and play facing away. The artist does what he isn't supposed to do. The artist dares to do what others don't. The artist sees song as a means of lateral thinking. The artist makes performance a personal invention. Hendrix is able to do *his* dance.

Ambitious as he was, Hendrix was always liable to push the envelope especially as his coming of age coincides with the greater press coverage of the rock festival, as exemplified by iconic late 1960s events such as Woodstock, Isle of Wight and Monterrey where the onus was on him to make the greatest possible impact on a bill that included stars of the day such as Otis Redding, The Byrds and Simon & Garfunkel.

Indeed it shouldn't be forgotten that he was of a generation of performers acutely aware of competition and for which the line between artistry and gimmickry could be crossed at will. Setting alight the guitar was actually an idea dreamed up by one of Hendrix's road crew in order to lend a startlingly literal meaning to the song 'Fire'. Having either played with or seen the greatest stage wizards up close and personal, Hendrix had every reason to acquiesce to the strategy in question. If Little Richard was the Human Atom Bomb and James Brown Mr Dynamite, he was the Firestarter.

We expected a black soul band from the USA

Although Hendrix the performer, or rather the performer who learned from other performers, is pivotal to the wider story of Hendrix the artist, there is also Hendrix the listener to consider. Not just the singer and guitarist who would lend an ear to the pulse of the bass guitar and drums in his own band, but the curious mind who is intent on studying in detail the methodology of others whose work could feed his fertile imagination.

Testimonies of close friends in New York such as the Allen twins, as well as documentation of his life in London, point to a central pillar in his life: his record collection. Although unable to read or transcribe music, Hendrix spent countless hours listening to the albums of others. He was a serious student of song. He realized that the songs of others could decisively shape his growth as a creator of original songs.

Luckily, the record collection from his British home survived largely intact and the contents highlight wide-ranging tastes. He owned albums by many of his peers at the cutting edge of late 1960s rock and pop, from Cream to

Spencer Davis and The Beatles but of great significance is his acquisition of music that was not contemporary.

The music of Sonny Boy Williamson, Leadbelly and Elmore James was in his possession. As was that of Muddy Waters and Lightnin' Hopkins. Hendrix owned copies of the former's *Down On Stovall's Plantation* and the latter's *Earth Blues*. These albums contain songs recorded in the early and mid-1940s. They showed Hendrix the roots of the R&B in which he was fully engaged as a sideman, providing priceless insights on the phrasing, articulation and timbral nuance of the voice and guitar in the blues, and highlighting the immense emotion and musical interest generated by fluctuations of line length and the acuity of even the most brief of improvisations.

Hopkins, in particular, takes Hendrix into a key performance space in music, that of the storyteller unadorned rather than embellished, the agent of superior charisma who needs the most minimal backdrop on which to cast his overwhelming sense of self. On one hand that means that he is mesmerizing with nothing more than voice and guitar. On the other it means that he is the antithesis of the song and dance tradition in R&B. Lightnin' sits down to play. Lightnin' doesn't do any of the slick moves that create a sense of spectacle. Lightnin' gets his groove on without all the latest steps.

Watch footage of him performing a timeless piece such as 'Mojo Hand' with nothing more than an acoustic six-string as he gently rocks back and forth on a stool, tapping his foot to keep time, and the effect is striking. His pure magnetism is the stage show.

In the context of the burgeoning rock culture with which Hendrix became associated, such a restrained stance would have been anomalous. A young man was not supposed to be parked on a chair when the underlying image he conveyed was one of freedom of expression. Sitting would have had the effect of impugning a would-be *wild thing*.

Yet one of the most iconic of Hendrix images is that of him sitting à la Lightnin'. In the revealing documentary *A Film About Jimi Hendrix*,[23] he is perched on a high stool, playing a 12-string guitar, his red patterned jacket and black fedora with purple band and yellow feather brought into sharp relief by an enamel white backdrop. He is looking studiously at the neck of the instrument. In several other clips in the film he is on stage, wheeling, strutting and swirling with abandon, but here he is calm personified.

Whether or not it is apparent to viewers, he is the embodiment of spirits who have come before him. He recognizes and acquires a rootedness in music that actually serves his own evolution. The history thus courses through his body and his mind.

Of all the things that a musician can do in order to further his progress as a creative being, broadening and deepening his knowledge of music is as vital as mastering a given instrument. The primary advantage of untold hours of listening is the creation of historical context. Master musicians do not pop out of vacuums. They all have formative periods in which they seek to develop their own sense of self, and their recognition of artistic ancestry enables them to do so because the boundary between past and present in music has never been set in stone. Old and new *product* exists but as much as a song belongs to one era it can just as easily be transmuted to another, or at least shown to be relevant to it by way of interpretation and presentation, which is something that both jazz and hip-hop have done at different times in recent history. Surely Hendrix, when listening to James Brown's *Showtime*, noted that the artist was absorbing and revitalizing the energy of the past through his choice of covers.

Songs such as Louis Jordan's 'Caldonia' and 'Ain't Nobody Here But Us Chickens' covered by Brown were written and recorded in the mid-1940s, so they were almost 20 years old. The point is that the wonderfully pithy horn and vocal riffs, brimming with zestful humour as well as popping rhythmic effervescence, were grist to Brown's daringly evolutionary mill.

This bridging of eras is pivotal. Hendrix spinning records over and over in order to improve his own technique, as guitarist, vocalist and songwriter, can be seen as a demanding academic exercise as well as pursuit of pleasure at the time he came of age, where vinyl was assuming great cultural currency but where large swathes of musical history were out of the reach for many consumers given the absence of yet to be invented platforms such as Spotify and YouTube. Instead of Googling he went into bouts of hard study of all available resources. He had a thirst for knowledge.

Hendrix mythology has a tendency to depict the prodigy or force of nature. But to all intents and purposes he was as wedded to learning by way of listening as he was by playing. The consensus is that almost every waking hour was spent working on his guitar technique, but that discipline was supplemented by an intense focus on albums by artists he found interesting to the extent that there are stories that a pre-fame Hendrix in New York lugged around a stack of albums as part of his worldly goods when he was of no fixed abode. A collection of songs was his home.

Significantly Hendrix's tastes were wide ranging. His deep admiration for Bob Dylan is well known and well represented by the presence of several of his LPs in his later record collection but what is also instructive is his interest in artists, apart from Dylan, who were from outside the blues canon. On one hand there was Indian sitar virtuoso Ravi Shankar. On the other French avant-garde composer Pierre Henry.

In other words Hendrix was not confined by any expectations that pertained to ethnic minority consumers, or the racist notion that blacks only listened to black music. Hendrix embraced artists like Shankar, who made *other sounds*, and Henry who was experimenting with sound design, as can be heard on his 1962 album *Le Voyage: D'Apres Le Livre Des Morts Tibetain*. In other words Hendrix the listener is travelling in two directions at once, back to the scrape of the guitar and forward to the slur of electronic effects, ambient noise and the excitingly ambiguous textural patchworks of *musique concrete*. Hendrix was thus investigating the time-honoured narratives in black pop and the more open-ended form of European art music. While it would be too glib to ascribe his brilliance to an elision of the two there is no doubt that his desire to go deep and broad in his research of music he deemed to be relevant to his development, to be part of his culture, was decisive. His musical education was multi-layered. The database at his disposal was thus impressively wide. Hendrix studied the figurative and abstract; the mechanics of song and the minutiae of sound.

More than anybody, musicians and those who chronicle their lives and careers know that the history of music is far from complete. From the vantage point of the twenty-first century where vast amounts of old as well as new music are available it may seem we know it all and have heard it all, but Hendrix's comprehensive exploration and singular interpretation of the songs of both his predecessors and peers underlines the ongoing need to assemble and accurately put together all the pieces of the jigsaw of real history in the field, meaning that forgotten, overlooked or unrecorded musicians may have actually broken new ground before others who came after them.

As a musician who had the invaluable first-hand experience of an intensely vibrant strand of culture, post-war R&B, which greatly affected the rock genre with which he became synonymous, Hendrix is a vital prism though which we can unpack all of the many complex sociological and political layers that surround the phenomenon of the modern-day pop song, both as a means of artistic expression and industrial product.

Hendrix appears in many guises and the challenge he poses to any observers who attempt to analyse his work is this range of constituent parts in the artistic whole. There is Hendrix the singer; Hendrix the lyric writer; Hendrix the composer; Hendrix the guitar player; Hendrix the improviser; Hendrix the bandleader; Hendrix the listener and researcher; Hendrix the technophile; Hendrix the entertainer; Hendrix the dancer, or rather the showman with his own take on black song and dance traditions. Instead of trying to make sense of all of these facets of his life it is easy to become fixated on any single one, especially that of Hendrix the guitar deity, a temptation hard to resist, given the way the instrument has become such a totem in rock lore.

The border between virtuosity and gimmickry, the suspicion that a player can pull a few scene-stealing moves from a "bag of tricks" as much as he can genuinely push the envelope in terms of creativity, was being crossed long before the advent of Hendrix, but the tension between these two realities crystallized very conspicuously in him, to the extent that his profound relationship with a fundamental form of contemporary expression, the song, was perhaps obfuscated. When David Crosby, another musical legend who knew and played with Hendrix said, "Jimi Hendrix could play better than our best guys, and he did it while dancing and while being completely outrageous", he further emphasized the depth of debate around him. Did "our best guys" include the pace setters of jazz as well as any cutting-edge rock and pop musicians in America?

Was "dancing" to be taken literally as well as more figuratively, as in an ability to create a number of interesting sensations in the rhythmic content of composition as well as moving one's body in the heat of performance? Did "outrageous" mean daring and innovative in the studio as well as visually provocative and compelling on stage? Whatever the viewfinder through which Hendrix is seen, the portrait that comes into clear and sharp focus is that of the maverick, the original, the iconoclast, for whom a prevailing format of American R&B or British rock is by no means a comfortable fit.

Of all the genres of music relevant to his imagination and personal sensibility it is the blues that appears most appropriate, but as much as he draws on its historical models he is interested in extending, and more importantly asserting, what the term itself means to him personally, from a musical, emotional and intellectual standpoint.

A spell on those two white boys?

Try as he might have done to rule it out of his life as musician, Hendrix had to contend with the racial politics of both the music industry and society as a whole. Over time it has become commonplace to assert that he was a "black man in a white man's world", implying that as an exponent of rock he had strayed onto territory that was beyond his expected boundary as an ethnic minority artist, but this is far too vague an assertion. Hendrix was an unorthodox black man in a black man's world prior to being considered an outsider in a white man's world, and the difficulty in assessing his life and work stems to a certain extent from a refusal to even acknowledge just how complex a black man's world is before any other race is slotted into the equation.

Still, Hendrix was well aware that by playing with two white musicians in The Experience he could not but stoke an inferno of controversy on "black magic" and the like. He and the incumbents threw some humorous oil onto the fire in a deleted scene from *A Film About Jimi Hendrix*. Mitch Mitchell enquires: "Jimi, did you put a spell on those two white boys?" Hendrix shoots back: "Well, I think they put a spell on *me*. We're all brothers and sisters, aren't we?" The nervous giggles that punctuate the rhetoric flag up his awareness that there is anything but equality in his lifetime, a standpoint that chimed with Hendrix's numerous statements on the iniquities of the establishment and the subsequent importance of music as a vehicle for the truth.

One of the most thought-provoking of all the hundreds of pictures of Hendrix, Mitchell and Noel Redding together is a kind of "candid camera" moment of the three men in a dressing room prior to a TV appearance in 1967. Given the importance of image for budding pop stars at this time, as is still the case today, it is no surprise that there is a barber in attendance.

Hendrix is in the chair while his bandmates look on. They all have Afros. But only Hendrix has "proper" black hair, or *nappy roots*, puffed into the full-bodied sphere that sat atop the rainbow of threads that adorned his body.

Smiling boyishly, Mitchell and Redding are distanced from Hendrix at that moment. Whether or not they are in admiration of his hair or awestruck at the sight of a black man in a barber's chair, possibly the first time they had ever seen such a thing, the fact is that one of Hendrix's defining physical features is highlighted as "other", even though his colleagues have copped his style as a reinforcement of the musical alliance formed between the three. The Experience is a group that crosses the border of ethnicity, yet at the same time there is no denying the differentiations of African-American and Caucasian among musicians who exist in a world where skin colour and hair texture cannot escape scrutiny. Hendrix the artist intent on creating his own credo through music still had to deal with judgements and perceptions of him, both positive and negative, because he dared to buck convention in the company of blacks and whites alike. It is commonplace to hold up The Experience as a multi-racial model in a racially divided music industry, but that does not mean that the group was idealistically de-racialized, or that the cultural assumptions that attended Hendrix magically vanished.

His anomalous ways also occasionally gave rise to misunderstandings from certain audiences. Presumptions on what black musicians presented on stage still died hard, regardless of whether they were being their own kind of black. Here is a very telling anecdote from a British punter, 18-year-old Brian Wallace, who recalls the confusion of seeing the Jimi Hendrix Experience at the Imperial Hotel in Darlington in 1967:

> According to people who say they were there the Imperial must have held 2,000 people. But there was only about 100 to 150 there. I saw loads of bands every Thursday night. Hendrix was a bit of a let down for me and a few others as Thursday night was a soul night, so we expected a black soul band from the USA. Normally the soul bands were good to dance to. Hendrix was completely different.[24]

Hence a substantial socio-cultural and political charge is ignited by the question of the song and Jimi Hendrix due to the artist's challenge to the norms in a world that was stratified along many different lines. The song and Jimi Hendrix is about the complexities of race, the fluidity of genre, the blurring of lines between art and entertainment, the vagaries of the music industry, the disorientation of society in flux, the self-assertion of the individual who is willing to flout all prevailing conventions.

Right in the midst of these live-wire debates, he still created. The song was a key form of expression. But it was not free of complications – for himself and several others.

Part 2: The Songs of Jimi Hendrix

Playing (and losing) the name game

Making records has always been fraught with risk, reward, and recrimination. Numerous are the tales of barefaced exploitation of budding artists; this has led to an insider's jargon as expressively rich as some victims are heartbreakingly poor.

Ghosting is a term that has been in circulation for so long it is hard to pinpoint its genesis. Certainly at the time when pop music started to become a lucrative business it was understood all too well by musicians, but rarely used outside of the world of entertainment for the simple reason that it would have caused at best embarrassment and at worse scandal. Ghosting was essentially faking, cheating and lying to the general public; an illusion that what consumers heard was the work of who they thought they were listening to. Ghosting was the practice of having a lesser-known musician or singer cut a track that would later be released under the name of a star performer. To paraphrase a timeless socio-political maxim: the first casualty of the music industry is the truth.

Other areas of entertainment had long adopted such counterfeit, and the technique was fairly widespread in film. But the disbelief that the public was invited to suspend in some instances was perhaps not something that would cause outrage or, more importantly, lessen the impact of the work. Numerous Hollywood musicals featured ghost singers who intoned the parts that were mouthed on screen by matinee idols and popular actors, sometimes becoming legends among their peers while consigned to a life of obscurity. For example, Bill Lee dubbed for John Kerr (*South Pacific*), Matt Mattox (*Seven Brides for Seven Brothers*) and Christopher Plummer (*The Sound of Music*) while the "playback singer" for icons such as Deborah Kerr (*The King and I*), Marilyn Monroe (*Gentlemen Prefer Blondes*) and Natalie Wood (*West Side Story*) was Marni Nixon. With its dazzling score by Leonard Bernstein and glamour plated depiction of youth subculture, *West Side Story* put the onus on the dramatic substance and visual panache of Wood and fellow cast members. The songs were crucial but so was the snappy choreography and narrative drive of the movie. Wood looked the part. Nixon gave her character the requisite voice for a musical.

However, the ethical magnitude of ghosting in the world of pop is immense because it collapsed the very foundation on which not just the music but the culture of its constituency, which from the mid-1950s, was the teenager, rested. The fetish object on which this hugely important new group of consumers began to increasingly define its identity – the vinyl recording – led to the hero worship and deification of its creators, who would gradually become not so much genies let out of the fabled bottle as geniuses stamped on a small circle of black wax. Building a "gramophone library" of 78s was what older folks did. Collecting records, and emulating those who made them, above all their style of dress, thus cementing the synergy between music and the fashion industry, raised the stakes. An older jazz fan once told me that as a boy in the 1950s, seeing the sleeve of Miles Davis's *Milestones* with the trumpeter strikingly cool in his green button-down shirt was as instrumental as the music in the construction of the artist's mystique. The appearance of pop stars was of paramount importance, and although they were generally not expected to provide the same degree of virtuosity as Davis and his ilk they were *believed* to be the players featured on their own records. If the sounds we hear seeping out of the radio are in fact not the work of whom we are told is the performer then the entire validity of broadcast media and the precious commodity of a 45 rpm single is impugned beyond redemption. The players play to the public but the players cannot *play* the public because the public can end the game any time it sees fit.

Simulation in the service of make-believe kicked into touch the dream that pop could be a force to be reckoned with in an evolving consumer society. Those who instigated and perpetrated the act of ghosting were lying to listeners. Pop stars weren't allowed to be homosexual when singing love songs for teenage girls because the edifice of romanticism constructed around them would come tumbling down if they were outed.

At the moment Hendrix hit the deliciously sunny chords of 'Twist And Shout' during his audition for the Isley Brothers in the early 1960s he may not have been aware that he was making an indirect connection to a man who was directly involved in one of the most notorious ghosting affairs of the time: Phil Spector. He had produced the original version of the song 'He's A Rebel' that was recorded by a group called The Top Notes in the winter of 1961. By the time spring had sprung The Blossoms, a girl group led by the fine vocalist Darlene Love, recorded the same song for Spector, but the music was subsequently credited to another group, The Crystals, and the record's runaway success led to a quite surreal state of affairs. It was a scam of truly epic proportions.

While The Crystals were out on tour, the single started picking up major airplay. As the buzz became deafening, the "hitmakers" in question were congratulated for something into which they had absolutely no input. The singers who did not sing on the precious product then had to learn to imitate the singers who did, so that they could convincingly bring to life, in future, live performances of *their* big tune; this caused problems because Love's finesse in the high register was not easy to negotiate.

Ironically, 'He's A Rebel' was meant for neither The Blossoms, who recorded it, nor The Crystals, who became the faces of the song. Composer Gene Pitney had The Shirelles in mind, which makes a great deal of sense given that they were one of the most successful of the wave of "girl groups" that became part of the pop landscape in the 1950s and '60s, but for whatever reason they declined, or were advised to do so.

Thereafter, twists of fate as well as the sheer cynicism of the music industry took on a sharp focus. Smelling success upon hearing the song, Spector was keen to record it but his sense of urgency went into overdrive when he learned that Vicki Carr was also about to cut a version for Liberty records. Having recently bought out his partner Lester Sill to become head of the Philles label, Spector had to score a hit to shore up his reputation and finances. Competition thus began hotting up. With multiple renditions of the same song set to come into existence, the onus was on claiming the birth of a hit.

Spector wanted to be the all-powerful midwife. Because The Crystals were touring the east coast, he turned to a group that, like him, was based in Los Angeles, and that happened to be The Blossoms. They were in the right place at the right time, though they would find they had trusted the wrong man when it came to their rights.

While the lead singer of The Blossoms provided what could be termed foreground moments by way of melody, the contribution of the backing vocalists added extra authority or sensuality to a key phrase in a verse, and was not an element of an arrangement to be discounted.

The hierarchical relationship between female accompanists and male bandleaders was complex. There could be the absolute power of a James Brown, right down to fines for missed notes, lack of punctuality or slovenly appearance. Ray Charles went so far as to facilitate the making of the album, *Yesterday, Today, Tomorrow,* that his backing vocalists, the Raelettes, made under their own name. The fact that he had a long-running affair, and fathered a child, with one of the group, Margie Hendrix, suggests his intentions may not have been purely magnanimous.

In any case the tendency of male bandleaders to thrust their own names upon their backing vocalists, as in The Raelettes or Ike Turner & the Ikettes, reflected both egos and a deep-seated patriarchy in the music business that would not have made life any easier for women who, as Mick Jagger condescendingly sniffed, did "those oohs and aahs", and were rarely given the chance to fully exercise their talents on their own terms. The relative absence of female writers and producers ensured the status quo.

Ironically, black women were highly valued as backing vocalists because of their ability to improvise and embellish in a way that was not common for their white counterparts who usually stuck rigidly to parts that were written in advance for them. Black women were more than *readers*. They added something of themselves, their personalities and their own response to a written piece of music, which was noted by composers, arrangers and producers who trusted their ability to extemporize and imbue additional feeling into a song. But this was not reflected in their status.

When interviewed for Morgan Neville's *20 Feet From Stardom* (2014), the excellent documentary that tells the story of the background vocalists who were a notable part of the pop landscape, while often working in disadvantageous conditions, Love said: "What hurt was when people hear it on the radio and go that's The Crystals, that's a great song, and they're sitting there telling that to me, not knowing I did it."

Having said that, they had to get real. Love understood all too well that Spector was a major hitmaker and it was in her interests to keep working with him, hoping that the pendulum might swing back in her favour with him deigning to release a song in *her* name. She decided to persevere. "We go in the studio I'm signed with him now ... everything's legal. We record 'He's Sure The Boy I Love'", she recalls. "I'm tootling down the street a couple of months later and I hear the disc jockey say well, here's the new record by The Crystals. I'm going The Crystals ... what did he do? Fly them in and didn't tell us. No, it was my voice on 'He's Sure The Boy I Love'. I was *pissed*."[1]

What gave Spector the upper hand was the fact that he lorded it in the studio. It was a controlled environment. A recording could be made and then take on a life of its own, right down to incorrect authorship being thrust upon it. Taped audio had an essential quality that raised the prospect of misuse and exploitation: permanence. It captured sound for posterity. This was diametrically opposed to the impermanence, the perishable nature of the stage performance. The concert was to be experienced in the moment. The 45 rpm single or album was to be enjoyed over and over. This meant that once music was on tape it could be placed in a new timeframe and invested with a different identity. It could be "rush-released" under the name of an impostor, or made available at a later date in such a way that appeared "authentic" but presented a version of events that was contentious if not actually disadvantageous to some parties.

Such was the situation Jimi Hendrix encountered at a crucial stage of his career. In the autumn of 1967, a year that had seen the vocalist-guitarist-songwriter take giant steps in his career by way of several successful singles, a debut album, *Are You Experienced?* and a lengthy bout of touring in Britain, Europe and the USA, he was hit by a blast from the past in a manner he had not anticipated. Musical skeletons started waltzing out of the cupboard of obscurity to enter the full glare of unwanted notoriety.

Songs he had previously recorded with singer Curtis Knight in 1965, who had hired Hendrix when he was a struggling session musician, were issued by a production company, PPX, which was run by Ed Chalpin. Tellingly, the material was billed in such a way as to clearly capitalize on the name that Hendrix was busy making for himself. The single 'Hush Now/Flashing' was attributed to Curtis Knight and Jimi Hendrix, thus clearly implying that the work was that of a partnership of equals. Hendrix, his management and legal team didn't see it that way, and, upon learning of the product, immediately took court action, "restraining the defendants from passing off 'Hush Now/Flashing' as my recording and from issuing or publishing 'Hush Now/Flashing' under my name at all".[2] The matter was hugely important because artistic endeavour, quality control and standing in the market place were at stake.

In a nutshell Hendrix considered the music to be sub-standard, falling well short of the high bar that he had raised in the whirlwind ten months that he had been in England where he succeeded in winning a large fanbase by way of the singles 'Hey Joe', 'Purple Haze' and 'The Wind Cries Mary', pieces that offered proof of his ability to both imaginatively recast material written by another and compose original songs of his own. These three releases broach the themes of infidelity, the liberation and desperation brought on by narcotics, and the deep pathos caused by friction in a couple's relationship with a masterful blend of vivid imagery and observational acuity. All the aforementioned tracks are consolidated by a series of grippingly novel sonic backdrops. Hendrix reveals himself to be a pop artist who nonetheless has a certain gravitas.

By all accounts the songs yielded by the Knight–Hendrix collaboration did not pass muster. It would be unfair to condemn them as irretrievably poor work but compared to what Hendrix had released under his own name, more to the point what he wanted to present to the public, they were in no way the optimal representation of his talents. Unsurprisingly the legal wrangling that ensued between Hendrix's manager, Michael Jeffrey, and Chalpin became acrimonious, and the dispute was finally settled in 1969, with the granting to Chalpin of the distribution rights of the *Band of Gypsys* album.

As a cautionary tale the events are instructive. On the one hand Hendrix comes across as at best naïve, at worse downright lackadaisical given that he put his name to a contract with Chalpin without properly weighing up its implications, but the key component of the case is the fact that it was seen – by the artist in any case – as a "practice session" rather than an official recording date. Hendrix's own deposition confirmed this in no uncertain terms: "I verily believe that without my knowledge, consent or approval the said practice session, or a part of it, was recorded at the time and I verily believe that the defendants have incorporated or caused it to be incorporated in the recording, which they now intend to release for sale under the name 'Hush Now/Flashing'. At no time during the said practice session did I sing a song as such and from the beginning of such a session I was under the impression that I was 'jamming' with old acquaintances".[3] Jam at your peril, Jimi.

Much as Hendrix could be collared with head-in-the-clouds unprofessionalism for letting the situation arise in the first place, there is a question of trust to consider. As is made clear from the above statement the guitarist, who also played an uncommon instrument for the sessions – eight-string bass – believed that what was taking place was an informal reunion with an artist who had previously employed him, and with whom, by common consent, he had enjoyed a good working relationship and friendship. Recordings of the sessions in which there is a conversation between Hendrix and Knight, in the live room, and Chalpin, in the control booth, reveal that the guitarist did indeed have misgivings about the possible use of any material from the "practice" or jam that was about to take place, and clearly voiced his concerns. To Hendrix's demand that "you can't you know, use my name for none of this stuff, though. Right?", which is reiterated by Knight – "You can't use his name for any of this" – there is a nonchalant dismissal from Chalpin: "Oh, don't worry about it".

Doubts still assail Hendrix and he can't refrain from further pressing the issue – "No serious though, serious though, you know?", so Chalpin becomes more insistent to the point of being prickly – "Like I said, don't worry about it". There's one final splutter of resistance from Hendrix – "Huh?"– before Chalpin then moves to swiftly silence any rising dissent for good: "I won't use it, don't worry". Except that he did, and there was much more than a furrowed brow from the artist as a result.

With the benefit of hindsight it is not unreasonable to argue that Hendrix, his suspicion creeping into full view, shouldn't have let the tapes roll, something of which he was fully aware, but the whole scenario, and certainly the exchange that took place between him, Knight and Chalpin, makes an essential point about power dynamics in the music industry in the period during which the guitarist was in the ascendant. The means of production, namely the studio, the quarter-inch reels, the mikes, amps and mixing desk, was largely not in the hands of musicians. Executives, label bosses, A&R and producers could and did place an iron grip on careers, which inevitably meant that any artist could be manipulated simply for the sake of product.

Bearing that in mind, it is important to place the Hendrix–Chalpin affair in the lineage of the Spector–Blossoms scandal. The common denominators are a betrayal of trust and the absence of a transparent legal framework for the recording of music in the first place. Reckless as he may have been, Hendrix sought and was duly given reassurances. They were not honoured. Unfortunately we don't have a recording of conversations that may have taken place between Spector and The Blossoms prior to the studio date for 'He's A Rebel' but, as Love tells it, the producer gave them no idea that he was about to tell the wider world that the fruits of their labour would be placed on another tree. To paraphrase an infamous British courtroom testimony, *well he wouldn't, would he.* Spector–Blossoms and Hendrix–Chalpin form a tragic symmetry of manipulation and exploitation. Musical contributions were presented as half-truths.

Just six years separate Spector–Blossoms (1961) from Hendrix–Chalpin (1967). Yet in that time much change took place. The exponential growth of pop as a commercial phenomenon was accompanied by an increasing interest if not obsession with genre and sub-genre. The decisive split between pop and rock, and the splintering of rock into the precise strains of acid, space, country, psychedelic and garage, yielded a substantial new cultural harvest that was not for fans of chart toppers like Doris Day.

Furthermore, the album was growing in importance to rival if not exceed that of the single. Hendrix's immense contribution to the art of the long player makes his anguish over the Chalpin affair all the more understandable because the unsuspecting public would believe that he was just banging out sub-standard songs, which were really loose jams, rather than thinking carefully about composition, arrangement and engineering. As his *real* work showed, there were high production values to uphold.

Hence in the greater scheme of things the twin scandals of The Blossoms–Spector and Hendrix–Chalpin being duped by dodgy producers with self-serving agendas was about considerably more than dollars lost by the unfortunate artists in question. It concerned careers and the heartlessly cruel irony of forced invisibility and visibility.

The Blossoms were an omission. Hendrix an unwilling inclusion. The Blossoms were heard and not seen while Hendrix was seen against his wishes and heard to his disadvantage, the ghost of himself rather than the ghost who stood in for others.

Where Spector saw The Blossoms as a footnote and a song they performed as a headline, Chalpin viewed Hendrix as a major, potentially lucrative story even though he was a minor player in somebody else's session. As this policy shift occurred there were commentators in the media who were savvy enough to spot the stunt that was being pulled, and realize that a reputation was being traded on, a growing stature was being exploited. To see an artist as a major draw beyond music they were part of, in some capacity or another – as a casual jam session attendee rather than an established member of a group – was to take the general public for patsies. The *Los Angeles Times* decided to cry wolf. "Beware when an album shrinks the featured vocalist's name into small type beneath the twice as large name of a backup musician."[4] In this case the songs of Jimi Hendrix were not exactly the songs of Jimi Hendrix.

Indeed, the fact that Hendrix's name overshadowed Knight's spoke of the clear perception of the guitarist as a cash cow and the intent to milk him for all he was worth. The songs were neither here nor there. Quality wise there may have been little cream to skim but, over a number of years, the original yield was watered down way beyond what anybody could have reasonably imagined. Hendrix's work as a one-time member of Curtis Knight & The Squires and his occasional jam sessions with them gradually elided into a body of work that is anything but consistent and coherent.

Noted Hendrix biographer John McDermott has the pertinent facts and figures:

> More than a hundred albums have been crafted from some 40 studio recordings and a handful of live appearances. None of these albums justify the extravagant claims their titles boast, and most feature low fidelity variations, remixes, edited versions and instrumentals of the same material – often with their song titles changed.[5]

Got my mojo working

Whether in the book publishing or music industry, putting old material in a new jacket has been standard practice for many years. Changing the name of an album is more insidious, and there can't be a record collector alive who hasn't been caught out at least once when it comes to buying a "new" item by an artist only to find out that they already own it. Fandom is a form of devotion, though, and professing faith in an artist can easily lead to submitting to the mysterious ways of the capitalist Supreme Being of a record label or producer who can play god with the incumbent's heavenly offerings.

Hendrix is an extreme case of an artist whose comprehensive output has reached a volume that is wildly out of proportion with what might pass as the representation of himself that *he* would have been happy to endorse. The distance between the poles of authorized Hendrix and bootlegged Hendrix, in-his-lifetime Hendrix and posthumous Hendrix, intended-for-release Hendrix and taped-regardless Hendrix, leader session Hendrix and sideman session Hendrix, is significant, to say the least.

This means that defining Hendrix as a recording artist is actually much less straightforward than the standard narrative that holds that he cut three studio albums and several live records in the mesmerizing years between his commercial "breakout" in 1967 and his tragic death in 1970. Exactly how many Hendrix releases on vinyl and CD are in circulation is a moot point to this day, with McDermott's calculation on the exponential harvesting of the Curtis Knight sessions alone giving a useful clue as to why the Hendrix catalogue has gone on to reach quite a sprawling, unhealthy surplus.

To all intents and purposes, *Are You Experienced?*, *Axis: Bold As Love*, *Electric Ladyland*, *Smash Hits* and *Band of Gypsys* are the *real* Hendrix discography. This is the kind of statement that puts us on solid ground as observers of his work. It doesn't necessarily further our understanding of Hendrix as a creative force, though. As problematic as all of those other releases are, because they are mostly of varying quality, they nonetheless contain songs that still underline his great depth of talent. Tunes that were not part of a sequence of tracks of which Hendrix himself conceived, such as 'Drifting' and 'Ezy Ryder' (from 1971's *The Cry of Love*), or 'Hear My Train A Comin'' (from 1971's *Rainbow Bridge*) or 'Earth Blues' and 'Izabella' (from 1972's *War Heroes*) are hardly disposable fare. They are anything but *filler*. There is an argument that several of the tracks on these posthumous albums would actually make more narrative sense if they were moved around and featured on different releases, and it stands to reason that the sprawl of material beyond the "classic albums" has not been as well overseen and curated as it could have been. But the fact of the matter is that these additional pieces broaden our portrait of Hendrix as an extraordinary talent who proved himself capable of generating a wealth of material in a relatively short time.

Musicians secure their place in history by defining moments, a single composition or set of songs, as well as an output sustained over a number of years. In the grand scheme of things Hendrix was here and gone in a flash, his star extinguished just as it appeared to still have a long, potentially limitless trajectory ahead of it. Yet his artistic life in numbers does not suggest idleness or a desire to shirk a strong work ethic. Discounting multiple versions and reprises, there are at least 73 songs for which he is credited as composer. Then there are pieces of which he is co-composer and where his input is so substantial that the music deserves a place in the Hendrix canon. The obvious case in point is *Doriella Du Fontaine*, a startling hybrid of rap, rock and funk that was the result of a jam session between Hendrix, Buddy Miles and Jalal Mansur Nuriddin of The Last Poets, under the moniker of Lightnin' Rod. Or how about 'Mojo Man' by The Ghetto Fighters? It is more than a curio in any Hendrix record collection.

'Mojo Man' is a thrilling piece of tough, taut rock-funk that resulted from the enduring simpatico relationship Hendrix enjoyed with two twins, Albert and Arthur Allen aka The Ghetto Fighters, who knew him when he was down on his luck in New York, trying to make the all-important jump from session player to bandleader. They had seen him go on to enjoy stratospheric success with The Experience in England and reconnected with him upon his return to America. The story of Hendrix's involvement in 'Mojo Man' is highly instructive of his ability to push the creative envelope in circumstances that are far from ideal. The basic rhythm and vocal tracks were cut by the Allens at the storied Fame studio in Muscle Shoals, Alabama run by Rick Hall, the man who had produced epochal soul music for giants such as Aretha Franklin, Otis Redding and Etta James, among others. Featured on the session was the New Orleans piano legend James Booker, a superb player from whom Dr. John learned a great deal.

At the time Hendrix was in Los Angeles with his trusty engineer Eddie Kramer. They were about to mix tapes for a live album. Allen played him the songs from the Muscle Shoals session, which the guitarist liked but he was too busy with his own material. However, upon his return to New York, Hendrix did ask the Allen brothers to contribute backing vocals to two new songs, 'Freedom' and 'Dolly Dagger', and thereafter he rekindled his interest in the track they had played him.

> When we were in the studio with him he asked about 'Mojo Man'. He asked me to get the tape because he had ideas that he wanted to record for it. I told him I didn't have the master tape, I only had the mix that had been made. Jimi said: "That's okay. We can make a new master. Eddie knows how to do that." I went home, got the tape and came straight back. Jimi put on some incredible guitar and transformed the song.[6]

This is the flipside of the same coin – the informal musical gathering – that almost thoroughly compromised Hendrix when the collaborators were not on his level. The creative energy was reactive as well as proactive, participative as well as instinctive. While the immense individuality and strength of character he stamps on what can reasonably be deemed his high watermarks, the pieces which he wrote and either produced or co-produced, form the backbone of his legacy, the contributions he made in much more desultory circumstances, the fleeting moments squeezed in between busy studio dates, are not without consequence. As Allen said, 'Mojo Man' became *something else* after Hendrix had laid down his guitar tracks. That is no hyperbole. Hendrix brings a kind of rhythmic and textural agitation to bear on the melody that, crucially, does not derail the all-important vocal carriage of the song. It is a superlative display of much more than attention-seeking virtuosity. The flurries of sound added by Hendrix, like fireflies in a night sky, cohere with the arrangement.

Even after making it as a leader, Hendrix proved a frequent guest in the company of others. The ego that drove him to become a star in his own right was held in check by a musical intelligence and humility that led to continual sessions with friends such as the Allen brothers, or, as he said of Curtis Knight, "old acquaintances", making it clear that the creation of music in varying capacities, as leader and accompanist, remained the central dynamic of his life, even as his ascent to the run of megastar in the music industry exerted enormous pressure on his personal life. A near relentless round of taxing, international tours as well as a hedonistic lifestyle would sadly take their toll, but any putative depiction of Hendrix as a victim of rock 'n' roll excess cannot mask the relentless productivity he sustained in the heady days prior to his untimely demise.

All credible sources, from lovers and bandmates to family and friends, concur that Hendrix spent inordinate amounts of time attempting to unlock and master every secret the guitar had to offer a curious mind. His commitment to the command of his instrument led to countless hours of practice as well as forensic study of the songs made by a host of other artists he admired.

Central to Hendrix's life is a love of the world of sound, especially the realm opened up by new technology, and a deep-seated fascination with the process of playing and matching appropriate lyric to melody.

Collaborating with others was central to both his lifestyle and ethos. The jam session, as Hendrix himself saw it, was by no means an inconsequential endeavour. Although the circumstances were informal there could be valid musical ideas sparked by the symbiosis of strong personalities, or perhaps more importantly, an initial fuse of musical understanding between players could be lit with a view to an even more memorable creative combustion further down the line.

Are You Experienced? and *Axis: Bold As Love* are the two albums that cemented the Jimi Hendrix Experience as the most compelling new act in pop, with the added attraction of being a combo that cut across the lines of race, culture and geography. On the one hand the albums were made in Britain, following Hendrix's relocation to London in September 1966. On the other hand it was a one-man American invasion to rival Britain's incursion into entertainment USA a few years before. Whether Hendrix on the BBC was a fair trade for The Beatles on the Ed Sullivan show was not the point, though. What really mattered was the rapid progress made by the group due to their incendiary live shows as well as work in the studio.

By all accounts Hendrix had a stroke of fortune insofar as he found a manager in Chas Chandler, who was genuinely as interested in nurturing the talent that astounded him when he first heard the guitarist in Greenwich Village, New York as he was securing him the kind of stardom that would result in financial gain as well as celebrity status. Furthermore, Chandler was a more benign presence than that of his successor Michael Jeffrey, who had previously managed Chandler when he was the bassist in the successful Newcastle R&B band, The Animals. Chandler had been obliged to turn to Jeffrey when he went into management, even though there had been major disputes over his apparent manipulation of the group as well as alleged financial impropriety.

In any case Chandler was Hendrix's producer as well as manager and kept his musician head on in their working relationship. He was largely responsive to the originality of his new charge. He noticed something in Hendrix that several others did not.

Writing and recording aside, Hendrix saw playing in an impromptu manner as an integral part of his musical culture, which was something Chandler could well turn to his advantage. He knew that his new charge had to become a face and fixture on the pop scene in London so he judiciously made a point of taking him to clubs such as the Speakeasy, the Cromwellian, the Bag O' Nails and other haunts, where sitting in with whoever was on stage was seen as the norm. It was a way to be seen and heard. After auditioning several musicians with Chandler, Hendrix formed The Experience, comprising Noel Redding on bass and Mitch Mitchell on drums, though the Liverpudlian

Aynsley Dunbar came close to securing the latter berth. Getting gigs, getting into the studio and getting a deal were next on the to-do list.

Such an approach has to be cast against the backdrop of a music industry that was vastly different in mechanics than what it is today. The recording contract, which in Britain was harder to secure, given the fewer number of labels in operation compared to America, became something of a Holy Grail, and it was not won without considerable endeavour in most cases. Being signed, for the most part, involved being able to prove that one could play songs in real time rather than create them in the surroundings of a studio, which in the early to mid-1960s, was still largely an environment for the capture of a performance rather than the extensive manipulation of audio in delayed time. Post-production, as a concept, was nowhere near as developed then as it is now.

This is one of the reasons why many of the artists who were signed often landed their deal on the back of a gig to which an A&R executive, impresario or manager was invited. An artist, Hendrix being the epitome thereof, had to be entirely committed to the idea of playing as there was a potential professional advantage to be gained by whosoever had clocked up sufficient stage time to be able to give the best account of themselves if a "kingmaker" took an interest. Musicians who jammed frequently were, if they had any semblance of talent, staying in good shape should a chance come their way. Hendrix played a lot on his way up, and apparently did not deviate from that praxis even after he had *made* it. His essential cultural foundation did not erode. It was a major part of his creative DNA.

Korner stone

Stories of Hendrix "cutting" other guitarists and leaving audiences open mouthed have been told ad infinitum to the extent that they have almost tipped the guitarist's legend into the tiresome mythology of the extra-terrestrial force. But what is perhaps more revealing is the observation of how self-possessed he was prior to taking to the stage, as if he was intent on bringing the light of artistry amidst the heat of spectacle, and that the inevitable competitive undercurrent that might flow through a room, where any number of "name musicians" had convened, did not appear to faze him in any way.

Certainly in the early days of life in London he did not travel with a star's entourage and the lack of fuss may have been entirely to his liking. Jam session culture was sufficiently well established in the city for gatherings to be plentiful, several of which revolved around the guitarist-vocalist and bandleader, Alexis Korner. A child of Greek and Austrian migrants, Korner had developed a great passion for older forms of black music, and started his career playing the kind of languorous folk-blues epitomized by the legendary 12-string guitarist, vocalist and composer Leadbelly.

Korner formed his first band, Alexis Korner's Breakdown Group, which featured harmonica player-vocalist Cyril Davies in 1959, and they continued their association when Korner launched Blues Incorporated in 1962, where a much more explicit influence of electric blues came into play. Between them Davies and Korner were able to develop an audience for the hard, muscular sound of urban black America, as pioneered by legends such as Muddy Waters and Howlin' Wolf, that was increasingly capturing the imagination of young British musicians who related more to the sense of invigoration and ignition in both their electric instruments and sexually charged voices than they did the harmonic gymnastics of modern jazz. Korner and Davies's residency at the buzzing Marquee Club in Wardour Street, Soho, central London in the early 1960s was a turning point in appreciation for the blues and its outgrowths such as R&B in post-war Britain. Blues Incorporated's 1962 recorded debut *R&B From The Marquee*, which was actually laid down at Decca studios in London rather than the named venue, remains a key entry in the canon of blues in Britain. Perhaps more importantly Blues Incorporated served as a springboard to many an aspiring musician in London and Korner acted as an informal mentor to members of the Rolling Stones, The Yardbirds and Cream, groups whose considerable international success eventually eclipsed his own work.

A prolific recording artist, Korner reprised anthems such as Waters' 'I Got My Mojo Working' and Son House's 'Preachin' The Blues', but they were supplemented by originals such as 'Keep Your Hands Off Her', a vocal piece and 'Downtown', an instrumental number. In other words there was a respectful application of the tried and tested American model of mixing old and new material, or rather showing how the former could give rise to the latter. The seminal references to the blues such as in 'I Got My Mojo Working' took pride of place but Korner's own personality was allowed to shine through, as he had an understanding of the mechanics of the genre and, more importantly, its underlying role as a reflection of a range of life experiences. One of his most engaging strategies was to present direct anglicizations of blues titles or African-American cultural references that aficionados would have very little trouble spotting, so that 'Stormy Monday' became 'Rainy Tuesday' and 'Collard Greens' became 'Cabbage Greens'.

Historically speaking, the advent of Korner, Davies and Blues Incorporated did more than bring new names to post-war British popular music which was coming to terms with the fact it could be shaped, comprehensively and irrevocably, by the cultural ingenuity of what in the early 1960s was an ethnic minority group across the Atlantic still relatively shrouded in mystery. What the descendants of slaves were doing, not just as players of music, but sound adventurers who realized that the guitar, mouth organ and voice were sources of tremendous narrative depth, and alchemists of language, capable of investing a supposedly mundane word such as "baby" with an immense new emotional capital, was nothing short of a bold, revolutionary act. Acknowledging the blues as a space for self-realization in the fullest sense of the term, from the announcement to the world of both joy and pain to the affirmation of fever-pitch sexuality as well as low-key drudgery, empowered a generation of British musicians for whom a model of chaste investigation of feeling and meaning, as epitomized by crooners and the more sedate dance bands, did not bring satisfaction.

The blues brought to the stage by Korner and his acolytes was a necessary form of raw material for an industrial-scale pop culture phenomenon. Indeed, the very name Blues Incorporated implied influence beyond the parochial. Blues Appreciated by the masses that wanted something new. Blues Implanted into the fabric of society in flux.

Korner and Davies's gigs at the Marquee, as well as their indefatigable work in bringing influential blues musicians to Britain, created a climate that was conducive for the likes of Hendrix to put forward his own interpretation of the blues. There had to be a fundamental belief in the value of the idiom so that an audience would even accept in the first place that an exceptional American guitarist newly arrived in Britain who could negotiate and invigorate the known characteristics of the 12-bar form was a sensational authority rather than an illegitimate anomaly. Hendrix was able to stand as an essentially progressive High Priest of the music because it had evangelists who had proved themselves to be more than willing to preach the virtues of a song in which emotionally naked lyric and clearly mapped sounds, their sensuality and intensity wrought by nothing more than a downbeat, a bend of pitch and a pentatonic phrase of guitar or harmonica, could evoke celebration or damnation of a lover so vividly that it could move the most hardy of souls to tears, even when a man ain't s'posed to cry.

These adopter disciples doggedly built an audience of converts prior to the coming of an artist messiah who could take the blues to thrilling new places. Korner helped to prepare hearts and minds for the likes of Hendrix to both captivate and capture.

Inevitably, their paths crossed. Symbolically, the meeting would take place at a transatlantic gathering in London where informal rather than formal circumstances were able to create magic. It was all about the "after hours" rather than the booked gig, Korner's biographer Harry Shapiro notes:

> In the autumn of 1966 the American blues festival came to town, to the Royal Albert Hall. After the show several artists on the bill, which included Little Brother Montgomery and Roosevelt Sykes, made a point of going to the all-nighter at Cousins in Greek Street, Soho to play with Alexis. Jimi turned up at Cousins, paid his entrance money and quietly walked in.[7]

Hendrix made a big impression on all present when he played, though apparently Korner conceded almost begrudgingly that the new arrival was not just another contender. "Pretty good, yeah, pretty good". Maybe he saw a kindred spirit who had unquestionable authenticity as a bluesman while also spotting a subversive who was seeking to reach new musical horizons from an ages-old idiomatic headland.

While Korner did not dive into the same mercurial technological waters that became a defining feature of Hendrix's career, he wrote and performed some outstanding original songs, an obvious highlight being 'Am I My Brother's Keeper', and his considerable strength of character has made the bulk of his work age particularly well. Korner and Hendrix were both inveterate storytellers who were able to couch thought-provoking, often poetic lyrics, in a sound world that scored highly on contrasts, dynamics and originality of texture. In fact, one of Korner's great achievements was the fact that he managed to retain the softer folds of an unmistakably British accent all the while embracing the standard tropes of blues vocal delivery, right down to the sighs and growls, without sounding corny. His status as "Father of the Blues in Britain" was consolidated by his development of a blues voice that was not apishly American.

Like Hendrix, Korner also had a marked sensitivity in his performances when the moment called for it, bringing out a fraught melancholy that was highly effective when the material was of an ethereal folk-rock quality, as in Nick Drake's 'Saturday Sun', a piece Korner covered brilliantly. He knew how to flicker as well as fire up.

Born in Paris in 1928, Korner was Hendrix's senior by 14 years, but the age gap did not mean that they did not have things in common. The link was one of experience, specifically the apprenticeships that both had served with older musicians who were influential in their given fields. Korner played with British stars of "trad jazz" such as Ken Colyer and Chris Barber, himself a great promoter of the blues in the UK who had brought the likes of Muddy Waters to tour, whereas Hendrix, as previously noted, gigged with rock 'n' roll and R&B pioneers such as Little Richard and the Isley Brothers. In other words Korner and Hendrix had had the all-important opportunity to play older genres of black music, and, most interestingly, gain a direct understanding of the foundation that was laid for new schools of thought. Engagement with this past had the effect of strengthening their grip on the present.

The itineraries of these musicians serve as a reminder of how wide-ranging, unpredictable and at times plain bizarre was their professional experience. Korner had what could be described, with some justification, as a colourful journey through the world of the post-war professional player, quite simply because he was not in a position to refuse a variety of work due to fluctuating income. Critical acclaim was not in short supply for his body of work, yet he never achieved the commercial success commensurate with his talent, and live gigs as well as radio work sustained him throughout his career. Opportunities to play to dedicated blues and R&B audiences were not unlimited, so it was inevitable that he would appear at various "function" events, which aroused his curiosity as much as they tried his patience.

His bands could play society events in plush dining rooms as well as basement clubs with beer-stained floors, venues that attracted vastly different audiences and impromptu jam sessioners. Korner's combo performed for the Marquis and Marchioness of Londonderry in July 1962 at a reception for whom the guest of honour was a "little white-haired man with glasses". He happened to be the legendary American clarinettist Benny Goodman, on a brief stopover in Britain following a tour of Russia. He promptly sat in with the band.

Another engagement offered by aristocrats was considerably more fractious. When Baron Rothschild hired Korner's band the guest of honour was His Royal Highness Prince Philip, and court jester for the evening was the comedian Jimmy Edwards, who much to the dismay of the players on stage insisted on joining the musicians to blow his "hunting horn" so that he could provide some jolly high jinks for the delectation of the guests. Ronnie Jones, the vocalist in the band, recalls how events then unfolded.

> Alexis smiled and muttered: "Oh, god there's no way I can tell him to get off the stage". Behind me Ginger [Baker] was playing away and he leaned across his drum kit and said "Ronnie, tell him to piss off". I turned to Ginger, shrugged my shoulders: what can I do? We'd almost got to the end of the song, when still playing in tempo, Ginger stood up and shouted "Fuck off, bugger!" There was a huge hush, with only the band still trying to play because we were all laughing our heads off. Prince Philip was standing about twenty yards away turning two or three different colours. I could no longer sing, Alexis nearly swallowed his guitar. Jimmy Edwards just disappeared and didn't return to the bandstand at any point during the evening.[8]

As much as the culture clash of blues/R&B musicians, used to forthright profanities, and royal blood, with its supposed airs and graces, lends itself to humour, there is a very serious point to be made. Essentially there was a real lack of understanding of and respect for the artistry of the musicians who had been booked for the evening, the underlying intent of which may have been to provide a kind of light relief or "background music" which was considered to be insubstantial enough for the appointed funnyman to hi-jack.

Stories of musicians having to deal with this kind of inconvenience, which sometimes crossed the line to incivility, are legion. The blues as a space for both emotional release and musical expression did not insulate its practitioners from casual verbal and physical abuse when they were plying their trade in working-class venues such as clubs on the Chitlin circuit in America and small pubs in Britain. The more fantastical tales may have been exaggerated for effect, but the anecdote of a trombonist in Manchester booting a punter who, under the influence of alcohol, had attempted to aggressively rush the stage, rings true, primarily because it comes with the rejoinder that the musician managed to stay in tune while delivering the decisive cranial kick.

Whether or not the blues was still consigned to the status of noise or lowbrow entertainment, it is unlikely the indignities suffered by Korner and his musicians would have been visited upon a string quartet booked to play classical music. Then again the scenario of either an aristocrat or a member of his entourage acting up is not a million miles from stories of British royals taking it upon themselves to sit in on drums at London clubs, which were very much perceived as dens of vice, when American jazz musicians such as Coleman Hawkins and Benny Carter visited the capital in the 1930s, and had a significant effect on the development of the local scene.

Dialling in

Placing artists in the right circumstances to perform, so that their music fulfils both audience expectations and suits the practical characteristics of a venue, such as the acoustics and sightlines, was, and in some cases to this day, remains a thorny issue in the world of entertainment. The extensive segmentation of the market in popular music means that even eclectic live events such as the all-important outdoor summer festival circuit will partition artists into specific areas such as the rock stage, dance arena or world tent. In the broadest of broad church there are still divisions of faith.

The high watermarks of late 1960s festival culture such as Woodstock evoke an image of inspiring open-mindedness with regard to the array of artists, which led to Richie Havens, Ravi Shankar, Sly & The Family Stone, Janis Joplin, Grateful Dead and Hendrix being on the same stage over three days. Yet there was coherence in the programming of this event where common denominators, explicitly blues-rock, and implicitly a culture of strong instrumentalists, were able to hold the bill together.

On other occasions Hendrix found himself doing gigs where the discrepancy between himself and other artists did not play out so favourably. In April 1967 the Jimi Hendrix Experience was booked on a multi-artist tour that featured Cat Stevens, the Walker Brothers and Engelbert Humperdinck. Hendrix was aware of how differing perceptions of the artists in question could be problematic, but even more troublesome was the remonstrations of the road manager with regard to Hendrix's stage show.

> Most will come to see the Walkers. Those who come to see Englebert sing *Rescue Me* may not dig me, but that's not tragic, we'll play for ourselves, we've done it before where the audience stands about with their mouths open and you wait ten minutes

> before they clap. The tour manager Don Finlayson told me to stop using all this [sexually charged gestures] in my act because he said it was obscene and vulgar. I have been threatened every night of the tour so far and I'm not going to stop for him. There's nothing vulgar about it at all. I've been using this act all the way since I've been in Britain. I just don't know where people get the idea from that it's an obscene act.[9]

If that experience brought home to Hendrix the contempt in which he was held by some powerbrokers in the music industry then there was even greater friction generated by the decision, which with the benefit of hindsight seemed incongruous if not ludicrous, to secure him a support slot on a US tour with The Monkees, every bit a manufactured studio act as some of the groups assembled by Phil Spector, whose pre-pubescent fanbase was totally incompatible with that of Hendrix. To the relief of all concerned parties, it was an ill-conceived venture that was quickly cut short.

That debacle demonstrated in no uncertain terms the need for coherence in programming musicians beyond purely commercial considerations. The idea of shared culture, if not artistic values, was not a high-minded principle to be discarded, if it meant that a "boy band" with bubblegum appeal would be part of a bill with a group whose music was altogether more mature, adventurous and challenging.

Supporting artists whose music was different to his own was not necessarily the issue for Hendrix. To suggest that he could only relate to guitar players and singers with a blues background makes a dangerous implication of narrow mindedness, and it is well known that Hendrix actually learned a great deal from warming up for a star who had real stagecraft, the French icon Johnny Hallyday, who The Experience supported on a tour throughout October 1966 (including a show at the prestigious L'Olympia, Paris).

As noted above, live performances often unfolded in conditions that were sometimes far from adequate for artists such as Hendrix and Korner who were developing popular music with a blues base. Nonetheless gigs remained important because they provided both a means of promotion and reputation building as well as income, though fees could vary considerably according to the management that the artists were under. In any case, Hendrix, as he hit superstardom, had a gruelling touring schedule, which saw him rack up an astonishing 600 dates between 1966 and 1970.

However, the tail end of the 1950s saw the advent of a format that would assume great importance for exponents of popular music in Britain: the radio and TV show that featured short sets played live by guest artists. Back in the 1930s BBC radio had broadcast substantial amounts of music performed in real time by both classical artists and exponents of what was deemed light entertainment such as big band jazz and swing.

However, when the market for this music started to decline it was deemed appropriate to showcase other genres that were resonating strongly with young people in post-war Britain. Skiffle, an offshoot of New Orleans jazz, folk and blues enjoyed a surge in popularity through artists such as Lonnie Donegan who scored a number one hit in 1956 when he covered Leadbelly's 'Rock Island Line'. With its emphasis on manufactured and homemade instruments such as guitar, banjo, tub bass and washboard the genre had a carefree spirit that exerted great appeal on some, prompting many teenagers to form bands and also foreshadowing interest in an altogether more robust, "heavier" sounding electric blues and rock in the 1960s. Alexis Korner (who played skiffle with Ken Colyer and the aforesaid Donegan), as well as Jimmy Page and John Lennon, were just a few of many to follow this path.

First broadcast in 1957, the TV show *Six Five Special* exposed skiffle to the general public and in June the same year a new radio show was launched. *Saturday Skiffle Club* further cemented the genre and, more importantly, the idea of a music programme for young people. The likes of trad stars Humphrey Lyttleton, George Melly and Kenny Ball were all guests. Gradually more R&B and rock 'n' roll was programmed, the highpoint of which was the appearance of Bo Diddley, Gene Vincent and Eddie Cochran. The show was accommodating artists who believed in plugging in. The increasing amplification reflected a shift towards an appreciation of music that was not only louder but played by artists with a more aggressive energy.

Skiffle went out of fashion, so *Saturday Skiffle Club* morphed into *Saturday Club*, and it became one of several BBC youth music shows on which Hendrix performed between 1967 and 1969. That musicians were asked to play live on these programmes stemmed from an agreement with the Musicians' Union to substantially limit the "needle time" on a show, which was a colloquialism that referred to the minutes a stylus spent on a piece of black vinyl spinning on a turntable. In other words there would be restrictions placed on the amount of records that could be played on air because the Union argued that this would dent record sales as the music had already been heard at no extra charge, a reasoning that was a gross misunderstanding of the essential place the single and album would have in the pop constituency. Furthermore, broadcasting recorded music lessened the number of opportunities for musicians to play on air, which undermined the BBC's longstanding commitment to live performance.[10]

Ironically, this meant that audiences sometimes had a chance to hear new music live on the radio before it was even released on vinyl, which was a state of affairs that would have given performer and audience a certain frisson of excitement. The prospect of something exclusive was a major draw. For the most part the BBC radio and TV sessions were recorded quickly without many retakes or overdubbing, so the onus was on the artist to nail the performance first time round. When one considers that the Jimi Hendrix Experience was debuting songs such as 'Love Or Confusion' in February 1967 before the release of the full-length album *Are You Experienced?* in May of that year the BBC sessions[11] are nothing less than fascinating. They capture an artist at an early stage of his career, but he already has the self-confidence of a seasoned one. Furthermore, these live performances are interesting insofar as we hear Hendrix's original songs sitting alongside songs that were drawn from a wide range of sources. In a nutshell, Hendrix the writer-performer adjoins Hendrix the listener and lover of music who cannot resist the urge to play covers from both the past and present day.

Trawl through the tapes that Hendrix recorded for these broadcasts, which included shows such as *Saturday Club*, and what stands out is the blend of both original material and cover versions, but perhaps more importantly there was a spontaneity and playfulness, if not sense of mischief that pervaded many of the sessions. The most well-known is the turn on Lulu's TV show in January 1969 where the scheduled 'Hey Joe' was given an unrecognizable incendiary introduction before Hendrix hollers: "We're gonna stop playing this rubbish and dedicate a song to Cream." They launch into a rugged instrumental version of 'Sunshine Of Your Love', to the dismay of the producers whose careful time management of the show was now rapidly unravelling. Hendrix is heard saying wryly: "We're being put off the air."[12]

Put it down to the exuberance of youth or a flight of non-conformism: the fact of the matter is that the incident would not have occurred had Hendrix been a less imaginative musician, or rather an artist who could not think beyond parameters set by others. It is actually a fundamental behavioural trait that says much about Hendrix as a strong-willed individual and possibly dissident force in popular culture who would not always simply toe the line if his heart told him to do otherwise.

However, his actions were not just whimsical or self-indulgent at the expense of the BBC. Hendrix played 'Sunshine Of Your Love' as a tribute to Cream because the band's break up had just been announced. In other words he was marking the occasion with an act of reverence wrapped up in an act of irreverence. While putting the BBC's proverbial nose out of joint he raised his arms in salute to his peers for whom he had genuine admiration, enshrining their excellence in the annals of broadcasting by way of a performance on a programme pushed abruptly off script. In this way Hendrix underlined the importance of context for a song, making a choice of material according to what he thought was a meaningful emotional moment.

Another example of Hendrix the agent provocateur came during a session for *Top Gear* in December 1967, two years before the Lulu show, an important radio programme insofar as it marked the BBC's desire to try to play catch-up with the pirate radio stations, Caroline and Luxembourg. The illegal offshore broadcasters realized that pop music was the essential cultural currency of young people; this was far removed from the Corporation's reductively binary division of light entertainment and classical music.

Top Gear was a dual pun that referred to the height of fashion – gear meaning clothes – as well as glamorous fast cars, and although the programme, presented by Brian Matthews, did feature records, there was also a session played by a band in the studio. As well as Hendrix, The Beatles, Manfred Mann, Cream and The Who all appeared.

During their session Hendrix and The Experience performed a short burst of music that both acknowledged and parodied a small but integral part of the identity of any show on air – the jingle. But this key radio production technique was still fresh out of the conceptual womb. Launched in September 1967, Radio 1 was just a few weeks old, and the press made a point of stating that the first sound that hit the airwaves was a jingle, actually recorded in Texas. Hendrix's improvised incidental music thus thrust him straight to the frontline of events as he put something new on a new something.

Although by no means as subversive an episode as the off-piste antics of the Lulu show there is nonetheless a teasing undercurrent to the way Hendrix informed the producers he and the band had some surprising music to share. He is heard on tape: "Hey, we made a little radio jingle for you ok? Is there anybody back there? We got a little radio jingle for you ok, it's called Radio One ... you're the one for me!" After which the band launches into a tough hard-wrought groove in which the guitars and bass slash and grind on two chords while the kick drum pounds with the same degree of belligerence, so that all three instruments conspire to project as much sinister energy as vulgar eroticism. Hendrix's voice cuts in soon enough, but his tone is distinctly higher than it is on most of his other material. He has just a few lines to sing, but he is sneering and spluttering rather than attempting a melodious delivery.

"Radio One", he cries, "you're the only one for me", before throwing in the pithy rhyme, "Just turn that dial/make your music worthwhile", to then sign off with the stark accusation, "you stole my gal" and quick absolution, "I love you just the same".

Clocking in at just 1:33 the piece is something of a blink and miss episode. Tempting as it is to pass off the moment as the schoolboy in Hendrix coming to the surface and knocking the focused adult artist off his stride, 'Radio One' is not an entirely inconsequential song. It is parody on several levels. On the one hand Hendrix is biting the hand of the broadcasting establishment that feeds him in a light-hearted way by imbuing the whole concept of the jingle with a jocularity that does not serve the usual purpose of promoting the given show on which the artist has been chosen to perform, a privilege not to be scoffed at when such appearances were at a very high premium.

The initial praise Hendrix gives to Radio 1 in the jingle is very much drawn from the standard vocabulary of blues and R&B love songs. 'You're the One', 'You're the Only One', or more precisely, 'You're the One for Me', is exactly the kind of tried and tested declaration a suitor makes to any object of their affection, regardless of whether the apparent devotion can be substantiated by consistent behaviour, as another love, "new love" or "a new baby" is also a great enduring staple of this kind of lyric writing.

However, Hendrix does not lapse into ready-made cliché thereafter. He has done nothing less than issue a demand for quality control. Radio 1 has a responsibility not to be shirked: it has to make its music *worthwhile.* That is no disposable sentiment given that the essential purpose of the airwaves is to relay information that is worth listening to as opposed to information for information's sake. Hendrix is taking it upon himself to make songs, great songs, songs that have value, songs people will want to hear, the central remit of a broadcaster that is the powerful cultural gatekeeper of the day, an organization that set much greater store by classical music not pop.

When cast against the prevailing landscape of pop in the mid-1960s, when the BBC was still coming to terms with the idea that it would do well to cater for a teenage market, the statement is anything but anodyne. It is a rhyme that presents a sign of the times. For Radio 1 to be relevant in any way, to be down with the kids, then it had to shape up and make sure that they could tune in and hear sounds that were *not* what their parents felt comfortable with or related to, whether it was the thunder crack of a guitar, the lupine howl of a middle-aged American bluesman's voice or the screeching "yeah, yeah, yeah" of young British groups lighting their own fire from the embers of US R&B.

Furthermore, Hendrix is picking up on themes that most probably marked his psyche as a youth. By his own admission he spent hours learning the repertoire of Chuck Berry, during which he may have absorbed his lyrics as well as riffs. What is the chance that Berry's promise to send 'Roll Over Beethoven' to his local radio station – "It's a rockin' rhythm record I want my DJ to play" – settled into the subconscious of Jimi Hendrix and resurfaced in another form of demand on the 'Radio One' jingle? What is the chance that Hendrix is rechannelling earlier tropes?

The radio station, one of whose imaginative paeans comes in the form of "Do not attempt to adjust your radio" or "Don't touch that dial" by 70s and 80s funk innovators such as Parliament and Captain Skyy, is something to love, for the sheer joy it brings. A throwaway jingle that deigns to turn that inanimate object of affection into a fantasy romantic rival is not so trite a proposition. A girl could love a radio station a whole lot more than a boyfriend if it played the *right* music, after all. A radio station could break her heart if it did not. Hendrix is riffing heartily on these notions.

Without warning, Hendrix turns accuser, casting himself as the cuckolded lover who has fallen victim to the station's philandering ways. "You stole my gal." This is the sort of candid version of events that conveys the transparent nature of the blues, where communicative power, inscrutability of thought and feeling, and above all, unshakeable conviction, reign supreme, although the way the perpetrator of the misdeed is soon absolved of guilt underlines the emotional ambiguity that can also be at the heart of the genre. Studied in isolation, the fleeting verse intrigues for its casual approach to the hazards of the rather unique love triangle of girl–boy–broadcaster.

What makes the station-as-lover scenario nonetheless compelling is the musical accompaniment to the piece. The contrast between the clipped, curt, throaty staccato chords in the opening bars, which are not so much strummed as spat into life, and the higher, hissing screech of the repeated riff that follows it, creates a tension that is not given any release in the brief life cycle of the performance. There is no time for a key change or any major shift in the textural canvas as the players proceed to crank up their attack soon after the final part of Hendrix's sniggering quasi-pantomime vocal.

Harder, louder, tougher than in the first part of the song, the final part of the jingle essentially offers an on-the-spot encapsulation of what the band might be capable of in the setting of a stadium or festival, when they would have had sufficient time and inclination to really let rip and push the performance into something more daring and confrontational.

However, what does happen is a tongue-in-cheek finale. The band threatens to lose the pulse as Hendrix's guitar trips over the downbeat, coming in too early as if he'd been knocked off balance by his own theatrical snarl into the microphone. Rhythmically, the performance derails, and momentarily the piece freewheels into twitchy rubato.

With an abrupt, final burst of energy the piece skids to its conclusion before the band does a sharp U-turn into a merry jig, which sounds like a variation on the *Loony Tunes* cartoon theme, and instantly any seriousness of the thought-provoking cultural commentary in the short lyric that preceded it is dashed by the sweeping change of mood. Without hesitation the guitarist-vocalist informs the control room that this is a part of the performance that doesn't need to be heard. "You can fade it out before that part", says Hendrix, his voice brimming with a salty mockery. The music simply implodes just as any fit of laughter has to eventually peter out. The fast and loose nature of the sign-off lets us know that Hendrix is pulling his tongue firmly from his cheek.

A R&B classic

Hendrix the humorist is writ large over the jingle but the joke is perhaps not just at the expense of the BBC. Upon repeat listening it becomes clear that the song 'Radio One' is as much an exercise in *self-mockery* as it is parody, as if the players were happy to take the heaving animal attraction of 'Foxy Lady' and puncture it with a tale of adolescent angst at the fearsome pulling powers of an inanimate object, just as one might caricature a rock star who might simulate sex with a guitar or amplifier.

Where and how this piece of fantasia was conceived is not known. Did Hendrix, Noel Redding and Mitch Mitchell knock it out before they arrived at the studio or when they were on the premises? Were the lyrics improvised on the spot? Regardless of the answer, the defining characteristic of 'Radio One' is that it really feels like a riff that is disposable but still redolent of the signature sound of the Jimi Hendrix Experience.

To all intents and purposes, the band had sufficient competence to subvert the jingle format because they could fall back on a vocabulary they had fashioned in the relatively short time they had been together – all the sessions taking place in a few months after the formation of the group. On the one hand they were winging it, deploying their ability to groove on the relatively flimsy premise of a jingle with just a few words and rhythmic motifs that grind to a halt after a short span of time. On the other hand they are actually upholding a fundamental principle in the culture as opposed to simply the music of the blues insofar as they are making something out of nothing, turning a disposable moment into a memorable one through sheer force of wit as well as a store of musical knowledge borne from lengthy hours of engagement.

The Hendrix jingle is a resonant blues because there is so little to it, in a similar way that Muddy Waters, John Lee Hooker or Howlin' Wolf can straddle the border between the literary and colloquial over one chord to devastating effect on the listener. For example, Hooker's 'Moses Smote The Water' recasts a biblical tale to convey a message of hope and salvation, whereas his 'Crawling King Snake' is a sly metaphor for a man's irrepressible urge for sexual conquest, as he's "just gonna keep on crawlin' now, baby," until the day he dies. The psychological and emotional depth of these words would not have been lost on Hendrix, given the depth of his immersion in the blues. Tellingly the moments of zany originality heard at the BBC such as 'Radio One', laid to tape in December 1967, were prefigured by his own very accomplished interpretation of some of the defining moments of the aforementioned icons. On *Saturday Club* in March of that year he and The Experience cut a quite scintillating version of Wolf's 'Killing Floor' and a few months prior, in October, they did Muddy's '(I'm Your) Hoochie Coochie Man'.

'(I'm Your) Hoochie Coochie Man', one of Waters' most enduring anthems, was performed by Hendrix on *Rhythm & Blues*, the show Alexis Korner presented on the World Service. It is another example of Hendrix's tight grip on the vocabulary of the blues and his ability to personalize a performance of "a standard" that had already been in circulation for a number of years. Waters first recorded the song in 1954, when it became one of his best-selling records, so 13 years had passed when Hendrix decided to make it part of his set for the BBC session he did in October 1967.

Certain superlative compositions gain additional magnitude when they are covered by other artists, as well as being recorded several times by the original artist, and this is certainly true of '(I'm Your) Hoochie Coochie Man'. It was reprised by a range of performers, which included blues man B.B. King, jazz organist Jimmy Smith and rock 'n' roller Chuck Berry. Waters himself, on his 1960 *Live At Newport* album (recorded at the renowned Newport jazz festival), also played the song with Korner's former boss, Chris Barber, who backed the singer when he appeared in Britain in 1958.

Korner himself also recorded an excellent version of the song in 1964, so when he introduced Hendrix on the World Service, "*Rhythm & Blues* is what this show is called" – before promising "a classic in that field, 'The Hoochie Coochie Man'" – he was announcing a song with which he had a personal relationship. This familiarity may well have led to the minor alteration of the title. (Aficionados would have been quick to cry '(I'm Your) Hoochie Coochie Man'.)

More importantly, Hendrix made a request to his host, which, according to the studio producer Jeff Griffin, reflected a distinct informality in the very format of the programme that was intended to lead to a greater degree of spontaneity in the performances:

> I had this idea: instead of Alexis just doing the speech bits it would be fun if he played guitar behind the links and half-chatted the links. So we always used to have him with his guitar in the studio. We recorded all of the links and then once we knew what the keys of the numbers were then he would modulate from one to the other. But of course the fact that he had the guitar in the studio more often than not the band would say "Hey do you want to sit in, Alexis?" One of the best moments I can ever remember was when we did Jimi Hendrix. We'd already got a couple of tracks down and then Jimi said "Hey man, I want to do *Hoochie Coochie Man* and it'd be great if we had slide guitar on it".[13]

Korner duly obliged, and the artistic choice was an astute one as the glissando and tremolo lines created by the guest musician bring a kind of effete sensuality to the rendition which combines very vividly with the gruff, at times grating, sound of Hendrix's guitar while Mitchell's drums and Redding's bass maintain a steady pulse with appropriately discreet peaks in their attack and volume. There is a distinct pizzicato quality in the wispy, needle-like timbre Korner produces, and his sustaining of notes is enough to create the sensation of liquidity in contrast to the solidity of the rhythm section. One guitar streams into life while the other grinds.

This duality is a bold and inventive variation on the original textural framework of the original Waters version of '(I'm Your) Hoochie Coochie Man'. Its primary feature is the combined resonance of electric guitar and harmonica. These two instruments form a slow-moving carriage that feels both threatening and beckoning, as the difference in pitch and timbre on the uncoiling pentatonic phrase has immense sensory power. Lower, harder and thicker, the guitar hauls the line along. Higher, lighter and brighter the harmonica arrows it into being, and it is through this entwining of a gruff bass and shrill tenor that the rhythm section acquires a rich sound spectrum which underlines the authority of Waters' voice as well as the impact of his words. All the bulk of the guitar props up his warning, "I'm gonna mess with you", while the sharp cry of the harmonica colours the sight of "pretty womens" who "jump and shout". By including Korner's slide guitar in his version, Hendrix is actually bringing significantly more delicacy as well as a mild sense of sombre mystery to the table.

The blues element of Korner's performance, his bending of notes, part of a game of emotional push, pull and tease, is entirely appropriate for the arrangement, but the patent fragility of the guitar induces an additional tension. It is like a ghostly figure on the surface of dark water that can be eclipsed by the bullying nature of Hendrix's guitar. It is indeed drowned out altogether when the rhythm section kicks into the chorus.

Following two choruses, Hendrix takes a 12-bar solo marked by a smart alternation of hard-edged chording and rapier single notes, and the form starts to loosen up. Instead of returning to the 8-bar verse Hendrix's voice drops out and Redding embarks on a bout of brief riffing, allowing the heaviness of tone to come to the fore, swinging his line just for a few beats before Hendrix comes back in to state the melody on the guitar and round it off with a few variations. He then launches into a final solo in which his whole notes have a scratchy thickness to them, which makes the piercing quality of Korner's slides more impactful when he re-enters the fray for the final climactic verse-chorus.

If a certain heaviness defined the bottom end of the track then listeners with sharp ears would not have been surprised. In his announcement of the band, Korner pointed out that Noel Redding was on 8-string bass guitar, "a pretty rare instrument with a pretty rare sound".[14] Across the broad canvas of Hendrix's life, especially the more tumultuous aspects of his journey through the music industry, this was not just a colourful detail for any fetishist or obsessive of musical paraphernalia of the less common variety. The instrument in question actually symbolized strife for Hendrix.

On the infamous Curtis Knight sessions from 1965, which later turned into a legal millstone around his neck, Hendrix had played an 8-string bass. The music generated by that meeting was something that he expressed a distinct desire to shelve as he considered it to be sub-standard quality whereas the BBC broadcasts, the version of '(I'm Your) Hoochie Coochie Man' in particular, was anything but. Both dates were connected by the presence of the same unusual axe but in Hendrix's view one was worth keeping and the other deserved to be shelved. Taken together the two sets of music say a lot about the mindset of musicians in post-war pop who were determined to play and develop their craft at every available opportunity, and how artistic choices of the musicians and producers with whom they worked as well as the instruments they used could have consequences that had wildly varying degrees of significance.

Listening not just to Korner perform with Hendrix but also introduce him on the radio is hugely instructive because of the socio-cultural context it provides, and those fleeting asides about the place of '(I'm Your) Hoochie Coochie Man' in the blues canon are important as they bring the gravitas of history into view, shoring up this black popular music in the minds of new British listeners who by way of the radio were discovering this "old" music that sounded nonetheless new, such was its vitality.

Korner excels himself with his brief, pithy closing statement for the Hendrix session:

> Ladies and gentlemen, this ridiculous crew, that's the Jimi Hendrix Experience, are now off, and I'm going with them. Hope we'll all make it. Tell 'em we went that a way … 'Drivin' South'.

The final words were the title of a song written by none other than Curtis Knight, which add a further thread to the entwining of Hendrix's past and present. Korner consciously hammed up his voice to spell out the clearly implied image of the journey, which in the African-American psyche, is intriguing because the South represents a genesis of black history, which is infinitely bittersweet insofar as it is a place to flee from the most brutal historic oppression as well as an essential familial heartland and cultural repository, the place where the blues began, no less. The first part of Korner's closing statement is not devoid of interest. He bestows a great compliment on the musicians. "Ridiculous crew" is to be taken as extraordinary in the sense of uncommonly, outrageously or "stupidly" good.

A jam, but in a very specific way

Interestingly, one of his peers who emerged as one of the most credible exponents of blue-based pop in Britain, Eric Burdon, lead singer of The Animals, whose bass player Chas Chandler was Hendrix's first manager, also used the image of travel when airing his views on spontaneous playing. "Music in action is taking a band on stage, calling the key and taking off without a detailed expectation of what is going to happen, but knowing that the musicians are good enough to carry it off."[15]

To all intents and purposes Burdon, Korner and Hendrix understood that there was much to be gained from *not* controlling all the variables of an event where people came together to jam. The spontaneity of having several players together, choosing a tune and seeing *where* the music might go, how players would interact, what old and new riffs might surface as a result, was a basic glue that bound personalities of this ilk.

Jam session is such an evocative term that it is important to separate the reality from the mythology of the event. For the most part it calls to mind musicians ambling on stage at a venue in an impromptu and unregulated manner and playing as the muse dictated, somehow finding a magical alchemy in the process. While jam sessions are, generally speaking, much looser affairs than a studio date, where both musicians and managers are mindful of charges per hour, jam sessions are usually not anarchic free-for-alls where *anybody* and everybody can just get up and do their thing. There is usually an appointed director of traffic who decides who will be next to sit in with a house band, and any new unknowns are introduced by other tried and trusted players.

Linguistically, jam is intriguing for its multiple meanings. Used as a verb it specifically referred to rhythmic regularity. Clapping hands to keep time was known as "jamming the beat", implying that the incumbents are fully engaged in the process, just as today one might talk of "feeling" it. The sense of plenitude of emotion as well as physical engagement is conveyed by a variant expression such as "jam on the groove", which is an ear-catching turn of phrase insofar as it vividly conveys both musical and sensual fulfilment, an evocation of the act of reaching a level of satisfaction which concerned parties want to maintain and possibly push farther. It is about hitting the "sweet spot", where all the players in the session by way of musical communication are able to lock in to the same energy, the same intent and purpose.

Jam as a springboard for linguistic and semantic variation in the African-American vernacular is rich. A "bad mamajamma" is a "traffic stopper" sexy woman who inspires adulation in rhyme or song, inspiring at least one cry of "Lord have mercy!", whereas ramjam could designate anything from the name of a club to a band in which, again, the underlying meaning is one of exuberance, energy and enjoyment. A ramjam session is a gathering, musical or otherwise, which is packed, and by implication, a moment that is marked by a sense of wellbeing for all in the house.

Used as a compound noun, jam session is even more colourful. According to Mezz Mezzrow, the Chicago clarinettist-saxophonist who played a major role in the New Orleans revival with Sidney Bechet, the term originated from a pun on the title of the song 'Ain't Gonna Give You None of My Jellyroll' which he adapted to "Jelly's gonna jam some now".[16] In other words, something memorable may happen when the musicians in question come together and play with a degree of freedom. Jamming is about uplifting creative release as well as communal energy.

Historically, the jam session was an established praxis in African-American music that has very deep roots, reflecting the fact that the first players to emerge from slavery often played makeshift or home-made instruments, and that lessons on banjo, washboard or a range of percussion instruments, such as tambourine and bones, did not yet take place in institutions. The idea of mastering and developing techniques was closely linked to live performance as much as players began to learn theory on piano, brass and reeds. Knowing a number of songs thus became a pre-requisite for anybody who hoped to be able to mix it with *boss* musicians, with the hope of learning invaluable tips on how to produce a memorable version of a tune.

More important still is the musician's state of mind. The jam session was not just about responding to an impulse to perform. One also has to think of those band members who were subject to the rigours of life on the road that could be stultifying at best and debilitating at worse. How individuals dealt with those impositions from the 1930s to 1970s – the peak years of live playing where the changing face of black popular music in America produced swing, R&B, soul and funk, which were performed by bands of various sizes, sometimes with dancers and comedians – is worth considering, as it highlights important underlying behavioural traits of the "gigging" musician, as Alyn Shipton explains in *A New History of Jazz*:

> From the earliest days of jazz musicians had got together to jam: there were sparring matches, tests of instrumental skill and long solos wringing the last drop of inspiration out of well-known chord sequences. In the swing era there was an added incentive for those who played nothing but third or fourth brass or reed parts in a section to flex their improvisatory muscles. In most big bands it was easy to get typecast, and never be offered a solo. For such musicians the jam session was a safety valve and a social interaction for those who travelled with different line-ups to meet one another and play together.[17]

This is hugely important to Hendrix's story. When considering the phenomenon of the jam in his psyche as well as his modus operandi as a musician one has to reiterate and evaluate his formative years. As a sideman to R&B and soul stars in the 1960s Hendrix was subject to a considerable amount of constraints and, as detailed in Part 1, indignities. Being a band member, especially in a multi-artist "revue" that was on tour, entailed a gruelling schedule that could sometimes see musicians play several shows a night, where they stuck to an established routine with carefully rehearsed parts from which they were not supposed to deviate, certainly not when as demanding a star as Little Richard was on the bandstand. Extended solos were frowned upon, especially if they drew attention to the musician at the expense of the singer. Showboating did not go down well at all. Upstaging the star was a no-no.

Given that kind of iron-rod regimentation it stands to reason that Hendrix craved the looser scenario of the jam session. The pressure to conform eased up. The shackles came off. The constant need to stay on point with the big name artist was no longer an issue, and tellingly it has been reported by several credible sources that Hendrix didn't always play at a jam. Instead he would content himself to listen or even film the proceedings, making the point that the social occasion mattered a lot to him.

Yet Hendrix the player remained formidable in a jam session for a number of reasons. His virtuosity, expressed in lengthy solos, inventive rhythmic playing or expert choices of the moment in which to embellish a melodic line with a fleeting aside or punctuation, or simply launch into more abstract soundscapes, was certainly an asset.

What gave Hendrix a decisive advantage in these situations was the apprenticeship that had been tiresome on occasion for the impositions hitherto mentioned. The years spent with key figures in black music in the early 1960s had forced him to learn dozens of songs written and performed by substantial talents. As a musician who had not been taught to read scores or transcribe music he relied purely on his memory, and there are numerous classically trained artists who actually see this putative limitation in a positive light insofar as it can foster a greater absorption of the music in question, an internalization of the appropriate patterns of notes and the meter in which they sit as opposed to the convenience of refreshing one's mind by way of a written score. Being able to read the part put in front of you is an invaluable skill, especially for musicians in orchestral contexts, but it is to no avail in an improvised session without written material if a tune is called and you do not actually know its melody, rhythm and chord changes, or are not able to at least work out an accompaniment on the spot.

Hearing Hendrix turn in superlative renditions of blues standards such as 'Killing Floor' and '(I'm Your) Hoochie Coochie Man' is not only exhilarating listening. These performances, or more to the point, the absolute verve in which they are delivered, say a great deal about how they became part of the musician's core database. BBC listeners may have heard him play these songs for the first time when they tuned-in in 1967, but how many times had he listened to recordings of them and played them before, either in the privacy of his own home or at an after-hours jam session?

Any musician who related to the jam culture that was an integral part of Hendrix's world was bound to strike a chord with him. It is that simple but essential leap of faith that led to him playing outside of formal studio sessions with an impressively diverse range of musicians throughout his lifetime. To play without micro-management and extensive preparation is to entertain the very real possibility of artistic failure, which in the worse-case scenario can come back to haunt you, as demonstrated by the Curtis Knight affair. But the flipside is that openness can also lead to experiences that are far beyond expectation, such as the night when Hendrix jammed with the extraordinarily gifted multi-reed player Rahsaan Roland Kirk in London. To a certain extent, the meetings with Knight and Kirk represent the opposite sides of the same coin, and the tragedy is that it was the wrong session that was committed to tape.

What stands out from all accounts of Hendrix's gigs, and more importantly, his own emotional engagement with the act of performing on stage, was the extent to which he fed off interaction with like-minded souls, who could react in the moment to ideas that may have arisen impromptu, all the while being able to fall back on common musical ground if need be. Knowing tunes and being game for stretching them out. Playing the material and playing *with* it. Starting one song and veering into another.

The other thing to bear in mind is that there was a depth as well as breadth of knowledge gained by Hendrix during his formative years. It wasn't just the vast number of tunes but the shifting stylistic backdrop to them that was part of Hendrix's skillset, meaning that he had experienced first-hand how the specific structural properties of rock 'n' roll differed to those of R&B and then soul. These sub-genres were all related but it was the change of rhythmic and harmonic nuance from one to the next, the particular attack of music that had a more quarter-note feel of swing, with the insistent chatter of a ride cymbal or the eighth-note thump of a bass drum, creating that sense of solidity that would suit a proper "shouter", that had to be mastered by sidemen who survived in those years of rapid evolution in black pop.

As Hendrix was on the rise, the house bands of labels such as Motown became exemplars of how musicians could create magic in the studio as well as on stage for a variety of solo singers and vocal groups, sometimes from having nothing more than chord sheets, because of advanced craftsmanship, discipline and versatility, and it goes without saying that their desire to hone their ability by playing "after hours" sessions in jazz clubs in Detroit was also another asset of untold importance.

Interestingly, Hendrix would also find himself jamming at the BBC in the company of an artist who was proving to be a key member of the Motown roster, and the encounter makes an essential point about spontaneous performances. "Little" Stevie Wonder was the genius child of black music, staking his claim as both a writer for other artists such as Smokey Robinson & The Miracles and a hitmaker in his own right between the early and mid-1960s. In 1967 when the Jimi Hendrix Experience arrived at the Playhouse Theatre in central London to record *Top Gear* they found Wonder on the premises for an interview for another programme. According to bassist Noel Redding, a brief session came about in no time at all. "Mitch [Mitchell] nipped off to the loo, and some enterprising person suggested an informal jam between Jimi and myself, with Stevie on drums. They forgot to turn the tape machines off."[18]

That is not so much mordant self-deprecation as an honest admission that the results are inconsistent. Promising so much on paper, because of the brilliance of each individual, the Jimi–Stevie union delivers on the first piece they performed, an instrumental blues-funk number, which was just called 'Jammin'', presumably as a reflection of the fact that there was no agreed title. Wonder's timing is good, his crisp snare fills and tingling ride cymbal work lend the necessary momentum for the insistent attack of his new bandmates, but there are moments where he lacks a touch of fluency, conveying an all-too-real uncertainty as to how Hendrix and Redding were going to broach the remainder of the piece. When bassist and guitarist harden their attack in the latter half of the song, Wonder keeps up but he doesn't quite thrust forward as much as one might expect, and simply lacks a surge of the aggression that comes with familiarity of both material and fellow musicians. 'Jammin'' makes for an enjoyable 3:24 minutes of music, but it really feels like an alternate take, not a master.

Having said that, the piece goes to show how even great musicians can be compromised by difficult conditions. Wonder, as he has proved on many occasions in a unique career, is an excellent drummer and percussionist (not to mention harmonica and keyboard player), but here he was playing at very short notice on equipment that was set up for another player so it should come as no surprise that he struggled a touch.

After 'Jammin'' the newly convened trio had a stab at 'I Was Made To Love Her', a Billboard R&B chart topper in 1967 that also reached number five in the UK charts, and remains one of the great anthems of the burgeoning soul movement. It is very uneven. Again Wonder's drumming is beset by moments of hesitation that make him much more static than on the previous track, but what really stands out is the fact that Hendrix obviously doesn't know the original melody well enough to attempt to state it for at least one chorus. He avoids it altogether and quotes the irresistibly infectious, pinging electric sitar riff, one of the greatest opening fanfares in the history of pop, but doesn't manage to convey the tonal brightness and zest that make it the perfect vehicle for the song's message of pure, unadulterated romance written in the stars.

Sadly, Hendrix can't really build upon that motif to create an inspired arrangement in the moment, and the performance ambles into a few mildly funky interludes that are not knitted into a coherent narrative whole that can hold the listener's interest. Rhythmically the trio sags, and the piece fizzles out before it can really get going.

It was not so much an opportunity missed as an instructive reminder of what a jam session entails – the real possibility of creative failure as well as success. One might point to a lack of chemistry between Hendrix and Wonder, yet the choice of both material and instrumentation should also be taken into consideration, as it is clear that things weren't quite able to click. Bear in mind that these songs were knocked off quickly, very much as a stop-gap in between the serious duties each of the stars had to fulfil. With the benefit of hindsight, covering 'I Was Made To Love Her' was a wrong move because Hendrix clearly didn't relate to it, and it is surprising that nobody suggested the music of an artist who was the obvious common denominator between the two, Bob Dylan. Stevie and Jimi both greatly admired and covered his songs.

For all its ultimately underwhelming nature, the Jimi–Stevie jam is nonetheless of consequence because it underlines the recurrent incidence of collaboration in the vocalist-composer-guitarist's life and the relative ease with which other players could become part of his circle of accompanists. It was essentially a suck-it-and-see moment, but the fact of the matter is that

Hendrix agreed to it. His innate musical curiosity, belief in his own ability, and extensive jam experience dictated as much.

At a crucial juncture in his career, Hendrix's desire if not need to reach out to other musicians beyond an established nucleus of players enabled him to scale brilliant musical heights. What partly distinguishes *Are You Experienced?* and *Axis: Bold As Love*, the first two albums under his own name, from the third, *Electric Ladyland*, was the much expanded sonic palette, and the fact that, as Chas Chandler says of *Ladyland*, "As time went on they [Jimi and members of The Experience] were less and less prepared for the studio".[19] *Experienced?* and *Axis* are tightly confined to the expressive vocabulary of the guitar-lead vocal-drums-bass outfit, the limits of which were imaginatively pushed, it has to be said, especially when an unexpected, or at least non-rock instrument such as the glockenspiel was deployed. *Ladyland* unveiled a far broader lexicon by way of the inclusion of Hammond organ, harpsichord, piano, flute, tenor saxophone, congas, percussion, 12-string guitar and female backing vocals.

Musical personalities of renown such as Steve Winwood, Jack Casady, Buddy Miles, Brian Jones, Chris Wood, Dave Mason and The Sweet Inspirations, a fabulous gospel-soul trio featuring Cissy Houston, mother of Whitney, were among the guests who came in to augment the triumvirate of Hendrix, Noel Redding and Mitch Mitchell. The key point about their input is that it largely arose because of an atmosphere of spontaneity stoked up by Hendrix himself that ignited his creative fire.

Mitchell recalls that the idea of a revolving door of musical guests was a well-established working praxis. "So much in the studios was done with either just Jimi and myself or Jimi, myself, and we'd bring in some other people."[20]

To all intents and purposes Hendrix was constantly writing and refining songs, hence there was no clear dividing line between the three studio albums he cut. During sessions for *Are You Experienced?* songs for *Axis: Bold As Love* were penned, and during sessions for *Axis: Bold As Love* songs for *Electric Ladyland* were penned. The wheels of creativity kept relentlessly turning. "We didn't actually start out to do an album at any time", recalls Chandler. "We just kept rolling and as soon as we had enough songs for an album we put that one out, and then just get on with the rest of the stuff, that's how it was still going by the time we got to *Electric Ladyland*."[21]

After his sojourn in England, Hendrix moved back to New York in January 1968, and wasted little time in reintegrating into the live music scene. He would spend many nights at venues such as the Generation club, 52 West 8th Street, an extremely hip place he visited frequently, where he was known to jam with major figures in blues, R&B and rock, such as Elvin Bishop and Al Kooper. On 7 April 1968, a few days after the murder of Dr Martin Luther King, a musical "wake" was held at the club with a bill that included B.B. King, Buddy Guy, Joni Mitchell, Richie Havens and Hendrix. No definitive documentation exists on the interaction of the players at the jam that followed their sets but Hendrix is known to have played with Guy, a very gifted post-war guitarist whose expressive solos and fine voice have made him a blues legend.

All accounts of Hendrix's movements in the late 1960s suggest that he had a clear intent of living an artistic life where there would be no strict boundary between informal performance and the process of recording. He actually wanted to purchase the Generation club when it was put up for sale so that it could then be redesigned as a new club to incorporate an eight-track studio. Eddie Kramer, Hendrix's longstanding engineer, was subsequently called in for advice on the project and he urged him and manager Michael Jeffrey to build "the best studio in the world" because they were spending $300,000, a very substantial outlay for any artist in the late 1960s. They acquiesced and the new recording complex was named "Electric Lady Studios".

Construction was beset with numerous delays and would not be complete until the summer of 1970. While wrangling over site permits and dealing with the disastrous effects of a flood would have been no small distraction to the team Hendrix hired to oversee the project, he carried on developing the music for his next album.

Kramer has been very vocal about the clarity of Hendrix's vision when they were working together, and when the guitarist explicitly articulated a desire for a loose, improvised quality to a new song he had in mind he expressed himself thus. "I want this jam but it's gotta be done in a very specific way", Kramer recalls of what Hendrix said to him the first time he talked about doing the song 'Voodoo Chile', one of the many highlights of *Electric Ladyland*. "The way Jimi conceived of it was ... look I wanna jam, I know the guys ... I know the guys I want to play this."[22]

At the time Hendrix was doing sessions at the Record Plant on 44th & 8th in New York, but he was spending a lot of time – jamming – at a club called The Scene, which was just a few blocks away on 8th Avenue, so he, somewhat logically, given his intent on capturing things in the moment, undertook to transfer the energy of the club to the studio. Kramer has this memorable recollection of the 'Voodoo Chile' session, as he hunkered down at the console waiting for Hendrix – and guests – to arrive:

> Imagine that you're on 44th and 8th and two blocks away is this famous nightclub that Jimi used to go jamming in a club called The Scene, that's on 46th Jimi would be there from like 8, 9, 10, 11, 12. We're sitting in the studio, everything's all set up, all the mikes are ready to go, checked out ... he comes strolling in at midnight dragging behind him 20 people. You imagine him walking down 8th Avenue stopping traffic, it's a big scene. He comes into the studio dragging in Steve Winwood, Jack Casady, whoever, a couple of rehearsals, one take, two takes, maybe and there's 'Voodoo Chile', done finished, thank you very much live from the floor. There it is.[23]

It is an invaluable insight, a light shone on the circumstances in which one of Hendrix's signature pieces came to life. Above all Kramer's anecdote captures something of the essence of the artist as a creative spirit wedded to spontaneity as well as, and this is crucial, the chemistry that could be achieved with the appropriate musical collaborators. Out of the original members of The Experience, Mitch Mitchell bought into this but Noel Redding was far more reluctant, and the frustration if not exasperation at Hendrix's methodology made him a troublesome voice of dissent. "Hendrix was jamming far too much in the studio", he said with a somewhat salty tone when talking about his time in the group years later. "And I told him so."

In other words, there was a gap between the two men, or rather a lack of understanding on Redding's part, of the primacy of the jam session in Hendrix's musical culture. The irony was that as much as Hendrix welcomed the prospect of musical newness and the excitement of spur-of-the-moment interaction he also had a perfectionist streak that would lead him to endless retakes of both his own lines and those of the bassist that would drive his first producer and manager Chas Chandler to absolute distraction. Therein lies a fascinating duality in Hendrix's approach to conceiving and making music. Spontaneity and micro-management came to co-exist.

From this conceptual base, a platform that upheld both an adventurer and control freak, there grew one of the most enduring songbooks in post-war pop, a body of work that has dozens of songs that could be deemed landmarks as well as others that could be called minor classics, and others that could be termed outright curios. The hits, the anthems, the big tunes and the lesser-known pieces are certainly worthy of in-depth analysis, yet before undertaking that, I would like to make some observations about several stylistic and structural features of Hendrix's music that say much about his development as a musician who was at the intersection of several key creative roads.

Variety of duration is a salient feature of Hendrix's repertoire. The longest piece he ever recorded was, at 15:00 mins, 'Voodoo Chile', and the shortest, at 1:21, 'And The Gods Made Love'. In between these two poles are a number of notable mid-length pieces (5–6 mins) such as 'Third Stone From The Sun', 'If 6 Was 9', 'Voodoo Child (Slight Return)' and 'Message Of Love'. But the bulk of Hendrix's songs fall in the 2.30–3.45 min bracket, and would include the likes of 'Foxy Lady', 'Fire', 'Stone Free', 'Purple Haze', 'I Don't Live Today', 'Spanish Castle Magic', 'Little Miss Lover' and 'Belly Button Window'.

The existence of shortform and longform Hendrix works, as well as this middle ground, reveals conceptual variety, and above all an awareness of concise, 45 rpm single radio-friendly formats as well as an affinity to the extended arrangement with its possibilities for longer improvisations, interludes, exchanges between specific instruments and an overall sense of the band following their muse as the tape rolls. There is something of a healthy tension between shortform and longform Hendrix.

Introductions with inspiration

Everything that we know about Hendrix's love of jam culture makes the long-form song an inevitable part of his development, but if there is an expectation that more musical information could be packed into a 15-minute workout then that doesn't mean that the arrangements for the shorter pieces were always simple. In some cases they had structures that were marvels of light and shade, textural diversity and dynamics. If we put some of them under the microscope we see fine architecture in miniature.

Perhaps it would be more appropriate to say that there is a beauty of construction in Hendrix's songs that reflects the workings of a quite unique mind insofar as it brought together both disparate talents and interests. Hendrix the composer, Hendrix the improviser, Hendrix the singer, Hendrix the student of sound, Hendrix the explorer of the studio, and post-production technique, were all integral to his output. All these strands of his artistic persona coalesce on the highlights of his work, but the core is really a series of structural choices that both excel within the accepted parameters of pop vocabulary, and also subvert them on a number of occasions.

Artists of his generation, who came to prominence during the heyday of R&B and rock 'n' roll, had a range of paradigms they could reference. As a musician who had first-hand experience of working with the pioneers of the genres, from Little Richard to the Isley Brothers, Hendrix was well aware of the models of songs that had become the archetypal soundtrack to post-war teens. These artists, and their peers who had shaped Hendrix as a youth, such as Chuck Berry, had won over listeners by way of the irresistibly vibrant character of their voices, the cut and thrust of their rhythms and the high standard of their musicianship. Yet all of these elements were framed by the central concern of arrangement. The number of sections; the bar counts allocated to these particular segments; the way the song (or story) unfolds from one part (or chapter) to another; the relationship between verse and chorus; the balance between instrumental and vocal passages; the introduction, the "outroduction" or conclusion.

Such were the decisions that faced artists, as they had done for decades, but also weighing on their minds was the constraint of time as dictated by the single that in the best-case scenario would reach a mass market through airplay. Brevity was at a premium in the art not just of writing songs but of hopefully making hit records.

Berry's 'Roll Over Beethoven' was a paragon of excellence in this respect. It deserves the mantle of one of the greatest songs of all time for its unforgettable beat, bold and brash lyric that does nothing less than posit African-American blues-based music as a legitimate and worthy challenger to European classical music, whose lauded champions, from Beethoven to Tchaikovsky, are bluntly told to vacate their thrones.

Significantly, the song clocks in at 2:23 mins. It is a ball of energy that bounces into life and retains momentum until it finally eases to a halt. The combination of Berry's zestful vocal and pummelling guitar catch the ear straightaway, but the cyclical form of the arrangement consolidates the feeling of unerring steadiness of the narrative. It is a 12-bar blues, so the chord changes are reassuringly regular and anchor the sense of the lyrical and musical vehicle coming round again and again, settling firmly in the listener's consciousness. Berry's guitar solo is a model of focused phrasing within the allotted harmonic framework but one of the most notable features of 'Roll Over Beethoven' is how Berry chooses to start the performance. We hear solo guitar for four bars before the entrance of the rhythm section of drums, double bass and piano. In other words the guitar is decisively placed in the spotlight ahead of all other instruments that will feature in the performance. This running order is a simple but remarkably effective way of creating a degree of dramatic charge. A sound in isolation is a sound in accentuation. There are no competing noises. It is impossible not to notice the presence of the instrument that is chosen to open proceedings just as a presenter at a concert commands attention prior to the appearance of the artist.

Tellingly, those who were Berry's peers or immediate successors found their own way of creating comparable impact in their introductions. Think of the joyous solo vocal wail that starts the Isley Brothers' 'Shout' (1959), James Brown's curt but startling scream on 'I Got You (I Feel Good)' (1964), the sole languorous chord of The Beatles' 'A Hard Day's Night' (1964), the grinding, if not snarling guitar riff of the Rolling Stones' '(I Can't Get No) Satisfaction' (1965) or the wonderfully tumbling, teasing horn motif of Sam & Dave's 'Hold On I'm Coming' (1966). These are all object lessons in how to start a pop song. These are introductions that are brief but brilliantly effective. Many producers were of the mind that a song had to capture the imagination in two to four bars. Berry Gordy, Motown's founder-visionary, gave his artists just ten seconds to nail it. Hendrix operated within such guidelines but also went significantly beyond them.

Complexity, a relative notion to say the least, has been a vexed issue in pop for many years, because of the received wisdom of losing a mass audience if the music is too challenging. Yet the issue of duration of performance has been no less important. The prevailing norm of the three-minute song that Hendrix was inured to, meant that he was acutely aware of the need to make an impactful statement as soon as the tape was running and he and accompanists struck the downbeat. Thus the primacy and the potential difficulty of starting a song should not be underestimated, as, generally speaking, there was less time to map out a dense, developmental passage that could have the magnitude of an overture in classical music. Producing a showstopper moment that would resonate with an audience, or in the best-case scenario, become fully lodged in its consciousness, and also provide a coherent gateway to the main body of the piece, was part of the songwriter's mission. The art of the introduction is an arduous one.

Hendrix's oeuvre has a rich gamut of approaches to the discipline. On one hand he could be direct, deciding that just a few measures were sufficient for him to present a kind of sonic appetizer before the main course. Yet the mini intro also displayed advanced musicality whereby he deployed his technical gifts with such diligence that a statement made in two or four bars nonetheless had phrasal richness to match emotional depth. In other words he was able to write so as not to waste any notes. Or rather, isolate a sound so that it becomes a punctuation or peak of interest in a succession of other statements, as is the case on 'Can You See Me'. A brash three-chord blues is punched out in four bars, and then a single tone on the guitar, bending to a hiss that becomes a tantalizing trail into the distance, is heard before Hendrix's voice comes in and the song starts in earnest. Midway through the piece the pattern is reprised and the isolated note is again heard and acquires further weight as a form of plea in line with the key image of the lover "begging you on my knees". That single note grows in impact, gaining a graceful sadness that adds to the theme of solitude.

Trawl through all of the material Hendrix recorded on *Are You Experienced?*, *Axis: Bold As Love*, *Electric Ladyland* and *Band of Gypsys* and you'll find many other examples of an introduction that establishes a rich harmonic or rhythmic framework of a piece as well as splashing on to this canvas an additional colour that may have some meaning in the overarching narrative, or act as a kind of fleeting, yet notable vignette that catches the attention before the performance gets underway.

'Them Changes' is an object lesson in how to create a kind of micro-overture for a song. The introduction for the original Buddy Miles studio recording is excellent – a sizzle of guitar feedback that is shattered by a two-bar fuzz bass motif which is then doubled by two bars of brass. It is a leisurely yet surging fanfare, which, through its changes of texture set over these 16 beats, is highly consequential. Hendrix and Band of Gypsys add a new section altogether, before they play the original horn figure. We hear a delightful melodic line in which the guitar plays sprightly octaves.

The four-bar line has a lovely sway to it, a kind of seesaw-like motion that is enhanced by a certain degree of restraint from the two string players, who hover mindfully over the energy of the drummer's snare rolls. There is an airy, carefree quality in this initial statement. Hendrix's tone is thin and metallic, picking lightly at the line rather than crunching it into life. Then the calm is brutally shattered by the reprise of the well-known horn line from the Buddy Miles version. Hendrix plays the phrase as a wah-wah groove. What was originally a gentle sigh turns to a tetchy growl, and the overall energy of the performance raises right up, as if to jolt the listener out of any possible slumber that may have been induced by the relative tranquillity of the previous part.

This introduction to the introduction, a kind of false prelude, is easy to overlook because it is a fleeting moment, but its creation of a significant emotional charge to the entire composition should not be dismissed because it says so much about the understanding Hendrix and his accompanists had of economy in the process of arranging. Write a part, however short or long it may be, and place it at the *right* stage of the arrangement; produce a coup de theatre; take the listener down an unexpected path; draw some unfamiliarity from familiarity – this is what 'Them Changes' tells us about bringing freshness to a tune, one that may have already been known to the audience. In the greater scheme of things the prelude is something of a footnote in the larger story of the song but it is by no means a meaningless or redundant element.

If the guitar-led intro of 'Them Changes' underlines astute editorial praxis then elsewhere Hendrix showed just how his creativity excelled when he put even greater temporal constraints on his song introductions. What can he do in less than ten seconds? Craft the rattling, scraping rise of sound in 'Foxy Lady'. The tonal manipulation of the guitar is masterful, producing one long whirl from which emanates a metallic judder and jangle, a kind of strange, almost honky-tonk piano transplanted from keyboard to fretboard, that is then swallowed up by a far bigger clang of feedback before the crash of a power chord, a dark summons to action.

What does Hendrix do in less than eight seconds? Produce the charmingly spindly chords that flutter and flounce over the hefty, bulky bass stabs in 'Wait Until Tomorrow'.

What does Hendrix do in less than seven seconds? Evoke a high, keening tanpura drone against an unsteady, almost blurred sound of a violin in 'Love Or Confusion', as if a disturbing blast of heat is somehow managing to warp the wood of the instrument.

What does Hendrix do in less than five seconds? Hit two chords then immediately punctuate them with a stark detuned note, which is then cut short by the hard, dry snap of a snare drum in 'Ain't No Telling'.

The sounds don't so much follow one another as set off a kind of chain reaction that nonetheless remains perfectly controlled. Timing, to the half-beat, particularly in the case of the last song with its snatches of silence, is of the essence. The attention to detail in the patchworking of elements, how the guitars, effects and percussion all knit together with such little opportunity for any sustained growth, is superlative. These introductions are unerringly focused and concise but they do not stifle Hendrix's overall creative drive.

All of the above are examples of Hendrix creating a maximum impact in a minimum amount of time, by way of very fine judgement on the proportion of information in an arrangement. Knowing how long to sustain a note, when to make a chord voicing subtle or emphatic, what draught of feedback will suffice to imbue the song with the necessary non-musicality to complement the musicality. Such questions were pondered by Hendrix, accompanists, engineers and producers, and if the introductions sound strikingly modern, decades after they were recorded, then that is also down to the input of the likes of Chas Chandler and Eddie Kramer, who advised on what parts might be effective, and how to sonically enhance them.

Interesting as these moments of tightly channelled creativity are, the real achievement of the Hendrix introduction is its role of scene setting. There are songs in which the opening array of sounds is a vivid foreshadowing of the tale that the singer will subsequently tell, and the range of thoughts and feelings he sets out to explore. The beginning really lends credence to the middle and end of the story.

Rough guidelines for pop songwriting generally place an emphasis on well-defined sections and the sacrosanct verse-chorus structure in order to enable the listener to have readily digestible data, usually a combination of words and music, that will lodge in the sub-conscious either during or after the life cycle of the arrangement.

Much more demanding, and much less easily computed, is the symbiosis of what is played and what is sung, how the common resources of guitar, bass, drums, keys, horns and strings, can actually be deployed in such a way as to sound or feel inextricably linked to the character of a voice and content of a lyric. A cymbal crash or a piano arpeggio may catch the ear of the listener when a song begins but it acquires additional power, certainly on repeat listening to the piece, if it transpires that a voice and the story it tells are launched and well supported by what is first heard.

'May This Be Love' is one of the most striking examples of this art. Mitch Mitchell's constant roll on the toms strikes a fine balance of momentum and delicacy, a distinct sensation of sound pushing forward without crushing all in its path. The drummer placed a device known as a ching ring on his hi-hat, which produced a kind of bell-like sound that softened and cushioned the lower pitch of the drums. This dreamy, slightly mesmeric purr is heard unaccompanied for just over a bar before Hendrix enters with a series of elongated single notes that form into a bizarrely beautiful melody. Initially, they pierce the upper register but soon curl to the middle, then sensually drift downwards in halftime, practically evoking a seductive slow haze.

Hendrix starts to gently strum a chord, as if he wants to channel those slivers of sound into a sensual vapour. The whole passage has a vague surf guitar or Hawaiian feel to it, and it could feasibly be interpreted as some kind of invocation of sun rays dancing on the sand or another earthly backdrop. However, the other portrait of nature that is suggested, perhaps even more so, is the flow of river or sea, primarily because of the radiant, glistening quality of the guitar and the wavering of pitch at several moments. Something is streaming but not with the cold efficiency of a man-made device such as a reservoir or tap. The music is a resoundingly vivid conveyance of the natural world.

Mitchell finally punctuates his toms with a cymbal crash, a decisive sound to signal the close of the chapter, or rather that the tableau thus far painted will be supplemented with something new. In a gentle tone Hendrix then sings: "Waterfall nothing can harm me at all/My worries seem so very small/ With my waterfall". There may be a spirit, creature or soul mate embodied in this wonder of nature but the point is that sound and word sync up.

The image of falling water in the musical introduction thus leads to a direct statement on the place of falling water in the lyric. The implicit is made explicit. The figurative is made literal. The strength of the narrative is then enhanced at various points throughout the song. After eight bars the music stops and Hendrix lightly bends a note. The moment is fleeting, like a single droplet of water glimpsed and then gone. After another eight bars he creates a similar effect but it is a slightly longer pizzicato sensation. The splash evoked in the previous interlude has turned to a brief ripple.

One of the less celebrated tracks in the Hendrix canon, 'May This Be Love' is nonetheless an important example of his skill at closely allying his work on the guitar with lyrical content. The considerable intricacy of the opening musical statement is not an end in itself but a well-crafted launching pad for what is to come, and a reminder that Hendrix had an ability to build a coherent synthesis of many elements.

Super genre buster

More attentive audiences would have heard that ambition from the early stages of Hendrix's solo career. Hendrix himself had made it clear that the pursuit of musical originality was at a premium, and that the desire to write and arrange songs which carved out a fresh space within the prevailing vocabulary of popular music moulded by the blues and R&B and that deployed state-of-the-art technology largely flowed from his boundless imagination. Tellingly, he stated that the breakout single of The Experience, a cover of Billy Roberts' folk blues ballad 'Hey Joe', was not entirely representative of the band's direction, even though the morbid tale of infidelity is well rendered by the performance.[24] The Hendrix version presents effective embellishments, particularly the guitar adlibs, but it remains mostly true to the song's original structure.

Moreover, the question of writing original material arose with that debut 45. Chas Chandler resolutely demanded that Hendrix exit his comfort zone when it came to the B-side. Hendrix had originally opted for a Wilson Pickett hit he knew all too well, but Chandler, showing tough love at just the right moment, flatly vetoed the idea. "Jimi wanted to put *Land of a 1000 Dances* on the B side, but I said absolutely no way – you will sit down tonight and write a new song. So he sat down that night and composed *Stone Free*, the first Experience song he ever wrote."[25]

'Purple Haze', the second single Hendrix released in March 1967, saw him emphatically develop his uncommon gifts as a purveyor of original words and music. A high point both in the Hendrix songbook and 1960s popular music that has stayed impressively contemporary, the composition stands out for the richness of the individual sections, and, as is the case with 'May This Be Love', the coherence of sound and lyric. A listener can home in on any number of moments in the piece, from the intro to the coda, but the whole is greater than the sum of its parts.

The song boasts an unforgettable introduction: the grinding rhythm of Hendrix's stark, snarly B-flat octaves bolstered by Noel Redding playing the same interval in E. From a theoretical point of view the effect of these figures is considerable dissonance but that alone does not explain both the structural interest and emotional charge of the music. While the choice of pitches may induce a deep unease, it is a juxtaposition of this and a new line that pushes the piece into a heightened state of anxiety. The guitar and bass riffs are solidly clamped on the 4/4 beat and are executed with a metronomic coldness, a sinister tick-tock that threatens to keep running without any pause. Then a guitar melody comes in which has a markedly different character. Whereas the first riff was delivered in terse eighth notes this new line is in elegant quarter-notes given additional glissando and vibrato, which lend a distinct grandeur. There is something heraldic about this theme, which is not hard to imagine being played on a medieval horn in order to announce an event of importance at a court gathering of nobles.

Finally, after 10 fraught measures, the jarring rhythm gives way to a new pulse as Mitchell starts to syncopate on his snare and ride cymbal, and guitar and bass pivot on a chord sequence of E, G, A. The band drives the piece forward in earnest. They play the harmony for four bars and then Hendrix succinctly conveys his state of recent disorientation: *Purple haze all in my brain/ Lately, things don't seem the same.*

For any listener who is really paying attention and who has a degree of imagination, it is not hard to hear and appreciate the coherent whole created by the coming together of words and music. The troublesome harmonic clash of the intro, the gnash and grind of the chords, the blend of staccato and legato notes, abrupt riffs and fluent lines, static and dynamic rhythms in that early part of the arrangement, consolidate the singer's overall state of disorientation. But the song becomes magical when it enters its breakdown phase after seven bars of lyrics. At the start of bar 8 the solo lyric "Scuse me while I kiss" rings out, then the guitar bursts back in with short, punchy triplets that stand as a perfect complement to what has come before, giving the impression that the electric instrument is somehow flowing out of the acoustic voice.

The sung line has seven notes and the guitar riffs, initially accenting hard on the D and G, are in sets of three, thus creating a consistency of odd numbers that imparts to the vocal-instrumental palette a superlative sense of cohesion. Hendrix smartly judges the length and tone of the various individual fragments of the song's architecture, and more importantly, how the parts should be locked together.

After the spookiness of the Bb/E dissonance in the intro there comes a series of shapes and colours that create spikes of tension. It is all fills, string bends, slides into notes, sharpenings of pitch, and vivid embellishments of phrase. Nonetheless, the stream of ideas is absolutely contained within a crystal-clear narrative. This is Hendrix displaying an ability to develop songs to match his introductions.

Put simply, a piece with such a charged atmosphere is made all the more impactful because the composer reins things in. The tightness of construction is actually the key to its richness. That discipline vaguely reminds me of the way Booker T. Jones's organ and Steve Cropper's guitar interact on Booker T. & The MG's peerless 'Green Onions', whereby the two elements support each other so sympathetically as to become one magical alloy. The whole of the instrumental sounds is greater than the very rich parts.

'Purple Haze' is a triumph of melodic clarity, or rather how to complement and embellish the voice with resonant guitar riffs, and it is a major part of Hendrix's legacy as a writer who is sensitive to overarching story as well as specific episode. When asked about the meaning of 'Purple Haze' he said: "Well, it's about this guy. This girl turns this cat on, you know, and he doesn't know which way he's going. But he doesn't know what's happening really. He doesn't know if it's bad or good, that's all, and he doesn't know if it's no tomorrow or just the end of time for instance."[26]

A coded narco hymn or an off-centre love song, the piece vividly projects feelings of ambiguity and uncertainty. And there is no conclusion to the torture. 'Purple Haze' fades out at 2:48 minutes, leaving the anxiety unresolved, the dilemma maintained.

What is significant is the way Hendrix still manages to overturn pop convention within this radio-friendly duration. There are exactly 14 bars of instrumental music before the lead vocal enters, which means that just over 30 seconds of airtime has *no* singing at all. Roughly one-fifth of the piece does not feature the frontman on the mike.

The song says many things about Hendrix the artist. Firstly, the player and the singer, two primary elements of his being, along with the composer, stand in a complex, mutable relationship. Hendrix *played* and sang. On 'Purple Haze' he deemed it important to feature guitar figures for longer than two or four bars before it was time to sing. To his great credit, producer Chas Chandler, as far as we know, did not attempt to shoehorn him into a more standard form, with an intro under 10 let alone 14 bars.

It is not so much that Hendrix is creating dissonance as that he is doing it for *so* long. Many may have expected him to curtail it after four bars and start the verse, as befits the argument that the pop audience sets great store by a melody in the form of words. Getting to the point without too lengthy a prologue was thus an essential strategy.

There were dozens of singles in the mid-1960s that were 2:30–3:00 minutes long, but very few had extended introductions. (Shocking Blue's wonderful

'Venus' has 10 bars and Procul Harum's 'A Whiter Shade Of Pale' has 8 bars that feel like a mini-eternity because of the slow-medium tempo dominated by the church organ, whose haunting melody is presented as the star feature for 29 seconds prior to the entry of the lead vocal.)

Through the structure of 'Purple Haze' Hendrix reveals an earnest interest in questions of pacing and proportion. He wants the track to breathe adequately. There is no rushing through a section if more running time is necessary to let the ideas unfold to their full extent. An 11-bar guitar solo is a highlight of the second half of the song, and there is a reprise of the intro, this time for eight bars. Yet the song still comes in at under three minutes. Hendrix is balancing concision and elaboration, opting for detail within a small picture frame, constructing music that, from its initial disturbing ambiance to the irresistible pull of its riffs, deftly straddles the line between the experimental and the accessible. It is avant-garde blues.

As he showed on 'Third Stone From The Sun' (duration 6:40), Hendrix broke out of the straitjacket of the 3-minute pop song, but on 'Purple Haze' he was subverting from *within.* He eschewed the orthodoxy of foregrounding the central rhythm or chords that underpin verse and chorus and made that unforgettable introduction a key gambit. 'Purple Haze' could have burst straight into life without the instrumental introduction. It would have been much more radio-friendly. But it would have been a lesser work.

Perverse as it may seem to listeners who, over years of repeat listening, are inured to the initial 14 bars of the song, the groove the band lays into for the second phase of the piece has sufficient character to sustain the potential absence of the gem of an introduction. This means that the first part of the song is practically a stand-alone entity. It would have made for a worthwhile reprise, a re-visitation and development on *Are You Experienced?* had Hendrix actually decided to use the idea of self-reference as he did with the "slight return" of 'Voodoo Child' on *Electric Ladyland.*

Given the richness of the specific constituent parts of some of Hendrix's best songs, it is little wonder that the stories of him being at pains to actually finish material abound. His attention to detail is of the highest order. Other pieces that are firm favourites in the Hendrix songbook also have opening salvoes whose craftsmanship is such that they bear repeat listening in spite of the notable beauty of what follows.

Released as a (US) single in November 1968, 'Crosstown Traffic' is notable for the expanded textural palette beyond the guitar-vocals-bass-drums that was the core of Hendrix's sound. The piano was the idea of Eddie Kramer, who, although Hendrix's trusted engineer, had studied classical music in his native South Africa prior to relocating to London in the early 1960s and liked nothing better than to play a few jazz licks in between recording sessions in studios such as Olympia. "This is one of the last tracks Chas really had a tight hand on", recalls Kramer.[27]

As with several other songs, there is a prelude to a prelude. The tracks kick into life with a sturdy B-flat piano chord which pounds away, supplemented by a screech of C-minor guitar underpinned by bass and a quasi-march beat on drums, and then abruptly gives way to another part after two bars. Bang, blink and gone. It is just a brief rap of knuckles on a door that then swings open. A moment of insistence quickly fulfilled.

Things move harmonically as a IV progression (C to F) and Hendrix then strikes up a strutting pentatonic riff that is given a breezy, almost insouciant character by an overdub of kazoo and wordless vocal. The blend of the three sounds – the thickness of the guitar, the pinched, nasal kazoo and the chirpy, whistle-like vocal – produces a sensation, which, from an emotional standpoint, is intriguing to say the least. There is a whimsy, a capricious sensuality and implied flirtation primarily because of an overwhelming softness in the texture, even though Hendrix colours the sound canvas with additional guitar figures that are quite thorny. Repeat listening underlines a point that is easy to miss. The title designates urban hustle and bustle, which becomes a metaphor for hit'n'run sexual escapades, and the tempo is a jaunty 113 bpm. Yet, despite its regular thrusts forward, the feel of the song is not that of a runaway train.

It is a more sophisticated than gentle introduction. There is a drive to the way the piece starts but it is calibrated in order to retain an element of playfulness. Hendrix is essentially teasing us – or the lover who has him in a state of confusion.

There are six bars of riffing before a quick resumption of the two bars of B-flat pedal, but in the very last measure Hendrix injects a new energy by doubling the hits of piano with the vocal and kazoo. It is a fleeting shot of adrenalin over four beats. However, the arrival of the verse dramatically raises the temperature of the whole piece. Hendrix's vocal does not so much ring out as crash right through the air. A woman jumps straight in front of his car, which he is driving at "90 miles an hour".

Music serves as a metaphor for confrontation and its attendant thrill. Hendrix gives an impassioned vocal performance, roaring out his words but what increases his impact is a simple but effective editorial decision. Mitch Mitchell's syncopated drumming moves right to the foreground as guitar, bass and piano hit the downbeat. Yet they play just two notes then drop out for the second half of the bar, giving additional space to Hendrix's voice and Mitchell's drums in the remaining two beats. They become the dominant sounds in a strange kind of micro-break rather than full breakdown. The result is a new spike of aggression within aggression, as if Hendrix is conducting an agitated monologue where he pours out his pent-up frustrations in a small, noisy room, or perhaps a busy, loud street. The burst of unaccompanied drums is a potent reinforcement of the singer's fractiousness.

When the chorus arrives and the harmony of the introduction returns there is a definite release of tension as the textural palette brings noticeably lighter strains into focus. There is thus a back and forth motion between a number of emotional states that are paralleled by the alternations of sounds of differing volume and intensity.

Through the timbres created by the band and his own lyric, Hendrix expresses tetchy surliness rather than outright anger, where a primary theme is a resentful lover – "Crosstown traffic ... so hard to get through to you" – as he sings in the chorus. Yet eroticism is also a key facet of the song, lyrically, through risqué imagery such as "tyre tracks all across your back/I can see you had your fun" and sonically, by way of the patchworks created in the instrumental passages. There is a slinkiness, sexiness and seduction in the meld of piano, kazoo and vocal, which stand in opposition to the ferocity of the drums. These textural contrasts and shifting moods, and the balance of melodic statement and rhythmic propulsion in 'Crosstown Traffic', are engrossing.

Furthermore, another distinct shift of character happens on the chorus. After the barrage of noise created by the guitar-drums-bass onslaught, a volley of backing vocals streams into life with an altogether gentler character. Members of The Experience are joined by Traffic's Dave Mason to create close harmony vocals that have a markedly boyish nature, loosely reminiscent of a 1950s doo wop group, thus creating a brightness, a buoyancy that offsets the distinct belligerence of the verse.

What the piece says about the musical culture of Jimi Hendrix is also worth consideration. Stylistically, it is not at all easy to categorize. Or rather the arrangement references several genres and sub-genres in an interesting way. The A section is very much in the vein of early 1960s soul jazz as pioneered by the likes of Cannonball Adderley and Horace Silver. In fact if the intro of 'Crosstown Traffic' were looped and pitched up to +2 on a turntable it would sit well in a mix with Adderley's 'Money In The Pocket' and Silver's 'Psychedelic Sally'. Both these compositions have bluesy, rousing horn figures that pack a greater punch than the piano-vocal-kazoo combination in the Hendrix piece, but that choice was made in the first place because the guitarist was obviously searching for a texture that was much more redolent of wind rather than string instruments. Ironically, it took him right back to some of the early practitioners of black music in America who used kazoos when they did not have brass or reeds.

If the intro of 'Crosstown Traffic' puts Hendrix in line with jazz present and past, the verse, which signals the dramatic surge of Mitchell's drums, is a form of funk. The overall jumpiness of the rhythm, the percolation of the snare, and the unbroken momentum of the beat, its ceaseless waves of energy, have clear dance implications.

An outstanding musician who had cut his teeth with British jazz, blues and R&B groups such as the Pretty Things and Georgie Famie & The Blue Flames, Mitchell had a super solid groove and a fine sense of swing, and his ability to alternate effectively between eighth and quarter-note led rhythms was essential for the dexterity Hendrix required for his more demanding arrangements.

As a disciple of jazz greats such as Elvin Jones and Roy Haynes, Mitchell was entirely at ease with the idea of being thrust into the spotlight even if his virtuosity had to be much more concise.

The verses of 'Crosstown Traffic' excel in percussive energy, showcasing the polyrhythmic and sonic richness of the drums that has a similar impact to the inspired pre-chorus of Wilson Pickett's 1966 soul classic 'Land Of A Thousand Dances', a song that Hendrix greatly admired and had previously wanted to cover. Here the horns, bass and guitar fall silent and there is a lengthy passage of drums and chanting of the percussively looping "nah nah nah nah nah" phrase. Apart from the infectiously communicative nature of the wordless line, which infuses a child-like, nursery rhyme innocence to the grown-up hedonism of a song that celebrates the infinite riches of black choreography, the drums-vocal duet is notable for the way it is placed in the arrangement. All the other instruments drop out very sharply, and the heavy punch of the kick and snare, and deep, dangerous growl of Pickett's voice, take centre stage. Consequently the drama of the song is invigorated by this quick change of scenery.

There is also no warning of the Mitchell explosion in 'Crosstown Traffic'. It happens with a head-turning abruptness, thereby becoming a stark disruption rather than smooth conjunction to what preceded, as if the caress of the jazz in the intro was unceremoniously kicked into touch by the hefty stamp of the funk in the verse. One style displaces another. Or rather there is a collision of schools of black music. An artist who has played many genres is letting his broad knowledge take its own course.

Whether Hendrix was consciously attempting to achieve a multi-genre eclecticism is a moot point, though. He was largely ambivalent about the whole issue of categorization, and exactly what market he should be placed in, and the continual questioning from pundits about appropriate descriptions for The Experience led to him emphasize the need to see beyond idiomatic boundaries. For example, when interviewed by Terry David Mulligan in Vancouver (7 September 1968), he explained his preferred modus operandi was to play with musicians of various backgrounds in the hope that the result may be something *beyond* any recognized genre. "Rock cats and jazz people ... when we jam all these things come about, they come up to another music we haven't even named yet. The only thing you can go by now is ... call it a jam."[28] That's a well-chosen word from somebody devoted to the culture of jamming.

Furthermore, the statement serves as a reminder that the Jimi Hendrix Experience was a band that had personnel with a variety of musical backgrounds. Noel Redding, born in Folkestone, Kent and originally a guitarist-vocalist for bands such as The Lonely Ones and The Loving Kind, was identified mostly with rock, Mitch Mitchell had a strong R&B and jazz C.V., while Hendrix was the American with a prodigious gift for blues and a virtuosity that put him on a par with jazz artists. It was precisely the differences as well as common ground that galvanized the group.

In the same interview Mitchell also made a case for the gathering of diverse creative spirits. "Musicians from different so-called categories … who expects dear Louis Armstrong playing with John Coltrane? Who knows one day? Because a lot of the cats we've been playing with lately have been on different scenes entirely."[29]

It was a timely reminder of the backstory of The Experience, and as good an explanation as any as to how a piece such as 'Crosstown Traffic' could have been created. More importantly it signals the real possibility of the large amount of musical information held by Hendrix, Mitchell, Redding and other collaborators leading them to conceptual places that would fall between rather than directly into pigeonholes. In the greater scheme of things rock is a highly approximate definition of the oeuvre of Jimi Hendrix because of the fusing of the many elements named above, as well as the significant impact on his work of state-of-the-art technology.

What is clear from extensive analysis of his songbook is just how imaginatively a wide range of black music was absorbed and deeply personalized by the artist. To state that Hendrix could play in a number of different styles is not wholly inaccurate, but it might be more appropriate to argue that his knowledge of the many rhythmic approaches to which he was exposed in his formative years came to organically surface in his solo work in a way that created something entirely personal.

Technically speaking, 'Crosstown Traffic' is a soul-jazz-funk-rock synthesis, yet above all it is a bold, boisterous depiction of a tempestuous relationship, a tale of the highs and lows of casual sex, where each party is 'accused of hit and run', that uses the attention-grabbing gear changes of the beat and striking timbral shifts to create pop that feels *beyond* soul, jazz, funk and rock as we perceive each single entity. The song is hybridized. The song is idiosyncratic. The song is in a genre all of its own.

Black music: access all areas

Look elsewhere in the Hendrix songbook and we see or rather hear other cunning adaptations of the vocabulary of black music. 'Ain't No Telling' is Motown soul with a shot of adrenalin. The pumping repeated bassline and sustained drive of the groove makes it kith and kin to Junior Walker's 'Shotgun', a piece that Hendrix had played numerous times as a young sideman with various bands when on the chitlin circuit, and that to this day remains an absolutely formidable piece of dance music.

'Stone Free' starts life as a crisp Latin boogaloo, with the hard resonance of Mitchell's eighth notes on the cowbell creating the percussive power that came to characterize the glorious music of New York's Cuban and Puerto

Rican communities of Spanish Harlem, before storming into an R&B-style chorus. 'Dolly Dagger' has a similarly strong Latin feel in the intro but settles much earlier into a punchy soul groove.

'Gypsy Eyes' presents vaguely similar elements to 'Crosstown Traffic' in reverse order. In the A section the drums, particularly Mitchell's kick, is marshalled to a 4/4 with such force as to convey the high-voltage energy of a marching band, before taking off into Stax soul on the B and then swirling into an airborne, jazzy swing on the C.

'Little Miss Lover' is another spotlight for the brilliance of Mitch Mitchell's drumming that also shows how the Jimi Hendrix Experience was referencing and extending the vocabulary of mid-1960s Stax soul, again with a particular focus on artists such as Otis Redding. Here Mitchell's steadily vaulting kick drum, whose pattern of nine notes in the bar is so clearly articulated that the phrasal grouping of 2.4.3 forms a micro-melody, is a more strident, aggressive relative to the groove of Al Jackson Jr on Redding and Carla Thomas's slacker funk gem 'Tramp'. Mitchell astutely brings great splashes of cymbals to the beat that act as a cooling airstream to offset the heat cooked up in the low register. The drum set is presented here as a source of multiple streams of sound, a cogent unit of basic but incisive orchestration as well as an engine of polyrhythms. Needless to say, this is prime sample fodder, one of many precious raw materials that would be liberally deployed in the development of hip-hop many years down the line.

There are certain songs where Hendrix deployed age-old methodologies in a context that managed to avoid being hackneyed. A great example is 'Rainy Day, Dream Away', an often-overlooked piece from *Electric Ladyland*. This is a beautiful investigation of the kind of style developed by soul-jazz organists such as Jimmy Smith. The gospel-infused sound he drew from the instrument blended well with the timbre of a tenor saxophone or guitar with a thin, sharp, piercing tone such as that of Wes Montgomery or Kenny Burrell, a player Hendrix was known to greatly admire. On 'Rainy Day' Hendrix steps into the Burrell role very convincingly with Mike Finnigan cast as Smith and Fred Smith (as Stanley Turrentine perhaps) on tenor saxophone. It is one of the most overtly jazzy sounds that Hendrix ever produced in his discography, and the first part of the song has some wonderfully vivid trading of licks as the players settle into a hearty shuffle and steadily cook up a deeply smoky, sultry ambience.

However, what is more important is the element of irreverence introduced at an early stage of the arrangement. As the players start to improvise there is a casual remark about falling rain, to which the solution is to play. "We'll get into something real nice".

The dialogue is fairly low in the mix, with the voices whispered and the response to the opening line close to the bassy slur of a cartoon character. Soon enough the talking ends and the music builds a head of steam before halting sharply. Hendrix then starts to sing, "Rainy day, dream away, let the sun take a holiday!" There are more verses in this carefree vein, but, interestingly, Hendrix dramatically alters the tone of his guitar in the final stages of the piece. The fluttering delicacy of the introduction is replaced by a heavier, bulker sound with a hard, stinging attack. As previously noted there is a liberal negotiation of genres, facilitated by the artist's sense of playfulness, openness and willingness to push an arrangement towards directions that collaborators, regular or irregular, may have deemed incoherent.

All of which makes possible several interpretations of Hendrix's relationship with the history of black music. On the one hand he has a firm grip on much of its vocabulary. On the other hand he has maverick ways. Like all artists who manage to shift paradigms, he doesn't keep on applying formulae, or act according to expectation.

If 'Crosstown Traffic' is the archetypal example of a song that feels emphatically Hendrix, but which has several constituent parts that clearly relate to musicians with whom he is not usually associated, then there are other songs that have a similar kind of transformation-personalization through clever musical structuring.

'Spanish Castle Magic' has a fraught, tense verse where a descending chromatic guitar line plunges into a pronounced sense of mystery before subsequently exploding into a kind of dread on the chorus, as the combination of an almost anguished vocal cry and a violently hissing guitar imbues the atmosphere with a distinct menace. What adds to the overall enigma of the song, though? On the verse Mitchell plays a hefty stomping pattern on the bass drum that is vaguely reminiscent of a Native American rhythm. The piece takes a turn into a cultural space that coherently bridges indigenous and African-American cultures, both of which were part of Hendrix's own heritage. The prevailing sensation is of something that is both deeply ancestral and modern.

'Fire' also works on artful dynamics and astute contrasts of phrasal length and tonal densities between verse and chorus. It basically moves from sparse to full. By starting with a rapid-fire rhythmic line, where guitar and bass stab sharply in and out of life, Hendrix gives the song a febrile, agitated energy in keeping with the title, a metaphor for sexual attraction. But the chorus wheels into the kind of swinging, boogieing blues that links anybody from Count Basie to John Lee Hooker and Muddy Waters.

'Up From The Skies' is more swing. The skipping, strolling beat has all the brightness of a banjo-driven piece of black music from the 1920s, and the overall lightness of touch is enhanced by the fact that Mitchell is playing brushes rather than sticks, which is an entirely unusual strategy for a late '60s band marketed as rock rather than jazz. Hendrix has a fantastically sensual growl of wah-wah on his guitar that makes the dominant hook of the song vividly playful. It is an additional form of percussion, a brawny shadow on Mitchell's fluttering beat, but it does not weigh the piece down.

Once again the music is straddling various perceptions of both genre and era. It is taking us back in time, suggesting an early form of jazz, yet it is also capturing and evoking a sound of its time, that of a recently invented keyboard, the Hohner clavinet, that would prove to be hugely influential, thanks to Stevie Wonder, in a time to come.

Get ur freakish blues on

Finding words to describe a style of music has never been an exact science, and it is worth reflecting on the genealogy of terms that may be associated with certain acts.

Just as swing was a noun and verb, a genre and a form of rhythm, rock was also a highly emblematic term in black culture and music prior to becoming synonymous with the likes of Hendrix. When jazz icon Duke Ellington recorded 'Rockin' In Rhythm' back in 1931 he was essentially celebrating the joyous sensation produced by music, which had the requisite snap to make inter-war audiences take to dance floors. An altogether more sexually charged connotation was attached to a variation on the language that became common in blues songs, "rock me baby, roll all over me", a metaphor for love making that was expressive without being overly crude. Rock 'n' roll as a genre in its own right still carried that current of profanity, which understandably provoked condemnation from men of the cloth, black and white.

A black R&B star promising "There's gonna be good rockin' tonight" was simply a liberating and semantically gymnastic way of aligning sound and sex, an inventive levelling of the ground between two universal impulses: making music and making love.

Solomon Burke, no slouch in the art of seduction and procreation – he fathered *at least* 14 children in his lifetime – was exactly the embodiment of rock(in') and soul. Ironically, rock had been a term used to describe the sensation of African-American church services at their most ecstatic, as the folk blues singer Leadbelly has pointed out. But nowhere was the interconnectedness of genres across the sacred–profane divide more striking than in the moniker applied to Burke, a preacher in his youth. He was the "king of Rock 'n' Soul".[30] This could be seen as a barefaced ploy to put a new spin on the term rock 'n' roll but it was not entirely meaningless, as the music of the likes of Burke, and his peers such as Wilson Pickett, Otis Redding and Aretha Franklin was absolutely imbued with the energy of rock and the feeling of soul. To rock was to move, both oneself and others, to impact, to affect, to disrupt, to push, to drive, to pump up with adrenalin, to embolden, to execute, to make happen.

The idea of rock as conviction is deeply rooted in the Afro-Diasporan vernacular; it is a term that pervades territories shaped by the slave experience, subsequently fashioning complex relationships with standard and creolized

English that have proved evolutionary according to the specifics of time and place. Hence in 1970s Jamaica a "rocker" is a wholly committed music head whereas in 1990s hip-hop stamped America you *rock* a pair of trainers when it looks so *phat* that you *feel* it. More imaginative rappers have further riffed on semantic history, turning the recognized formulation of rock 'n' roll into the affirmation of "I rock, I roll".[31]

Our understanding of rock as a genre that evolved from the blues necessarily puts under the spotlight this complex, interrelated network of psychological, behavioural and emotional impulses as well as musical strategies. The reductive, hackneyed definition of rock, and rock 'n' roll for that matter, usually places the emphasis on rebellion, swagger and *attitude* as well as a modicum of musical ability but no amount of posturing in the world will win over an audience that demands substance as well as style. The power of rock and the thrill of a soul or gospel show are not incompatible. Burke's rock is his voice. Hendrix's is his guitar.

Seeing Hendrix as a putative rock artist does not detach him from a host of R&B and soul practitioners who were able *to rock*, even if they were not marketed as rock. This became synonymous with British artists in the mid-1960s such as the Rolling Stones, The Yardbirds, The Who and Cream who Hendrix happily claimed as an influence.

The advent of large-scale amplification at outdoor festivals such as Magic Mountain, Monterrey and Woodstock consolidated the idea of the rock artist as loud, heavy and dangerous, if not destructive, complete with ritual sacrifice of equipment, moving one notch up from the scandalous wildness previously embodied by rock 'n' roll.

Regardless of the primacy of rock as a new genre and social phenomenon that coincided with Hendrix's arrival as a major solo artist, black music had already claimed intellectual and philosophical ownership of it in a comprehensive way years prior. Record industry tastemakers and critics may have prided themselves on trying to pinpoint what Hendrix was doing with the coining of sub-genres on a regular basis, but they were simply playing catch-up with history. Blues rock became a hip term in the late '60s, but T-Bone Walker recorded 'Blues Rock' a decade before that. The relationship between black language and music was both complex and dynamic.

Walker would have surely been aware that a black church service was known to *rock* as much as a roadside jook joint, and that rock as concept, verb and noun was like a roaming energy in African-American culture, which is one of the reasons why R&B and rock 'n' roll could be knitted together. Hendrix once described Little Richard, one of his significant early employers, as the "king of rock & rhythm".[32]

More revealingly, Hendrix *was* marketed as an exponent of black music and culture, on occasion. He would come to embody rock but it is a myth to think that the record industry *exclusively* defined him as such from the outset. No greater proof of this can be found than on a 12-track compilation that was released by Polydor in 1968. The album was called *Soul Party*, and featured Hendrix's 'Hey Joe' and 'Stone Free' alongside songs by Edwin Starr, Donnie Elbert, The Soulrunners, Suzie & Big Dee Irwin and The Ikettes, among others. The programme was entirely coherent, essentially showing Hendrix's music in the wider context of the R&B of his formative years. It is interesting to hear the common denominators between him and other artists, such as strong blues inflections and Latin rhythms, and his already strong marks of distinction, above all a wild, explosive energy, which clearly pushes away from any neat orchestration. He has managed to find a new junction on an old road.

Heard today, Hendrix's body of work essentially makes the point that he was part of an extensive amount of cross-referencing that was taking place over stylistic lines at the time of his rise to prominence. The importance of his music is that it invariably conveys the essence of a particular genre without being a direct or straight example thereof. Hendrix is funky without being standard funk. He is jazzy without being standard jazz. He is soulful without being standard soul. He presents rock as something that is a strange synthesis of these satellites of the mothership of the blues.

No clearer summary of this was presented than by Hendrix himself in an interview in London during February 1967: "What we're trying to do is, we're trying to get our own particular sound, you know, like a freakish blues with, you know, this rave like almost, only with a little more feeling than what's been happening lately."[33]

The importance of the statement cannot be overstated, and it is worth reflecting on the precise insight that can be gleaned from Hendrix on Hendrix. When he talks of "our own particular sound" he's not thinking in terms of genres but really broaching the specifics of what might be achieved by, for the most part, a guitar-vocal-bass-drums combo in terms of the audio canvas created by the synergy of those four elements, enhanced by engineering and studio production. The fact that he qualifies that as "freakish blues" reflects both a historical lineage and subversion thereof, because for all his command of older forms of black music Hendrix wants to draw new sensations from them. And he knows that in order to attain that goal he has to be open to whatever he hears around him. It is a case for tradition and modernity in alliance.

The time it is a stopping and a starting

What we hear at the cutting edge of post-war black popular music is greater rhythmic and textural ingenuity, as R&B gradually evolves into soul and funk, a brash new sub-genre that affects audiences through visceral, syncopated power and an aggressive use of amplified instruments. Beats are heavier, harder, tougher. The structure of soul songs that marked a leap forward between the mid- and late '60s such as James Brown's 'Cold Sweat', Sly & The Family Stone's 'Dance To The Music', and the Isley Brothers' 'It's Your Thing' made much of the interlocking of drums, bass, guitars and horns so that the focused criss-crossing of riffs created a new excitement. There was also a lengthening of guitar lines, which had a considerable metronomic solidity and added to the greater sense of dynamism and invigoration in the polyrhythms against which lead and backing vocals would be cast. This was very intricately constructed, multi-faceted electric dance music.

Hendrix is in and out of step with his movement. He brings greater density to his music through the mosaic of effects and a plethora of overdubs, so that they become as incident-packed as Brown's even though they may not be as overtly percussive. His raucous, insistent rhythm guitar phrasing sends high voltage excitement through unforgettable songs such as 'Gypsy Eyes', 'Little Miss Lover', 'Beginnings' and 'Izabella'.

Having said that, Hendrix keeps a handle on a rudiment of black music that is used by Brown, Stone, the Isleys and countless others in soul: a variety of breakdowns, whereby one or a few instruments drops out or the whole band might come to a halt. There is thus a simple but highly effective structural conceit: the dynamic range of the performance broadens, as specific elements of the horn and rhythm sections come in and out of focus amid varying levels of volume, from high to mid to low, all the way down to a theatrical silence.

A change in the configuration of an ensemble during an arrangement is a core principle of African-American music that reaches right back to the earliest known jazz ensembles of the first part of the twentieth century. This convention held sway for musicians working in R&B in the 1960s, where the use of a rhythm section that might include keyboards, guitar, bass and drums as well as horn and possibly string sections meant that there were more opportunities for light and shade when certain instruments were withdrawn at various points in a song.

Having worked with groups that had these expanded line-ups in his formative years Hendrix would have been obliged to learn precise cues, and it is interesting to see how he applied that knowledge to his own songs. Above all there is a sense that Hendrix the arranger as well as writer wants to make sometimes simple but highly effective shifts in the flow of a piece, that he takes the tune momentarily off piste.

For example, in the middle of the first section of 'Power Of Soul' there is a wonderful moment of respite, a kind of sudden end to the momentum after bar 12. Or a false start before the groove kicks back in. Drums and bass drop out and guitar swoons into silence on bar 13 before all three ferociously burst into life on the next measure. The use of pause performs a basic but highly effective theatrical function. It is a playfulness, a gamesmanship, a teasing with time, or with its expected regularity.

The momentary breathing space in the opening of 'Power Of Soul' is all the more conspicuous because of the sonic violence that is unleashed thereafter, and this is by no means an isolated case in Hendrix's oeuvre. Numerous are the songs where the intervention of silence is almost like the blink of a flash-light to grab the attention. 'May This Be Love', 'Fire' and 'Can You See Me' all set great store by the precise disappearance of the rhythm section to leave the vocal unaccompanied at regular intervals in the songs, usually so as to clearly signal the end of a particular verse.

However, the song where Hendrix really plays "mind the gap" is 'If 6 Was 9'. It could be filed in the sub-category of weird Jimi insofar as the arrangement creates a distinct sense of foreboding if not oppressive unease, as if the array of quite sinister sounds is being suppressed and bottled up before breaking through the silence.

What defines the song is the substantial amount of space and lengthy rests between notes, as voice, guitar, bass and drums move tentatively across what at times feels like a dry, arid landscape, if not parched desert. The ambiance is as airless as it is fraught. Each guitar lick or vocal cry has considerable weight in this vista of barren emptiness.

'If 6 Was 9' really skulks into life, with harsh guitar stabs announcing a strange tale. At various points in the composition you hear what sounds like an E-flat, or Gb, or Bb but these are not so much power chords as heated little explosions that appear all the more dangerous because of the way the other musical elements are spread out around them.

The fragmentation is marked. Mostly, the guitar grinds on beat 1 while the bass guitar and cymbals stretch over 2, 3 and 4, as a wry rejoinder. If we liken that set-up to a speech pattern the guitar is a snarl and the cymbals are sighs. Hostility is juxtaposed with lethargy. There is a clear sense of angsty in-breath and more relaxed out-breath.

These riffs are delivered over a four-bar introduction, at a low, languorous tempo, and the tantalization is made explicit by Hendrix mouthing an elongated "yeaahhh" at the end of the third bar and "sing the song" a few moments later. As with several other aforementioned compositions the momentary isolation of the voice, caught in an open space between beats, is a way of creating signposts in the course of an arrangement. Yet all the stark flits and flashes of sound make the entire performance feel on edge.

As 'If 6 Was 9' progresses, the initial stutters turn to steady movement on the chorus, which has a vividly distorted, almost hoarse first guitar chord that releases tension, but the two-bar sequence rolls in 7/4, so the oddity of the meter reinforces the strangeness of the prevailing atmosphere. There is then a return to the aching slow drag on the verse but with a slightly longer bass line that infuses a teasing energy.

The playing is still markedly staccato. There is a quasi-statuesque, slightly frozen quality to the groove as if the musicians really wanted the notes to linger in the air as long as possible. Mitchell hits the snare on the fourth beat of every bar in a simple but resonant act of temporary closure, rounding off each miniature episode in the song.

Hendrix ends the second chorus with a line that delivers a message of defiance: "Cause I got my own world to live through and I ain't gonna copy you" and then a real *coup de theatre* occurs. There is a pause for just over a bar, almost five beats, before the band adopts an entirely different pulse. After a burst of chords they fly into a double time swing with Redding laying down a fast walking bassline under a shower of guitar flurries and sparkling effects before they fall back into the two-chord verse, which is now nothing other than a foil for a tremendously kinetic Mitch Mitchell drum solo. Hendrix's vocal gradually takes prominence as he whispers he "wants to live my life the way I want to" and there is a slightly looser use of the main riff which is given an even more outlandish percussive framework due to a novel idea Hendrix had during recording.

Eddie Kramer recalls:

> Because Olympic [studios] recorded a lot of classical sessions we had these different platforms. We pulled one forward to put Mitch's drums on it and on another we put microphones on top and underneath to record a foot-stomping track. Jimi was the gang leader, and people were laughing and falling all over each other. Graham Nash was also in the studio and was recruited by Hendrix to contribute. Jimi said "Can you walk?" I said I had been known to in the past. He then said to Gary Leeds of The Walker Brothers "Hey Leeds can you walk as well? I need the sound of people walking". So Jimi, Chas [Chandler], Gary Leeds and I stomped on the platform. I compressed the foot stomps so much that you can hear the compression kick in and out.[34]

This makes the weighty thud of all those famous feet noticeable, as if they are marching ever closer to the listener. The whole thing has a brilliantly woozy, wavering quality, ambling artfully out of time with the guitar.

Finally, the piece fans out into improvisations from Mitchell and Hendrix, whose textural effects are wonderful, before the unexpected arrival of a recorder solo that the guitarist overdubbed. It is one of the most ambitious, if not avant-garde entries in the Hendrix songbook but at its core is the charged hesitation of the main verse-chorus.

This is an utterly original composition and arrangement but it has recourse to a deeply historical staple of blues and R&B: stop-time. The use of pause, the drop out of certain instruments, the isolation and emphasis of a single sound, the deliberate use of space within song, have produced key moments of the musical history of which Hendrix was a part and that he sought to enrich in his own way. Musicians who used the technique of halting momentarily, sometimes for no more than half a beat, before playing again were lending rudimentary dramatic tension to a song insofar as a discreet opening of silence served to bring further focus to a returning sound. The constant flow of rhythm in a shuffle is a thing of great beauty for its momentum-as-seduction. Stop-time is an alternative strategy, a kind of omission-as-seduction whereby the blink of zero decibels also provides stimulus quite simply because it is a contrasting energy to the very idea that music is an unbroken manifestation of noise.

Of all the tunes that Hendrix performed in his formative years the stop-time blues that may have impacted on him the most is Muddy Waters' '(I'm Your) Hoochie Coochie Man'. Hendrix's rendition of it at the BBC's *Saturday Club* was supreme, showing complete investment in the music, and it is worth bearing in mind that the original version of the song is a seminal entry in the canon of blues and popular music because it is an example of the powerful emotional and sonic impact of stop-time. The opening bars unveil the guitar, harmonica, drums and bass as four conjoined elements that move as one single, laboured vehicle. The pause after each phrase simply makes us feel the drag all the more. The motion is stuttered and uneasy. Walking basslines in blues and jazz create a sensation of fluency. Here we have fragmentation. If there are three tones to be heard then they will be heard as foregrounded objects that are bearing a certain weight, a mass, a heaviness that the musician will emphasize instead of attenuating. The gaps underline tonal character.

When Muddy's band comes back in after each pause they crash hard into earshot. Hendrix captures this perfectly in his rendition of '(I'm Your) Hoochie Coochie Man' and in terms of the central structure of 'If 6 Was 9' it is obvious that the song owes a conceptual debt to the Waters classic. However, Hendrix is tapping into and personalizing a kind of stop-time that dares to use extended pause and silence in a kind of cheeky gamesmanship where there is a challenge to the listener with regard to both listening and responding to the music. With easy humour the artist throws down a gauntlet.

Reaching back to the roots of the blues one sees that musicians such as Clarence "Pinetop" Smith, an Alabama-born Chicago-based pianist who, in his formative years, was also a singer and comedian on the vaudeville circuit, made records such as 1928's 'Pinetop's Boogie Woogie', where he uses stop-time as an opportunity to tell the audience that they have to pay attention and be ready to spring into dance action. On his cue he wants everybody to "get ready to stop and don't move a peg", and then when he says "git it" it's action time as everybody has to "do a boogie woogie".

Some thirty years on vocalist Henry Talbert, a more obscure figure of 1950s R&B whose sketchy biographical details state that he may have worked on both the New Orleans and Mississippi scenes, recorded a piece called 'Shake It Baby'[35] that had a spoken introduction which clearly invoked the spirit of Pinetop Smith. The piece boasts a snappy groove, particularly busy piano, conversely lazy saxophone and lyrics that are about paying close attention to instructions he is about to call out. When he says "shake it" he wants "everybody to shake it", but when he calls them to halt he wants "everybody to stop right with me". Listening, moving and halting – in time – are crucial.

When he reaches the first break, just on the words *'Let's stop!'*, Talbert makes a radical move. He leaves a sizeable hole in the music, choosing to resume his vocal on the third beat of the second bar of silence. He starts to draw out the syllable *Aaaah* to the first beat of the fifth bar before the rhythm section kicks back in. That extended pause is an enrichment of R&B vocabulary insofar as it shows how musicians could and did take licence with the recognized handling of a song's pulse.

Unlike Talbert's tune, 'If 6 Was 9' does not have any explicit instructions to the audience. Hendrix does not tell listeners to shake or stop in line with the appearance and disappearance of the beat. This isn't about boogie woogie as it is sonic cat and mouse.

However, the song is a puzzle of sorts and the very title that imagines a world where things are turned on their heads is powerfully conveyed by the central break in the piece in which a huge gap appears out of nowhere, so whoever is listening actually does have to *hold it* in some way and immediately process that pregnant pause. The extended silence in the middle of 'If 6 Was 9' is an even more meaningful scrambling of stop-time because it is striking, metrically and intellectually.

There is confusion expressed through the prolonged delay, the incapacitation, the inactivity. It is not so much a mess around as a mess with your head moment, which chimes with the song's conceptual core. The arrival of the downbeat, which duly announces silence rather than sound, has an all the more disorientating impact. Stop-time is a start of strange times, a lack of continuity and a lurch into otherness.

Sadly, there are no interviews on record of the artist talking precisely about the roles of time, pulse and meter in his songs, or about the power of silence and the muting of specific sounds. However, the moments where Hendrix did choose to cut all noise are sufficiently consequential in the music to be identified as part of an aesthetic that steadily evolved. Part of the explanation for the daringly long pause in 'If 6 Was 9' may well be the trust that Hendrix placed in his collaborators, from his band members to his producer and engineer, who did not exercise constraints that, certainly for some of their modern-day counterparts, would have been justified. Tellingly, the song presents a challenging relationship between sound and silence within the arrangement.

Having his guitar and rhythm section drop out so dramatically is a notable example of Hendrix upholding a longstanding blues tradition, but he also uses a related technique on a few of his most iconic songs that is simpler but no less impactful: the isolation of the voice. Since a very early stage of the history of black music in America, singers had been heard a cappella in both secular and sacred contexts and to a great extent the complex relationship between singer and player, with each influencing the phrasing and timbre of the other, has proved a major building block of blues and jazz, as heard in innovators such as trumpeter-vocalist Louis Armstrong.

If a voice could copy the timbre of a horn, and a horn the phrasing of a voice, then the use of a voice as a stand-alone element among horns was a prevalent strategy deployed by many R&B and soul singers to whom Hendrix would have been exposed in his formative years. The key example is James Brown. In the mid-1960s he recorded a string of groundbreaking sounds that gradually marked his evolution into the culturally and politically significant Soul Brother No.1 and the musically innovative Godfather Of Funk, but it was his explosive delivery at strategic points of an arrangement that raised the emotional temperature of dynamite performances.

In 'I Got You (I Feel Good)', he momentarily roars, "So good ... so good ... I got you" (first chorus) "So nice ... so nice ... I got you" (second chorus) as the horns withdraw. In 'Papa's Got A Brand New Bag' he punches out the immortal line "Ain't no drag" to mark a pause for the band to drop out before delivering the title "Papa's got a brand new bag", which signals a burst of rhythm guitar. In 'Cold Sweat' he ends each verse by singing "I wake up", which announces four stabs of horns, then hollers "In a cold sweat" before the re-entry of the horns with three staccato yelps and one conclusive legato drawl.

Such is the devastating effectiveness of the construction it is tempting to argue that the genius of the arrangement lies in its simplicity. While not entirely untrue, it is more a question of absolute clarity of the alliance of voice and horns. There is a deployment of another key aspect of black music, call and response, given the succinct exchange between the elements, but what also creates the magic is the triumph of the solo voice over sound, and the fact that the listener hears the words as a self-contained statement that has greater emotional weight and narrative magnitude. Solo voice: "I wake up". Tantalization of horns: "In a cold sweat". Conclusion of horns.

Now listen to 'Purple Haze'. As previously noted this is an extremely fraught piece of music that plays greatly on the use of dissonance and a brilliant combination of melodic lead and rhythm guitar parts, but nonetheless one of the pivotal moments of the song occurs when the whole band drops out for Hendrix to sing solo "Scuse me while I kiss the sky". It has become one of the most quoted lines in pop history, and stands as a kind of leitmotif for Hendrix as an exponent of tripped-out psychedelic music, which makes sense because of the great surrealism freighted by the words. Nevertheless the power of the statement is enhanced by its solo foregrounding in the arrangement that is well in line with the music of James Brown. For a split second it is the voice alone that will hold up the whole song. "Scuse me while I kiss the sky." "In a cold sweat."

On 'Foxy Lady' Hendrix uses the pause as an obvious metaphor for a lover being incapacitated by the sight of great beauty, the "cute little heartbreaker ... sweet little lovemaker", to whom he is obliged to bow. The momentary restraint before the naming of the titular sex bomb increases the sensory explosion. The narrative is emboldened by this simple anticipation. The sound of silence is the lover boy jaw-dropped and dumbstruck. The song starts with the guitar way in the foreground. As soon as the chorus arrives all other sounds extinguish. "Ooh, foxy lady". Flicker of pause. Band is back in.

Structurally, there is nothing overly complex about the technique but it is effective because the contrast of a small, intimate voice and large flood of guitar-generated noise upholds whisper-to-bang dynamics, which, in the narrative context of the piece, carries an erotic implication, the age-old summoning of desire through hesitation and anticipation. It is the briefest prelude to a kiss, or foreplay before the main event.

Similarly, the hard whack of the snare that announces the unaccompanied vocal line "Scuse me while I kiss the sky" in 'Purple Haze' is a deep inhalation before the guitar exhalation and storm of emotional confusion that fogs the narrator's mind. The vocal line is in seven notes dispensed over eight beats. Hendrix takes his time. Every word counts.

These manoeuvres mattered because they were a foretelling of the future. One of the most ingenious aspects of the history of black music is not just the recurrence or revival of sounds, rhythms and words, from one era to the next, but the imagination with which some of these elements are deployed to create refreshingly new sensations. Inevitably, any artist who lent an ear to Hendrix and really absorbed his spirit, or maybe something of his way of thinking, would be able to deploy some of this twisted stop-time with a smart turn of their own. They would pull freaky new from funky old.

Prince's 'Alphabet Street' is an obvious candidate. Commentators tend to focus on the sartorial flamboyance and prowess with guitar when drawing any kind of parallel between Hendrix and one of the defining artists of the 1980s, but that particular song shows just how astutely Prince could do his version of stop-time in a manner that his predecessor (and an avowed major influence) would have surely found interesting.

Clocking in at 5:40, 'Alphabet Street' is one of Prince's great mid-length masterpieces. It is far longer than 'Purple Haze' and boasts a circuitous arrangement that pushes the initial structure into a series of unexpected highways and byways that Hendrix himself may have marvelled at, given the totally outré character of the performance.

Lyrically, 'Alphabet Street' is more on the wavelength of 'Foxy Lady' or 'Fire' insofar as it sees Prince in "horny pony" mode, joyfully announcing to the world that his unrepressed sexual energy will lead him to "crown the first girl that I meet" on 'Alphabet Street' and "talk so sexy". The stop-time moments are vividly suggestive. Prince reduces them to a snarky little grunt at the end of the "yeah, yeah, yeah". Then on the second verse he throws a curveball that puts him right on 'Purple Haze' territory. Confusion reigns. Lately things don't seem the same. Sexy becomes sexless. No grand performance will take place from the performer supreme in the carnal arena.

There will now be a very different kind of bedroom action for Mr. 'Private Joy' with the 'Dirty Mind'. "Excuse me", he beckons politely, he doesn't "mean to be rude", before then admitting that tonight he's "just not in the mood", and, actually, he "would like to ... watch".

Tellingly, Prince starts the lines with Hendrix's trope from 'Purple Haze' – "Excuse me" as in "Scuse me while I kiss the sky" – but the new context for the words again reveals the conceptual depth of the original lick. "Excuse me" is more than an announcement. It is an interruption. It is a conscious break with the prevailing action, be it verbal or physical. It is actually a perfect introduction to the use of stop-time.

As the above words pass Prince's lips the riotous guitar fanfare that had exploded into life a few bars before comes to a grinding halt. He assumes a consciously theatrical delivery, leaving a pantomime pause between *I would like to* and *watch*. He can even be heard licking his lips just as his backing vocalist wails "oooh ooooh" alongside him.

It is one of the great alliances of eroticism and impishness in the recent history of popular music not simply because of the brilliance of the artistic execution. 'Alphabet Street' stands in a lineage of both concrete and abstract thought that binds Talbert's demand to "Shake that thing", which is carnal as well as choreographic, and Hendrix's vision of himself as a super being able to "Kiss the sky", which is the prevalence of the extraordinary over the ordinary. What is not supposed to happen comes to happen.

All these songs underline how much their creators understood about the art of manipulation in performance. It is not just that stop-time has an effect. It *is* an effect.

With Hendrix availing himself of state-of-the-art technology in so much of his work the moments where he affects us by nothing more than a decision to keep his hands *off* the guitar or his voice from the mike are anything but insignificant. Precise pause and silence in Hendrix's songs reflect an interconnectedness of the man-made and the machine-led, a symbiosis of acoustic and electric worlds, a reminder that switching off amplification is the ally of switching on. Stop, and people might well listen just a little bit mo'.

Try to imagine the climactic moment of 'Purple Haze' *without* the planned omission of the plugged-in rhythm section. Try to imagine the words "Scuse me while I kiss the sky" cast against the backdrop of guitar, bass and drums. Try to imagine the rhythm of the verse that precedes that iconic exclamation pursuing its course rather than halting. The result would have been a reduction and neutralization of the grandeur that is achieved when the words ring out a cappella, backed by the weightlessness of air.

More tea, rocker?

From the vantage point of popular music in the mid-1960s, Hendrix was engaged in a hugely significant burst of cross-cultural exchange which produced music that would be an integral part of a contemporary pop vocabulary.

The American guitarist-vocalist in London would also draw inspiration from the climate of experimentation greatly fostered by several notable British artists, especially Cream and the visionary Beatles.

As thus far discussed, Hendrix's ability to draw sweepingly from the rich database of black music in America, all the while adding his own personal customizations, enabled him to create a songbook that is notable for the richness of the arrangements as well as the overall skill of its execution. Above all he succeeds in widening the idiomatic scope of popular music whereby core values are still applied without becoming constraints that an artist with less imagination, not to mention a more narrow-minded management team, would surely not have been able to transcend.

What really shapes the creativity of any artist is notoriously hard to pinpoint. One of the most interesting exponents of contemporary blues, the guitarist-singer Otis Taylor, once expressed a certain amount of resentment at the way assumptions were made about artists, particularly African-Americans, with regard to the wellspring of information from which they might draw during their formative years and beyond.

> A lot of the time it's like 'Oh, your influences are the blues, you grew up listening to all the stuff that black guys like or are *supposed* to like'. I mean that stuff is hugely important to me, but I'm not sure that's *really* an influence, because to me it's the stuff from outside, where I have a *choice*, that I might really think 'Oh this is about something I don't know, or this is what I come across, what I discover' and it impacts on me in a different way to the stuff that is just there in my own world.[36]

Listen to any of Otis Taylor's excellent albums recorded in the late 1990s and early millennium, such as 'White African', 'Below The Fold' or 'Definition of A Circle', and you'll hear a worthwhile application of what he sees as influences, which sway artfully between modern African trance-like grooves and Native American riffs. This raises an equally interesting question of access to *stuff* in the first place.

Taylor's statement is deeply pertinent to the case of Jimi Hendrix insofar as he was not what is perceived as a classic case of somebody born into the blues, namely a black man from the southern states of America such as Mississippi, Texas or Georgia. Hendrix was a northerner, though his hometown of Seattle, Washington, had fostered the careers of artists of the immense stature of Ray Charles and Quincy Jones.

How members of a black community in any given space relate to and develop culture could be the basis of a study in its own right, and the nurture/nature debate surely becomes more complex when the element of ethnicity is factored into a deeply racalized if not polarized environment such as the United States of America. Maybe a major part of the story of black America that still needs to be told is that not *all* black people live in the cities that are seen as traditionally black. Brits of a pre-Google generation may recall having to learn to spell Minneapolis correctly in the wake of the phenomenon that was Prince, the city's famous son, who was black.

Then again extremes of talent will out, especially when it is leavened with determination in equal measure. Hendrix spent inordinate amounts of time listening, learning and practising to accelerate his musicianship and command of blues-related music at a breathtaking rate. Chas Chandler recalls that Hendrix would be "wearing a guitar" for anything between eight and ten hours a day such was his dedication to the instrument that was complemented by a marked curiosity about culture and aesthetics in general that extended to the worlds of fashion, photography and the visual arts.

Crucially, Hendrix had the opportunity to *live* abroad as well as simply work there. After being accommodated by Chandler in London for the first part of his sojourn in London, in a lower-ground-floor flat (owned by Ringo Starr and previously sub-let to Paul McCartney) at 34 Montagu Square in Marylebone, Hendrix and his girlfriend Kathy Etchingham moved into a top-floor flat at 23 Brook Street, Mayfair in July 1968 and lived there until January 1969. The apartment was in a large townhouse next door to the building that had been previously occupied by the German-born British baroque composer George Frideric Handel in the eighteenth century.

This was Hendrix's first home of his own. Domestic stability was a major asset to someone who had hitherto experienced great instability during life on the road, which in the worst cases had left him without a roof over his head following gigs organized by untrustworthy promoters. Hendrix's sojourn in London enabled him to gain a more than superficial view of a culture that was new to him. He and Etchingham were known to socialize extensively with a near-constant stream of friends, including musicians such as Brian Jones, dropping by for parties and jams, but also dear to Hendrix was a record player, his large vinyl collection, and a television set in his front room, colourfully adorned with eastern rugs and wall hangings acquired from Portobello market in west London. Hendrix thus discovered British soap operas.

Apparently the guitarist was an avid fan of *Coronation Street*. The idiosyncrasies of the characters must have intrigued him. One can only speculate further on how Hendrix perceived Mancunians as a cultural entity in relation to his native America, but the obvious statement to make about this episode in his life is that if he, as a black man in post-war Britain, could be seen as exotic to whites who had not readily engaged with the West Indians and Africans, then he was also in an environment that was undoubtedly exotic to *him*. Whether he could understand every phrase that passed the lips of the patrons of the Rovers Return is arguably not as important as the fact that he may well have pricked up an ear as words and idioms as unAmerican as *nowt*, *eh* and *chuck* rang out while he munched on the contents of a box of *Quality*

Street, perhaps being informed by the natives that he was enjoying a confectionary called sweets.

Hendrix also stuck to his vernacular. At a gig at City Hall, Newcastle in 1967 some excitable female fans thought that the best way of showing their appreciation would be to shower the stage with jelly babies. Hendrix snapped up a few of the small sugary stimulants and then thanked his new dealers: "I dig your candy, keep throwing it".[37]

In a modern globalized Information Age where everybody seemingly knows everything about everything, such cultural dissonances may seem quaint or insignificant but the minutiae of experience of any stranger in a strange land is not to be downplayed, primarily because they contribute to the development of the individual in question, sometimes with moments of real gravity as well as levity. For example, the American in London had a near miss with the grim reaper due to a lack of road sense necessary for his new surroundings. Hendrix had to remember that the English drove on the left rather than the right. Etchingham recalls that when he was hailing a taxi after his London debut performance, he was almost run over because, looking the wrong way, he stepped into the path of oncoming traffic. "I grabbed him by the back of his jacket just in time", she says.[38]

On one hand Hendrix's interest in satirical takes on English language and culture can be heard on the mock interviews on 'EXP', the opening track of *Axis: Bold As Love* where Mitch Mitchell plays a newscaster with BBC gravitas, but there is a much more meaningful and surprising indication of Hendrix's absorption of all things British in one of his most beautiful ballads, 'Angel'. The most well-known version of the song was recorded with bassist Billy Cox and drummer Mitch Mitchell at Electric Lady Studios in July 1970 and it featured an emotionally charged opening couplet in which the heavenly creature is a saviour. She stays "long enough to rescue me".

However, on a demo previously recorded in a hotel room in New York in March 1968 (the very first was done at Olympic, London in December 1967) the second line Hendrix sang was very different. An ode to the American cult of coffee it was not. This time round Angel has decided to stay "just long enough for afternoon tea".

This is a striking piece of leftfield humour, a juxtaposition of the sublime and the mundane that speaks of the impact on Hendrix of his sojourn in the UK, or how something as typically British as the nation's favourite "brew", offered to a celestial being no less, had crept into his anglophile subconscious. Although a relatively minor detail in Hendrix's oeuvre the line is nonetheless significant for what it says about his sense of humour and his process of revisiting, adjusting and finetuning his material over a period of time. A few weeks after laying down the first version of 'Angel' with a lyric, Hendrix returned to Olympic and performed an instrumental version of the song, renaming it 'Sweet Angel'. Hendrix's interest in the quirks of Britain also surfaced in the truly oddball title of another song, 'The Dragon From Carlisle', which also featured his bassist Noel Redding's own band Fat Mattress. It is also possible that the Dragon was a pub in Carlisle that The Experience had frequented following a performance.

In the popular imagination Hendrix arrived in London at a time when the advent of a new generation of blues-influenced groups generated audiences, and fellow artists were overwhelmingly receptive to the presence of somebody deemed an authentic representation of the source material that was precious to the young pretenders.

However, the skill with which the locals found pockets of originality within the vocabulary of Waters, Berry and Charles would have provided undoubted stimulus to a musician such as Hendrix who was intent on sounding as personal as possible. The decision to perform The Beatles' 'Sgt. Pepper's Lonely Hearts Club Band' at the Saville Theatre just three days after it was released can be held up as a sign of self-confidence and respect to the original artist, as did the off-script rendition of Cream's 'Sunshine Of Your Love' on Lulu's BBC show in January 1969. The more pertinent line of enquiry is what was the relationship Hendrix had with these songs, what did they mean to him, both as a musician and as an American expatriate in Britain. Chances are that he recognized and was excited by a novel sensibility, an exoticism, an otherness, a Britishness. He was hearing something outside of his own culture.

Long since evolved from skiffle and R&B covers, The Beatles had brought startling idiosyncrasies to recordings such as *Revolver, Magical Mystery Tour* and *Sgt. Pepper's Lonely Hearts Club Band* that could not but catch an ear as attentive as that of Hendrix – though the Fab Four's status as the most famous band in Britain at the time made it virtually impossible to avoid exposure to any of the aforesaid albums.

On one hand The Beatles embraced the idea of studio as instrument so as to view a basic performance, with the input of a skilled producer George Martin and the genius of sound engineers Norman "Hurricane" Smith, until 1965 and Geoff Emerick, thereafter, as a canvas on which unconventional new colours could be splashed in post-production, the apex of which was the arresting futurism of 'Tomorrow Never Knows', a piece in which a central drone creates a kind of charged static energy around which buzz and hiss a number of accelerating, decelerating and detuning phrases that suggest a mechanism in the process of unravelling to create a sense of deep tension. On the other hand their melodic sensibilities became increasingly broader to include Victorian music hall, circus, folk, military music and baroque as the vivid personalities of the band came through in their unpredictable original compositions.

Yet even as The Beatles significantly expanded their textural scope through the use of anything from cellos to sitars and brass, the guitar remained a core value that could be hugely effective when deployed to impart a blues undercurrent to a tune, as was the case on 'Sgt. Pepper' or 'Daytripper', another Beatles' number Hendrix covered. Such unrestrained imagination could be nothing but a breath of fresh air to a spirit such as Hendrix whose own music evinced ambition in no small measure, and whose interest in the work of his peers and predecessors was known to be all-consuming.

At more or less its halfway point *Electric Ladyland* has a run of three fine songs, 'Little Miss Strange', 'Long Hot Summer Night' and 'Come On Let The Good Times Roll', that define Hendrix as a transatlantic artist. The first piece, which features a lead vocal from Noel Redding, is very much in Beatles mode whereas the second is a brawny funk-rocker that Sly & The Family Stone could have made their own with the addition of horns. The latter is unabashedly a nod to the heritage of R&B and rock 'n' roll, right down to the old-school title, but fuel-injected with electric energy.

The other piece on the album where there is a clear sense of Hendrix's transatlantic identity playing out to thrilling effect is 'Burning Of The Midnight Lamp'. The intricately crafted opening harpsichord riff, a defining feature of the song, plants it firmly on European classical soil, but after Hendrix's mellow vocal skims over the funky wah-wah guitar of the verse there is a deep soulfulness that streams into the chorus as the Sweet Inspirations sing a gorgeous wordless vocal. The ensemble brings a glowing intensity to the arrangement that momentarily repositions it in the realm of gospel, thus creating a very perceptible shift to the timeless bedrock of African-American culture, the church. The transition is utterly seamless, and therein lies the genius of the composition. Geographical and stylistic waters are coherently crossed.

As noted previously, Hendrix had a large and eclectic record collection which included dozens of blues albums as well as many releases by Bob Dylan, for whom he also had a huge amount of admiration. He was absorbing music from disparate sources with the added stimulus of the alien environment that was London in the mid-1960s, a city that had formerly been behind Liverpool, once dubbed the New York of Europe, in terms of availability of black music, but was now able to supply ears as eager as those of Hendrix and his peers with a wide selection of blues, R&B, jazz and pop by way of outlets such as Dobells in Charing Cross Road.

Hours spent listening to Muddy Waters, Elmore James and Dylan would have no doubt consolidated Hendrix's feelings on the emotional and musical depth of the blues and the narrative scope of folk-rock, but one can only imagine how intrigued he would have been at the sound of the more outré items on his turntable such as Red Krayola's *The Parable of Arable Land*, The Mothers of Invention's *Freak Out!* or the soundtrack to the movie *The Trip*, which was performed by The Electric Flag, whose drummer-vocalist Buddy Miles would eventually join Hendrix in Band of Gypsys.

Now they call it psychedelic ... but there's no such thing as a "blues revival"

With rock being a kind of blanket term, the coining of sub-genres reflected a growing sophistication in both the cultural definition and marketing of new additions to popular music. The strain that increasingly applied to Hendrix and the aforementioned artists was psychedelic rock. The growth of drug use, particularly the prevalence of hallucinogens, the ritual of the acid trip and the arrival of riots of colour in fashion as well as an extended range of new sounds, all fed into a vision of music that could accommodate greater abstraction if not defy structural convention, as the likes of Red Krayola and the Mothers did with their off-the-wall melodies and zany harmonic patchworks. They sang about odd things as they ran a gamut of strange sounds.

Original as these groups seemed, they were not detached from what could be seen as a wider movement of young, mostly white artists who all drew from the deep well of the blues. From our vantage point of the twenty-first century we have every right to make observations about the currents of cross-fertilization in this pivotal period of culture in the mid-twentieth century but one would do well to heed the word of a black artist who is one of the great musicians of the years in question. He fashioned an entirely personal aesthetic through his ability to build coherent bridges between the genre and idioms from outside of North America, particularly the Caribbean and latterly West Africa.

He is a New Yorker whose birth name is Harry Saint Clair Fredericks, but is better known as Taj Mahal. Here he appraises the context in which Hendrix came of age:

> At this time The Byrds was happening ... The Association was going together. The Turtles, the Lovin' Spoonful, Tracy Nelson, Janis Joplin, The Pair Extraordinaire, Arthur Lee and Love, The Dillards, Hoyt Axton were all there. The Stones were kicking in with the blues. Paul Butterfield was playing in that direction. Mike Bloomfield was coming. Jimi Hendrix popped up in the middle of the whole thing. The stuff was blowing up all over the place. The bulk of the musicians came from the background of listening to the blues and Appalachian music. They were starting to mix it up with musicians who came out of rhythm & blues, or the gospel bag, so the music was starting to grow. It was like a hybrid that was going towards something.[39]

This something sounded new for a new generation. Or rather *something else* that really demonstrated how the blues could produce all manner of interesting mutations in the hands of artists from a range of different backgrounds who nonetheless had some semblance of personality, or at least ideas on how to twist a standard song structure, with familiar pentatonic riffs, or vigorous shuffle rhythms, into pop, which critics, fans and music industry executives would seek to accurately define.

Taj Mahal's insightful list of "happening" artists is lengthy but by no means definitive. Jefferson Airplane could have featured. As could have Traffic. As could have The Doors. All of the above have their place in history because they managed to create songbooks that have sufficient strength of character to distinguish them from their peers. Yet the presence of the blues, in varying degrees of explicitness, is pervasive.

For Hendrix covering Muddy Waters' 'Hoochie Coochie Man' there is The Doors reprising John Lee Hooker's 'Crawling King Snake', but the more interesting intersection of the two artists is by way of their respective original songs. Recorded in 1971 The Doors' 'The Changeling' is naggingly familiar to any Hendrix fans who wish to listen hard because it is essentially a revamp of his 'Ain't No Telling', cut in 1967, which is an extrapolation of Junior Walker's 'Shotgun', itself a pithy acceleration and re-accenting of any number of Waters songs. Such adaptations were part of an organic line of evolution, whereby songs were channelled from one generation to the next, thus extending the life of well-established materials and also providing any number of musicians with an expedient solution to the problem of producing their "own" songs.

Liberally "borrowing" riffs from other artists was an integral part of the fabric of black popular music in which songs were often taught informally rather than in institutions, and the grafting of new lyrics on existing melodies or chord sequences, or the editing of one artist's turn of phrase by another, led to wonderful new creations. Hence the real significance of Clarence Pinetop Smith asking an audience to "mess around" in 1928 is that Ray Charles would do his own 'Mess Around' 25 years later. With that in mind Hendrix doing Junior Walker or Sly & The Family Stone, whose 'Sing A Simple Song' formed the backbone of Hendrix's 'We Gotta Live Together', is not so much a transgression as it is a concession to a heritage that is dynamic rather than static.

In the greater scheme of things Hendrix's whole aesthetic is one of the great examples of an artist who has a complex relationship not just with the statements that have preceded his own, but with the very notions of new and old. Hendrix's pronouncements in interviews reflect a sharp awareness of how multiple readings or misreadings of history, and how what is presented in a new guise, can arise from one geographical area that has not been exposed to mass audiences in another. He made a thought-provoking statement in London about what he heard during his days as a musician touring across America in the early 1960s: "We played on the west coast and in Washington and down South. We had guys ten years ago in the States playing what groups are playing here now. Now they call it psychedelic."[40]

Willing as he was to acknowledge the musical bedrock from which his own work was sculpted, Hendrix had nonetheless trenchant views on the way scenes or movements in pop were identified and championed by either the record industry or the media. Acknowledging the founding fathers was one thing but attempting to coast on their backs was quite another. When the Canadian journalist Terry Mulligan put the notion of a "revival in the blues" to Hendrix during an interview for the TV show *Let's Go* on 7 September 1968, he did not suppress his deep irritation and instantly chided his host.

> There's no such thing as a revival [Hendrix snapped]. I'm just playing the way I feel, if it sounds like blues then call it anything you want, but there's no revival here, because why go back into the past, why go back there and drag up 'Blue Suede Shoes' because it's supposed to be hip to revive ... which is a drag in the first place because those people have done their thing, they're not offering you anything that's very instant, are they? There's so many musicians right now playing 20 times better than any Chuck Berry or any Fats Domino. I'm not putting these people down, I'm just saying that the music's better now, and people just don't even know it, it's right in their faces, they don't even know how to accept it, it's just so much better. They have to have gimmicks and imagery to go by. If they don't have these things they don't really think about music, that's the way some people think, which is a big fat drag sometimes.

There is so much substance in this outburst it warrants careful deconstruction. In keeping with many significant artists Hendrix is decidedly ambivalent about genre segmentation, so the blues is not something he has a pressing need to claim even though others may do so on his behalf. As far as he's concerned the appropriate terminology for his music is of a far more abstract order. There are those who apply a formula and those who opt for spontaneity, or "just playing the way I feel", which in the greater scheme of things, is the effective means to foster a degree of artistic evolution rather than the regression or lazy derivations for which he has little time.

It would have been interesting to know if Hendrix agreed with the assertion that the British blues movement gave a respect to the blues that was missing in America, given that the claim has grown into a much-quoted orthodoxy over the years. Hendrix may have been equivocal on the issue. Or he may well have argued that the blues was moving on, evolving into many other areas, and that black audiences and artists had as much right as anybody to look forward as whites, in turn, had to look back.

Commentators could well point to the irony of Hendrix questioning the relevance of Chuck Berry when he carried on performing his music right to the end of his life as well as during his formative years, but the less than charitable dismissal is done in the name of raising musical standards, which he actually sees in a purist perspective, unsaddled by stagecraft and "gimmicks".

Again, this is ironic for a consummate showman who once set fire to his instrument and simulated sex with an amplifier.

In other words Hendrix is laying bare his own contradictions and aspirations. He is actually revealing a central quandary in which he is caught, uncomfortably straddling pop success and creative ambition, just as the media is, in his view, making the cardinal sin of confusing an avowed interest in the finer points of black music made in the past, which he genuinely had, with a nostalgia trip, which was anathema to him.

What is even more interesting are the references he makes. By naming Chuck Berry and Fats Domino he is identifying two architects of rock 'n' roll and R&B, exciting branches of the ancestral tree of the blues. These artists showed how musical roots manoeuvre into sensational new areas by way of daring jolts of tempo and overall intensity but they also underlined the sonic breadth of black popular music. Put simply, Berry highlights the place of the guitarist in blues-derived music while Domino is a champion of the piano, but the no less interesting common denominator between the two is their use of brass and reeds. They used horns to excellent effect.

Chances are Hendrix was not looking to make this point in the Mulligan interview, certainly not in an explicit way, but he nonetheless points to numerous paradigms rather than a single one in his off-the-cuff overview of the blues, or rather his dismissal of its revival. That awareness of the sonic range of music from which he drew also came across in other interviews, sometimes in quite a puckish way. For example, when asked, for the umpteenth time, about six-string players he admired he gave an incisive answer that did not have an obvious qualification. "Well I always tend to the blues as far as guitar players, I like things from Bach to Roland Kirk."[41]

Naming a classical pianist-composer and a jazz saxophonist-composer in relation to a blues guitarist could be taken as wilfully cryptic if not mischievous behaviour. However, the references also reflect an interest in orchestral and harmonic prowess, which is relevant to a genre of black folk music like the blues.

"I mean the cat, he gets all those sounds and so forth", Hendrix gushed after his jam session with Kirk in his London flat in 1967. Simple as it may be, the statement is immensely significant because it underlines the dual role the guitarist had as a musical adventurer and child of the blues who had grown up to write original songs that were precisely driven by a desire to present novel timbres as well as memorable narratives. His mindset was not unique. Among his peers who had achieved similar things by drawing extensively on blues and R&B one could cite James Brown and Sly Stone.

The bedrock on which they stood was not just about rhythm, groove or the ecstatic energy of the church. There was also the question of how an artist interacted with audience and environment, how both parties perceived the unfolding of time, and the wide range of meanings that could be applied to the blues that are far beyond music.

Blues epic: no very clear beginning and certainly no ending at all

Some of the earliest manifestations of the genre in southern African-American communities altered the course of black music history, and individuals savvy enough to understand this actually helped to pave the way for Jimi Hendrix. The trumpeter and pianist W.C. Handy was one of the first composers of what would become known as jazz to draw inspiration from the blues and use the word in his song titles, such as pieces that were rooted in a strong sense of place, 'Memphis Blues', 'Beale Street Blues' and 'St. Louis Blues'.

Born in Florence, Alabama in 1873 Handy joined a local band as a teenager and later toured the South as a member of a Mahara Colored minstrel troupe, though he also did short stints as a teacher at the Alabama Agricultural and Mechanical College. Handy and his family spent several years living in Clarksdale, Mississippi, later the heartland of Son House among other significant blues artists, which put him within priceless proximity to the blues as a means of expression that was decisively shaped by improvisation in terms of instrumentation as well as the location for performance, or rather the manifestation of an individual's feeling.

Handy, whose religious father forbade the presence of a guitar in the family home, had a chance to hear blues guitarists in the early 1900s, noting the trading of lines between voice and guitar as well as the intervals on which phrases were built. Though initially baffled, he was astute enough and sufficiently free of prejudice to realize that these musicians who performed without notation could still open doors, stylistically. His inclusion of 12-bar blues patterns in his own compositions attests to as much.

By no means the sole inventor of the blues insofar as no form of music can ever be attributed to one person, Handy greatly facilitated its dissemination and permeation into other areas of black music. The issue is complex to say the least, for while his role as a key chronicler of black culture and collector of folk music is largely accepted, doubt is still cast on whether his songs are entirely original, or merely transcriptions of what he heard.

The movement of rhythms and accents, from the guitar or banjo to the piano, or the piano to the double bass, the voice to brass and brass to the voice, is precisely what makes the notion of genres such as gospel, blues, R&B and jazz so fascinating. The interconnectedness, the relationships *between* instruments as well as the multiple combinations of them, also has to be seen in a wider context of oppression from without as well as within ex-slave communities. The discernible narrative in the music of (the) black America(s) is also one of unparalleled resourcefulness and ingenuity fuelled by tension and exchange between the sacred and profane, town and country, dark-skinned African and light-skinned Creole, downtown and uptown constituencies, uneducated and educated singers and players, small groups and big bands. Handy had a grand epiphany when his orchestra appeared at a black venue in Cleveland, Mississippi and he was asked to let a "local coloured band" take over for a few dances.

> They were led by a long-legged chocolate boy, and their band consisted of just three pieces, a battered guitar, a mandolin and a worn-out bass. The music they made was pretty well in keeping with their looks. They struck up one of those over and over strains that seemed to have no clear beginning and certainly no ending at all. The strumming maintained a disturbing monotony, but on and on it went, a kind of stuff that has long been associated with cane rows and levee camps. Thump-thump-thump went their feet on the floor. Their eyes rolled. Their shoulders swayed. And through it all that agonizing little strain persisted. It was not really annoying or unpleasant, perhaps "haunting" is a better word. A rain of silver dollars began to fall around the outlandish, stomping feet. The dancers went wild. Then I saw the beauty of primitive music. They had the stuff people wanted. It touched the spot. Their music needed polishing but it contained the essence. That night a composer was born: an American composer.[42]

This engrossing account pinpoints key foundations of modern popular music as both art and industry. In plain and simple terms an audience is willing to pay for entertainment of the most direct kind, a sound able to more than *move the crowd*. The prehistory of early jazz through to R&B, soul, funk, rock, hip-hop, garage and house, and numerous variants thereof, are right there in Handy's vital testimony.

When he talks of the birth of an "American composer" that night he reveals his own ego and self-importance but if he is brazenly placing himself in the crucible of history then the source of his inspiration should not be discarded. Tellingly the "long-legged chocolate boy" and his combo provide the blueprint for black performers who are bound by a mission statement to "get the party started right". The dancers go wild and the musicians are strikingly expressive creatures, "rolling eyes, swaying shoulders".

Hendrix too had that physical engagement, and, as discussed in Part 1, developed it far beyond what Handy saw in his lifetime. He put his whole body under the spotlight. More interestingly there is an absolutely crucial observation made on the nature of the music Handy heard. It is not constrained by temporal *limits*. "No very clear beginning and certainly no ending at all": this conveys spontaneity and a freewheeling energy rather than adhesion to a preconceived set list. It could be argued that this is an African retention that connects the afrobeat, mbalaax and soukous bands that are known to do marathon sets from Lagos to Dakar to Kinshasa without a break, as well as Washington DC go-goers who keep their percussion rolling for hours at a time. Hip-hop also acknowledges this unflagging spirit by way of one of its most musically meaningful and emotionally charged lyrical axioms: *Ya don't stop, ya don't quit.*

This unceasing strumming and "disturbing monotony" could also be a notable early description of a jam session (decades after the gatherings in Congo Square, New Orleans), the creative platform that would prove vital to future generations of innovators such as Jimi Hendrix. Making music in the kind of loose, unpredictable circumstances described above was, as previously noted, an integral part of his culture, this desire to play with other like-minded souls without any clock watching. Hendrix embraced this aesthetic, falling right into the historical slipstream of the Mississippi players that Handy had so memorably encountered. As much as Hendrix eschews a "blues revival" he still carries with him a deep blues history.

The sense of the unbroken rather than curtailed sound that will not come to a halt is very real. An important part of the Hendrix songbook, both his studio and live recordings, is indeed the longform piece. One could call it the surrender of music to unstoppable feeling, the desire for an endless vibration, the irresistibility of a rhythm eternal. In any case it gives rise to an extended song that is a kind of *blues epic.*

For the most part this was a slow blues, a song played at a relaxed if not lazy tempo, which provides an opportunity to dig right into the marrow of the piece and greatly improvise around lyrics rather than squeeze a short solo in between several verses.

'Red House' is a case in point. It was omitted from the US version of *Are You Experienced?* for fear that it might make Hendrix be seen as passé rather than progressive, which really misunderstood his profound affinity to the blues and desire to find his own personal space within it. The take featured on the UK/international version of the aforesaid album lasts only 3:45 mins but a later studio version ran to 8:20 (there was also a very good performance, lasting 5:40, at Woodstock in 1969).

To all intents and purposes the form is a dyed-in-the-wool slow blues in which the unhurried, crawling pace of the song serves to magnify every element of the piece's construction, meaning that a single chord change is a mini event rather than a fleeting moment in the narrative arc of the harmony. But because more time elapses before the return to the root note, there is also a greater onus on the performer to create the widest possible spectrum of musical colour and emotion within this would-be eternity of a song. Just as Handy explained, there is not supposed to be a precise indication of the life cycle, the birth and death of the music, but quite simply the sensation created is meant to be all engulfing, thus taking the audience *out* of time. This is one of the reasons why this kind of marathon is such a challenge for any musician who sees the value of performance as an act that is a kind of liberation rather than a regulation, something that is allowed to happen and to then go on by any means necessary.

For the long studio cut of 'Red House', with Mitch Mitchell on drums and Noel Redding on bass, Hendrix improvises around a short lyric that details the troublesome scenario of him returning home to find changed locks and an absent girlfriend. Into this sea of misfortune the guitarist wades and engages the listener with a series of compelling solo statements that fluctuate sufficiently in length and shape to hold the interest. Hendrix introduces the piece with a texture on the guitar that has the delicacy of a mandolin, an instrument Handy saw black blues bands use when he first heard them in the South, and the phrase is in a glistening cascade of triplets, flowing down in semi-tones, before coming to a wry, almost irksome halt after which he gives a heart-rending cry to the guitar by several stark note bends before launching the song in earnest. The sense of intensity created amid a relaxed leisurely tempo is masterful.

Hendrix presents the blues as an evolved creature since Handy's time. He shows, in these ethereal four bars, that he does know how to make a song's beginning very *clear*. It convincingly sets the tone for the entire performance, during which he shows his ability to move from lines that are short, sharp shocks, occasionally ending with an off-the-cuff brusqueness, to drawn-out sinewy phrases, like threads entwining on a gust of wind. His tone on some riffs is light and pebbly, on others the notes are bouncing boulders. Elsewhere he stacks rhythmic figure upon rhythmic figure, slipping into will-o'-the-wisp double time to create a notable tension against the drag of the drums and bass. Hendrix pits dynamic against static, pronounced activity against relative inactivity, to make the whole performance simmer with unresolved tension.

As is the case in the best examples of a slow blues, the improvisations around the vocal lines shift in character a great deal, sometimes anticipating the last words of a phrase, sometimes delaying a few beats to increase the mercurial nature of a song where something can and does happen while little *seems* to happen. It is the legacy of Handy's understanding of the value of the *monotony* he had witnessed decades before.

Clocking in at 15 minutes 'Voodoo Chile' is almost twice as long as 'Red House', and shares similarities and marked differences. Tempo-wise it is in a comparable area but rather than being a showcase for Hendrix the piece sets up a fabulously intense dialogue between the guitarist and organist Steve Winwood that reveals both their advanced empathy as well as the strong personality of each individual. The constant rocking back and forth over one chord creates a springboard for a series of engrossing exchanges, whereby a line from one player is skilfully completed by the other, or becomes a direct echo of or subtle variation on it, so that guitar and organ engage in a complex bout of dovetailing that has appropriately impassioned crescendos. Winwood really highlights how aggressive the organ can be, drawing from the instrument a snarling, almost nasal whine that is able to match Hendrix's hottest blues.

This is Hendrix's music once again in genre-crossing mode because it shows the continuum between blues and jazz whereby the players observe the guiding principles of interaction and spontaneous composition. Whether this materializes as the pithy exchange of four-bar phrases – trading fours – or spurring each other on to creative heights, there is an edge of excitement generated by strong personalities on the same wavelength. They are painting on a spare harmonic canvas but the colours, and the different levels of energy and ebb and flow of invention, justify the decision not to try and curtail the performance so that it could then fit a radio-friendly format.

On numerous occasions throughout the piece each man makes his instrument scream, creating emotional peaks that do not encroach upon the other while the rhythm section also gathers a head of steam. Jack Casady's bass makes for a springy, quite trebly dynamo while Mitch Mitchell moves from heavy shuffles to a trippingly funky solo in the latter stage of the song. After ten minutes the band breaks down and there is a long, tantalizing whistle of feedback, before jabbering voices, a scrambling dialogue of revellers at a party, come into earshot. It could be the crowd of people that Hendrix dragged from The Scene to the Record Plant for the recording, or the voices could have been overdubbed. It matters little. The moment breaks the solemnity of the performance, lending the whole event an unpredictable edge. It starts again and runs for five more minutes in which there is more compelling musical conversation. The piece finally concludes with the sound of people talking, further breaking the barrier between formal performance and informal social gathering. The jam ends. For now.

Therein lies the currency of what Handy observed and was enthralled by decades before. Because it is so strongly suggestive of an infinite, irrepressibly human experience the blues epic, whether 8, 10 or 15 minutes long, still sounds incomplete, whereas the 2–3 minute Hendrix masterpiece can sound utterly complete.

If 'Voodoo Chile' has a shadowy, subterranean ambiance then 'Machine Gun' is the Hendrix blues epic that is as grippingly lugubrious as it is languid. The anti-war anthem, with its introduction conjuring up the sound of flying bullets, is also a momentous example of the repetition that Handy once dismissed as a strategy of little musical value before he had his head turned by musicians who applied it effectively. 'Machine Gun' also marks a degree of continuity between the two major groups Hendrix led, The Experience and Band of Gypsys. It is tempting to see the latter, formed in New York in 1969, as the moment where the expat anglophile "brought it all back home" and made a more direct connection with black musicians and the burgeoning new strains of soul and funk. For the most part there is a rootsier sound at play but there was not a total overhaul of the Experience vocabulary, which, as I have previously argued, already had a considerable amount of soul and funk at its core.

The great shame is that Band of Gypsys did not have time to record a full-length studio album, in which Hendrix and Eddie Kramer may have had the opportunity to bring to the table the detailed sonic embroidery that marked The Experience's oeuvre.

As Hendrix was in a kind of transitional period and still searching for a direction with which he felt entirely comfortable, he trialled various line-ups where the arrival of new players beyond the guitar-bass-drums trio enabled him to create a sound that was occasionally very dense. At his iconic Woodstock appearance Hendrix led an expanded multi-racial combo Gypsy, Sun & Rainbows, which included percussionists Juma Sultan and Jerry Velez, second guitarist Larry Lee, bassist Billy Cox, who met Hendrix in the early 1960s when both were in the military in Kentucky and had played with him in Clarksville and Nashville, and Experience drummer Mitch Mitchell, who would later depart to be replaced by Buddy Miles in Band of Gypsys. 'Machine Gun' was one of several new pieces from that period that became a kind of work in progress, and was performed in the studio with Mitchell and in concert with Miles.

Both the live and studio versions stretch to just under 13 minutes, during which, especially in the former case, Hendrix unleashes some exceedingly violent chording and volleys of equally frightening riffs that paint a 3D picture of the horrors of war. In fact, the studio cut features a shift to a higher tempo around the middle of the arrangement that brings greater interaction between percussion, mostly cowbell, and guitar, bass and drums. While not uninteresting, this acceleration is not quite as emotionally charged as the much more steady tempo maintained on the live jam.

What Hendrix is doing in terms of his guitar textures comes across all the more powerfully in a much less busy atmosphere. His tone moves liberally from a hard, almost icy piercing in the upper register to globular, gluey distortions in the mid-range, to clunking thuds in the low, the kind of treacle-like sub-bass that is extensively used by contemporary producers who work in the fields of hip-hop and electronic music. This array of singular noises, roaring and roaming at will, is given a superlative supporting platform by the deep and rotund tone of Cox's bass guitar. It is an essential reminder of the place of regularity and clarity within any ongoing flurry of activity.

Hendrix is the lead but Cox's rock-solid anchor, his tight grip on time, enhances the guitarist's freedom of movement. He has solidity all around him. He can stretch out. Cox also starts to shift around but his central riff is an irresistible statement of intent. He rocks back and forth between E-flat and D-flat then makes a downward chromatic run from B-flat, to provide a shape that has just the right amount of movement to push forward without ever becoming overly busy. There is enormous ballast in the line, which is all the more charged for its lack of any excessive speed.

This combination of low tempo and tonal bulk imbues 'Machine Gun' with a distinct grandeur, if not majesty, that one would associate with an adagio movement in classical music, or perhaps the relentless surge of Ravel's 'Bolero', where the wide spectrum of melodic and harmonic colour benefits significantly from the constant momentum of the metronomic snare drum. The investment in repetition is integral. The effect is one of irresistibility. On the moments when Hendrix's guitar doubles Cox's bass the two become an army on the advance, pushing on with sufficient force to sweep away all in their path. Buddy Miles's steady marching beat adds to the procession.

Also striking is the immense sustain of certain sounds so that what is an already slow song threatens to freeze in time. Hendrix plays a slew of long tones in each version of the piece at the two Filmore East gigs in 1969–70, but in the second show he hits an emotional peak with a guitar scream held for 16 beats before he launches a ferocious bout of rhythmic somersaults and tremolo manipulations that lasts for two whole minutes. More withering, hoarse legatos are heard at 6:17, another moment of climax prior to an improvisation that embarks on a new course of melodic wavering.

Throughout there are careful shifts in volume as well as timbre so that the bi-polarities of soft–loud and thin–dense keep the listener fully engaged. At 7:34 the firestorm cools down, and Miles starts to hum a honeyish, almost boyish wordless vocal. It may seem initially incongruous amid the audio brutality. On the other hand it is very welcome: an antidote to the miasmic maelstrom of sounds, a shaft of light in the darkness, a plea for the case of innocence amid the relentless loss of it. There is a hint of doo-wop sweetness that fleetingly nestles in the dark heart of this blues epic.

Although each song is very different, 'Red House', 'Voodoo Chile' and 'Machine Gun' make for a crucial trinity in the Hendrix songbook. They illustrate his ability to create what Handy called "the essence", and to varying degrees have the haunting character that made such a lasting impression on him the first time he heard Southern blues.

Furthermore, these songs put Hendrix in line with the growth of the rock album in the 1970s with its extended tracks as well as with many jazz musicians, who from the mid- to late 1950s, had begun to push songs well past the 10-minute mark to accommodate longer solos, although sometimes they used significantly more complex arrangements.

Guitar and voice; voice and guitar; two is one; one is two

As much as his blues epics showcase Hendrix as a superb improviser they also reveal how seamlessly he blended his guitar and vocal lines, sometimes with the guitar framing every note of a sung phrase, sometimes just a portion of it. The overture of 'Voodoo Chile' is a good example of guitar and vocal in fleeting unison whereas the live version of 'Machine Gun' (first show) has a terribly moving passage of vocal-guitar at around the 7:50 mark as Hendrix starts to holler "Your brother ain't evil" and every note of his voice is matched by the melody played on the six-string. Voice and guitar are wailing and weeping *as one*, just as the song conveys achingly deep pathos.

It may be a received wisdom that a classic bluesman will use the guitar to provide a chordal bed for the voice, so that the musician's singing takes pride of place, often with a short guitar phrase played in response to a line of words. Instrument and voice are thus presented as two elements that talk to one another in a musical conversation.

That is not the only historical model, though. There are many examples of voice–guitar unison, of voice and guitar talking simultaneously and inseparably that Hendrix most probably heard, was able to decisively learn from, and then develop in his own work.

Robert Johnson's 1936 masterpiece 'Come On In My Kitchen' is an emblematic song not just for the irresistibly strong emotional fibre of the lyric, which hovers artfully between regret and solace, but because of the skilled layering of sounds. Throughout the piece there is a steady pulse set by lightly strummed chords and the words of the title are closely doubled by the guitar, which proceeds to weave in and out of the verse often playing the same four or five notes as the voice sings on the line ending. Hence the guitar is both a moving shadow and echo of the voice, which gains additional textural substance, but also has a more defined movement over the harmony of the song. The rise and fall of Johnson's vocal inflections glow and fade more emphatically as the guitar rises and falls in pitch, which is wonderfully sensual on a vivid line such as "cause it's gonna be raining outdoors". The narrative explanation is heightened by these concise yet potent musical resolutions. Voice and guitar colour each other. The words that ache over the vagaries of love and the supremacy of nature, where the elements make music of their own that cannot be ignored – "Can't you hear that wind howl?" – are bolstered by their synthesis with the instrument that is used for more than accompaniment. 'Come On In My Kitchen' thus works on a potent sonic duality. The vocal is complemented by *both* rhythm and lead guitar lines. Apart from the doubling of the vocal by the guitar in specific places there are some memorable "micro-solos", a short, single note line in which glissando and vibrato are deployed to bring enormous feeling to the piece.

One of the defining figures of Delta blues, Johnson is rightly deified for the brilliance of his work and the reach of his legacy, which has exerted an influence on everyone from Bob Dylan to Hendrix, and his importance lies as much in his musicianship as it does his devilishly good storytelling. The co-existence of these different functions of the guitar in relation to the voice significantly broadened the scope of blues artists who sought to communicate by way of a lyric as well as music because there is a much less clearly defined hierarchy between the elements in question. In the aforementioned example, Johnson's voice is prominent but it is not exclusively in the *foreground*, opening space for the guitar to play a key role in the arrangement.

By the mid-1940s the likes of Lightnin' Hopkins brought further invention to the vocal–guitar template by bringing more pronounced percussive effects and bass lines to the matrix of rhythm, lead and vocal lines. His vast body of work contains numerous examples of his ability to embellish the blues with a striking range of melodic asides of varying intricacy, but one of his definitive performances is his version of the Big Joe Williams standard 'Baby Please Don't Go' where he liberally doubles his vocal lines with guitar. What makes this memorable is the shifting emphasis between vocal and instrumental. Throughout he weaves in more fleeting solos than was the case in the Williams version, and generates drama by using stop-time to leave his vocal or guitar momentarily unaccompanied. He also unfurls a range of timbres on his electric guitar, from finely picked soprano curls to heavier, bulkier basso roars, that provides a fascinating mosaic of sound for the tale of foreboding and mistrust of what might come to pass if a convict's lover dares to venture down to New Orleans before his release from prison. The song is a tremendously earnest plea in the face of danger.

Hendrix employed similar techniques in several of his songs. Given his virtuosity as a guitarist this is hardly surprising, as he was more than able to play interestingly shaped phrases, as was evidenced by the abundance of hooks and riffs in his catalogue. However, when his voice and guitar were wedded over the same line the effect was quite startling, often because of the textural richness of the parts that came before or after. An obvious example is 'Voodoo Child (Slight Return)'. The unforgettably growling, Muddy Waters-inspired intro then gives way to one of Hendrix's most impassioned vocals, during which he punches out his lines with a confrontational potency, and this is decisively boosted by the doubling of the melody with a fibrous guitar on certain parts of the lyric. He plays on the guitar every note of "So I stand up next to a mountain" and then just adds a chordal bed for "chop it down with the edge of my hand". Everything simmers momentarily. But when he repeats the whole phrase he stalks it in its entirety on the guitar, raising a massive tonal alloy in which the acoustic roar of the voice and electric squall of the guitar coalesce. It is one of the great examples of layering, spacing, wrapping and entwining of notes in 1960s pop.

Because of the abundance of power chords and snapping, scything riffs throughout the piece it is easy to overlook how the voice and guitar join forces so effectively on this first phrase, but maybe that is the whole point. The weaving of one sound into the other is seamless and thoroughly integrated into the audio patchwork. Is it the guitar that is doubling the voice or the voice that is doubling the guitar? Come what may, the result is something that has a much greater effect than the widespread technique of unison statements for two or more instruments, first and foremost because of the precise timing with which guitar and voice intersect, as if they *breathe* together.

Furthermore, the fact that Hendrix recorded instrumental versions of several of his songs reinforces the point that the place of the guitar and voice was not set in a clear hierarchy in his mind and that the co-existence of the guitarist who sings and singer who plays guitar to a virtuosic level remained an essential part of the artist's aesthetic.

The verses of 'If 6 Was 9' also feature guitar and vocal blended together with such cohesion they have a weightiness which is highlighted by the daring amounts of space and silence, as well as minimal harmonic movement and a teasingly low tempo.

'Gypsy Eyes' entwines guitar and vocal at a much higher pace. The soaring attack of the opening verse catches the ear because Hendrix is not just playing over the chords of an A minor pentatonic scale but powerfully underpinning the vocal melody with the instrument. "Well I realize that I've been hypnotized" and the accompanying rhyme "I love your gypsy eyes" are thus not heard in isolation. The two lines are fully clothed in sound. But what makes the unison even richer is that Hendrix chose to overdub two guitar lines an octave apart, so that the voice is framed by a high and low guitar accompaniment. If there is a casing of the voice by the guitar then the use of two lines rather than one creates a simple but effective splitting and spreading of the instrumental sound across the register, the effect of which is to make the passage broader and fuller in sensation. There is a succinct but very rich timbral spectrum. Everything is also that much clearer for the conspicuous absence of the bass guitar.

After that opening, the song evolves through a shifting structure with the verse being delivered over a rhythm with decidedly more swing than the stark kick drum-led intro. Interestingly, Hendrix chooses to reprise the vocal–guitar doubling at the very end of the stanza, picking up on lines such as "Do you still think about me?" In other words the sonic combination is used as a form of punctuation, a clear underlining.

In fact the technique crops up time and again in the Hendrix oeuvre as a clear form of dramatic announcement, as if the guitarist wants to put the vocalist or songwriter in a temporary spotlight. Think of the way he starts the epic 'Voodoo Chile'. The very first sound heard is the guitar bolstering the dramatic vocal declamation, "I'm a voodoo chile ... lord I'm a voodoo chile", then Hendrix and combo embark on what is a heated workout, which has incendiary solos from the leader and organist Steve Winwood.

How Hendrix took decisions on when to bring his voice and guitar into close alignment does not conform to a rigid pattern. 'Lover Man' is a striking demonstration of the guitar threading in and out of the vocal in a semi-regular way, so the six-string is posited as a joint lead instrument should Hendrix deem it suitable at any given time.

The aforementioned songs reflect a pronounced spontaneity in his decision-making that resonates with his deeply held belief in the jam aesthetic. Moreover, different versions of the same song support this view. For example, there are three cuts of 'Hear My Train A Comin" and each has its own pattern of voice–guitar synthesis. The two trio versions, cut with Noel

Redding and Mitch Mitchell (on 7 and 9 April 1969), see Hendrix play fragments of the melody on guitar, and in a manner not dissimilar to 'Voodoo Chile' he uses the unison technique as a grand opening fanfare before he goes on to do the same at the halfway point. Due to the concise but incendiary licks that Hendrix plays in between the vocal phrases there is an enormous amount of sonic information and emotional angst thrust in to the first part of the song, above all through the charged image of "tears burning me in my eyes". It is as if he is walking on a minefield of tension. When the guitar–vocal unison returns on the line *Hear my train a comin'* there is an explosion of optimism, a sense of release from the inner torture.

The solo version of the song finds Hendrix on a 12-string and his approach is markedly different. He scraps the chorus altogether and after a brief instrumental intro moves straight to the verse where he doubles many of the lines before framing the arrangement with more strummed chords. Then, he sings "My Girl ...", before doubling the remainder of the line "... call me a disgrace" with the guitar. The punctuation is at a key point in the narrative. A conspicuous new sonic thread wraps around the words; a kind of heavy, steely sensation increases the theatrical quality and overall urgency of the piece.

In fact, what stands out on 'Hear My Train A Comin" is just how little Hendrix sings. The lyrics are nothing more than a few statements on the familiar theme of sorrow, heartbreak and the chance of redemption, and proportionally, they play a relatively secondary role in the arrangement. It is as if the guitar that doubles the voice is actually a creeping presence that then emerges into the spotlight around the halfway mark. The solo arrives in earnest and unfolds over an epic 46 bars before a brief reprise of the vocal which serves as a concluding statement of the song. In other words Hendrix the player kicks the singer roundly into touch, as what starts as a vocal turns for the most part into an instrumental, or rather the vocal is like the "head" in jazz terms, that is a melodic statement, which is a springboard for an improvisation.

How he came to this decision would have been intriguing to know but there are numerous other entries in his body of work that reflect a pivotal aspect of the songs of Jimi Hendrix: an ever-intriguing, shifting relationship between voice and guitar, an unpredictability in the priority given to each element that emphasizes the creative multiplicities of the artist and his questioning of appropriate methods of expression.

Of guitar, beyond guitar

As is to be expected, the guitar features prominently on the extended compositions where Hendrix bucked the 3-minute pop song convention with bravado – as on 'Voodoo Chile', 'All Along The Watchtower' and any number of live versions of his other songs, notably those featured on *Band Of Gypsys* – but what is also striking is the vocal–guitar ratio in several of the "radio-friendly" pieces that are around 3 minutes in duration. 'The Wind Cries Mary' has an 11-bar solo, 'Izabella' a 12-bar solo, 'Little Miss Lover' a 13-bar solo, and as for 'Little Wing' it starts to fade on the 14th bar of a solo.

In each case the improvisations are anything but perfunctory. They are constructed with sufficient phrasal variety and timbral richness to make it clear that Hendrix does not view the solo as a throwaway convenience for the middle eight in pop orthodoxy.

Rather than attempt to shoehorn his playing into this standard unit of measure he is minded to play longer and, in the case of 'Little Wing', defy expectations by fleetingly breaking into a line of scat vocal and then a few muffled words as the solo moves to its conclusion. It is a small but not insignificant detail insofar as it flags up the presence of Hendrix the singer who is not entirely silenced by Hendrix the player.

Exclamations and exhortations to play, the statement of intent, from a simple "C'mon now" to a more explicit "Here we go!" have been an integral part of the vocabulary of the blues improviser since the genesis of the music, and Hendrix simply found his own place in the history. That teasing vocal interjection in the coda of 'Little Wing' is nothing other than a demonstration of spontaneity and expressive restlessness.

Of all the songs Hendrix recorded that show his desire to use the guitar as a source of compelling colour that takes equal billing with his vocal, without losing the momentum of the arrangement, it is 'All Along The Watchtower'. From the point of view of a black music tradition it is possible to argue that the version of the Bob Dylan piece is a case of an artist playing another's material with such verve that they wrest ownership of it, as could be said of John Coltrane's 'My Favourite Things'.

Hendrix fits right into that mould of the improvising artist who reshapes material so as to reinvent, but what makes his case all the more impressive is the fact that he retains his duality as a player who sings and a singer who plays. The listener isn't entirely sure how much weight each particular entity will take in the arrangement.

The introduction to the song signals Hendrix's serious creative thinking and musicianship. Two bars of languid 12-string guitar chords ring out over the snake-like hiss of the vibraslap, but suddenly we hear a stinging electric guitar line in which a busy rhythmic push gradually draws down to a relaxed melodic conclusion. Hendrix sings the first verse and then takes an 8-bar guitar solo, which, unlike the opening fanfare, has more of an emphasis on legato phrasing that induces a degree of respite in relation to the preceding activity. Hendrix sings the second verse and then the piece undergoes a grandiose transformation. The main guitar solo runs to 32 bars of incident-packed action before the final verse and a closing guitar solo that fades out after 18 bars.

All the additional writing and arranging in the piece stems from the undeniable bravado of the artist but the overwhelming spotlight afforded the guitar is actually not the grand achievement of Hendrix's 'All Along The Watchtower'. What really makes the piece special is the second guitar solo for the simple reason that the first stage of its development has such a tight melodic focus and resolves so decisively after eight bars that it gives the distinct impression that it has made way for the return of the vocal. But this is a *false ending*. It is fabulous trickery, a superlative example of music as drama by way of nothing more than a wily, witty dashing of expectations.

Just before Dylanites start singing the final verse, Hendrix, after a two-beat rest where the 12-string pops back into earshot, takes the solo to an entirely new place, by way of a wavering note that has the sensuality of a long sigh on an endless summer's day. Hendrix has hit a delay pedal and the note becomes a downward floating cloud that then splits into languorous streaks of Hawaiian guitar, which, legend has it, were created by him sliding a cigarette lighter on a single string. The phrases have such pronounced sustain that they plunge into a dream state and also push Hendrix into twenty-first-century proto-electronica as well as twentieth-century pop. It is one of the guitarist's accomplished pieces of soundscaping but as steeped as it is in post-modernism there is a deep strain of blues history in the process. What comes into play is the idea of altering timbre through the most makeshift of technology, and that essentially means using anything from a bottleneck to a tube or glass fingerpick in order to produce more levity in the note.

If we reach back to the pre-war era and refer to the testimony of the "Father of the Blues", W.C. Handy, we find the roots of Jimi Hendrix. In 1903, while the bandleader was travelling with his orchestra in the South, he heard something extraordinary at a train station in Tutwiler in the Mississippi Delta.

> A lean, loose-jointed Negro had commenced plunking a guitar beside me while I slept. As he played he pressed a knife on the strings of the guitar in a manner popularized by Hawaiian guitarists who used steel bars. The effect was unforgettable. The singer repeated the line three times, accompanying himself on the guitar with the weirdest music I had ever heard. The tune stayed in my mind.[43]

Admirably perceptive, Handy notes the beauty of the indefinable. Nothing could be more relevant to Hendrix's brilliance than the word *effect*, an indication of resonance and character of note. Hendrix takes things much further and benefits from the use of an amplified instrument, but nonetheless he is crafting a majesty of strangeness for the age in which he lives by way of touch and string manipulation as well as the use of machinery. Or maybe what Handy is saying is that the guitar is a machine that can be modified with the crudest implement, nothing other than a knife, to produce "the weirdest music I had ever heard". Hendrix retains that spirit, blurring as he does the line between acoustic and electric, organic and synthetic, thus making us question what is understood by a genre such as techno and the very concept of technology in music. Is contemporary electronica reducible to a computer-generated click or is it about the lateral thinking that leads to sonic novelty by way of a household object shoved onto a fretboard gripped by a human hand? Does the machine lead the man or vice versa? Do they dance as one? Maybe the liveliest of wires is really in the mind. Handy put his finger on a deep-rooted blues hankering for adulterated sound, the beauty of the impure, and Hendrix honours that with his object-assisted oddness.

During the central instrumental section of 'All Along The Watchtower' there is a clear change of ambiance and narrative. The shift of both mood and audio landscape is absolutely masterful. A hazy ambiance is increased by two and three note phrases with the sharp, rapier-like tone associated with jazz guitarists. But this passage of thinner, steelier sounds soon comes to an end and Hendrix shouts "Hey!" to signal the next stage of the solo, which introduces a molten, wah wah lick that evolves into a viscose, almost squelchy theme before there is yet another bold change of timbre. Now strumming hard and fast in the upper register, Hendrix gives chromatic lines a glinting metallic quality and pushes his attack to a torrid vigour that foretells of the master rhythm players of 1970s funk and disco, from Marlon "The Magician" McClain to Roger Troutman to Nile Rodgers.[44] When Hendrix starts singing the final verse it makes sense for him to scream "All along the watchtower" because of the feverish climax of the long instrumental section.

This performance is a highpoint in his oeuvre for its sense of daring as well as technical brilliance. While riding roughshod over the pop orthodoxy of the short solo it also undermines any potential cliché of the guitar solo itself, for the visionary construction in that extended suite-like passage. Dividing it into a series of such distinct *episodes* increases the amount of light and shade in the piece tenfold, so that even though Hendrix is putting his obvious improvisatory gifts to good use he is also drawing on his skill as an arranger-producer with an eye for creating a lengthy score in which each constituent part can stand as a work of art in its own right. The guitar solo is a self-contained, multi-faceted concerto, a suite of perfect conception.

As a summary of Hendrix's gifts as a guitarist, 'All Along The Watchtower' is terribly important because of the musicality as well as the virtuosity that is deployed. It is an object lesson in how to weave instrumental interludes into a vocal song without the wordless feature becoming too self-indulgent or detached from the source itself.

Hendrix's guitar triumphs in timbral flourish but he also reins in the burst of ideas. In other words he achieves the all too elusive ideal of conveying spontaneity in his playing all the while producing phrases that have a composer's discipline, so that the whole guitar break has several moments that listeners can feasibly sing just as they might the words of the verse. Hendrix matches in guitar, Dylan's bravado in lyric.

Of no less significance in the song is what happens during the sung verses. Hendrix's accompaniment is a masterful display of commentary on and embellishment of a central melody through mostly short phrases that uphold the classic blues call and response tradition. But what impresses is the degree of variation, which takes him from clenched three to four note phrases, the darker of which are like vocal asides to longer runs that finish with a brash chord. The sense of agitation is further enhanced by the stabbing bass lines that Hendrix himself played, which brings a kind of paradox to the verses. They unfold in an ambling halftime, but the criss-crossing of the multiple guitar lines nonetheless imbues the piece with a degree of nervy activity.

There is one sound in particular that exemplifies the abundance of ideas that can be heard, and it comes under the line 'There are many here among us/who feel that life is but a joke". Just as the last word rings out, a low-pitched muffle, a kind of ungainly, slightly queasy wobble of noise, wafts by and is held for a whole measure before the next line is sung. It is a small but devastatingly effective texture, because it both breaks the previous pattern and creates a sonic oddity that is not overly obtrusive.

'All Along The Watchtower' is a superlative display of the art of rhythm guitar as well as lead playing, or more to the point, the means of blurring the line between those two skills. Too often, they are presented as distinct entities that are connected only by the harmony of a song, but Hendrix makes his rhythm and lead playing so seamlessly unified that they can become part of a coherent overarching story in which the footnotes are as important as the main paragraphs and statements. What the guitar is doing alongside the vocal is as crucial as what it does when used for a solo.

Facilitating his development were any number of important historical models. The finer points of the relationship any musician has with an instrument usually differs from one individual to the next, bar the usually common incidence of a large investment of time in the pursuit of mastery, which certainly held true for Hendrix. What is so obvious that it may be overlooked is the fact that the guitar served an invaluable dual purpose for him. On the one hand it allowed him to launch into often startling improvisations. On the other hand the instrument, as previously argued, formed part of a complex musical relationship with his voice. This placed him in a lineage of post-war blues vocalist-guitarists that included B.B. King, Buddy Guy, Otis Rush, Magic Sam, Elmore James, Freddie King, Albert King and Albert Collins, to name but some. In B.B. King, Hendrix had a superlative role model with regard to how to play fills between lines, how to move between fortissimo and pianissimo phrases to bring nuance to the table, how to articulate precisely, how to seal gaps without breaking momentum. There is immense expression in King's playing, as there had been in that of the great T-Bone Walker.

These players had a broad vision of the guitar as a vehicle for additional detail as well as the enunciation of chords. Complementing a vocal line with a two note lick or a bent pitch hinges on the ability to use skill and imagination but it is also an exercise in self-editing because the trick is not to detract attention from the lyric while bringing a range of hopefully interesting hues to it. The aforementioned musicians provide these moments, these flashes of drama on a song without major disruption to the central narrative.

On occasion Walker would hold the guitar practically at a right angle to his hip and bring his hand down onto the fretboard from up above as opposed to the more conventional method of playing with the guitar clamped to the body. It is an example of the importance of an individual's physical engagement with an instrument, and in Hendrix's case the very way he touched the guitar, from the active use of the thumb to the hard shaking of the neck, is also part of his development of a personal sound. The Kings had engaged in pronounced pitch bending prior to Hendrix, but Jimi brought more expression to it on an electric guitar with lighter strings and also used hammer-ons and pull-offs, and dampening and sliding with immense bravado so that a phrase could acquire more implied vocalization than if the notes were just fretted "straight".

Perhaps the best way to understand Hendrix as a key architect of contemporary guitar is to listen to how a player in 2019 hears his work from 1967. Chris Montague is an excellent British guitarist who has distinguished himself in a wide variety of contexts that run from jazz to electronica in bands led by Trish Clowes and Squarepusher as well as in the collaborative trio Troika. He has a simple but essential acid test to explain Hendrix's significance.

> He's a whole conundrum to get your head around. He's *very, very* hard to transcribe ... I still find him the hardest to transcribe because with his playing there's a deliberate kind of scrappiness in the way, it's so hard to talk about because he had such an idiosyncratic style and sometimes a scratching round the edges roughness to it, to get that ... if you try to play it like him to get all those little bits, the feel around his playing it's very hard to do. There's a lot of guitar players who play with a more sophisticated harmonic and melodic palette now in the jazz world but because their articulation is so much more even and clean they're a lot easier to transcribe whereas with Hendrix it's more murky, more misty, and you've just gotta really dig into it to try and pull out what he was doing.
>
> It's harder to put your finger on a wider dynamic range for guitar players. That thing of having crushing volume, blood-curdling screams, the pain from the guitar, mixed with unbelievably serene, angelic, gentle, tender quality to his playing.
>
> It's a really broad palette. B.B. King is subtle and nuanced ... he has an instant fingerprint. He's one of the few players who, when

he plays that one note, you know it's definitely B.B. Hendrix, however, has such a big bag of tricks to draw upon that his palette is so wide. He's doing rhythm and lead guitar at the same time. Being able to play a melody with one string and really reed-like almost. He really developed the idea of vibrato for guitar, having a very personal thing. That was another physical innovation he had on the guitar. He would bring his thumb over the top, all these little idiosyncrasies he has. If you can play bass notes with your thumb you got four fingers available to play melodies or other parts of chords, it's specific to his physiology.

> The thing that amazes me in Hendrix's playing is that no matter how experimental it became there's still this DNA, this lineage that goes right the way back to those much earlier players, right back to T-Bone Walker and Robert Johnson, all the Delta blues stuff, who just vamp on one chord. You can hear that on something like 'Voodoo Chile,' it's a Delta blues, he just sits and vamps on one chord pretty much with variations and moves harmonically when he feels like it, not within a form or structure, it's super sophisticated stuff but it's very *old*. It's bringing all this old school stuff back into the thing but like any innovator of his day he's embracing the technology that's around.[45]

Curiosity, autonomy, daring. Beyond the specific techniques employed by Hendrix there is the fundamental question of his state of mind and sense of self that must be factored into his achievements as a player. The confidence to know musical history and roam through it at will, remould and customize, embrace the unorthodox. The ability to evoke a sense of oldness within a cast of newness, to blur perceptions of age.

Another contemporary British guitarist, Chris Sharkey, who has, since the 1990s, compiled an excellent body of work as a member of groups such as Trio VD and Roller Trio as well as a leader of his own projects such as Sharkestra, argues that Hendrix was able to really assert himself as an individual precisely because of his desire to take liberties with any notion of a correct way of doing things. Discerning the richness of lines he drew from scales and modes, or the skill with which he used an E7 sharp 9, a chord he favoured a lot, is maybe not as important as recognizing the way he brought a vast amount of ancillary textures and harmonics into play, like an artist using a range of inventive brush strokes on a canvas.

> The great British guitarists influenced by American blues are great but to my ear when I hear [Eric] Clapton or Peter Green or [Jimmy] Page, as much as I admire and respect the guitar playing it still sounds very "square", almost in a box, or very orderly, very in the pocket. I'm generalizing to an extent but if you imagine that they're

playing these tidy, neat phrases you hear the respect for the music, like a homage kind of. Hendrix comes along and just blows it all open ... the boundaries around the notes and phrases evaporate, rather than just being stuck in the squares. There are spirals ... it's kaleidoscopic and impressionistic and vocal.

When he plays a slow blues the phrasing is this very emotive, impressionistic and vocal style of playing, so super expressive. *Live at Filmore*, he plays like that all-night rhythm section are locked, he's painting over the top. It's random but it's tied to the rhythm section. He's like a kite flying above this rhythm section. He plays like that with the Experience too, he had this sense of freedom, I think probably because he didn't feel as shackled to the history in the way some of the British players did.[46]

First manufactured in 1952 the Fender Stratocaster is the electric guitar with which Hendrix became largely synonymous. With its three single coil picks, streamlined body that facilitated access to the upper reaches of the neck and tremolo arm, the device would have been understandably stimulating for a player as adventurous as Hendrix and he indeed made extensive use of the myriad possibilities of these particular features, as well as the numerous settings of the tone controls.

Yet as much as the "Strat" was a modern industrial device, a machine with a number of electronic components, it was also a string instrument, which could be most effective in the hands of a player who understood the necessity of dynamics and the precise way the instrument was manipulated. One can gain an insight into Hendrix's achievements on the electric guitar simply by studying him on the acoustic.

Homemade film footage of Hendrix on the bed of his Mayfair flat playing an "unplugged" jam session surrounded by Kathy Etchingham and others is a priceless document because, despite the lo-fi quality of the recording, the richness of his sound can be clearly heard. Big Mama Thornton's 'Hound Dog' is re-harmonized with a languorous, mildly flamenco flavour but Hendrix alters the ambiance of the piece significantly throughout by the shifts in his attack. You can hear a changing weight of his picking hand on the strings, making some chords slender and others rotund, so that the landscape of notes created has a real sense of foreground and background image.

His timekeeping is faultless, but there is much graduation in the palette of colours. Before he starts to sing he breaks into a percussive strum as the assembled guests make their handclaps more insistent. He occasionally centres his energy right on the soundhole and his chords have a sharpness, a kind of metallic quality that is immediately contrasted by the heavier bass drawl produced when he moves his hand towards the bridge. Then, in a moment of intense drama, he breaks the rolling rhythm by punching a single note through a minor third that brings everything to the boil. The sound screams into life. When the immortal opening accusation "You ain't nothing but a hound dog" is finally sung by Hendrix it makes a real impact because there has been such a build-up of tension in the preceding lines. Just as he did on numerous other songs, he doubles his voice with the guitar to create a glowing rhapsodic unison.

The range of character of notes, the spikes of volume, the shifts of tonal density make the performance more memorable than one would expect from a singer using the guitar as a perfunctory backdrop for the voice. Although devoid of amplification, the instrument, by dint of the player's ingenuity, acquires the aggression and physicality associated with amplified music. All the available films of Hendrix in performance are deeply instructive because they bring home the lack of timidity he had when handling the guitar, the way he makes it an extension of his body – which is an aphorism beloved of horn players in jazz – that chimes so closely with the vivid nature of the music he made.

Why a Hendrix glissando or sustain can acquire a depth of colour that lifts it beyond the adornment of a note achieved by the bulk of guitarists becomes all the clearer when you see the close-ups of how far on the fretboard he might bend the strings or how long he grips the tremolo arm. The sense of him pushing sound to breaking point and not conforming to prevailing vocabulary translates perhaps most fully in the way he achieved a distinct vocalization in his guitar tone. He is standing fully in the blues tradition of the "cry" or the wail but also managing to impart additional nuance and emotional charge. For example the initial flurries on the A section of 'Voodoo Child (Slight Return)' are deeply disturbing because they have a reedy, distressing quality that vividly serves the subtext of a life shrouded in both mystery and mysticism.

Also relevant to Hendrix's whole identity as a guitarist is the fact that he was already unconventional if not abnormal by dint of the workings of his own body. He was a left-handed player who took a right-handed instrument, flipped it over and restrung it. The resulting changes in string tension and positioning of components all made a difference to his sound. Roger Mayer, the visionary audio engineer who built pedals and accessories for Hendrix that also increased his timbral range, gives this insight.

> When you flip the guitar, the actual cavities in the guitar now appear on the bass strings, right? Because the volume control is facing toward your head. So the actual resonances of the cavity do change. Now you're faced with the fact that the actual length of the bass string is the other way round, and conversely on the treble strings. So yeah, that will make the guitar feel slightly different because the actual string length affects the kind of strength needed to bend the strings. That's one of the reasons why we used to tune the guitar down a little bit.[47]

Chris Sharkey also has illuminating views on how Hendrix actually made the flipped-over right-hand Strat an integral part of his aesthetic as a player that would have been impossible to recreate had he used a left-handed instrument better suited to him in theory.

> I seem to remember hearing a story that Fender wanted to build him a left-handed Strat, but he didn't like it – understandably the shape felt wrong to him, and crucially the volume and tone knobs, rather than being behind his picking hand, where he could subtly manipulate the parameters of his sound mid-flow, they were now at the bottom of the instrument and he had to reach down and break the flow to change his sound. Jimi was a master of using the volume knob of the guitar to control the amount of signal going to the amp to create magical changes in energy, tone, volume and emotion – he wouldn't have wanted to sacrifice any of that.
>
> Similarly the vibrato bar of the left-handed model would be at the bottom of the bridge rather than the top, where he was used to. This would have felt physically awkward and changed the "envelope" or shape of the vibrato he was able to get from the instrument. These are subtle differences, imperceptible to the layman – but monumental for the player.[48]

Castles made of quotes

Of the historical templates that Hendrix used on the road to creating his own vocabulary, the one that might be most relevant is that of Albert King because he too was able to create belligerent, frankly often violent sounds that contrasted somewhat with the fluid, swirling phrasing and lustrous tone of B.B. King. Yet to assume that there was a clear boundary between those who played lines and those who made *sounds* would be to misrepresent the history of the guitar in black music reaching back to 1930s innovator Charlie Christian. Those who succeeded him, from Wes Montgomery and Barney Kessel to Grant Green and Kenny Burrell, added to the growth of the guitar as a lyrical instrument on which the lengthy, often acrobatic melodic lines and complex chord sequences of horn players could be brought to life.

But some of the members of this school also did *effects*. Three years before Hendrix made his way to Britain, soul jazz organ legend Brother Jack McDuff took a quartet on tour in Europe. His brand of hard-swinging dance music pulled a large audience as he built a bridge between the sophistry of bebop and the immediacy of the blues. A recording of a gig in France in the mid-1960s has a standout moment during the exchange of solos between McDuff and his hotshot young guitarist, George Benson, on a piece called 'One On Eight'. Benson plays several choruses where his lightning runs and rapier intonation take the breath away but there is a moment that tops that. He responds to one of McDuff's sizzling solos by stuttering on one note then hitting a new chord change, but with a slight fattening of his tone on the end of the phrase. In the space of two bars the guitar becomes animal. It imitates a squawking rooster. The sound is vocalized, rough-edged and humorous. It is the guitar as character.

As a symbol of the complexity of the relationship between what is understood to be jazz, soul and blues the moment is instructive. According to received wisdom, a player as eloquent as Benson isn't supposed to be so rugged, so brash, so imaginatively gutsy. Yet he stands in the lineage of swing-era horn players evoking the sound of anything from quacking ducks to speeding trains and the general interest that successive generations of African-American artists have shown in non-musical contexts as a springboard for musical statement. We know about black convicts breaking rocks and wielding pickaxes for state enrichment, we know about the chants to hard labour for those born on the wrong side of the tracks, we know about the *sound of the men working on the chain gang* because Sam Cooke hummed it to us. Hendrix broadens the scope of this metaphorical praxis by way of more industrial-age references: the power chords and distortion evoke the screech and revving of engines or the sturm and drang of city life. Yet it is the depiction of the terror of modern warfare, and the relentless, staccato rattling of the deadly weaponry that came to define the great wars of the twentieth century, which marks Hendrix out as a very gifted sound symbolist.

'Machine Gun' produces startling metaphorical bullets on a glacier, slow beat. Taking the tempo down has the effect of summoning an oppressive, almost frozen-fear stillness, as if the everyman soldiers, the ill-fated protagonists in the horrific tableau of combat, are automatons devoid of emotion. The dehumanization is underscored by the sound of mechanization: the relentless rat tat tat of the machine gun, the invention that helped to revolutionize combat for its ability to inflict large-scale casualties, is evoked by the rhythmic scraping of Hendrix's guitar and pummelling march of Buddy Miles's drums. Together they *become* the faultless killing machine, the deadly device that won't stop. Closely entwined, the two sounds make for a stark pneumatic force that encapsulates the theme of unstoppable evil that Hendrix describes in the verses.

This grippingly lucid musical strategy, the drilled rhythmic overlap of guitar and drums, made a substantial impact because of the particular performance space in which the concert took place. Eddie Kramer, who recorded *Band Of Gypsys*, recalls how the venue came into play. "I was so fortunate to be able to have the acoustics of the Filmore East, so when you open up the room mikes you really hear that taka taka tak ... the snare and Jimi's guitar is just an explosion, which is what it was."[49]

Hendrix's 'Machine Gun' is far removed from Benson's 'One On Eight' but the songs are linked because they exhibit the players' ability to use sound to summon image. For the most part Benson could not be a more different character to Hendrix – neatly suited, booted and primped, a product of the whole "grooming bit" the latter had to once endure as a sideman – but nonetheless the two men are part of an extensive nexus of players that essentially shows how apparent stylistic opposites can overlap in unexpected ways. Benson has a love of fluid, fluttering lines where speed of movement and skim of hands on the strings almost turns the six-string into an amplified harp whereas Hendrix has a considerably brasher signature even when he is opting for prolixity in a solo.

Yet the blues is still the common denominator between the two men. While Benson is predominantly characterized as the urbane demi-god of jazz-inclined soul, typified by hits with big production values such as his perennial floor filler 'Give Me The Night', one only has to reach back to some of his early 1970s works for the CTI label such as *Bad Benson* and *White Rabbit* to hear how tight a grip he has on older forms of black music. It is a testimony to the strength of the foundation of the blues, and its nurturing of jazz and rock, that players as distinct as Benson and Hendrix could nonetheless share similarities in both their source materials and artistic strategies.

Imitating the noise of farmyard poultry brings humour to a performance, as can be seen by the reaction of Brother Jack McDuff to Benson's high jinks, but it would be remiss to just pass this off as a musician playing to the gallery. The populist slant of the action should not detract from the fundamental truth that Benson exercises an artistic choice for which he has no obligation. He decides to take the music out of one register and into another, and therein lies the achievement. He is not part of a vaudeville act for whom a prank is a sine que non, but a highly skilled musician, who has decided that the rooster squawk is an appropriate manoeuvre in the setting of a jazz performance where band and audience are formally attired. To an extent Benson is throwing a curveball into the air just as Hendrix did, often resulting in censure.

However, Hendrix struck another parallel with Benson's wider history that is often overlooked. He came up with one of the most ingenious examples of the jazz praxis of quotation to which his peer would have been well inured. During a gig at the Atlanta Pop Festival on 4 July 1970, Hendrix played 'Spanish Castle Magic'. The mysterious, nightfall ambience of the studio version is convincingly recreated, but at around the three-quarter mark of his solo Hendrix plays a new melody that would have been familiar to Latin music aficionados. It is 'The Breeze And I', composed by Ernesto Lecuona, a founding father of modern Cuban music whose 1920s and '30s themes laid the foundation for post-war artists who developed son and mambo.

Popularized by bandleaders and singers from Xavier Cugat to Caterina Valente, 'The Breeze And I' is an affectingly romantic piece that has the kind of deep sense of longing that would have appealed to Hendrix. Yet that is not the ultimate significance of the quote. The alternative title of the song was 'Andalucia', and it was part of a sequence of related themes called *Suite*

Espanola. In other words the guitarist is purposely riffing on Spain, making an entirely knowing reference to the title of his song through the title of another song, the meaning of which may not have been known to less discerning pop audiences. Hence the improvisation on 'Spanish Castle Magic' was given another resonance by the integration of an element of the *Spanish Suite*.

Yet what scenario does Hendrix create in the first verse of 'Spanish Castle Magic'?

It takes "about half a day", travelling "by dragonfly" to reach the Spanish Castle. Intriguingly Hendrix also makes it clear that the destination is "really not in Spain". He explicitly reveals the song as a "trip". The magic has nothing to do with the land of flamenco and bullfighting. Insiders would have known that the Spanish Castle was a ballroom near Hendrix's hometown of Seattle that he had played, so the song was an opportunity for him to pun on the far from glamorous aspect of his life as a former itinerant musician en route to a particular venue. He puts a surrealist spin on the scenario by citing as his mode of transport the dragonfly. This may have been just a flight of fancy or Hendrix making a very subtle reference to his own Native American heritage as its mythology associated the insect with stealth and swiftness. Or maybe tales of castles and dragonflies reflect an interest in mediaeval folklore?

Whatever subtext the writer really intended, the image of the people carrier dragonfly is reinforced by the mention of the wind. This twists the significance of the Lecuona song back to its English title of 'The Breeze And I'. It is possible that this is coincidental and Hendrix didn't think about setting any puzzles, yet if he was simply interested in the beautiful romantic melody of the Latin classic he would surely have played it as a stand-alone feature, given how steeped he was in a culture of covering material. The decision to integrate *Suite Espanola* into 'Spanish Castle Magic' thus appears as a highly conscious piece of oblique referencing. Hendrix is indulging in an exercise of on-the-spot guessing games that only those who recognize the musical quote at the gig and then crosscheck it against the lyric will be able to win. Whether thousands of stoned, half-naked hippies left baking in the searing southern sun, much to the despair of horrified responsible adults, appreciated that ruse is a moot point.

Regardless, Hendrix is serving notice of extensive musical knowledge beyond that of the bulk of his peers in the pop world. More importantly, he is showing his ability as a thinker, reminding us that all creative journeys begin in his mind. With the songs of Jimi Hendrix come the virtuosity of Jimi Hendrix and the intellect of Jimi Hendrix. If he upholds the blues then he reveals it as a cerebral and emotional space. If he is nurturing a future genre called heavy metal then here he is also doing *heavy meta*.

Fleeting as the Lecuona moment is in Hendrix's oeuvre it is nonetheless a highly significant one because of what it says about the range of musical references he was able to make in his work and the conceptual richness he created as a result. To quote another song has been a fundamental part of the jazz aesthetic since its genesis but to make connections as a result of a specific, rather than superficial premise of meaning, lends that much more credence to the endeavour. Another example is the case of Sonny Rollins mischievously playing a snatch of 'Anything You Can Do I Can Do Better' when the young pretender of the sax shared the stage with older champion Charlie Parker.

Ballads built for comfort not for speed

From a purely musical point of view, what is striking about the quote from 'The Breeze And I' is that it is used as a form of release following a barrage of faster, vaulting runs where Hendrix's rhythmic attack hits peak energy. There is a vague similarity to the construction of the second guitar break on 'All Along The Watchtower' insofar as a clear, direct contrast of note lengths and shape of line is used to good effect. When Hendrix plays Lecuona's melody he puts the trajectory of notes through a warp and weft of distortion, especially the fourth and fifth chords at the start of the theme, to retain the sensuality of the original, but imbues it with a fraught, sombre intent.

A variety of phrasing, from a sustained, percussive double-time drive, a heated rhythmic whirlwind, to a decidedly leisurely attack, where the notes are floating metal, is one of the major appeals of Hendrix as not so much soloist as soundscaper. The punctuation of a barrage of fast triplets by a legato or lento phrase was by no means new but in Hendrix it acquired an altogether more striking countenance because of the thick, almost marble-like cast he gave his whole notes, so that they become all the more statuesque when heard in isolation after a stream of eighths.

Interestingly he expressed ambivalence on how he might fit into the "art-house" end of black music, that of the performance-athlete improvisers synonymous with bebop who were admired for their ability to negotiate complex chord changes at high tempo. "I always felt so insecure about jazz and all because they could play so fast ... dooo doo doo adat dat dat dat", Hendrix told Niels Olaf Gudme in 1969. "Jazz is a thing, like for some musicians it might scare them first ... when you say jazz, just the term."[50]

It could be argued that Hendrix was wrong to reduce the genre to this characterization, and that he was wholly qualified to be regarded as an improvising musician precisely because of his ability to think outside the box and express a strong personality, which the more progressive end of jazz would actually applaud both in his lifetime and thereafter. Nonetheless, he mostly shied away from speed, or an excess of it.

A tendency to play not so much slowly, but with *leisurely energy*, a steady authority rather than manic urgency, defines some of Hendrix's highpoints on record. The unforgettable central melody of 'Third Stone From The Sun' has just 12 notes spread out over eight bars, which provides a distinct breathing space for the statement, rather than rushing it to any conclusion. He plays far more notes on 'Burning Of The Midnight Lamp's four-bar theme but the effect is similar. There is tranquil poise.

As for the gorgeous chromatic curls at the beginning of 'The Wind Cries Mary', they are so nonchalant, so unabashed that they appear almost to be an earnest invitation to sit down and listen to a grown man pour his heart out even if he ain't s'posed to cry. Detailing the emotional fallout of a lover's tiff the song is deeply reflective and poetic, but what makes it such a rich textural as well as lyrical construct is the immense skill of Hendrix's rhythm guitar lines that brilliantly hover between airy fluttered phrases and bulkier hefts of bass, so that the piece feels paradoxically light and heavy, as if it is able to both skip and drag, questioning our notion of what is a medium or a slow tempo, or how both can be simultaneously implied.

After two sung verses the guitar solo vividly enhances the ambiguity. The instrument is placed in the spotlight but the improvisation is built more on rhythmic variation of a central figure than an unfurling of harmonic ideas. The motifs switch compellingly between emphasis and restraint, again by the interplay of high, mid and low range, before concluding with brief crescendos that are anything but overpowering. The climax is in whispers rather than screams. It is a stunning example of a guitar solo that stays deeply mindful of pacing and proportion, and the need to focus ideas rather than display them for effect. The life cycle of the guitar break serves the prevailing mood of the song in the manner of great soul players such as Steve Cropper or Curtis Mayfield. This does not mean that, when necessary, things went straight towards a deluge of sounds.

The other thing to bear in mind is how extensively and effectively Hendrix used the opportunity to overdub multiple lines in the studio. As many as four or five parts could be stacked up in order to create an orchestral richness that would impress any arranger of brass and reeds in a jazz ensemble. For example, the way he made the multi-tracking of 'Night Bird Flying' into a complex but entirely coherent matrix of overlapping lines has the layered richness of a four-part vocal harmony group.

None of these songs scales the heights of 'Little Wing'. It remains one of Hendrix's supreme achievements as a guitarist, first and foremost because it is a performance in which he once again brilliantly straddles the line between rhythm and lead playing, so that the only thing that really matters is the immense amount of detail in all the guitar parts, rather than whether some are played in the foreground and others in the background.

As Hendrix moves through the chords he adds, in his trademark way, a whole catalogue of tangling pentatonic runs of differing lengths to create a vast amount of additional detail so that the chords themselves are a canvas upon which he casts brush strokes as his imagination and musical intelligence dictate. While the sense of ornamentation, of each chord being a colour for which there will be relevant shades, light and dark, is part of the magic of the piece, and the way he chooses to start the song is simply beautiful. Hendrix does a dampened slide, his fingers pressing down lightly on the strings before the plectrum sweeps across, which conjures a distinct but not overpowering shudder, a discreet jolt, almost like a staccato tap on a table. He has our attention by way of a flicker of sound. Now he proceeds to stoke a quiet fire.

'Little Wing' begins in earnest and the tempo is set at just over 70 bpm, a slow amble forward where everything can be heard with the utmost clarity. No rush, no urgency, no quick lurch forward to the finishing line. Everything unfolds in a slow motion that feels almost static because of the easing of some notes from silence and their steady linger, their deliberate glide and flow through the air before they gently ebb away. The finesse and graduated softness of the playing coheres with the sensitivity of Hendrix's voice and a lyric that casts the titular woman, 'Little Wing', a name that possibly reflects an interest in Native American culture, in a spellbound scenario. She is spirit-like, "walking through the clouds" with a "circus mind running round". Yet the song has peaks of energy, notably the guitar solo's opening attack which raises the emotional temperature above what is created in the song's two short sung verses.

More importantly, the form is as subversive as it is attractive, which makes the song a rare example of a piece of popular music that stands on its own peculiar logic rather than bowing to convention all the while retaining commercial appeal. The guitar phrases, with sensual twists and turns, are mapped out over ten bars, the first eight of which are in 4/4, followed by one bar in 2/4 and a closing bar in 4/4. Alternatively, it can be counted as a 9-bar sequence where eight bars of 4 are rounded off by one bar in 6.

Mitch Mitchell's pounding drum fill on that last measure is a concise but resonantly forceful conclusion to the song's unusual structure, the asymmetry of which becomes more pronounced when the piece unfolds and reveals that it has no discernible vocal chorus or hook for the listener. The 38 beats, with the sole bar of 2/4 like a wrinkle in time, provide the framework for a series of guitar chords in the key of E minor that by dint of the beauty of execution and embellishment is as much the story as an exposition for the forthcoming story. The sonic-emotional depth of that gambit is a testament to Hendrix's genius as a lyrical player whose spontaneity takes him wherever his muse dictates. The slight lopsidedness of the final stage of the sequence gives it a one-off grace, as the relaxed forward motion is made to hover ever so slightly at the very end.

Therein lies one of the great achievements of 'Little Wing', and Hendrix as a writer and thinker. The 10 (or 9) bar structure is a life cycle that is sufficiently rich to sustain the entire performance. It has the episodic depth of a 12-bar blues but the elements are linked in a less familiar chain. A sense of journey, of progress and outcome remain but there is a road map that is interestingly tangential. The net result is a piece that ingeniously straddles eras, harking back to the kind of conceptual looseness of early blues, where bar counts and meters may not have been rigid, yet pushing forward to something ear-catchingly contemporary in both the textures and chord progressions.

Active since the mid-1980s, British guitarist Tony Remy is a superlative player whose long list of credits as a sideman include rock, pop and jazz artists such as Jack Bruce (on his post-Cream solo albums), Annie Lennox and Sarah Jane Morris. His roots are very much in the blues and he counts Hendrix as a major influence. He explains how the guitarist-composer threw a few effective curveballs into the harmony of 'Little Wing'.

> That's what makes the tune special, the unusual note choices. When he goes up to the B minor at that point in the song you don't expect it. That's the special, that's what they call "the rise" in gospel, you'll have a verse and chorus and just before a chorus they'll be a 4 or 8 bar thing to give it that lift into the chorus, and that's what he does with the B minor through to A minor C, G, F, C, D. It's got that move away from the normal blues in E of E, A, B. The way he's worked it is he's added the G in there and the B minor chromatic down to the A minor ... that's what gives it that big lift that's the unconventional part of that tune. You really know something is coming after that.
>
> At that point in the tune you have the expectation it's gonna go into something else, or another verse ... You can feel it at that point, like "oh, no, where is it gonna go now?" It's the element of surprise ... gospel music has that, a little bridge that says we're going somewhere now.[51]

As rich as its movement is within its 10-bar structure, 'Little Wing' flatly refuses to take off in an overtly dramatic way. There are just two short verses with a slight but decisive variation in scansion, which convey a deep spontaneity, as if Hendrix, giving himself over to a confessional impulse, has decided to shorten the final line and slide into repetition on verse 2 – "anything ... anything" – but the second rendition of the word is a passionate yearning as Hendrix draws out the last syllable. Just as the note falls silent he makes the guitar quiver in the upper register, sustaining for just over three beats, and the sense of emotional release is enormous. He starts his solo with a melodic motif before one last vocal message, a tender farewell: "Fly on, little wing".

What Hendrix achieved on 'Little Wing' is the symbiosis of text and subtext, primary and secondary colour, emotive foreground and no less touching background. The essence of the song is distilled in the first eight bars, a round trip where the start and finish are perfectly satisfying. The introduction is, in many ways, the conclusion.

There is such a beauty in the choice and handling of the notes that they represent an emphatically melodic progression in their own right and would make an intelligent musician (and listener) question the need for further development that may actually end up compromising what is conveyed by the very foundation of the song. This is after all a concise but potent solo guitar feature rather than a grandstand guitar solo.

The chord sequence acts as the narrative journey as well as the point of departure. In other words there is an immense amount of musical *judgement* as well as technique in the song. Hendrix could have played more. Given the effective key changes he wrote for other pieces it is entirely feasible to imagine him doing so again but the genius lay in knowing when a pattern of notes is actually fully formed rather than incomplete. There is thus a real artistry that underpinned the decision to take a step back, exercise editorial intelligence and actually avoid overstating what needs no further elaboration.

As much as 'Purple Haze' is crying out for its B section, such is the tension stoked in the A, 'Little Wing' requires no further adjustments because it has such apt tonal light and shade and rise and fall of emotional pitch in its 10-bar corpus. It is a masterpiece of self-containment, a balance of the weight of flourish by the measure of discipline.

In addition to the structural logic there is also the advanced dynamics of the piece to consider. It is a slow song, a meditation, a ballad, a lament even. There is restraint as well as emphasis in the string of sounds but it is not entirely soft or muted. To all intents and purposes a piece with as much sensitivity could have been well suited to the acoustic realm but it is nonetheless an electric elegy, which definitely has an edge, especially on the closing instrumental guitar break where Hendrix "blows", whilst at the same time retaining the melodic core of the song, making the initial phrase sing out by way of clear spacing between notes. He has just the right amount of fortissimo on the shorter figures, particularly the higher tempo flurries that bring a new burst of energy.

When he jumps to the high E in the coda the guitar really sings, complementing the voice that has preceded, and then in the very final bars he uses a previously discussed trademark technique: he doubles the guitar with a "yeh, yeh" which then trails off into more breathy, muffled words. This is a brief surge of intimacy. It is as if the artist, who has already shared so much, wants to keep his innermost thoughts to himself, leaving something in the air for us to *not* know as we contemplate the brilliant portrait of beauty that he has somehow managed to paint in just under two and a half minutes.

Recalling the sessions for 'Little Wing', Eddie Kramer shared some important unreleased material. Spooling back through the master tapes he found a second take of the song and made this insightful comment about exactly what Hendrix, Redding and Mitchell really needed to do performance wise so as to nail the take.

> This is live from the floor, the three of them just playing as if it was a live concert performance. It's obviously Jimi just stretching out, feeling his way. It's raw, it's in your face, it's bleeding, it's

really just heavy. It's just to establish the ground rules. I think the delicacy comes as a result of him having got this out of his system and Chas [Chandler] making the suggestion, "You know we gotta take it down lads."[52]

What happened on the final take was a distillation of the requisite emotional charge and sonic attack of the song. The "heaviness", as Kramer says, is still there but it is channelled into a form of power that is not overwrought. This challenges our perceptions of the suitability of certain sounds to a particular atmosphere, as well as the appropriate combinations of instruments for an accompanying arrangement. With that in mind it should not be forgotten that the other very decisive element of 'Little Wing' is the glockenspiel. It chimes away, sketching out the twists and turns of the harmony, along with Hendrix's guitar, and it becomes a miniature sound to the grandiose stature of the chords. Hendrix's instrument is put through a Leslie speaker so it envelops the audio but, partly because of Kramer's superlative mix, it doesn't swamp the smaller instrument. The weight of some of Hendrix's fills is clearly felt but the glockenspiel peeks through. A child-like innocence nestles in adult eminence.

Here, then, is Hendrix creating music that achieves many things at once. Lodged as the music is in the marrow of the blues, it has elements that create a certain idiomatic ambiguity which is fascinating. The combination of floating, spacious vocal, yearning guitar licks and distillation of heaviness without necessarily being heavy, create a ballad that has the emotional depth but not the sonic sheen of orchestral R&B or soul.

There is a raw edge to 'Little Wing', just as there is to 'Angel', just as there is to 'The Wind Cries Mary'. These ballads are practically a sub-set in Hendrix's songbook; the lament that has a peculiar languor that is so personal, so intimate, so vulnerable, so fragile, so exposed, so naked, so full of risk that it can't be neatly classified in a specific genre. It is black music in mutation, cross-fertilizing with anything from folk to country so that the end result is akin to what the French call *chanson pathetique*, a song of pathos.

Some of the songs of the great soul men of the 1960s that Hendrix was known to admire, Curtis Mayfield and Otis Redding, are mildly comparable. As much as Redding's songs could be well layered by the superlative organ-based rhythm section of Booker T & The MGs, there was a heavenly clarity in the backdrop of anthems such as 'Sittin' On The Dock Of The Bay'. This is a landmark musical moment because, on careful listening, it is not a straight application of R&B methodology. Like 'The Wind Cries Mary' there is an artful levity in its pulse. Like 'Little Wing' it has a child-like gambol. All these songs are triumphs of slow music; considered, studious performance and unfettered emotional honesty. One of the key testaments to Hendrix as a mature and serious artist as well as perceptive human being is that he was not afraid to create a certain gravitas in his work, to reveal his inner feelings in sound and lyric.

The outstanding ornamentations that can be discerned on 'Little Wing', from the double stops and slurs to the curled line endings and perfectly judged sustain of notes, are integral to the fine architecture of the track but the solid foundation remains the absolute sense of contemplation if not meditation in the performance, as if the song was a moment for Hendrix to bare his soul without reaching for a big drama chorus. It is the antithesis of the modern power ballad. It is a ballad with power. And control.

As much as he might have distanced himself from jazz because of its high tempo, Hendrix put his finger on a fundamental aspect of the art form that is perhaps underrated. He proved himself a master ballad player, a true storyteller who is wont to move a listener in the intense scrutiny of a slow arrangement, where success hinges on the technique of not hiding behind technique, of making every note and pause something that *has* to be played rather than something the musician is able to play.

Finding the sweet spot … feet first

The very subject of intent and motivation, of why he was even making music in the first place, was addressed many times by Hendrix in interviews. One could deride his belief that music was a higher form of communication as the view of a spliffed-out dreamer who came of age in the late 1960s where flower power, the counter-culture and the hazy and hedonistic idealism of the fabled "summer of love" held sway. However, Hendrix was very consistent with his statements and perhaps the most emphatic was the following:

> It's all pure feeling. What we're playing is complete honesty; we're playing nothing but 100% honesty. It's up to the people to dig it, or not dig it. The verbal language is going out of style anyway, it's too two-faced if you listen … sometimes you can get a whole conversation from maybe two bars of a song. That's what music's all about. It's not a play thing, with us it's all serious.[53]

His decision to play 'Star-Spangled Banner' at the Woodstock festival in August 1969 could not have been a more direct manifestation of that claim. Hendrix's sense of occasion, and perhaps irreverence, was such that he also played 'God Save The Queen' at other gigs. However, taking on the American national anthem was an altogether more audacious move, given the fever-pitch tension of a country convulsing with the folly of engagement in Vietnam, pacifist movements, nationwide race riots and student unrest.

The performance is an extraordinary feat of artistry, which has rightfully prompted countless observers to see it through an anti-war prism whereby

Hendrix proceeded to pass comment on what he regarded to be the alarming state of his heartland at that point in time. He made this clear to reinforce the notion of music as a form of truth. "Did you hear those bullets in the middle of it? That's our interpretation of America, what we've seen the last time around, it's everything, it's extremes, everything, the sign of a country right on the brink of going mad and right on the brink of exploding."

Although there is some initial accompaniment from Mitch Mitchell on drums and a barely audible Juma Sultan on percussion, this is very much a solo guitar feature. Lasting just under four minutes, 'Star-Spangled Banner' shows how enormous was Hendrix's creative depth and breadth of imagination. First and foremost, the guitar is orchestration. From the opening few bars the multiple layers of sound, contrasts of tone, bursts of distortion and changing levels of attack and volume conspire to fulfil the ideal of a single instrument that somehow acquires the range of several drawn from different families of instruments both in and out of the western classical convention that would be deployed for a symphony. His initial statement of the melody has liberal sprinklings of vibrato and phrasal variations that reflect a desire to use the anthem as a launching pad for a volley of subversive, if not dissident ideas rather than make a faithful rendition that would appeal to all apple-pie patriots.

The central guitar tone has a piercing, searing, viola-like quality to it but the passing scrambles of noise are like hissing brass, yet on so many phrases there is also a distinct implication of metal on metal, the austere sound of the cold and crushing mechanization that has come to define much of the western world, whose strict regimentation and order Hendrix unseats by way of his spontaneity and whimsy. The chords left to judder under many parts of the main melody add to the sense of a central protagonist in a play being assailed, which is heighted by the fragmentation of the theme with aggressive trilling that is as percussive as it is disruptive to the line.

As the performance unfolds, the changes of direction are increasingly more daring and unpredictable but still held together by the skill of the execution and the richness of the narrative. There are sustains which seem to last an age, then Hendrix bends the note, dashes to the wah wah pedal and pumps it to make his tone harden and sizzle, before his hand races up the neck to a screaming crescendo that is followed by several rapid-fire slides up and down that are redolent of the grind of industrial apparatus or the roar of an engine. Executed at such speed this double glissando is another notable sign of Hendrix taking the guitar into the realm of abstract noise rather than keeping his thinking tied to the principle of melody and rhythmic ingenuity. The notes are so jaggedly violent that they act as fleeting, shocking explosions in the performance.

Thereafter he starts to work the tremolo arm of the instrument and the improvisation goes to another level both sonically and structurally. The howl is now one of immense anguish, intercut with faster slides so that a new urgency is introduced and further enhanced by the alternation of long notes and phrases pummelled into a sonic blur. Metaphorical war has broken out and feedback grenades are going off with abandon.

Momentarily, Hendrix teases with a variation of the melody, so long abandoned it could act as the metaphor of a body left behind on the battlefield, as if a good tune is also a casualty of war, but he spikes it with a sinister riff that plunges into atonality. Several times thereafter he conjures a shower of oscillations that melt into the air with such drama that the effect is that of exclamatory voices in the darkest echo chamber. There are moments when some of the textures he creates are frighteningly sinister.

Roughly 1:40 minutes into the performance he tears into the melody again but breaks off and for a fleeting moment he plays a handful of eighth notes that are intriguingly familiar. It is more of a half phrase than phrase but what rings out is a universal urban rhythm. It is close to the sound of a police siren, the shrill, almost nasal whine jarring the ear.

That moment is so ephemeral it is easy to miss, like a word slipped under the breath in a heated conversation, but it has immense weight as a subtext. For if 'Star-Spangled Banner' is the national anthem of America then Hendrix's reference to the most recognized element of state authority in civic life, the police, is an act of provocation that far exceeds his reprise of Ernesto Lecuona's *Suite Espanola* during his rendition of 'Spanish Castle Magic' at Atlanta. The quotation again specifically reflects a love of enigma. The music has codes. The artist invites the listener to turn on, tune in and *not* drop out of a conversation that concerns any audience with a degree of consciousness.

As previously noted, Hendrix talked of distilling truth in "maybe two bars of a song". Well, here is an essential debate that is posed by the artist in just over three beats. He evokes law and order amid the rhythm and noise of death and disorder. Is this the sound of the police or the sound of the beast, as KRS-One would remind us years later? Who is safe in America? Who will save America? Who will be saved by America? Who will be saved from America?

Next the tremolo arm is deployed for new extremes of distortion, with Hendrix shaking the metal rod so vigorously that his hands blur. Throughout the performance all this sound-scrambling is liberally marked by moments of detuning, where his guitar is like the voice on a tape slowing down so the pitch becomes a sludge-slur. This was nothing new for Hendrix. He frequently used Eb as well as E tuning, and would detune mid-song, aware of the additional dramatic effects he could bring to the table. On the memorable appearance of The Experience on the Lulu television show in January 1969, he can be seen doing so with the most mischievous grin during 'Hey Joe', and the ensuing wobble of noise is like a metaphorical curveball thrown at the producers before the band then launch into the unscripted reprise of Cream's 'Sunshine Of Your Love'. The detuning is about deviating from what has been agreed.

On 'Star-Spangled Banner' Hendrix takes things to another creative level, possibly because he had set out to turn an old national anthem into a new nation of sound. The series of closing vocalized riffs is nothing less than operatic, the sensation heightened by the way Hendrix throws his whole body back and then crouches down just as he brings more bass into play. The descent from the high to low register is paralleled by this up and down physical movement that is anything but superficial. The visual spectacle is compelling because Hendrix strongly suggests that he is feeling every sound to his very core, and pulling it from mind, body and soul.

He returns to the melody and also keeps this dynamic, playing it both low down the neck and then up high, producing jolting, threatening reverberations before he signs off with power chords moved up a step then plunged into bass, like a movie show theme finale, a sharply ironic coda that paints America as a day-glo tragi-comedy.

"All I did was play it, I'm American, so I played it," he later said of the 'Star-Spangled Banner' solo. "I used to have to sing it in school, they made me sing it in school, it's a flashback. I thought it was beautiful."[54] This can be seen as the beauty of honesty, a reality that, due to the subject matter, had to entail a degree of unfettered brutality. The recasting of the national anthem as a theatre of cruelty as well as sonic drama thus asks pertinent questions of what patriotic symbols really represent, and to whom they belong. A year later, the revolutionary African-American artist Faith Ringgold would assert that "the American people are the only people who can interpret the American flag", right down to deciding that it should be "burned and forgotten". She found herself rewarded with an arrest and charge for her patriotism.[55]

Hendrix did not pay a similar price but the great subversive power he brought to bear on 'Star-Spangled Banner' was no less of a threat to any establishment that seeks to gain the loyalty of its citizens without standing up to due scrutiny. As a sonic and intellectual statement, the performance is unrelentingly one of discourse, question, contention, assertion, challenge, of countless episodes in a raucous assembly of voices unleashed by one man with the range and invention of an orchestra. The idea of small groups with a big sound became prevalent in rock in the late 1960s, but Hendrix went one step further and *became* the whole band. Instead of power trio he did power solo.

As much as Hendrix created a striking continuum between voice and guitar on so much of his repertoire, here on this voiceless piece he is demonstrating his conception of the guitar as both instrument and technological apparatus that can be used for soundscapes not within the realm of commonly used notes and chords. This underscores Chris Montague's point about the challenge of transcribing Hendrix, and the observation made by Brian Eno and others that the Stratocaster and pedals were tantamount to a kind of synthesizer in the guitarist's hands (and under his feet).

Understandably, onlookers are impressed by the dexterity of any player's fingers on a fretboard, where the complex phrases or chords heard in real time are matched by the sight of hands stretching and curling into unwieldy shapes. The digit gymnastics are eye-catching. However, the use of other parts of the guitar such as the tremolo arm should not be underestimated simply because of the lack of spectacle. It is tempting to fall into the trap of thinking that *all* Hendrix is doing is holding the "wammy bar" to scramble a note rather than taking extreme care when *using* a component of the guitar that is far more difficult to manipulate than one might think. Montague explains:

> You can sound like a total wally if you get it wrong, you can sound so school assembly. It's pitching notes, you hit a note and then you need to either pull it back to raise the pitch, or push it down to lower the pitch but each string feels different. There's a different amount of tension on each string so you have to know what each string is gonna feel like before you commit to it. Integrating that into your playing is a wonderful way to make your playing more vocal. The way Jimi did it ... it could be very erratic, he would control feedback, he'd get a note going on the guitar, depress and raise it to get feedback, and nobody had seen that before.[56]

Feedback as a coherently placed part of the broad sound palette of the guitar is one of Hendrix's great achievements. Rather than being presented as some kind of eldritch, extraneous noise that stands in opposition to the proper notes of a phrase, the distortion fits into an overall narrative logic. The "dirty" and clean articulation of sound become interlocked, certainly in the most daring way in 'Star-Spangled Banner', where the whole point of the performance is the co-existence of the known melody and the unknown textures that frame it, like branches of differing length and shape wrapping around a solid tree trunk. In fact, all of the embellishments of phrasing hitherto discussed, from the double stops to the glissando, vibrato and string bends, are absolute manifestations of a desire to see a melodic line or chord sequence as raw material to shape what could pass as adulteration or corruption of sound rather than a base element to be refined and filleted of too harsh or rough a content. The result is a blend of musical and non-musical sound, of note and adjacent effect.

Hendrix the electric guitarist is also consciously and skilfully manipulating sound in relation to an amplifier. There is a pivotal relationship between the instrument and the box into which it is plugged in order to generate volume, as Chris Sharkey explains.

> Because the guitar and amp are in dialogue, what the skilled player is able to do is control and utilize distortion for musical purposes. The way Hendrix does it is by using volume control on his guitar. The idea is the amp turned all the way up so when the guitar is at full volume you can do rich sound with these long legato notes. But if you lower the volume control on the guitar to rescue the sound

going into the amp that changes the nature of the distortion. With high fidelity amplifiers you take a wave form of whatever signal and make it louder but when things start to distort, the top of the wave form becomes clipped off and that reduces dynamic range but creates more sustain and more harmonics. A pure sound becomes enriched by first, second and third order harmonics. The sound becomes richer and more detailed, and it becomes recognizable as distortion. It drastically affects the sound production of the guitar.

Imagine it as controlling the electricity going to the amp, changing the flow of energy to the amp. All the sounds Hendrix is famous for are a result of his technique of alternating and modulating the amount of energy going into the amp from the guitar. When the volume's all the way up and in front of the amp you're getting feedback but depending on where you're standing and the angle at which you hold the guitar you can change the pitch of feedback and that becomes another tool in your arsenal. On 'Star-Spangled Banner' you see him finding his sweet spot on stage. When the guitar is all the way up and amp is up you don't even have to touch it, you can rub it against the stand; it's creating sounds by itself. It's that fundamental relationship between guitar and amplifier.[57]

Numerous commentators have pointed out the advanced science behind much of Hendrix's feedback and his use of hugely powerful "overdriven" amplifiers, and it is fascinating to watch footage of him on stage precisely because of the clear intent with which he availed himself of the equipment around him. His positioning in relation to the amps was important as precise distance could affect the sound, as is evidenced at many gigs, particularly Woodstock in 1969. At the 1968 Miami Pop Festival the extended overture of 'Foxy Lady' has a surge of energy unleashed by Hendrix turning towards the stack of Marshals behind him just as he starts to grip the tremolo arm. It surpasses the record, and is almost like overtone throat singing done on the guitar.

The slow rise, the emergence of the notes from silence, is a thing of beauty, for the absolute steadiness with which their howl is sustained, almost like the wind held in the palm of a hand that opens and closes. The sense of tantalization, of a tremulous feeling as well as a tremolo of sound, is very vivid, and crucially conveys something undeniably human, a suggestion of breathing in the midst of a crackle of electricity.

One again his control of the sound is exemplary. There is a consensus that the sheer strength of his (large) hands was a major advantage in this respect, but the ability to graduate and *regulate* loudness, to create presence that could expand or contract, is what made Hendrix a kind of man-machine phenomenon. Those who saw him in concert, such as Mike Bloomfield, the guitarist known for his work with Bob Dylan among others, attest to the "organic" way Hendrix was able to make futurist noise.

> I have never heard a sound on a Hendrix record that I have not seen him create in front of my own eyes. Somehow by tapping the back of his guitar neck – which he constantly did – and by using the [vibrato] bar, Jimi could control feedback. You would hear a rumbling start – he knew which note would feedback and what harmonic he was shooting for, and then he controlled it.[58]

Furthermore, the invention of numerous pedals such as a "fuzz face" or Octavia, both custom made for Hendrix by the engineer Roger Mayer, which allowed the guitarist to raise or lower the pitch of a note and introduce distortion to further alter the colour, could only be grist to the guitarist's creative mill. More textures could come into play.

'Burning Of The Midnight Lamp' is a brilliant example of how the additional apparatus was used by Hendrix to craft a quite magical overture for a deeply evocative song. All the majesty of the shimmering harpsichord theme is strikingly counterpointed by the arc of beckoning, tantalizing reverberations of the guitar, which show Hendrix's great understanding of precise pitch manipulation as a vital form of musical tapestry. Essentially, the pedal-generated sounds allow Hendrix to create a series of fine brushstrokes around the broad strokes of a chord. The guitar releases additional specks of notes that momentarily flicker and hang in the air, like shifting shades on a canvas.

All these pedals brought an additional range of embellishments to Hendrix's phrases that put him on a par with other virtuosi, not just in music but in the visual arts such as painting, photography and cinema, who are intent on exploring how a note (or image) can be presented and then framed in a number of different ways. It is Hendrix responding to a deep impulse to do much more than articulate "straight".

As Sharkey explains:

> The fuzzface is so linked with his sound. And with the Octavia you have dialogue because of the way it works. Different frequency ranges have incredibly powerful harmonics when you play more than one note at once. And there are random pitches at times. What's interesting about all the pedals is that they respond to changes of volume in a similar way that an amp does. I think that's why he loved them. They worked in a similar way … another colour, another expression.
>
> Again it's all about how he engages mind and body with all this stuff. The wah wah gives this an even more expressive nod to the type of vowel sounds you make when singing. It's about making the guitar and voice closer, bringing them closer together.[59]

Inevitably, a piece of kit such as the wah wah would have greatly appealed to Hendrix precisely because it required such careful physical application. Because there is relatively little footage that really gives a close-up of exactly what he is doing when he puts his foot on the device it is tempting to think that it is a fairly straightforward technique to deploy, and that pressing up and down will do the job. The many iconic pieces on which the wah wah featured, from 'Burning Of The Midnight Lamp' to 'All Along The Watchtower' to 'Voodoo Child (Slight Return)', are proof positive that Hendrix made the pedal manipulation an art form, and exerted a huge influence on contemporary players who recognize how much ingenuity he brought to the table.

The vocalization offered – the growl, snarl and slur – did not come easy. Says Tony Remy:

> If you think using a wah wah pedal is just tapping your foot in time with the music, no, think again. There's much more to it than that. You've got to move it around as if you're playing with the clutch on your car, like you have to find the biting point, the sweet spot because if you've got your pedal on and you get the pedal in the right place you get some great feedback, then you can move your foot up and down slightly and you get different notes and in a lot Hendrix's tunes you can hear him do that. He's not just pressing it down in time with the beat. That "waaoooo" ... he's getting that tone by precise movement of the foot as if he's feeling out the lyric, it's another extension of the sound of the voice (that's implied). It's in the precise physical manipulation, and the absolute care and attention to detail.[60]

Chris Montague argues that Hendrix had to have a well-defined idea of what he wanted to hear before he went into action, and that ultimately he invested something of himself in pursuit of the required sound. As Remy did, he makes the point that using the pedal straight on the beat is really the way to kill any creativity. Hendrix was much more adventurous with his pulse, thus bringing more character to the fore.

> You see a lot of people with the wah wah pedal, they just rock it back and forth in time, it's awful. The best use of it is when it actually shapes the phrase so that it sounds more like a vocal. You don't just press it and it does *something*. You have to put something into that pedal in order to get a good result. It's inanimate; you have to control it. It doesn't know what to do. It's like another little instrument.
>
> With a wah wah the challenge is you have to shape the note convincingly, because when it's in its back position you've rolled all the top end of the sound and when you push it forward it puts

> all the top end into the sound so it rolls off at the bottom end. So you go between those two things and there's somewhere in the middle where there's a sweet spot with the note. You have to learn how to shape that. I suppose you have to hear it. 'Voodoo Child (Slight Return)' is a stunning example of that. That was the tune that made me want to be a guitar player, that intro ... it's where he's choking down the strings as well as using the pedal for that woka woka sound.[61]

While the Hendrix wah wah became another one of his musical signatures it also raised an intriguing question regarding where his music could be placed in a historical lineage. After all, the forerunner to the pedal was the hat, cup or mute used by swing-era brass players to make their instruments sing more explicitly and acquire the "wa wa" effect that broadens their expressive range. The likes of Duke Ellington's revered band members Bubber Miley and Joe "Tricky Sam" Nanton blazed an adventurous acoustic trail that gave a glimpse of Hendrix's grand electric wanderings to come.

Another ancestral acoustic vocabulary that the guitarist calls to mind is that of the harmonica players who sometimes trilled as outlandishly as possible, aggressively bending notes to make the little pocket device much favoured in early blues vocabulary, where it could be a highly effective complement to guitar and voice. Although harmonically limited, the instrument offered rich possibilities for vocalized timbres, and on occasion some exponents would closely alternate their own hollers and screams with vibrato-laden phrases played on the instrument, as in Sonny Terry's astounding 'Fox Chase', which evokes the country pursuit of the animal by way of fast rhythmic flurries that entwine with recurrent and impassioned yelping and whooping. How old and new music might be entwined in Hendrix's work is a complex subject. But their relationship was brought home to me in unexpected circumstances.

Sometime in the late 1990s I saw Ben Harper at the Shepherd's Bush Empire in London. The Californian had three excellent albums to his name, *Welcome To The Cruel World, Fight For Your Mind* and *The Will To Live*, which had made him one of the freshest things in rock, primarily because there was such a strong blues and folk element which inevitably drew comparisons to both Jimi Hendrix and Bob Dylan.

What was more significant was the rich seam of historical information Harper mined, for unlike most of his peers he played lapsteel guitar as well as slide and electric. In the middle of a pulsating set where he regaled the crowd with original songs such as 'Whipping Boy' and 'Like A King', Harper quoted Hendrix's 'Voodoo Child (Slight Return)' on the lapsteel. But what was even more interesting was the way he stretched out a hand and arched his fingers to mimic a DJ sliding a record back and forth on a turntable. Harper equated the wah wah of the late 1960s with the scratch of the early 1980s.

In many ways that single moment, for its audio-visual significance, its combination of sight and sound, its reinforcement of music by gesture, is one of the best summaries of Hendrix as a musical time traveller and boundary breaker. Here was Harper at the dawn of the second millennium calling forth the spirit of one of his forebears whose manipulation of an electric instrument, the guitar, in a genre commonly known as rock, prefigured one of the central sounds of a genre that was not invented in his lifetime, hip-hop. There was no DJ present on stage that night but Harper was essentially showing a continuum between Hendrix and the likes of Kool Herc, Theodore, Terminator X[62] and other pioneers of the art of crafting percussive sound, with that strangely alien *waka waka waka* scream of the most expressive of scratches, by the careful deployment of apparatus made for 7″ and 12″ discs. Hendrix uses his foot in order to vocalize tone whereas Terminator X hits the decks to speak with his hands.

Furthermore, listen back to the way Hendrix is dampening or "choking" his strings at the very beginning of 'Voodoo Child (Slight Return)' and it makes perfect sense for a DJ to relate to the sound because it evokes an extreme dryness, a kind of sandpaper scorch, that resonates closely with some of the peculiar textures fashioned by the skating of needles on vinyl and the back and forth of faders on a mixing desk.

Chances are that Harper chose 'Voodoo Child (Slight Return)' as a cipher for hip-hop not just because of the landmark wah-wah intro. Pay close attention to the opening bars of the song and what catches the ear apart from the guitar is Mitch Mitchell's skipping kick drum, which expertly frames the attack of the strings with a sturdy downbeat and sharply pummelled triplet that is a bass line in the absence of a bass guitar. There is something utterly primal about the meld of the drums and guitar, which creates the same kind of bullish thrust that spawned a term such as "boom bap" in order to convey the gargantuan mass in the low end, which largely defines hip-hop.

On one hand the music conjures up the era of two turntables and a mike. It supports the view that Hendrix prefigured a sound of the future, the shape of the groove to come. On the other hand a deeply ancestral quality can be heard in the propulsion generated by Hendrix and Mitchell. They are in forceful forward motion.

Says Chris Montague of 'Voodoo Child (Slight Return)':

> The thing I didn't get until a lot of years later, listening back to it, is how much it swings. It's like old swing band rhythms, it's way, way back in the lineage of stuff, like Hendrix had a strong sense of swing in his playing. Just him choking the strings down and using the wah wah pedal, it's got serious momentum when you listen back to it. It's really funky, really swinging; it's almost like a New Orleansy shuffle. It's quite extraordinary.[63]

There is no definitive answer to the question of where to place this pivotal piece of music on a historical timeline. The beauty of 'Voodoo Child (Slight Return)' is that it can be heard as an audacious bridge between old and new soundworlds, a reminder that the perception of where one musical epoch ends and another begins is by no means unequivocal, and that the whole point about Hendrix the creative being was that, as much as he was able to absorb the history of black music, he did not reduce it to pastiche. He invented from the deepest roots without getting stuck in passé soil.

Listening to his oeuvre as a whole, Hendrix stands as much more than a soloist or proponent of the role of "lead" instrumentalist. He is guitar hero and techno warrior combined, which has enabled him to impact on a wide range of different types of player. On the one hand he is essential listening for anybody interested in the evolution of the blues. On the other he provides a paradigm for sound adventurers who seek novel textures, and all those who do not see these schools as mutually exclusive. Hendrix can be heard in anybody from Americans Vernon Reid and Brandon Ross, to Europeans such as Marc Ducret and Noel Akotche, to Africans who are exponents of "desert blues" like Goumar "Bombino" Almoctar. Hendrix is the guitarist who questions what the guitar is and what it may also become.

It has been said by many jazz historians that virtuoso trumpeter Louis Armstrong was one of the most significant early jazz musicians because he was able to distil such a substantial amount of knowledge of his predecessors and craft his own identity as a result, which in somewhat romantic terms meant that it took hundreds of brass players marching through the streets of New Orleans for Armstrong to be able to simply exist. Hendrix also appears as a kind of manifestation of myriad players who came before him, from the unknown but spirited bluesmen in honky tonks and roadhouses to the forward-thinking sound scientists who experimented with technology as crude as rattlesnakes and tin pans to create the earliest resonators – think Eddie Durham and Charlie Christian – so that they could cut through a horn section in a swing combo. Hendrix is building on that legacy of risk and daring with tone and texture, all the while asserting a unique personality that excitingly blurs the line between rhythm, melody and harmony to create a sound world that is beyond the imagination of most.

At the board going crazy

Studio as instrument is a widely used term today, but it is by no means new. Musicians have used recording facilities to overdub and collage multiple tracks to create one-man bands, as in the case of jazz legend Sidney Bechet, since the 1940s, and Hendrix bought right into the idea of pushing the envelope with regard to sonic manipulation. If he was wont to obsessively dwell on the finer points of a song then he was lucky enough to stand in the headwind of a period of experimentation in popular music and be surrounded by collaborators who were also willing to get caught up in the swirl.

As Mitch Mitchell recalls, the head-turning adventures in sound undertaken by The Beatles in the mid-1960s made a major impact on musicians as well as music lovers. "*Sergeant Pepper* had just [come out] ... that started the ball rolling, really. Everyone was listening to everyone else's records and trying to ... oh, how did they get that effect?"[64] The idea of both devising sonic originality and using all technological means available to do so had well and truly taken hold of Hendrix and his collaborators. Chas Chandler was a notorious pragmatist who imposed discipline in the studio yet he nonetheless saw the immense potential value of another burst of creativity taking place *after* what he considered to be a good take of a particular song. The finished article could be finished again in a different way. "Once it was in the can then you started mucking with it for various effects and things," Chandler said.[65]

Post-production is an integral part of the process of making records. But the late 1960s was still a relatively early stage of this development and Hendrix was intent on not being left behind. It became increasingly clear that the extended creative team around a band in the studio could be of vital importance, if the individuals in question shared the same vision. Hendrix had an ally in engineer Eddie Kramer who was unabashedly proactive in pushing the idea of studio as instrument, and upping the ante on confecting original sounds in a spontaneous, freewheeling manner that was not in the mindset of the more disciplinarian Chandler, even though he did give substantial licence to Hendrix.

All accounts of the working relationship Hendrix and Kramer enjoyed point to a deeply shared interest in sound that often crossed the line into nascent ideas for song structures. Although employed as an engineer, Kramer was a classically trained pianist with a great love of jazz, and in between sessions with Hendrix, the Rolling Stones and Traffic (Kramer worked for London studios such as Advision, Pye and Olympic) he would riff on the keyboard, sometimes catching Hendrix's ear with a chord sequence from which a song might flower, as in the case of 'Crosstown Traffic'. Kramer's knowledge of harmony also led him to suggest the augmented ninth piano chords that underpinned 'Spanish Castle Magic'. The engineer was an able musician as well as an astute listener and sound sculptor.

It stands to reason that Hendrix respected Kramer as a musician as well as somebody who was capable of helping him mould the sonic environment of his songs, which again strikes another parallel with the relationship between The Beatles and George Martin. In any case, as Kramer recalls, he and Hendrix developed a bond in the studio based on their mutual love of adorning the canvas of each particular song. "I have so many great memories with Jimi and I at the board going like crazy, trying to get all these special effects, there's backwards guitars, there's percussion", Kramer recalls, before adding that the increased use of state-of-the-art studio techniques, certainly on longer arrangements, represented a degree of liberation from what was possible in the confines of the shorter, concise pieces done with Chas Chandler.[66]

> This is like huge sonic painting. It's the opposite of what he was doing with Chas. That's not to say that the stuff he did with Chas was bad. The stuff he did with Chas was magnificent, but it's just that it was the total other end of the spectrum. Chas has got these little tight songs ... Jimi wanted to go on a ride. And he did.[67]

Certainly, 'EXP', the opening salvo of *Axis: Bold As Love*, sets the agenda for these flights of fancy. This parody of a public service announcement reveals both the wry humour of Hendrix as well as an earnest desire to toy with recorded sound so as to subvert convention. A perfectly articulated statement (by Mitchell in the role of the presenter) mimics prevalent BBC norms but as soon as the promise of an interview with a "peculiar looking gentleman" who goes by the name of "Mr Paul Caruso" is made, the pitch on his voice starts to alter and continues as there is talk of "UFOS ... spaceships and even space people". Hendrix is then heard as Caruso and, in contrast to Mitchell's voice, which hit chipmunk high, his is pulled down to bullfrog low, as if Looney Tunes had overtaken the hallowed ground of Maida Vale studios. Hendrix's crashing power chords then go in and out of earshot, making us believe that this hallucinogenic adult cartoon is being scrambled by, heaven forfend, an alien invasion of the television set. This is followed by more orchestral, whistling feedback from Hendrix that flits heatedly around the ether like an insect flying blind. Audaciously, this barrage of disturbing noise goes on for the best part of 50 seconds with the guitar creating howls, hollers, hisses, a vague hint of a police siren, the distinct throaty roar of a motorcycle engine and finally the wheeze of a transistor radio whose aerial is being turned every which way to vainly overcome a maddeningly faulty reception.

There is a clear intent to bring satire to anything from the world of broadcasting to a news agenda hooked on outlandish stories, but the collaging of sounds, their careful implementation and sequencing is anything but amateurish. This is a bravura display of what can be achieved by a musician and engineer on the same wavelength, so to speak, who conceive of sound as modelling clay that can be pushed and pulled into abstract shapes rather than sticking to a clear linear narrative. The piece is important because it also provides a vague foretaste of Hendrix's rendition of 'Star-Spangled Banner', and equally importantly it reveals Kramer's ability to brilliantly mix and enhance the guitarist by bold panning and liberal doses of reverb and distortion.

Because Kramer was using equipment that is rudimentary by today's standards – many songs were recorded on 4-track and the mix "bounced down" to 2-track on another machine to free up two extra tracks to accommodate more sounds – he had to be resourceful in order to produce the soundscapes Hendrix envisioned, which meant the use of great amounts of compression, reverb and EQ so that a smaller sound such as a piano or vocal could cut through the mix amid the tidal wave of noise created by the electric guitars and "a bunch of bloody Marshalls", as Kramer put it when referring to the powerful amplifiers that Hendrix had deemed *de rigueur*.

The fact that Olympic studios had a capacious floor that enabled the musicians to play much louder than in previous studios Chandler had found for Hendrix, facilitated the character of performance the guitarist was intent on delivering, though even with this new-found advantage some simple but highly effective techniques were employed. When Hendrix thought that a sensual tone was needed for more intimate songs he would keep the amplifier turned up and turn down the volume on his guitar. When the child-like recorder which Hendrix played on 'If 6 Was 9' needed to be turned into a breathless blur, Kramer swamped the tape in echo which blended fantastically with the stomping of assembled studio guests that became a kind of jokey off-kilter saunter. When 'Purple Haze' was in need of another layer of disturbing textures the ghostly chanting of Hendrix, Mitchell and Redding was overdubbed in the song's coda with just the right amount of presence so that the words are more felt than they are heard.

Taken as a whole, the three studio albums that largely define Hendrix as an artist are also a high watermark in recorded music for what they represent about the ingenuity of all the contributors within the prevailing technological confines of the age. A desire for nuance and attention to detail were, by all accounts, common denominators between Hendrix and Kramer, and as maddening as was the former's tendency to retake a performance dozens of times, it nonetheless underlined the potential artificiality of the studio aesthetic, which, paradoxically, opened another door of creativity, one that facilitated the integration of unidentified sounds onto the matrix of drums, bass, guitars and vocals. The epic fantasia of '1983 (A Merman I Should Turn To Be)', which ran to just under 15 minutes, is a prime example of a song with a main guitar riff being a demonstration of legato phrasing imbued with such depth of feeling it has the grandeur of a requiem that evolves into extended tone poetry. The initial arrangement breaks down into daringly still soundscapes swept over by gusts of wind that are given a spectral character by the piercing boing of a vibraslap or the metallic ching of cymbals. Hendrix's guitar returns with a stupendously glistening tone as hushed currents of percussion form a haze around his slow riffing, which forms a gentle electric whirlpool before the bass and drums kick the piece into a kinetic blues-rock.

Yet, just as a backbeat beckons, the music starts to vaporize and the renewed levity is enhanced by a delicate, pastoral flute. An angry thrust of heavy guitar shatters the calm, then Hendrix's vocal comes back for the final stage of the piece, delivering the melody once more before a climactic disintegration during which Kramer's mix unveils swooping bird-like effects before a lengthy, sensual sizzle into silence.

It is an astonishing suite. A major part of its appeal is the conjunction of organic and synthetic components, or rather the use of sounds rendered in real time and those wrought from tape manipulation. The recording of instruments then turned backwards also imbues the palette with an otherworldly mystery, unravelling perceptions of a normal musical narrative through the peculiar movement of the note, which, on occasion, is so staccato and disjunctive it comes across as a scrape or scratch. Similar techniques had appeared on the title track of *Are You Experienced?* but they were deployed with even more daring. Again this is Hendrix, decisively assisted by Kramer, far out on an imaginative limb, to the extent that the composition and production occupy a unique space in the colourful landscape of Hendrix's songbook.

The track 'Are You Experienced?' has a deeply unsettling ambiance that suggests a dream state or form of semi-consciousness in which hearts and minds seek clarity. An intense sense of suspension if not stasis is created by Hendrix pounding out A flat octaves on the piano, shown to him by Kramer, of course, for the entire duration of the raga-ish piece. It is a metronome of ambiguity rather than certainty and the lack of movement in the harmony ratchets up static tension the more the clarion is heard. This eerie bell tolls away in steady time, but it stubbornly refuses to announce a melody.

Adding to the feeling of floating in space is the lack of clearly audible sounds in the low register. Kramer has stated that bass was recorded with drums and guitar but, if so, it is very difficult to make out, and may be part of a continuous hum or gurgling drone that conspires to curl itself like a discomfort blanket around the whole arrangement.

The unbroken clanging of the keyboard feels weighty and vaguely desolate in character. This is a real masterstroke. There is a kind of slender, filleted quality to the arrangement that brings the middle and upper register utterances of the lead vocal, guitar, drums and piano into sharp focus, but the music is still not overly flimsy. The result is a metallic mesh of sound marked by the jangle of Hendrix's arpeggios and the military beat of Mitch Mitchell's snare. The song reveals itself to be a twisted march at altitude; a procession through thin air rather than on solid ground.

Right in the middle of the parade there is a dazzling section of "backwards" music which takes the track to another level of enigma that potently reinforces the thought-provoking opening line of the first verse: "If you can just get your mind together". As Kramer recalls, the decision was made to edit a tape with drums and rhythm guitar running backwards to which Hendrix would then overdub a solo that had to be played in such a way as to make harmonic and metric sense heard in reverse.

Kramer explains how the process unfolded, and how ingenious Hendrix was:

> We would give him a tape every night if he was gonna do a backwards solo. He'd take it home and rehearse to it and he'd come in

the next day and say I know exactly where I wanna be and we'd wind the tape and sure enough bang! That's exactly where he's supposed to be. We'd drop in to record ... record it after the tape had been flipped over, and then flip it back the other way and it would be perfect. He knew exactly how far to go and what it would sound like. This was a creation in the studio.[68]

While the brilliance of Hendrix's timing and his ability to conceive chords that made sonic sense when run backwards in the mix is a technical feat, to say the least, the really ear-catching aspect of the whole passage is that there is such fluency where one might have expected disjuncture, which only adds to the overall oddity of the song 'Are You Experienced?' Disparate parts, benefiting from Frankenstein-ian tinkering, form a monster beauty. It is a highpoint of the Kramer–Hendrix creative chemistry insofar as the song feels highly produced yet still very performed. The distinct energy of "in the moment" playing and the more surgeon-like tape manipulation are thus in symbiosis.

Beyond all the specific technical skills that Kramer employed, the inventory of which could easily form the basis of another book altogether, the understanding he had of Hendrix's musical intentions appears pivotal to the ultimate success of the discography, from a sonic point of view. Kramer was able to handle and indeed enhance the large amount of sonic information that Hendrix threw at him, and achieve a degree of balance in the final produced mixes that is really quite astounding.

When discussing the recording sessions with Hendrix, Chas Chandler made a crucial point about Olympic studios, pointing out that it had a circular-shaped "wrap-around desk" so that whoever was manning it didn't need "arms six-foot long to reach all the buttons", which had presumably been the case in some of the previous places in which he had laid down tracks. The new layout thus offered a substantial practical advantage so that Kramer could manage the various levels of volume that were reached by Hendrix and his band with much more precision as a session unfolded.

What sets apart *Are You Experienced?* from *Axis: Bold As Love* and *Electric Ladyland* is the fact that Kramer compressed the drums in mono on the debut album and in stereo on the two that followed. Yet there is a pleasing coherence in the sound he achieved on all three, perhaps because there was already such a strong creative dynamic at play from the outset, which saw musicians and engineer move through a series of ideas where vision was matched by execution, from the backwards guitar solo of 'Are You Experienced?' to the astutely applied phasing techniques of 'Little Wing' to the vividly shaded tableau of '1983 (A Merman I Should Turn To Be)'.

However, there was also something of a delicious paradox in the way Hendrix thought about and engaged with technology. As enthusiastically as he embraced pedals, feedback, distortion and a general studio-as-instrument mindset, he insisted on maintaining a sense of the live "happening" within all the sonic manipulation. Man and machine had to somehow co-exist. "There's something that we want, it goes Sssshhhhwsshh, and we wanna make it sound like that", he stated. "But we don't wanna use tapes or jet airplanes. We want to have the music itself warped."[69] Record a band in the studio that sounds like more than a band but still is a band. Sure.

Hendrix was aware of the danger of going too far in the direction of sonic fantasia if it came at the expense of authenticity. He wanted music to retain a lived-in character. Perhaps unaware of the irony of an artist who was wont to stack up several guitar parts on a single track, Hendrix hurled a brickbat in the direction of the polished aesthetics of Motown[70] because he felt the large resources – strings, brass, reeds, rhythm section, lead and backing singers – had fallen into the arch trap of disproportionate gloss. "They put about a thousand people on tambourines and these bells, you know, they gotta thousand horns, a thousand violins and then a singer, he overdubs his voice millions of times, and he'll sing in an echo chamber full of this and that, and it comes out so artificial ... it's so synthetic, you know, synthetic soul."[71] In other words, Hendrix advocated outré production, not overproduction.

All the lights off in the studio ... that alright ... sure it's OK?

While recognition of the achievements of Hendrix and collaborators in the studio are absolutely necessary they often sadly cast into shadow another element of his artistry: his voice. If we are to gain any complete understanding of who he was musically then the fact that he was a singer as well as player and songwriter needs to be recognized. The lack of attention paid to this aspect of his creative persona is understandable because of his virtuosity on the guitar as well as the quality of his songwriting.

Hendrix used his voice extensively throughout his career as an artist in his own right, and although there are many pieces he wrote in which the arrangement decisively tips in favour of the guitar, as in the superb rendition of 'All Along The Watchtower', he actually recorded relatively few fully instrumental pieces.

Still, the very co-existence of the vocalist-guitarist and guitarist-vocalist in the one creative being was complex, quite simply because these skills were tightly interconnected. Yet those who had a close working relationship with him observed that there was a reluctance, if not a discomfort, he had to overcome before he even stepped to the mike and opened his mouth. Here is the testimony of Eddie Kramer on the subject of what needed to be done for Hendrix to psych himself up to sing a take, identifying a deep insecurity.

> He hated the way he sounded. He thought he had the worst voice in the world. He was embarrassed about his vocal performance, so much so that I had to build a series of screens – three sides

> – facing away from the control windows so nobody could see what he was doing. We'd turn all the lights off in the studio, except for a little light where he had his lyrics, and he would do the take and we would stop, and he would poke his head around the side of the screen and say "Hey, how was that? Was that alright? Are you sure it's OK?"[72]

Determining the precise reason for the unease is difficult because the subject was not openly discussed in any interviews, to my knowledge. One can speculate on a number of things, though. It is generally accepted that Hendrix was a shy individual and that his scene-stealing showmanship on stage was at odds with a mild countenance off stage. Maybe the antics were a form of escapism for his natural tendency was to be understated. There was no doubting his command of the guitar so it made sense for him to feel a degree of freedom if not self-empowerment when he was in the act of playing. After all, that was what drew no end of superlatives. That became the story. The *thing.* All of which could have exacerbated any misgivings about his ability to sing.

One might also bear in mind the vocalists he backed in his formative years: Wilson Pickett, Little Richard, Ronald Isley, Don Covay, Sam Cooke, Jackie Wilson. These regal gents helped to define the art of soul singing between the late 1950s and mid-1960s, and have a legacy that extends far into modern pop. Their voices are simply timeless. To Hendrix they could have been as much a source of intimidation as inspiration, for fear that he would not be able to reach the high bar they had set, which is entirely feasible given the fact that his focus was so taken by the task of complete mastery of the guitar. In Hendrix there was a *virtuoso* player who also sang rather than a singer who accompanied himself on guitar. He is thus comparable to the likes of T-Bone Walker, B.B. King and George Benson insofar as the guitar was not a secondary form of expression to his singing. The voice could easily be overshadowed by the guitar.

Perhaps the greatest sign of a certain ambivalence that Hendrix retained in the use of his voice was the decision to hand the role of lead vocalist to other musicians in the groups of which he was the clearly identified leader-frontman. Bassist Noel Redding sang lead on 'She's So Fine' (*Axis: Bold As Love*) and 'Little Miss Strange' (*Electric Ladyland*), as did drummer Buddy Miles on 'Them Changes' (*Band Of Gypsys*).

What are we to make of this? On one hand it could be seen as a sign of generosity from Hendrix insofar as he is allowing a sideman to temporarily occupy the bandleader's chair. On the other hand he is perhaps showing real strength of character because he knows that ultimately he is still the star attraction. Were he more narcissistic or indeed unsure of his own position he would not have relinquished the spotlight at all.

Tellingly, the above songs were not written by Hendrix. Redding and Miles had penned what they sang. And that may have been the decisive factor. To all intents and purposes Hendrix felt most comfortable singing the words he had written *himself*, unless covering a song which he felt very strongly about, and that could be anything by his peers such as Bob Dylan, Cream and The Beatles to several of his sources of inspiration such as Chuck Berry, Howlin' Wolf, Willie Dixon and Muddy Waters.

That said, Hendrix the singer appears to be, first and foremost, an exponent of his own way with an idiosyncratic lyric as opposed to a virtuoso vocalist who sets out to impress by the gymnastic phrasing and majesty of tone that have become synonymous with exponents of R&B, gospel and jazz. The diehard cliché about a soul singer being able to sing the contents of a phone book and nonetheless make the performance engaging if not deeply moving is not particularly helpful, yet it carries a grain of truth, especially when one considers how a master of the art such as Otis Redding, who Hendrix seriously revered, could bring immense emotional depth and artistic value to nothing other than a string of babyish syllables. Why sing Fa-Fa-Fa when you can sing Fa-Fa-Fa-Fa-Fa-Fa-Fa-Fa-Fa-Fa-Fa-Fa-Fa-Fa-Fa-Fa-Fa and make those 17 delicious idling notes of the chorus of his 1966 classic 'Sad Song' into a beguiling "sweet melody", "a lovely line" that tells a story.[73] The result is a thing of beauty.

Hendrix, however, did not aim to make blues purely from the sound of his voice. His primary intention was to bring carefully considered words to life, but that priority is not just vying for space with his guitar, which is a springboard for virtuosity. As previously mentioned, his voice and guitar often entwine so that the position of one element in the foreground and the other in the background is by no means cut and dried. This intermingling of sounds lends credence to the argument that Hendrix may have well seen the voice as a secondary rather than primary instrument, which completely chimes with Kramer's account of his shyness in front of the microphone.

Yet there are a few salient points about Hendrix's notable vocal performances that are worth bearing in mind. Firstly, for a singer who lacked the heaviness of a baritone such as Redding he was nonetheless capable of a strong attack when needed, upholding the blues tradition of the shout without necessarily hitting the levels of a classic shouter. Listen to the way he punches out the verses in 'Fire', 'Purple Haze', 'Crosstown Traffic' and 'Stone Free' or the way he tears into the choruses of 'If 6 Was 9' or the final sung part of 'All Along The Watchtower'. In each case there is an intensity in the vocal delivery that matches the vibrant colour of the work on the guitar, or perhaps either consciously or subconsciously draws a degree of inspiration from it.

At the other end of the spectrum, Hendrix is a singer who is soft and gentle. One could say that he has a sensitivity in performances at low tempo and an ability to convey a degree of thoughtfulness that closely align with the way that he came across in many interviews. The delicacy of his ballad singing matches the eloquence of his conversation. Think of the sharp melancholy he conveys in 'The Wind Cries Mary', where there is very little embellishment of the verses.

For the most part Hendrix is very economic and spare, hanging just long enough on line endings to bring a sense of melodic shape without going overboard to make the theme too dramatic. There is no melisma. Such sobriety absolutely works in the context of a song with such a deep melancholy, for Hendrix almost has an apologetic tone, a knowing contrition wrapped up in a voice that dare not be raised too loudly. In short he is entirely personal and strikingly confessional, bringing a range of impactful nuance to his delivery to ensure that every single word carries meaning and feeling.

Even more delicate are the gorgeous 'Angel', where Hendrix is convincingly blissed out and dreamy, and 'Drifting', which has a similarly hazy, smoky, almost slumbering ambiance. 'Little Wing' is another level of intimacy, which is again defined by the restraint and balance Hendrix brings to the song. He is often whispering the words rather than singing, making a virtue of a quiet, self-effacing character, the fragility of his voice to the fore as much as its ferocity is displayed on the other numbers in his songbook.

His elongation of notes, such as "through the clouds", is done with a tonal control so as to convey a peak of emotion without hitting a melodramatic high that one might expect from a more showboat vocalist. The ethereal nature of the image is mirrored by a notable lightness of timbre, which serves the unforced flow of the melody. The beauty of the phrasing, with its tentative, almost creeping carriage, is entirely appropriate, and although 'Little Wing' is far removed from an acoustic jazz ballad in terms of its sound canvas – bear in mind that Hendrix's guitar solo heats and hardens considerably in the latter stage of the piece – there is in the singer's poise a hint of the solemnity created by Billie Holiday on anthems such as 'God Bless The Child'. In other words, the vocal ends up floating with dignity over the chords and underlying pulse.

Amid the airy drift of the first verse is a significant event that says much about Hendrix's deep roots in black music. When he reaches the sixth line of the stanza his delivery alters. He does *not* sing "That's all she ever thinks about". He speaks the line. It marks a significant contrast with the phrases that precede and follow, creating a momentary informality whereby Hendrix steps out of his role as a singer and into one as a confidant to the listener. There is thus an added degree of intimacy as a result.

Then again a switch to spoken word can also convey aggression, as is the case on 'Crosstown Traffic' where Hendrix is spitting out many of the verses as a heated remonstration with a girlfriend in a tempestuous relationship. The sexual metaphor of "tyre tracks all across your back, I can see you had your fun" is very conversational, delivered as a kind of spontaneous comeback to a complaint during a lovers' tiff.

Throughout the song Hendrix slips freely between the roles of singer and speaker. This kind of "talking blues" reaches far back into African-American folk culture and has possibly its most influential exponents in the form of

Leadbelly and John Lee Hooker, and it can also be argued that the blues is such a medium for personal expression that a launch into monologue is an option available to any artist who knows the music's roots. The aforementioned could be emphatically verbose and blur the line between singing and talking much more frequently and conspicuously in their songs, such as Hooker's quite majestic 'Moses Smote The Water'. But this option of abandoning melody and launching into spoken word has considerable artistic value when deployed with care.

What is striking in Hendrix's work as a vocalist is how measured is his use of the technique. There are several instances in songs where it happens so seamlessly that it is easy to miss. Yet the way he exits singer mode and enters narrator mode adds to the detailed narrative patchwork knitted together by a musician who is also a storyteller. For example, 'Belly Button Window'[74] is an utterly charming, existential honky-tonk blues in which Hendrix has a notably relaxed, unhurried delivery in the sung lines that see him view life inside his mother's womb. There are short melodic phrases such as: "What seems to be the hang?" As the song unfolds Hendrix starts liberally dropping in wry spoken observations about how he sure remembers "the last time, baby" and that he won't be "coming down this way again" in the future.

Irregularity thus breaks the regularity of the scansion. Hendrix's alterations of delivery effectively loosen the song structure so that he comes across as a playful thinker who is philosophizing on conception, and related issues such as birth control and the embryonic setting in which he finds himself, of which he logically says "sure is dark in here". His none-too-cheery view is expressed as a frank spoken declaration about "looking out my belly button window" where he sees "nothing but a lot of frowns". Finally, he signs off with a sung line, a subtle hint at the (still) vexed subject of abortion: "I'm wondering if you want me around".

A minor entry in the Hendrix canon, 'Belly Button Window' is instructive of a certain mercurial quality, an unpredictability in the singer's phrasing, which parallels the spontaneity of his guitar playing. From a practical point of view the shifts from sung lines to spoken word enable Hendrix to create a much greater sense of dialogue in his performances, as if he wanted to be able to make a direct appeal to the listener in an unadorned way; this direct communication is a central tenet of the blues.

Sometimes the spoken-word moment can be fleeting and relatively easy to miss but it is by no means inconsequential. In 'Room Full Of Mirrors' the coda sees Hendrix move liberally between melodic phrase and spoken word and after singing "Lord, I know who will be for me", he quickly utters that the "meantime ... is a groovy time to me".

'If 6 Was 9' is memorable for its entire bridge section done as a monologue in which Hendrix denounces the white-collared conservatives "flashing down the street", while the majestic band version of 'Hear My Train A Comin'' is practically all spoken word with some fleeting interruptions of singing rather than the other way round. No greater summary of the beauty of this contrast can be found than in the first verse where Hendrix sings *take me* and then immediately speaks *take me.* The rendition of the same phrase in two different ways highlights the distinct nature of the two types of delivery Hendrix has at his disposal but also serves notice of how much freedom he allows himself with meter, for as the song progresses he constantly moves between options, repeating the technique again but in reverse. He speaks "tears burnin' me" and then sings "tears burnin' me in my eyes", giving the lines a clear twist in attack, making both the musical and emotional effect that much more powerful.

On the solo version of 'Hear My Train A Comin'', where Hendrix sang and accompanied himself on 12-string guitar, he again varies his delivery in the song's closing lines, moving liberally between spoken and sung lines, sometimes giving the same words – "Gonna buy this town" – a series of different inflections. His adlibs are unrestrained.

For the most part this is not at all on a par with the more ear-catching vocal gymnastics of jazz singers, particularly those who are skilled practitioners of the scat tradition, but these fairly simple, often minimal nuances imbue many a Hendrix song with different levels of intensity, as if he were deliberately choosing to create some additional breathing space, or a range of both colour and movement in his voice. Hendrix the singer and narrator therefore co-exist. Each appears bound to the other.

One of the great conjunctions of the two occurs on 'Burning Of The Midnight Lamp'. In the second verse the melodic pattern is well established by the striking opening two lines that evoke "the smiling portrait of you", which is seen "on my frownin' wall". Then Hendrix makes a decisive and dramatic change to the phrasing of an extended line that starts with "It really doesn't" and trips straight into "really doesn't bother me" as if the narrator falls into interior monologue, trying to convince himself he is in control of a situation fraught with distress caused by a sense of deep isolation.

What was previously a steady contemplation thus becomes something much more tetchy and agitated. This sudden burst of emphatic spoken repetition shatters the composure of the singing up until that point. Hendrix wilfully loses his cool, energizing his voice and heating his tone a touch to undermine all the apparent indifference expressed by the words. It is a simple but clever conceit. As the rhythmic feel of the verse jumps from a casual quarter note-led pulse to a busier eighth note thrust that resolves melodically with "too much at all", the narrator conveys marked tension. The new delivery of the words acts as a counterpoint to their stated meaning.

It *does* bother him. *Really.* The heavy solitude is in the key word of the song, "alone", that Hendrix elsewhere turns into the melodramatically elongated phrase, *ah ... loh ... oh ... one.* Here then is Hendrix the vocalist liberally playing with the shape of his verses, as many of his peers in the world of soul had done, on one of many subjects for which he would pen a quotable lyric.

Its crutch, its old age and its wisdom … the wind, writes Jimi

With Hendrix the singer who didn't believe he could sing came Hendrix the lyricist who did believe he could write lyrics. It is not unreasonable to argue that his flourish on paper aligns with his conversational skills and off-the-cuff repartee on stage.

Sometimes there would be irony and puckish word play, such as introducing a set of songs as a bunch of O.B.B. – "Oldies But Baddies", a twist on the black slang of O.B.G. – "Oldies But Goodies" – or a saltier riposte when he felt that some banter from an audience member or broadcaster crossed a line. On numerous occasions he was quizzed on the subject of the world's greatest guitarist, an all too obvious bait in reference to the graffiti *Eric Clapton Is God*, and he simply refused to be reeled in, shooting back with "whether there was something as the best girlfriend in the world".

Hendrix's ripostes could also be sexually provocative. When in 1968 a male audience member at a gig in Anaheim, California, hollered "Fuck you, Jimi!" Hendrix produced the quite majestic putdown of "You're not my type, man".[75]

These moments are instructive. Relatively little is known about Hendrix's formal education, although he is on record stating that he was a "high school dropout". How he fared in English lessons would have been interesting to know because what comes across in both his conversation and lyric writing is wit as well as an interest in debate, exposition, rhetoric, narrative and characterization, often with poetic inclinations.

At several points in my analysis thus far I have quoted lyrics to show how they often reinforce musical intent, but the words also require examination in their own right. 'Burning Of The Midnight Lamp' is as good place as any to investigate Hendrix's texts because it presents both his ability to create striking images and plot a strong narrative thread through a standard verse and chorus structure. Lyrically, this is a desolate if not bleak affair that starts with an incredibly stark piece of scene setting that conveys an utterly downcast atmosphere. His opening salvo is blunt in the extreme. An uncompromisingly maudlin view is presented in a few spare words. There is something of Baudelaire's spleen, a totally grim resignation to lifelessness. To start with something as irrevocably dismal as "The morning is dead" is clear enough notice of a troubled state of mind but to reinforce it with "And the day is too" really draws a very dark veil over the scene. The only thing on the horizon is despair.

Just a few lines on, Hendrix's first foray into a more fanciful world comes by way of the "velvet moon". Thereafter he presents emotionally charged images such as "the same old fireplace", of which he no doubt tires, and the "forgotten earring laying on the floor" which is "facing coldly towards the door", an arresting symbol of romance as a fading, spiteful force rather than sweet solace. Even more troubling is the abstract thought of "the circus in the wishing well". A place for fulfilment is actually now synonymous with uproarious clowns. This is musical theatre of pain not joy. Hendrix is projecting a life full of hazardous confusion rather than likely fulfilment.

The central image in the chorus finds the narrator in a state of dissatisfaction that is a subtle straddling of the two distinct worlds he conjures up. He continues to "burn the midnight lamp", which can be immediately understood as a cipher for his solitude, but it is an anachronism not a symbol of the modern world. The common metaphor is to burn the midnight oil, not the lamp, therefore Hendrix has given himself minor poetic license. The lamp is a decidedly archaic symbol, a word whose primary association is a candle housed in a curved glass holder, possibly held by hand by a Victorian gentleman wearing a bonnet or nightshirt in an age of dark winters, smoke-filled streets and chimney sweeps. Metaphorically the midnight lamp vividly speaks of a bygone era.

It could be argued that the language completely reinforces the specific sounds deployed on the song. After all, the central melodic theme is played on a harpsichord, an instrument associated with composers of the Renaissance and baroque eras. The subtext of working late into the night implied by the words is given a sharp emotional twist because Hendrix makes it clear from the first chorus what his condition is. He signs off with the simple but potent word "alone", and as the song reaches its climax he makes a passionate clarification: "Loneliness is such a drag".

Hendrix cuts right to the chase. Any doubt on what has really motivated the lyrics in the first place is cleared up. Hendrix would later confirm as much in an interview: "I wrote part of the song on a plane between L.A. and New York and finished it in the studios in America. There are some very personal things in there, but I think everyone can understand the feeling when you're travelling that no matter what your address there is no place you can call home."[76] This is one of the most honest and instructive statements Hendrix ever made about the reality of his short life, which surfaces powerfully in much of his lyrics. Hendrix the firestarter guitarist was also a great ballad player, and showed marked awareness of his emotional state amid the slings and arrows of an eventful career. Several other key songs address heartache.

The well-documented context for 'The Wind Cries Mary' – a row with girlfriend Kathy Etchingham who Hendrix often referred to by her middle name Mary (just as she used his, Marshall) – may make the piece in Hendrix's own words "nothing but a story about a break up". However, the imagery of the text carries far deeper meanings.

Hendrix's deconstruction of common language is notable. A popular child's toy is put away – "After all the jacks are in their boxes" – while another symbol of merriment is overturned – "clowns have gone to bed". (Or does he mean fools, people who are acting up, rather than benignly entertaining? Is he evoking a human circus, a domestic tragic-comedy? In any case the prevailing subtext is that laughter time is over.) Thereafter Hendrix evinces a deeply troubled state of mind, with a couplet in which the ideal of fulfilment is vividly personified as a drunken, if not wounded warrior. He tells us that what he hears is "happiness staggering down the street" and that what we see is no less alarming – something elegant but bloody: "Footprints dressed in red".

He then escalates the sadness through a truly brilliant tableau, with a touch of Dylanesque dramatic grandeur: "A broom is drearily sweeping" is a charged image of domestic ennui that is given a sharp existential twist as it turns out that what is on the floor are "broken pieces of yesterday's life". Suddenly the scene assumes real gravitas as we are asked to contemplate the misery of the highest members of the land ("Somewhere a queen is weeping") to such an extent that the Royal household is now coming apart ("Somewhere a king has no wife"). Next Hendrix flips back to everyman with a clever subversion of a common feature of modern urban life that enables him to bring a revealingly sharp focus to his inner turmoil and an overwhelming isolation. The traffic lights "turn blue tomorrow" and shine "their emptiness down on my bed".

Finally, there is a submission to nature, a force that endures but can also erase history. Hendrix pertinently asks if the wind will remember "names it has blown in the past?" He then imbues the element with everyday human accoutrements and virtues, "its crutch, its old age, its wisdom", before concluding that the sense of loss is definitive. He hears it whisper "no, this will be the last". The wind brings no act of remembrance.

From happiness to emptiness Hendrix touches on profound universal angst, locating it right on the floor of a kitchen or living room, the place where smashed crockery may end up following a row over a badly cooked meal. The traffic light turning blue, the colour of sadness, flows from the reality of Hendrix following Etchingham to a street corner after she stormed out of their flat in the midst of an argument. Like the best of writers Hendrix has decided to use real events and first-hand experience as a raw material to make observations of a great philosophical magnitude. His life is symbol.

Furthermore, his recourse to the near-divine supremacy of nature for the song's defining image – wind is a source of memory and wisdom and has powers of speech – puts him in the lineage of centuries of poets, novelists and songwriters who turned to the elements for characterization. 'The Wind Cries Mary' loosely aligns with any number of gospel or soul songs that evoke river and mountain, or a Broadway anthem such as Kern/Hammerstein's 'Ol' Man River', which is a silent witness to the plight of "darkies" in the 1927 musical *Showboat*. But what would have been much more personal to Hendrix is the superb lyric of a blues classic he recorded, Elmore James's 'Bleeding Heart'. Again loneliness is to the fore and the natural world is paramount. Every morning he hears "birds call my name" because his "heart is in so much pain".

'The Wind Cries Mary' is a graceful paean to nature built on the premise of a lovers' tiff and stands as one of Hendrix's most poetic outpourings, demonstrating that he had a real gift for conveying strong emotions by way of a range of imagery that could move seamlessly from concrete to abstract. It is a text that generates a strong, affecting emotional charge that also broached a greater philosophical discourse.

The life of a successful musician in the mid-1960s, when Hendrix rose to prominence, was becoming a subject of increasing social debate. The Beatles, the Rolling Stones and Cream were just a few of the British groups who travelled extensively in the wake of international success. Hendrix was well used to exactly what being on the road meant, given his extensive experience of the chitlin circuit in his formative years. He had endured Spartan living conditions when playing venues where sometimes there was no guarantee of either accommodation or remuneration if musicians had the misfortune of dealing with more unscrupulous promoters. As Hendrix's fame grew in the late 1960s he became a magnet for hangers-on of all descriptions, from groupies to other musicians, who wanted to bask in the glow of his success and a known generosity that would often lead him to indulge a friend such as Brian Jones, even though he would stop short of letting the Rolling Stone lay down a desperately out-of-tune piano part on an early take of 'All Along The Watchtower'.

Loneliness is one of the biggest clichés in the starry rock 'n' roll lifestyle but in Hendrix's case it appears to have been sadly true. He became surrounded by no end of people at the peak of his commercial powers, but whether he found *true* happiness, and more to the point stability, emotionally and mentally, is a moot point. Numerous musicians tell the story of groupies playing Hendrix in the most cynical of ways, sponging money off him and, most callously, walking away with prized items from his wardrobe. It is a soul-destroying downside of a celebrity lifestyle where material success did not automatically ensure peace of mind. Female fans who fleeced big-name musicians did not just spring up after the rise of the white rock star such as Mick Jagger et al. Black bandleaders were, in the worst-case scenario, known to have been held up at gunpoint by a "hoochie mama" who eyed their hard-won earnings. Making it could easily lead to others making off with it.

Transience and rootlessness were realities in Hendrix's daily life that extensively permeated his lyric writing, but what is interesting is the insecurity that attended his life of flights and hotel rooms is offset by a recognition that he nonetheless had a degree of freedom that eluded those who did not face the rigours of extensive touring. If the assertion of independence were not clear enough through the song title 'Stone Free', Hendrix spells out what life on the road means to him in the opening lines, and his need to keep moving on in order to avoid negative forces in his life. Whether he is talking about opportunistic women or exploitative music industry types isn't clear but he marks out what he sees as perils. He is shuttling from one city to another and if he does not stay in transit then he finds "people try[ing] to pull me down". There is a safety in gigging.

Call it the romance of the freewheeling hobo or wanderer, or the paranoia of an individual who is actually scared of responsibility. In any case the need to make a run for it surfaces in other pieces such as 'Lover Man' where the desperation is even more pronounced as Hendrix grabs his suitcase so that he can "get the hell out".

Therein lies a central paradox. Constant transit occasioned by life as an artist leads to loneliness and an inability to form meaningful relationships, yet that still cannot quell the restlessness Hendrix feels, the desire to stay on the road despite its concomitant hardships. In 'Gypsy Eyes' he makes it clear that his paramour is almost a reflection of himself, destined to be a vagabond, "one that rambles on for a million miles", which is one of Hendrix's most potent bursts of hyperbole.

Yet this existence on the fly could reflect more than the bitty lifestyle of an itinerant musician. When Hendrix says that he has no choice but to move on he is possibly talking about his development artistically so that his music keeps on evolving. And in the latter verses of 'Gypsy Eyes' he posits the interesting scenario of spiritual fulfilment. He's searching not just for "your love". What he really needs is "my soul too".

Hendrix is consistent with his references to existential concerns throughout his songbook. 'Manic Depression', after all, is not just mental pain. The hurt is "touching my soul". 'Drifter's Escape' presents the scenario of the titular anti-hero hauled before a court but the judge declares that there is more than jail time at stake. "Hey, you better leave that boy's soul alone." An even greater sense of Hendrix's metaphysical leanings comes in one of the most resonant lines in '1983 (A Merman I Should Turn To Be)', which heralds the prospect of reincarnation against a backdrop of alienation from a world of conflict as he seeks to be reborn away from "a life so battered and torn".

There are moments where Hendrix is just plain beguiling, as on 'Ain't No Telling' where he abruptly says of Cleopatra: "She's driving me insane/She's trying to put my body in her brain." On 'Castles Made of Sand' the fragility of life takes a strange and tragic turn when Hendrix describes the fate of the "little Indian brave" who would one day grow to be a "fearless warrior Indian Chief". On the eve of his first battle, a great tragedy struck as a "surprise attack killed him in his sleep that night". It is a resoundingly dark denouement, even more so because it marks a decisive shift of tone compared to the previous verse which depicts an altercation between a couple, possibly husband and wife, who draw attention from gossip-hungry neighbours.

Again the downcast, lugubrious strand of Hendrix's lyrics comes to the fore, and invites speculation on whether there is an intensity to the descriptive scenes because he has drawn on a deep well of personal experience to flesh out the song. 'Castles Made of Sand' are destined for destruction, to be washed away by the tide and disappear, and it is possible that the theme of dejection, if not defeat, and the uncertainty of the family unit and long-lasting relationships in general had been viewed through a more pessimistic prism as Hendrix felt the pressure of fame.

The reference to the "little Indian brave" is all the more intriguing because of the Cherokee heritage Hendrix claimed, which is relatively widespread among African-Americans, of which a notable example is jazz legend Wayne Shorter, a superlative improviser and composer, who, like Hendrix, also had a lifelong interest in science-fiction. Hendrix was vocal about his native American roots and spoke warmly of his Cherokee grandmother, with whom he spent summer vacations on a reservation in Vancouver where he witnessed a community in the grip of deprivation and prone to substance abuse. He would recall the shocking nature of what he saw years later. "There's some of them that have a lot of money. But a lot of them are on the reservation, man, it was really terrible. Every single house is the same, it's not even a house, it's like a hut. Ough. It's just a really bad scene for 'em, you know. Like half of them are down in skid row, drinking and completely out of their minds."[77]

Even more interesting is the fact that this first-hand experience of an ethnic minority group from which he was partly descended was compounded by a widespread stigmatization of Native Americans, which Hendrix became more aware of when he was still at high school. The racism was openly expressed. "I used to get so mad though 'cause of what the teachers was telling us ... 'Indians are bad!'"[78] Years later he found out how invisible and indistinguishable black artists were to some whites.

If there was an understanding of how deeply bigotry ran then there were also incidents that occurred that would have fuelled his sense of marginalization. His Cherokee grandmother made clothes for him such as shawls and ponchos that he wore to school only to be subjected to ridicule from other pupils. This laid the groundwork for self-definition as an individual who would not be cowed by officials whether it was the armed forces, which Hendrix joined because he didn't have "a cent in his pocket", or R&B bands whose frontmen were the centre of attention and brooked no flashy licks or threads that would upstage them. Although the extreme boredom of life in the barracks, especially the day-long sessions of potato peeling, drove him to distraction, the artistic constraints placed upon him by a tightly marshalled revue also induced a fair amount of resentment. Little Richard was more flamboyant than a drill sergeant but by no means any more tolerant of maverick guitarists. Although Hendrix counted himself lucky to be able to pursue a career in music, once he, to his great relief, managed to get discharged from the army he often still found himself in very difficult situations, where he would get "burned", as in reprimanded by the bandleader because what he did was deemed too outlandish.

As one might expect, the success enjoyed by Hendrix and The Experience emboldened him to pursue his own path with a vengeance, both artistically and sartorially. However, the adulation heaped on the American expatriate in London by both his British peers and audiences the world over did not necessarily quell some of the more negative, if not debilitating feelings that had regularly marked his personal life.

What comes across in Hendrix the interviewee as well as the artist on stage is a beguiling blend of energy and sensitivity. Extraversion and introversion are joined at the hip. Gifted and successful as he was, Hendrix continually recognized his own state of otherness during a short lifetime marked by the pressures induced by fame and the stress of having to generate product, be it in the guise of a stadium appearance or a new album.

There is a steeliness in some of his writing that often reflects substantial feelings of cynicism, an unabashed challenge to others and a defiance of authority. The lived reality of walking down Carnaby Street in London dressed in a hussar's jacket and drawing gawps from passers-by as if they were bearing witness to the arrival of *something* made it entirely logical that the character of the outsider-drifter-gypsy would feature in many Hendrix songs. Many pieces deal with a clash of views or conflict between either individuals or groups in society and in some of Hendrix's most thought-provoking lyrics he sometimes wraps layers of deep cynicism around this core theme.

For example, 'If 6 Was 9' has a basic premise of a world turned upside down and held in a state of confusion and illusion, where things are not what they seem. The juxtaposition of two different numbers that look alike when inverted is a clever conceit to evoke superficiality and the possibility of seismic events such as "the mountains fell in the sea". Hendrix also conjures up something close to class war by pitting white-collar conservatives with their "plastic finger" against "my kind", who wave the "freak flag". He goads Mr. Businessman who "can't dress like me", which is a line related to his bitchy detractors in 'Stone Free' who "talk about the clothes I wear".

However, 'If 6 Was 9' is not just a straightforward opposition between the flower children of liberal America and the starched suits of the right wing. Allegiance to the "freak flag" puts Hendrix in league with the hippies yet he refrains from taking sides in too peremptory a manner. He recognizes situations can change and that the act of social rebellion that can attract great censure, as Marvin Gaye points out in 'What's Going On' – "who are they to judge us just because our hair is long" – will not always prove to be a steadfast conviction. Showing a similar mistrust of middle-class whites as the brilliant black writer Sam Greenlee, author of the visionary *The Spook Who Sat by the Door*,[79] Hendrix implies that hippies are not necessarily righteous. After all, they could turn out to be tomorrow's businessman. The constant in the midst of such vagaries is the individual who takes responsibility for *himself*. There are intimations of mortality as Hendrix bucks against those around him. He is indifferent to a possible volte-face of the counterculture – "the hippies cut off their hair" – because he does not want to sheepishly follow any crowd – "I ain't going to copy." He is entirely resigned to the ultimate fate of death, and reasons that nobody can live his life "the way I want to". Again, one of the central statements in the Hendrix book of lyrics comes to the fore: the right to be a singular personality in a society that can be profoundly judgemental.

That the artist also raised the spectre of death just a few years before his own passing lends a disturbing but also poignant undertone to the above lines, and to 'If 6 Was 9' on the whole insofar as it suggests that the crushing wheels of destiny won't stop turning amid the prevailing draught of disorientation that is identified by the narrator. In no uncertain terms Hendrix is exercising his desire to make observations on the current, mostly turbulent state of the world, from his vantage point as a free spirit. Hence there is recognition of the place of the counter-culture that was gaining ground in the 1960s, yet at the same time a subtle distancing from it, or rather an expression of a certain mistrust of others that has already been alluded to in other compositions.

As can be heard in the numerous interviews he gave in his lifetime Hendrix was not reluctant to express opinions on a plethora of subjects, from reincarnation and astral travelling to drug use and government institutions. He spoke about the evolution of the human race and the need to legalize abortion, which was a courageous stance to take in the America of his day, as it still is today given that the debate continues to rage on.

There are many Hendrix songs that betray a desire to explore a theme laterally as well as literally, often without much restraint in content. On occasion Hendrix wrote a lot of words, even if he subsequently decided to edit them. He admitted to an epic streak.

> Oh, you should hear the real 'Purple Haze', it has about 10 verses. But it goes into different changes ... It had about a thousand words. You should have heard it man. I had it written out. It's about going through all these ... this land, you know.
>
> This mythical ... 'cos that's what I like to do is write a lot of mythical scenes. You know, like the history of the wars on Neptune and all this mess you know. And the reason why the ring, the rings were there; see like how they got the Greek gods and all that mythology. Well you can have your own mythology scene. Or write, you know, fiction. Complete fiction, though, you know. I mean anybody can say "Well I was walking down the street, and I see an elephant floating through the sky".[80]

Martian sunsets, a Venus witch's ring, Jupiter's sulphur mines

A cursory scan of Hendrix's lyrics shows that he absolutely did not restrict himself to the material world when it came to creating scenarios that he explored in his songs. What jumps out in so many texts is the breadth of references and statements that move from transparent to opaque, concrete to abstract, explicit to implicit in a sometimes unpredictable if not desultory way. Through his texts Hendrix displays both an interest in language and desire to fully indulge his imagination.

Numerous are the flights of fancy in his lyrics. In 'Have You Ever Been (To Electric Ladyland)' he promises that "the magic carpet waits for you". In 'Spanish Castle Magic' there is talk of reaching the titular destination – which is not in Spain – "by dragonfly". In 'Up From The Skies' there is a terrifying global meltdown – "the smell of a world that has burned" – and subsequent rebirth – "I want to know about the new Mother Earth", which acquires a notable resonance today, given the pressing climate change debate. Such flourishes of imagery can be seen as Hendrix's boldness and desire to put a signature on his work, in addition to a literary impulse that may have been triggered by his first few months in Britain, when manager-producer Chas Chandler, who accommodated him, lent him many science-fiction books, the most notable of which was George R. Stewart's *Earth Abides*, a post-apocalyptic tale published in 1949 which described the end of civilization by way of deadly disease.

Although it is clear that exposure to these works had a significant impact on Chandler's gifted protégé, it is also worth remembering that Hendrix himself claimed that his penchant for such subject matter ran much deeper in his personal history, right back to his childhood in fact. An abiding memory of his school days was his love of art classes. Part 1 of this volume referred to sketches of musicians that Hendrix made as a child but, looking back on those days he also made this intriguing revelation: "The teacher used to say 'Paint three scenes'. And I'd do abstract stuff like Martian sunsets."

Given these portents it stands to reason that Hendrix was such an audio-visual creative being and that the content of some of his work includes references that were extra-terrestrial, the obvious example of which is 'Third Stone From The Sun', with its talk of an alien spaceship en route to earth. There is a clear interest in science fiction. Hendrix can't resist a few turns of phrase that lighten the mood. So the spaceship is described as a "kinky machine" and instead of the visitors remarking on an expected landmark such as the pyramids, they single out "your majestic superior cackling hen", one of the most bizarre images in the Hendrix songbook. The piece ends with the threat of destruction wrapped up in a burst of wacky irreverence. The alien vows to do away with earthlings so "you'll never hear surf music again".

There is a playful, if not mischievous slant in Hendrix's thinking and writing. He can be puckish and sarcastic and serious if not portentous in the space of two or three verses, as 'Third Stone From The Sun' demonstrates. These frequent changes of register make some songs less accessible than others but a clearly mapped linear narrative is by no means a hard and fast rule for Hendrix when it comes to the process of lyric writing. One of the biggest clues he gave to his modus operandi was that he often set out to deliberately create "a clash between reality and fantasy mostly. You have to use fantasy to show different sides of reality."[81] In other words, he believes in the power of allegory and metaphor. He's taking us "out" in order to be able to go further "in".

Throwing off the straitjacket of the three-minute pop song was an inevitable consequence of that mission statement, so that he could record more than two or three verses. A song that was never recorded but which says much about Hendrix's aesthetic was 'Eyes and Imagination', a piece that he said was "about fourteen minutes long" and which shifted subject matter every two sentences. Furthermore, there was a creation-destruction dynamic captured in the contrast of various effects, from a baby crying to the ricochet of bullets, which served as a prelude to the song's four movements.

Against the disappointment of the piece never being committed to tape, one could weigh a composition that, lyrically, is one of Hendrix's most expressive. 'Bold As Love', which closes the album *Axis: Bold As Love*, is the songwriter at his most positive, if not idealistic and grandiose. The axis refers to the axis on which the earth spins, which as Hendrix posits, can bring about profound change for the better of humanity if it is invested with love. He assigns feelings to colours which have well-known literary associations – "Queen Jealousy has a fiery green gown"; "Red flashes trophies of war" – and there is talk of grand conflict and the raging battle of immense armies.

Yet if Hendrix is intent on achieving the gravitas of a mediaeval ballad or vaguely Arthurian legend by way of the bejewelled poetry of a line such as "Blue are the life-giving waters taken for granted", then true to form, he pulls off one of his most daring cultural and literary pirouettes in the final verse of the lengthy composition. He starts by stating his yellow is "not so mellow", admits that he is frightened, and that his emotional turmoil holds him back from "giving my life to a rainbow like you".

Because the prevailing tone of the lyrics is earnest it is easy to overlook the passing reference in the stanza's opening line to the folk-rock anthem 'Mellow Yellow' by Scottish singer Donovan, which was a hit in the winter of 1967, several months before the release of *Axis: Bold As Love*. Hendrix removes the levity from the other song title and replaces the blissed-out state of being mellow with that of being frightened, and then, in an impressively simple but effective psychodrama he asserts that the overriding reality of the human condition is complexity. The rollercoaster of feelings has incapacitated him in front of the beautiful but beguiling sight of "a rainbow like you". This movement from the many colours of emotion to an individual made of many colours is masterful. It invites all manner of interpretation. On one hand the image speaks of the unfathomable mystery of human nature, the fact that people are multi-faceted, multi-layered entities who can't be reduced to simple, one-dimensional creatures. On the other hand this could reflect a degree of idealism, for if a person is a rainbow, a beautiful spectacle in the sky following a downpour, then the divisive notion of race is impugned, as mooted by the yet-to-be-coined term "rainbow nation".

However, the writer could also be ultimately freighting pessimism. After all, a rainbow is ephemeral. It lights up the sky and then fades away. Hendrix is back in his world of vulnerability and transience, where good things are simply not set to last.

Close attention paid by Hendrix to the music of Bob Dylan, The Beatles and Cream would have inevitably had an effect on his lyric writing, and his penchant for characterization is in line with that of the aforementioned. However, Hendrix's ambition with regard to the breadth and depth of his texts did not mean that he entirely abandoned models of black popular music in which he was well versed.

So clear are the parallels between the lyrics of Cream's 'Tales of Brave Ulysses' and 'Bold As Love', it is not unreasonable to argue that Hendrix was on a similar wavelength as his peers. Where the former, whose text was actually penned by the Australian cartoonist and poet Martin Sharp, presented the tableau of "dancing through the turquoise", "sparkling waves" and "tiny purple fishes", the latter revelled in "shiny metallic purple armour", "turquoise armies" and "ribbons of euphoria". In both cases the result is a text that has a stirring baroque quality, which represents a departure from the quotidian observations that were found in the bulk of 1960s pop.

Although the more fantastical images that imbue the Hendrix songbook suggest a kinship with English folk imaginings or Greek mythology, the imaginative use of natural world and the animal kingdom is also a major part of the lyrical bedrock of the blues. If Hendrix is breaking out of some of the conventions of black pop texts then he does not entirely forgo the major tropes favoured by his direct sources of inspiration. We are so inured by names such as Muddy Waters and Howlin' Wolf that it is easy to forget how ingenious they are. These are two grand *noms de scène* which denote vivid characters, and the possibility of a musician engaging in role-play with a larger than life bravado. This is why another blues legend, the guitarist-vocalist Brownie McGhee, ends up with an alias that is as funny and downright funky as Spider Sam. And also why the peerless John Lee Hooker reaches a gracefully evocative finesse with a song title such as 'She's Long, She's Tall, She Weeps Like A Willow Tree'.

Hendrix is as interested in the supernatural as he is in the natural strain of blues imagery. When we hear him holler *I stand up next to a mountain and I chop it down with the edge of my hand* on 'Voodoo Child (Slight Return)' he is channelling the mysterious and mythical energies of the strain of mostly Louisiana-based cults in which spells are cast, "blackcat bones" are bared and a gypsy woman as well as a man with a mojo can orchestrate events that defy rationale, as detailed in the bewitching music of Waters, Robert Johnson, J.D. Short, Johnnie Temple, and Arthur "Big Boy" Crudup, to name but a few. The phenomenon of throwing a "hoodoo" on another individual or waking up to a destiny that could lead to all manner of ill fortune has roots as deep as tales of guitar players meeting the devil at the crossroads to learn unholy, invaluable musical tricks.

On 'Voodoo Chile' Hendrix makes explicit use of this rich metaphorical database with talk of how on the night of his birth, the "moon turned a fire red" and his mother invoked a strange destiny by crying to the heavens "Lord, the gypsy was right!" As much as he is in Muddy mode, Hendrix proceeds to embark upon a typically wild ride into abstraction, which resonates with the LSD trips and drug culture that became synonymous with artists of his ilk. He sees "mountain lions ... set me on an eagle's back", a "Venus witch's ring", "Jupiter's sulphur mines", "liquid gardens" and "methane sea". In other words, two cultural strands are entwining. Hendrix, the lyric poet drawn to all the portentous majesty of Greek mythology, joins hands with Hendrix the blues raconteur who is able to create a strong miasma by evoking all manner of prophesy and trickster manoeuvres proscribed by Christian religion.

With that in mind it is worth remembering that the chorus of 'Gypsy Eyes' also enters into a magical world where he is *hypnotized* by his paramour or that in the midst of a song in which he expresses lust, such as 'Little Miss Lover', he reverts to mysticism, explaining that it is the "gypsy in me" that has drawn him to a chosen woman.

One might also add that 'Gypsy Eyes', 'Foxy Lady', 'Fire' and 'Crosstown Traffic' are the songs where Hendrix, to use the language he employed himself, goes for "the sex angle", and in the process also occasionally succumbs to the casual misogyny found in the blues and R&B where the focus is very much on a man's wants and needs to the extent that a woman is ornamental or submissive, granted the right to "tag along", or may even be a troublesome presence to overcome: "you can't hold me down" is one of the most resonant lines of the independence anthem 'Stone Free'. Hendrix was simply joining a long lineage of male writers whose imagery could come down on either side of a fine line where woman can be both glorified and objectified. The woman who makes your nature rise or leaves you on the killing floor. The woman who is as liable to have what it takes and use what she has got to get what she wants. The woman who is a "sweet little lovemaker" and a "cute little heartbreaker". The woman who arouses a range of feelings from lust to mistrust, and even contempt.

Such depictions of the archetype of the "Foxy Lady" must be cast against the backdrop of a hectic and hedonistic lifestyle in which, for those who embodied the culture of rock as well as developed it as an art form, sexual conquest was one of the substantial fringe benefits way beyond the reach of most mere mortals.

The phenomenon of the groupie, or the "starfucker", who would target demi-gods seen on stage swivelling hips and wielding guitars is another force that would have fed into the experiential database on which a writer such as Hendrix could draw. His alpha-male status was enhanced not only by the extreme sexual charge of his performances but the knowing deployment of his powers of seduction in the company of his peers, the epitome of which is the pass he audaciously made at Mick Jagger's girlfriend Marianne Faithfull at a nightclub in London at a time when the Stones front man was the reigning lothario of pop for whom there were no serious rivals. The frankly racist statements made by Eric Clapton about people falling for "spades with big dicks" and "that magic thing" also serve as a depressingly stark reminder of how much additional political dynamite there was in the reality of an African-American such as Hendrix having his way with glamorous white women in the mid-1960s, only a decade after race riots had rocked Nottingham and Notting Hill because of tension aroused by the sight of racially mixed couples seen arguing in the street.

Black masculinity has long had to confront the threat it poses to white masculinity and repeated attempts to neuter it. An African-American blues artist singing 'I'm A Man' has to be perceived and understood against the immensely debilitating backdrop of centuries of black men being called "boy". Their perceived sexual threat, as delineated by Clapton, can be seen as part and parcel of a wider war waged for freedom. The bedroom was one of the few areas where a "spade" could feel power.

This in no way makes blatant sexism or sexist behaviour any less excusable. In some cases the woman herself could declare open acceptance of the violent ways of man. Whether or not Hendrix heard jazz legend Billie Holiday make the dolefully resigned plea *He isn't true/He beats me, too/What can I do?* on the song 'My Man' in 1949,[82] there was a widespread blanket of misogyny in culture that would have been impossible for such a sensitive and observant man as him to ignore. Interestingly, Holiday roared right back in defiance on 'Billie's Blues' with: *I've been your slave/Ever since I've been your babe/But before I'll be your dog/I'll see you in your grave.*

One might also add that the issue of the relative lack of autonomy for women, especially black women, in the music industry should not be discounted from any debate on how they were portrayed in song. The rise of songwriters, male and female, across many genres, from Odetta to Bob Dylan and Joni Mitchell, could not change the fact that Holiday was probably given little choice when it came to singing about a wife beater, just as Tina Turner would have felt utterly trapped in the shockingly abusive relationship she had with Ike Turner, which was an open secret that the likes of Hendrix, one of his former sidemen, would most probably have had some knowledge of. As far as post-war feminism is concerned the two compositions make it clear that the battle lines are drawn, and the conflict can swing back and forth between submission and resistance, the recognition of male power and the denigration of its very source.

When Hendrix enters the arena he occasionally betrays emotional impulses that do not stand up particularly well today, deriding his woman as an impediment to his freedom – to enjoy promiscuity – by placing him in a "plastic cage" in 'Stone Free', or suggesting she has ideas above her station in 'Are You Experienced?' that lead him to posture as a snarling Iceberg Slim street hustler who only sees a woman in dollar signs, accusing her of being "made out of gold and can't be sold". On 'Fire' he is typecast as loverman superstud who tells a hapless rival named Rover to move over so that he can "take over" and start to get hot with whoever his chosen conquest may be. It's all about Jimi thinking and acting with his dick.

Pitted against all these testosterone-charged manoeuvres is Hendrix the gentle partner, the exponent of tenderness, the man who worships woman rather than dominates her. The portraits drawn in 'Little Wing', 'Angel' and 'Have You Ever Been (To Electric Ladyland)' are striking because women are invested with uplifting, redemptive and divine powers, the greatest manifestation of which is an ability to resolve the age-old conflict of dark and light, and presumably heal the whole world by making "good and evil lay side by side" while "electric love penetrates the sky".

If that is one of Hendrix's most daring lines, a kind of biblical reckoning which still has a strong sexual undercurrent, then elsewhere in 'Have You Ever Been (To Electric Ladyland)' he pursues faith in a location called "Loveland", which could be seen as a heavenly place for earthly beings. Given that he had a string of girlfriends, not to mention countless encounters with groupies, it is tempting to cast aspersions on the belief Hendrix may have had in *real* love, though he clings firmly to the ideal of it. The affecting conviction with which he sings 'May This Be Love' is a further layer of complexity to Hendrix's vision of love because there is no explicit mention of woman but instead of the beauty of (Mother) nature, whereby woman could be waterfall, rainbow and misty breeze.

However, faith in emotional fulfilment is undermined by everyday life where the artist has to confront his inadequacy and self-doubt – he's "trying to be a man" on 'Stepping Stone' – as well as the poignant reminders of his stark condition as a loner. Often, the game of self-realization defeats Hendrix. The wide range of emotions and outlooks expressed throughout his songbook points to an individual who is deeply conflicted. To a certain extent one could argue that the sheer volume of lyrics Hendrix produced as well as the colourful palette of imagery are a sign of somebody who is struggling with all kinds of issues as much as a creative being who engages body and soul in the art of storytelling and its attendant discipline of sub-text and word play.

(Talkin') blues 'n' greenbacks

Looking back on the short but eventful life of Jimi Hendrix, especially the two-year period, 1967–69, of his meteoric rise and tragic demise, it is tempting to use the word confusion as an appropriate term to describe it. Having said that, electric will forever be associated with him. It has a dual meaning, referring to music played at high volume, to which the guitarist attached a spiritual power, and also evoking the hotly vibrant, thrilling nature of Hendrix as an artist, particularly in live performance.

Hendrix was nothing if not inventive with his use of language, as can be seen in his coining of neologisms such as *Ladyland*. Yet for all the literary flourish, he also used one of the oldest terms in the black vernacular: blues. They may not have featured on the albums released in his lifetime, but 'Earth Blues', 'Georgia Blues', 'Easy Blues' and 'Villanova Junction Blues' are all tracks that Hendrix recorded in the sessions that he was doing up until his death. One of his earliest original songs was 'Jimmy's Blues'.

For such a sophisticated writer, who was carefully *not* marketed as a blues artist, it may have been perceived as hackneyed for him to use a trope such as "I woke up this morning..." Yet his immersion in the form and grasp of the emotive power of key words deployed by its pioneers led him to explicitly use the term blues at times. He starts 'Look Over Yonder' by stating *here come the blues*, while 'Stepping Stone' (January 1970 version) is even more personal: "I sure got the blues this morning".

Rather than reject the classic language of the blues outright, Hendrix opts to make it part of a wide vocabulary that he draws on at will, coming back to it alongside the lyrics of a more fantastical bent elsewhere in his songbook. There is a perfect illustration of this double register character in a formal written assignment Hendrix was given: the sleeve notes for *Expressway To Your Skull*, a 1968 album recorded by Buddy Miles, a member of Band of Gypsys. He seamlessly blends "downhome" terms with trademark off-the-wall imagery. "The bro' ... kicking a can ... tryin' to kick out his blues and jealous hues and in his back pocket he carries a bootful of raw violent silk ... but he doesn't even have to cry because his natural soul shall be washed soon."

As a summary of Hendrix as a cultural coat of many colours the passage is significant, above all for the way he clothes his blackness in threads of abstract meaning and mysterious, if not mesmeric ideas that flow from the well of a mind that will not, or cannot, be confined to purely literal forms of expression. Whether this is tantamount to obfuscating posture or challenging mystique, there is a sense of humanity at the root. Hendrix ends with soul and starts with blues. The words are used here as principle and philosophy that are not to be taken lightly. When asked about his relationship with the blues he had several worthwhile insights, which were emphatically aired when he appeared on *The Dick Cavett Show* in 1969.

Referring to the guitarist's status as one of the highest paid rock stars of his generation, Cavett surmises that it must be hard to play the blues if "you're making hundreds of thousands of dollars [though this assumes you can't be unhappy and rich]". Hendrix is very quick to set him straight. He becomes unguardedly personal.

> Sometimes it gets to be really easy to sing the blues when you're supposed to be making all this much money, you know, because like money it's getting to be out of hand now. And musicians, especially young cats, you know, they get a chance to make all this

> money and say "wow, this is fantastic", and, like I said before, they lose themselves, and they forget about the music themselves, they forget about their talents, they forget about the other half of them, so therefore you can sing a whole lot of blues. The more money you make, the more blues sometimes you can sing.[83]

Hendrix's Afro and turquoise tunic – a material manifestation of the colour parade of 'Bold As Love' – stands in stark contrast to Cavett's side parting, sports jacket and tie. Distracted as the viewer may be by the visual clash between the two men who embody the characters of the gypsy and the square featured in several Hendrix songs, it is worth focusing closely on the artist's demeanour at that moment. He comes across as deeply wistful if not regretful when he utters the last line, which is essentially what a modern-day hip-hop artist might formulate as "mo' money, mo' problems". His argument is for artistic integrity but he's really providing a timely reminder that the blues is actually not just a function of being poor, broke and black. It is about the wherewithal to make something out of circumstances that would be inconceivably dehumanizing to the majority of people. Art may often be borne out of oppression but that doesn't mean the oppressed are automatically born artists. The extreme lack of choice should not be taken as a ticket to jump on an express train to songs that will change the world. African-American musicians who invented the blues were singing not only because they were disenfranchised in the extreme, but *in spite* of their position as chattel and beasts of burden wholly denied the exercise of free will, according to the principles on which slavery and plantation economies were built.

Much as the blues is a means of conveying deep emotion, of creating beauty by way of words and music that will affect others, it hinges on a lot more than spontaneous expression. It is also an act of mental fortitude and prowess. The exponent of the blues has to have the conviction that their own song, regardless of its apparent simplicity, moots the real possibility of optimism, salvation, relief and redemption in the midst of a life that has given them nothing but a "sack o' woe". And what the courageous individual does can grow into a resource for a whole community. Before the blues could even exist, a person so damned and downtrodden they were seen as less than nothing had to imagine they *were* something and could sing about anything.

Lasting just a few moments, the exchange between Hendrix and Cavett is nonetheless significant insofar as it frees any perception and definition of the blues from the straitjacket of assumption and muzzle of cliché. By arguing that the sadness with which the genre is synonymous is *not* confined to destitution, Hendrix is taking it beyond the transparent and superficial and into the realm of the truly universal. He who apparently has everything can actually be no better off than he who has nothing. The poor man's blues does not make impossible the advent of the rich man's blues. The common denominator between the two is the need to declaim: "I'm a man".

Given its conceptual strength and the great courage of its progenitors, it was thus inevitable that the blues would be a place for a range of intellectual pursuits despite the lack of formal education granted to slaves and their descendants. The blues does humour. The blues does sarcasm. The blues does satire. The blues does pathos. The blues does duplicity. The blues does irony. The blues does allegory. The blues has mordant imagination. So if the tale of a woman who *pours water on a drowning man* is a brilliant expression of love gone real bad, then so too is the story of another man who says that when he asked his woman for a cool drink of water on a hot day *she brought me gasoline.*

What is happening while this merry scene plays out? A godly church bell could be tolling or a man and woman could be engaging in the carnal art of rocking 'n' rolling. Sanctity and profanity in harmony warn you of the blues as sweet headspin trickery.

You may believe a sexually charged Hendrix when he says "Let me stand next to your fire!" but what you should really do is question what it means "to get burned" if you decide to play with him. The blues gives him the platform to tell all these life stories. And for you to also muse on your real wants, needs, desires, fears and fantasies. After all, why would you not want to feel the metaphorical heat the song can bring to a cold world? Why would you not want to be burned by a man such as Jimi Hendrix?

Quite apart from the fact that the blues is one of the most deeply expressive and emotionally rich forms of expression in human history, it has always had a vexed relationship with the primary constituency from which it was born because of the truths it may tell rather than the myths it cultivates. Whether Robert Johnson pimped himself with the angel cast out of heaven in exchange for tunes that were too hot for the Lord to handle is immaterial compared to his deep convictions that will leave no mortal soul unmoved. To reduce the blues to the cliché of "My baby done left me" is misrepresentation. It is not so much that the bluesman thinks his woman ain't coming back. It is that he is smart enough to think about how treacherous he was to get her in the first place, and how fate will then get him. He recognizes rather than resists the karma police and submits to poetic justice. Here is a majestic example of the praxis from Johnson's 'Come On In My Kitchen'. The narrator admits that the woman he loves is someone that he "took from my best friend", before the biter was bit: "Some joker got lucky, stole her back again".

Laying bare one's own futility is bad enough for a people already much maligned, but to do so in conjunction with one's own brazen betrayal is simply too much for some members of the aspirational and god-fearing strand of society, especially the black bourgeoisie, busy trying to "get over". For every "joker who got lucky" there is a nail driven into the heart of putative respectability as much as there is a weight lifted from a life of crushing inhumanity. Johnson is doing one of the most empowering things that can be done for the disadvantaged – he is making a game of his own existence, playing with the sanctity of love, stealing women and then having them stolen back from him, as if the ten commandments had a few killjoy regulations taken out to make sure that the night time is still the right time for people to do what they shouldn't be doing in the eyes of the good lord. Decades later a certain Jimi Hendrix would turn comic himself, pushing his behaviour into a post-Johnson bacchanal by shamelessly deciding to stoke up some underhand sibling rivalry when he reached the "Red House". If he should find out that his "baby don't love me no more" then "her sister will".

In 1926 when the great Harlem Renaissance poet Langston Hughes wrote *The Weary Blues*[84] he was identifying and conveying a deep-lying angst in the post-slavery black condition that went far beyond any material deprivation or the denial of civil rights. The way he frames melancholy and loneliness – "ain't got nobody in this world/ain't got nobody but myself" – has an absolutism that would certainly have appealed to Hendrix. Tellingly, the subject of Hughes' text is a musician, a pianist and vocalist, who is condemned to a never-ending cycle of torture that is mental: even after the singer has gone to bed he finds that the weary blues "echoed through his head".

Existential concerns pervade many of Hendrix's texts. If the blues defined by Hughes is crushing solitude then the guitarist has to contend with frightening alienation in the midst of affluence and adoration, and it is a lack of fulfilment from the trappings – or the trap – of fame that brings a sharp edge to Hendrix's brief exchange with Cavett. If he has no cause to worry about his cash flow his mind is still under great strain.

Feeling weary like Hughes' singer, making big money and singing *more* blues may have been a powerful dynamic in the final phase of the life of Jimi Hendrix, where his continual inability to create new music with which he was completely satisfied is well documented. But that did not stop him from writing new songs and, more to the point, exploring new subject matter. If he indirectly revealed the pressures exerted on his own life on that TV appearance then he was not entirely consumed by the trials and tribulations of maintaining his star status. There was life beyond the rock star bubble.

One question that repeatedly confronted Hendrix during his career was where he and his music fitted on the racial landscape of America. As a black artist who made his commercial breakthrough as the front man of a group with two white musicians playing music that was mostly marketed as rock, not blues or R&B, despite his deep affinities to those genres, Hendrix was bound to be an anomaly at a time of polarization.

Lest we forget, his rise to prominence coincided with a decisive phase in the Civil Rights movement, which was dealt a bitter blow by the death of Dr Martin Luther King Jr in April 1968, and Hendrix, whose *Electric Ladyland* was issued six months after the event, was one of many artists to take part in tribute concerts in his honour. "Well, it's so funny because even some coloured people look at my music and say 'is that white or black?' I say what do you want it ... you know, what are you trying to dissect that for?"[85]

His idealism was getting the better of him there. In a country with the biggest line drawn in the sand over ethnicity – one drop of black blood and you're condemned to be on the wrong side of the tracks – there was little chance of Hendrix, moving in racially mixed musical circles or not, ever escaping that kind of scrutiny. And he was well aware of the magnitude of the issues of equality, choosing not to bury his head in the sand when riots broke out in Detroit and Los Angeles over ongoing issues of police brutality, poor housing and ongoing disenfranchisement of black communities. Interestingly, Hendrix spoke out on occasion: "The race problem is something crazy. The black riots in American cities, that you can read so much about in the papers currently, are just as crazy. What they are doing is irresponsible. I think that we can also live quietly side by side. With violence; a problem like that has never been solved."[86]

Come on back to earth, my friend

Interpreting what Hendrix *really* thought about black identity was a far from easy undertaking because he rarely spelled things out in the sense of fist-in-the-air, brother-be-down-with-the-movement authority. A famous anecdote about him buying a Black Panther Party newspaper on a street corner in New York in order to be *seen* to do the right thing in the company of two African-American friends, the Allen twins (aka the Ghetto Fighters) rather than actually to read the contents himself suggests the artist had a certain ambivalence about racial politics. Apart from the tragic tale of the "little Indian brave" on 'Castles Made of Sand' there are no explicit references to race in his songs. The most recurrent and boldly claimed identity is the figure of the gypsy, which is not at all fanciful given the deeply peripatetic nature of Hendrix's life. The status of wilful outsider appears to mostly transcend a putative black–white divide.

Yet one of the key songs Hendrix cut in the final phase of his life did make an earnest connection with a dominant strand of contemporary black culture: 'Power Of Soul'. First appearing in the mid-1950s, soul referred to the gospel-infused genre, soul jazz, and in the mid-1960s soul came to encapsulate the exciting evolution of R&B. The word soul defined more than music, though. It was an entirely positivist mindset for African-Americans who could draw strength from *within*, defining their own music, aesthetics, food, fashion and overall system of values and humanity. In a civil rights context the idea of such a multi-faceted word that could capture and convey a certain spirit of resistance in the face of ongoing adversity was life-enhancing. Soul brought a sense of self that was not beholden to any of the edicts set by the white world, thus giving a greater currency to the idea of community and individuality. If there was a soul man, then there could also be a larger soul nation, at least in theory. On 'Power Of Soul' Hendrix wrote a chorus that conveyed that absolute can-do spirit. The power of soul is such that "Anything is possible", and those who really believe can achieve "Anything you want to do".

The song could be a loose rejoinder to the pressing urgency of James Brown's 'Soul Power',[87] where the singer progressively escalates demand for the life force of the title, from "we need it" to "we got to have it" to "give it to me" to "Hey you need it" to "Huh we want it" to "Got to have it". He leaves no doubt as to his priorities for himself and others. Both Hendrix and Brown establish a relationship between personal and collective achievement. There is the "power of you" (Jimi) and "you need it" (James), the fulfilment of all, "anything is possible" (Jimi) and the thought for the many not the few, "We got to have it" (James). Even though James is markedly more insistent on this priceless phenomenon he and others must acquire, Jimi nonetheless summons a similar feeling of something that is *happening*, something that makes things *happen.*

Ideological similarities between 'Soul Power' and 'Power of Soul' are not extensive, however. Brown's concise verses make it clear that his concern is also individual strength – "I'm still on the case and my rap is strong" – in a context where others, presumably people of colour or those who are sympathetic to "the movement", will understand his plea for collective thinking – "you need some soul/come on and get some then you'll understand where I'm coming from". Soul power is togetherness, triumph through solidarity, the intersection of "I'll get mine" and "we'll get ours".

Hendrix enters a more abstract, if not surreal space on the verses of 'Power Of Soul'. He talks about "shooting down some of those airplanes, you're flying too low", before extolling the virtues of floating, which is something a jellyfish will tell you about if need be. His mind is racing freely, as if the fanciful imagery is running away with itself as Hendrix offers a series of variations on these central themes.

The references to the animal kingdom, whether the butterflies and zebras of 'Little Wing' or the dragonfly by which one travels on 'Spanish Castle Magic' or the eagles, mountain lions and hummingbirds on 'Voodoo Chile', are sufficiently numerous in the Hendrix songbook to make a jellyfish not entirely surprising, but its appearance in a song entitled 'Power Of Soul' is intriguing. The shift in tone is abrupt. The strong ideological and political substance of the chorus is undercut by the frankly impish verse, delivered, true to Hendrix's well-established praxis, as spoken word. The whole passage has an element of stream-of-consciousness spontaneity about it, suggesting that it could have been partly if not totally improvised in the performance.

It is possible to interpret the lyrics as a strange reality check, as the opening couplets see Hendrix make a plea for his friend to "come on back to earth" yet this is offset against the violence of the image of airplanes being shot down. The jellyfish could be a symbol of nature that finds peace which eludes man who is "flying too much today", an ambiguous, open-ended line that can be decoded as a comment on the increasingly hectic nature of life in the jet age, or even a perspicacious environmental concern. It could even be self-reflexive, given the increasing amount of time Hendrix spent in transit – flying can also be moving fast in life generally as well as specifically travelling by plane – as he reached superstar status that saw him clock up many miles.

The subsequent verse can be seen as a freak nation oddity, complete with hipster speak – "Flotation is groovy, baby" – and pothead allusions – "Yeah, gettin' high every day is easy". Hendrix also invokes a very black, wholly blues vernacular by using the power of the church: "Lord he doesn't have a bone in his jelly back".

So what are we left with? Hendrix being wilfully, trippily opaque, or Hendrix slipping into a narrative that is plain self-indulgent high jinks? Starting a song with a strong, assertive declaration on the power of soul and then taking a tangent into the world of a jellyfish casts Hendrix in the role of lyrical court jester to his own musical monarch. By consciously steering the words of the song away from a clear ideological ground to a much more ambiguous space, Hendrix is putting forward a clear alternative to the prevailing imagery of the soul movement. James Brown presents a character that is absolutely driven in his desire to affect the status quo, or as he says to *get under your skin*, which can be seen as a penetrating comment on a racially polarized America.

A few years earlier, when the popular Stax records vocal duo Sam & Dave had a hit with 'Soul Man', they made a case for the redemption of those who were not born into privilege. Although it wasn't explicit, they could well have been addressing those who were poor, broke and black: "Got what I got the hard way/And I make it better, each and every day". As for Ben E. King, another mid-1960s African-American vocal hero, he lent his glorious tenor to lyrics that headed right into matters metaphysical: "Soul is something that comes from deep inside/soul is something that you can't hide". Hendrix and his jellyfish, flotation and grooviness thus stand at a considerable distance from both of the above. Was he gently ribbing the earnestness of the brothers?

If Sam & Dave claimed to be "educated from good stock" Hendrix, who raised the freak flag in 'If 6 Was 9', could have responded by saying he graduated at Woodstock.

'Power Of Soul' thus remains a conundrum, because Hendrix doesn't really stay on message according to the bulk of African-American artists at the time. He believes in soul power but he is not *profiling* as a soul man in the mould defined by most of his peers. To state that Hendrix, in that final phase of his life, was tuning in to black music and culture more explicitly than had previously been the case does not entirely stand up to scrutiny. For the most part the outsider-drifter-gypsy can't be held down to an official line on the power of soul as a concept that is standardized and identifiable. Hendrix feels the need to go and make some mischief with it, sea creatures and all.

Subversive as that may be, there is another argument for what he is doing. There can be no better indication of the strength of a political concept for a community, especially one languishing in a state of second-class citizenship, than its own desire to turn a spotlight of satire on itself. Trinidadians do it magnificently with calypso. African-Americans took it to heights of brilliance with "the dozens" where ingenuity of insult is the order of the day. Hendrix's irreverence does not necessarily equate to a defrocking of soul as a sanctified space. The levity can actually add to the humanity.

Other artists were on the same wavelength, and also became wary of the clichés that could be applied to the idea of soul and opted to bring a measure of hilarity into play. In February 1970, the month before the release of *Band Of Gypsys*, the album featuring 'Power Of Soul', George Clinton's group Funkadelic issued its eponymous debut album, and one of the highlights of the set was the song 'What Is Soul?'[88] Lyrically, it could not have been more different from the Ben E. King tune with the same name. The piece answered the rhetorical question with provocation aplenty – *Soul is a hamhock in your cornflakes/Soul is the ring around your bathtub/Soul is a joint rolled in toilet paper/Soul is rusty ankles and ashy kneecaps.*

Clinton didn't quite go as far as saying that "soul is a jellyfish in deep flotation" but there is nonetheless a connection between him and Hendrix insofar as they are taking soul on a bizarre ride to the far side. They can't resist some backsliding, and the reason the puncturing of solemnity works so well is because they are revealing a certain vulnerability and tongue-in-cheek comedy that has its place in any "movement".

Cast against the backdrop of Funkadelic's lyrics, Hendrix's 'Power Of Soul' is not such an anomaly. Together the two pieces serve notice of individuality and unpredictability even in the midst of a subject of socio-cultural and political magnitude. Hendrix was well aware of the limitations of the word soul when it was used to define a genre of music, and he openly objected to what he felt was an overblown ornamentation of it to the extent that he dissed Motown as "synthetic soul".

His rejection of music that had excessive veneer and orchestral pomp resonates with a refusal to write lyrics that are too "straight", so that whether or not Hendrix is expressing ambivalence towards soul is not really the point. What counts above all else is that Hendrix retains *his* version of freedom. *They* are the ones who are square. Who is to say that they could not be black as well as white? Assuming any black, especially a maverick, is somehow given the seal of approval of the self-appointed black establishment, whoever it may be, never mind the white establishment, is dangerous to say the least, and perhaps the ultimate goal set by Hendrix the lyric writer is to find space to "do my own thing". This is also part of the credo of soul.

Lest we forget, Hendrix singing a song with soul in the title is underscored by the powerful visual image of him flanked by other black musicians in Band of Gypsys, an obvious contrast to The Experience, where his accompanists were white. The received wisdom is that he is returning to black culture and black players. As much as there is something empowering for African-Americans about the Gypsys image it is significant that there was no definitive break with The Experience insofar as Mitch Mitchell still came in and out of the fold in 1970, and recorded and gigged with Hendrix and Billy Cox, notably at the Isle of Wight festival. 'Power Of Soul' is a deeply uplifting but also puckish song that casts blackness against a broader canvas of multi-racialism in the artist's life. Hendrix is asserting a brotherhood across borders.

Also integral to his notion of community is morality and ethics. The artist, campaigner, leader or counter-cultural figure who simply talked the talk drew nothing but contempt from Hendrix.

> There's gonna have to be some people to get off their asses and try to get their selves together. Instead of sitting around smoke dens, talking about: "Yeah, man this is groovy. Yeah, protest, protest". And then come up with no kind of solution. Or if they do come up with a solution, they realize there might be a sacrifice they might have to make like, some cat might have to give up his gig, which he calls "security", which is a slave thing; that's the worst drug in America today.[89]

This could well be an anti-capitalist rant as well as a plea for societal change. Or it might be Hendrix's avowed mistrust of human nature, a kind of residual bitterness of the trials and tribulations of his formative years, resurfacing. In any case it is an unfiltered social criticism which is sweeping in its range, applying as much to the world of entertainment as it does to the area of politics, levelling the ground between those who might appear "right on" and those who are "right off" in a more overt way.

Esoteric as some of his lyrics may have been and trapped as he increasingly became in a gilded cage, Hendrix did not entirely switch off from current events and international affairs. As the bulk of his oeuvre was being recorded, there was a groundswell of activity intended to bring about sweeping changes both in America and Europe. This included the Civil Rights movement; student riots in Paris; the growth of the anti-war and CND campaigns; women's liberation and the general sense of a widening generation gap that could lead to irrevocable societal breakdown. Armed conflict and the loss of young lives in particular, be it in demonstrations, riots or wars, were making headlines.

How he perceived the issues of the day was not entirely unequivocal. There were moments of great ideological contortion. On one hand he expressed firm support for America's engagement in Vietnam, arguing on the grounds that it was required for the good of "the complete free world". His hawkishness went emphatically further. "As soon as they move out they'll be at the mercy of the communists. For that matter the 'yellow danger' [China] should not be underestimated."[90] On the other hand his opposition to the shipping of young GIs to the killing fields was absolute, and in an extraordinary about-turn at a gig in Stockholm in 1969 he dared to make a wholly un-American statement: "I dedicate this show to the American Deserters Society".[91]

Amid the aforesaid cognitive dissonance it is tempting to conclude that Hendrix wasn't entirely sure how to make sense of what was an incredibly turbulent chapter in world history. But if there was a consistent pattern of behaviour throughout his life then it was a tendency to broach issues, such as race relations in America, with a certain cryptic attitude. On the subject of activists and militant groups he confined himself to declaring, "Everybody has their own way of saying things" rather than giving any outright endorsements. Yet he was emphatic in his condemnation of violence and aggression, and not simply in the physical sense. On numerous occasions he denounced the lack of straight talking in those who wielded executive power who had the ability to harm others through dishonest manifestos and "the art of words". He spelled out his utter contempt of those in the highest office. "Politics is really on an evil scene, you know. It's on a big fat evil scene."[92]

When Hendrix and Band of Gypsys performed at Filmore East in January 1970 the guitarist gave vent to anti-war and anti-establishment sentiment on 'Machine Gun'. It is the most explicit pacifist piece he ever recorded, and stands as a complement to his version of 'Star-Spangled Banner', which was meant to evoke the extreme violence and civil disturbances that marred America throughout the 1960s. Here Hendrix frames the bloodletting in quasi-biblical terms, reflecting soberly on the madness of brothers in arms: "Evil man will make me kill you/Even though we're only families apart". Lyrically, this is Hendrix at his most humane and empathetic. The tragedy of war is placed firmly at the feet of a powerful decision maker, presumably as much a politician as a commanding officer, for whom the artist has little or no regard at all.

In his brief introduction he makes clear reference to the riots and civil disturbances in America – "all the soldiers that are fighting in Chicago, Milwaukee and New York" – as well as Vietnam, which he mentions, almost as an afterthought. That may be his deep subconscious stirring into life, given the fact that the ex-U.S. Airborne private could have been one of the sacrificial teenage "grunts" subjected to unspeakable horror. The assertion of a real kinship between those who are involved in the massacre – "we're only families apart" – in the final line of the verse is incredibly poignant, and the searing anguish in Hendrix's voice is also powerfully underscored by the explosive music. The lyrics in the first part of the song are such a vivid portrayal of the horrors of war – "tearing my body all apart", "your bullets keep knocking me down", "you still blast me down to the ground" – it could be reasonably argued that there is nothing more to say, or at least to make explicit. However, in another verse he evokes "your mess" and "cheap talk" before rounding off with the simple but utterly damning moral indictment "you're wrong, baby". By using the word "baby" Hendrix, tapping into a deep blues vernacular, is bringing tenderness and familiarity into direct collision with violence, evoking countless songs that use the trope of "I shot my baby". In this way he cleverly imbues 'Machine Gun' with a personal resonance in the midst of the sweeping censure of all international wars.

Significantly, the lyric is a thinly veiled dig at social and political hypocrisy that may fuel conflict in the first place. The guitar is a searing, brutal presence in 'Machine Gun', but it may also be interpreted as an agent of truth.

Among the fans crammed into the Filmore, the more perceptive might have picked up on the subtlety of what the band was doing at that point. Yet as Billy Cox remembers, 'Machine Gun' sparked an intense reaction. "I looked out in the audience as far as I could see, maybe 10, 15 rows, and people were like in awe, like they were frozen in time, wondering this is unique, we've never heard anything like it."[93]

Therein lies an immense, if not deeply cruel irony. Everything that exploded into the air at that particular moment was, metaphorically speaking, the death and destruction that should have been defeated by the sound of silence. In a casual but entirely meaningful aside at the very end of the piece Hendrix made it crystal clear that the song was the most powerful of anti-war messages, an uncompromisingly visceral passion play on the sombre and sadly recurrent theme of man's inhumanity to man. This dark, theatrical slice of life is a sharp reminder of a deadly threat to life itself. "That's what we *don't* wanna hear anymore, right?" As the words pass Hendrix's lips, Buddy Miles is heard acquiescing in a much softer voice. "No bullets, no guns, no bombs."

Throughout his whole songbook Hendrix, by way of well-chosen words and daringly conceived and executed sounds, was able to fashion some of the great musical tableaux in the canon of mid-1960s popular music, from the fantasia of love as a dazzling rainbow to crushing loneliness to pulsating sexual enticement by way of hectic urban streets. The ability of the guitarist-vocalist-writer to create unique and original colours was consistently underscored by deeply personal lyrics that broached identity, society, relationships and cosmic imaginings. Yet here he was making a clear and heartfelt plea for human beings to reject the extreme impulse to kill one another. 'Machine Gun' remains a tour de force as a performance and political statement, a bold and uncompromising creation that stands up against any pure malice aforethought.

Taken as a whole, the songs of Jimi Hendrix still have much to offer any open minds and ears decades later. The melodies, sometimes rousing, sometimes contemplative, retain the quality of timelessness, of independent character that transcends an era rather than being beholden to it, while the embellishments, from the guitar and production, have seen their idiosyncrasy grow over the years, primarily because the way Hendrix stamped his multilayered personality on the instrument is so hard, if not impossible to recreate. His body of work has become its own genre beyond any notion of genre. It rests in a place the artist himself deemed an *electric church*, the doors wide open for all believers in an axis bold as love.

As a form of expression, song remains one of the most fascinating and emotionally (and for some) financially rewarding of artistic endeavours. Song is universal. Song is ancestral as well as modern. Song is democratic insofar as it can be passed relatively easily from one person to another. Yet song has the potential to be as esoteric and mystifying as it is populist and immediate in sensory impact. The late jazz pianist Geri Allen made this important statement on the subject: "Sure, a song is that thing we all know and sing. But a song can also be nothing more than one note."[94] Here she was talking about attention to detail and the creativity that can drive a skilled musician towards structures that are more unpredictable and abstract than the widely implemented verse-chorus paradigm. Hendrix's repertoire certainly has, on occasion, a strikingly opaque quality as well as an immediacy, which helped to make him immensely popular both during and after his lifetime. There was real artistry in his popular music, and not just as a result of the virtuosity of his guitar playing.

Hendrix brought his unlimited imagination to bear on the salient features of an arrangement such as the introduction, textures, dynamics, balance of instrumental and vocal content, and quirks in narrative such as leading the listener to believe a solo is about to end when in fact it isn't. That his ideas could be distilled into concise three-minute radio-friendly pieces or protracted into suites that could last up to fifteen minutes says much about both the artist's natural affinity to the pop aesthetic as well as his innate desire to challenge it when his muse dictated that it was appropriate to do so.

Above all, Hendrix was part of a generation of musicians who brought gravitas to popular music beyond the frivolity of teen-friendly models. When an 18-year-old Richard Ellis saw The Experience at the ABC theatre, Chesterfield in 1967 he was able to make a telling observation about a maturing process in the audience that would move it on from the mania induced by the Fab Four still saddled by boy band expectations.

> Just before that we'd seen the Beatles at Sheffield City Hall and you couldn't hear a thing. This wasn't anything like that. When Jimi was on stage it was more like a bit of reverence. A lot of people had gone to see him. It was as if people had actually gone to listen to him and watch him perform rather than women and girls screaming.[95]

In other words his legacy is songs worth singing and songs that warrant in-depth analysis as a result of an all-too-rare combination of musicianship, lyrical flourish, emotional charge and overall communicative energy. Hendrix had a great ability to touch listeners as well as impress them. He had the gift of knowing that, as straightforward a formula as the blues may appear, it is nonetheless very difficult to draw significant feeling from its core as well as its imaginative idiomatic outgrowths.

Regardless of what genre of music is used to classify Hendrix, he was able to create one of the most invaluable commodities imaginable for any artist – beautiful melody. For all his prowess as a soloist he had the precious ability to create phrases both on his guitar and with his voice that have the magical quality of emotional meaning as well as sonic substance. Hearts and minds are captured by the stealth and grace of a theme such as 'The Wind Cries Mary', a song that has the character of a centuries-old meditation, a sublime anthem for any lovers who have known the trials of an imperfect union. Aware of this, Hendrix deployed intellect as well as feeling and technique in his oeuvre, a complex multi-faceted songbook that was formed of several personae: Hendrix the guitarist meets Hendrix the vocalist meets Hendrix the lyricist meets Hendrix the composer meets Hendrix the producer meets Hendrix the soundscaper.

The unique songs of Jimi Hendrix flowed from the once-in-a-lifetime talent of Jimi Hendrix, which was itself inseparable from the unique mind of Jimi Hendrix. To reduce Hendrix to "greatest rock guitarist" is to sell short the sum of his achievements, which, tellingly, have captured the imagination of a very wide range of artists, from pop stars who put their faith in a good tune to jazz composers who focus on the finer points of an arrangement to hip-hop and techno producers who know a killer breakbeat when they hear one. The influence he would exert on others beyond his lifetime is substantial; his legacy strikingly rich, for after the songs of Jimi Hendrix came the songs from Jimi Hendrix.

Part 3: The Songs from Jimi Hendrix

That lady sings the blues, soul, funk and rock

Official causes of death may explain how a person lost their life but not necessarily how it unravelled. Knowing that Jimi Hendrix succumbed to an overdose of sleeping pills that led to him choking on his own vomit still leaves unanswered the question of why he felt the need for sedation in an existence increasingly resembling a goldfish bowl about to slip and shatter. Here are some salient facts. The endless round of gigs was exhausting; the attendant media circus debilitating. The demands of being a rock star, compounded by the high artistic standards he set himself, surely induced bouts of acute anxiety. Had Hendrix been able to take a break he may well not have snapped.

Adding to the stress of his life was an inability to finish a studio album with which he felt truly satisfied. There were numerous sessions undertaken with a variety of personnel in which Hendrix essayed many artistic directions without mapping out a clear road ahead, leaving tantalizing question marks over what may have happened had Band of Gypsys stayed together and evolved, or how a reunion with his first manager, Chas Chandler, could have revived Hendrix's mojo in his beloved Britain. Tragically, London was the scene of Hendrix's end rather than of a new beginning.

His age, 27, simply reinforced the "live fast die young" narrative that has underpinned several other iconic figures in the worlds of film as well as music. Hendrix passed on 18 September 1970, and roughly a fortnight later Janis Joplin, also three years shy of her 30th birthday, fell victim to a heroin overdose. The proximity of the two tragedies underlined the precarious pressure-cooker existence of glamorous musicians who, despite success, were forced to contend with no small amount of strife. Joplin had a voice with immense character, and made music that reflected personal adversity as well as a feisty and defiant spirit. She and Hendrix both played and had the blues.

The blues did not constrain Hendrix. If it was a tree then he was happy to embrace its numerous branches – R&B, rock 'n' roll, soul, funk and rock – in order to then create something that managed to convey the artist's distinct personality all the while recognizing this rich heritage and how it could effectively synthesize with other musical traditions and technological advances. The electric religion in which Hendrix passionately believed also enabled him to ascend to a unique musical firmament.

He was not alone in his convictions or endeavours. As Taj Mahal observed in Part 2, Hendrix was entering a musical space that remained difficult to define, just as several of his peers also gave vent to a spirit of experimentation between the mid- and late 1960s. Among the African-American or racially mixed groups who had a comparable creative verve, Parliament-Funkadelic, Sly & The Family Stone, Electric Flag, Eugene McDaniels and to a lesser extent the Chambers Brothers are all important names to mention insofar as their idiosyncratic music had varying degrees of rococo textural flourish as well as soaring lyricism, and an overall unpredictability in form and content. Terms such as hippie rock and psychedelic rock were applied to Hendrix while psychedelic soul became attached to Sly, maybe with Funkadelic somewhere in the middle, but all of these groups had common ground of sorts. Finding new sub-genres for any artist that managed to create a repertoire that had some semblance of originality as well as personality, regardless of the familiarity of the sources on which they drew, was inevitable given the increasing stratification of the record industry and the sacrosanct principle of presenting product that was new.

Parliament-Funkadelic alumni such as Bootsy Collins (and his marvellous Rubber Band), Junie Morrison and Eddie Hazel all made glorious music that drew on the base elements so skilfully used by Hendrix, above all funk-rock rhythms, rainbow-like textures and left-of-centre humour without sounding lazily derivative. The fact that Bootsy, a bassist, guitarist and drummer, had learned a significant amount of his craft as a member of James Brown's band, also gave him a discipline not unlike Hendrix's, while his magnetic stage presence and manchild cartoon humour made him one of the worthiest heirs of Hendrix in performance. And like Jimi, Bootsy loved to jam.

Knowing that there was a freedom within apparent formula, or that other more fluid desultory patterns were in the blues long before it settled into 12-bar paradigm, gave Hendrix a solid springboard for his own flights of fancy. A sense of possibility, a daring liberation and above all imagination, through word, sound and power, imbued his songs with a modernity that did not trash tradition. He became a mutation rather than an outright reiteration of what paved the way for him, and for all those with ears to hear Hendrix had an indelible impact. Most obviously, his embrace of state-of-the-art technology affected older musicians such as Muddy Waters, who went the way of Jimi on *Electric Mud* while Hendrix's direct influence on one of his old employers, the Isley Brothers, is clear in the timeless soul rocker 'That Lady'.

Ernie Isley's ecstatically screaming guitar is an obvious echo of Hendrix. However, the real tribute to him lies in the spotlight on the musicianship in the arrangement. Rhythmically and vocally the piece is "lighter" than most of what Hendrix recorded in his heyday, but it makes a dramatic turn into "heavy" territory around 2:25 minutes in, and Ernie starts to diligently work the fuzzbox, building tension in a way that is all too familiar to Hendrix fans. Significantly, the verse and chorus do not return. Ronald Isley's falsetto reveals itself to be incidental to the real action. Bearing in mind that the total duration is 5:36, over half of the entire song is guitar-centric. 'That Lady' also upholds the Parts 1&2 tradition of 7″ singles with a vocal on the A side and instrumental on the B, but taken as one whole performance, as it was presented on the Isleys' 1973 album *3+3*, the guitar solo emerges as the absolute raison d'etre. It comprehensively takes over, recalling the structure of 'All Along The Watchtower'.

Furthermore, 'That Lady'[1] was not a new song. It was a revamp of a 1964 soul bossa nova called 'Who's That Lady?', which was acoustic. Swooning horns provided the dominant harmonic colour. By the time of the remake Hendrix had been dead three years, but his spirit entirely frames and pervades the electric rebirth of the music, presenting the guitar as a lead instrument that could be as relevant to soul as to rock. Such a hardening of timbres characterizes the work of several of the Isleys' African-American peers. When you hear countless funk guitarists get on their wah-wah groove in order to bring a shot of adrenalin to their rhythm you're also hearing the legacy of Hendrix.

One group that bears a strong Hendrix imprint in terms of lyrical content, socio-cultural perspectives and visual panache is Bar-Kays. Formerly a house band for the highly influential Stax label in the 1960s, the group, after suffering the tragedy of losing several members in the same plane crash that claimed the life of Otis Redding, undertook a substantial overhaul of its sound in the early 1970s. They became louder and tougher, and acknowledged the cultural crossroads at which Hendrix stood by way of the thought-provoking title of one of their best ever albums – *Black Rock*.[2]

Also on a vaguely similar wavelength to Hendrix but largely overlooked is Jimi Castor. Although a vocalist and saxophonist rather than guitarist, he managed to coherently imbue his music with a wildness and urgency that built on some of the high points of the Experience catalogue, and his excellent reprise of 'Purple Haze' made explicit the influence of Hendrix that was implied elsewhere in his originals such as the quite scintillating 'It's Just Begun', a track whose pummelling, punishing rhythmic attack almost feels like an accelerated, hyperventilating take on 'Little Miss Lover'.

Even more obscure than Castor is a band that recorded little in the 1970s but nonetheless stepped into the melodic and sonic space opened up by several key pioneers of the late 1960s. Fresh Start, a very interesting multi-racial four-piece led by Michigan-based guitarist-vocalist Paul Frank, really comes across as a synthesis of the Jimi Hendrix Experience, Band of Gypsys and

Sly & The Family Stone, which means that the strong blues foundation of the music gelled with a funk-rock quality that is powerfully expressed on the band's excellent debut *What America Needs.*[3]

Incidentally, the other group Frank fronted, Head Over Heels, is an even noisier power trio that at times is almost like Hendrix meeting Cream or any number of acts that followed in their slipstream, notably Led Zeppelin and Mountain. The sole album the group issued in 1971 varies in quality but nonetheless is notable for its recognition of the blues musicians who opened the doors for all of the above, such as the legendary double bassist-composer Willie Dixon whose 'Red Rooster' is reprised to good effect.

A deep African thing, a deep African-American groove

Because Hendrix was such a striking example of black masculinity that is adventurous and daring, it is not commonplace to compare him to female artists, but Betty Davis, who he knew well – persistent rumours of a relationship between the two are not substantiated – is an important counterpart in so many ways. Lacking formal musical training, writing very much on instinct, performing with a sexual electricity but above all mining a deep, rich seam of the blues that remains pleasingly free of cliché: these characteristics define classic Davis recordings such as 'Anti Love Song',[4] where the boiling eroticism and sheer bravado and ballsiness of her performance is very much in the lineage of Hendrix at his most unfettered and boldly unapologetic.

Furthermore, Davis's blend of spoken word and sung vocal is something to which the guitarist would have surely been able to relate. No greater symbol of a musical kinship between the two artists can be found than in Davis's fine cover of Cream's 'Politician', which took her close to musicians who were significantly connected to Hendrix. The British trio was an integral part of his peer group, and he admired what Eric Clapton, Jack Bruce and Ginger Baker achieved as songwriters as well as players. To hear Davis breeze so nonchalantly through the song, retaining all the unhurried leisure and confidence of an artist intent on individuality rather than imitation, is to hear an inspired soul blur the line between blues, rock and funk. The electric music of Hendrix would be one of several key sources of inspiration to jazz musicians such as Miles Davis, husband of Betty, and who arranged the aforesaid track, in his pursuit of a new sound at the end of the 1960s.

Making the transition from the realm of acoustic, harmonically and metrically advanced compositions to an aesthetic that was much more visceral in impact and more redolent of an aggressive, combustible urban environment was partially triggered by the success of Hendrix, who Miles Davis discovered when, upon the recommendation of his band member, British guitarist John McLaughlin, he saw him appear in a documentary of the Monterrey Pop Festival. As much as Hendrix's spirit can be heard in some of the crunching riffs played by McLaughlin in Davis's work there is also a convincing evocation of the compellingly dark, fraught ambiences of The Experience and Band of Gypsys. In fact, the 1969 version of 'Spanish Castle Magic' live in Stockholm has an extended instrumental vamp that is quite startling in its hypnotic power and coherently prefigures the seminal Davis song 'Jack Johnson' as well as the explosive sound of Lifetime. This "power trio" was formed the same year by Davis alumnus, drummer Tony Williams, and featured McLaughlin and organist Larry Young, a superlative soloist and one-time Hendrix jam partner.

By the time Hendrix recorded his third album *Electric Ladyland*, Miles Davis had made over 40 albums, including the masterworks *Birth of The Cool*, *Milestones*, *Sketches of Spain*, *Kind of Blue*, *E.S.P.* and *Filles De Kilimanjaro*, all of which saw him cover a vast amount of stylistic ground while leading superlative bands. The above works spanned several schools of thought, from "cool" to hard bop and modal jazz, and made Davis much more than a gifted trumpeter and composer. He emerged as a great thinker, a perceptive enquirer and fearless adventurer of modern music. Yet there was something Hendrix had that Davis recognized as one of the most invaluable artistic commodities imaginable: a sense of creative freshness and spontaneity that was not necessarily based on a thorough command of music theory.

Hendrix's vocal and instrumental music would affect soloists such as Davis in a way that resonated with important events in the past. It is the relationship between the unschooled and the schooled that W.C. Handy actually witnessed at the dawn of the twentieth century when he was on tour in the South. A musically literate musician such as himself realized he had to give it up to those who were not. The moment was historic. "Those country black boys at Cleveland had taught me something that could not possibly have been gained from books, something that would, however, cause books to be written."[5]

Handy's illuminating testimony pinpoints a central development in the history of black music: the impact of one social class of artist upon another, and by extension the benefit of the academic taking an interest in and studying the work of the non-academic. The formally educated player who is skilled in the art of transcribing understands what is to be gained from the player who is not formally educated.

One could point to a legendary figure from the 1920s such as Duke Ellington who saw what beauty could arise from the meeting of the "schooled cats" and the "ear cats". One could also point to a legendary figure from the 1970s such as George Clinton whose ideal model of a band comprised two types of musician: the classically trained and the "ghetto trained". Handy intuited the value of this paradigm in his own lifetime.

Hendrix was not classically trained. He was self-taught and he did not sight read. Apparently this made him apprehensive about a possible musical encounter between him and Davis, for fear of being out of his depth, but nonetheless the fact that Davis was keen for a meeting of the two to happen was an endorsement of Hendrix's talent.

Regardless of his ambivalence towards jazz, or at least the high tempo action of the bebop school, Hendrix had a deeper alignment with the likes of Davis and his illustrious colleagues such as Wayne Shorter insofar as he was also fascinated by the idea of evolution, re-evaluation and re-visitation. Shorter insightfully said: "A song is like a person, it grows", and the idea of any artistic statement being definitive and not open to ongoing interpretation was anathema to him. Trawl through Hendrix's oeuvre and there are several instances of him presenting multiple versions of the same song – 'Red House', 'Hear My Train A Comin'', 'Angel', 'Little Wing' – but perhaps the most daring example of him assessing a given statement and extending it into another creative realm is 'Voodoo Chile' becoming 'Voodoo Child'. Nothing could be more jazz, conceptually. It is an "alternate take", as fans of Blue Note and Impulse! know only too well, given the amount of releases that feature versions of one piece. Look also at the language he uses. Hendrix calls 'Voodoo Child' a "slight return". That could be a form of the *reprise* that featured on 1970s soul albums or the *remix* in 1990s hip-hop.

All things considered, it is the towering personality of Hendrix, his abundance of melodic ideas as well as fearless pursuit of new sounds by way of technology that makes him part of an essential debate that progressive exponents of black music were engaged in when he rose to prominence. Davis had the wherewithal to know that jazz, for all its ascension towards what could be termed an art music, predicated on the virtuosity of its exponents, could have something substantial to gain if it stayed abreast of current events in the world of popular music that had embraced the possibilities of electric rather than purely acoustic instruments and studio production.

Miles and Jimi were both bound by an imagination that is too large for any categories. Ultimately, jazz is too small a word for Davis; rock is too small a word for Hendrix.

Davis and Hendrix both appeared at the Isle of Wight festival in August 1970, and there were plans for them to record soon afterwards but the guitarist would die before the session could take place. The two had had several jam sessions at Davis's house in New York. The trumpeter was taken with his playing, and the greatest posthumous compliment he paid to him was to make the guitar a more prominent component of the most adventurous bands of his electric period, with the incumbents including the aforesaid McLaughlin, Dominique Gaumont, Reggie Lucas, Cornell Dupree and Pete Cosey, the quite astounding Chicagoan who Davis felt was actually the closest approximation to Hendrix that he had heard. Having two if not three guitarists together on a single track enabled Davis to recreate some of the density of Hendrix's own rhythm-led conjunctions while the trumpeter's decision to use a wah-wah pedal with his instrument also nodded to one of Hendrix's most defining *signes particuliers*.

In his autobiography Davis made this very revealing statement about the character of his music at that time: "Now the band settled down into a deep African thing, a deep African-American groove with a lot of emphasis on drums and rhythm, and not on individual solos. From the time that Jimi Hendrix and I had gotten tight I had wanted that kind of sound because the guitar can take you deep into the blues."[6]

Or rather the electric version of the instrument is capable of reaching an emotional as well as sonic intensity that he felt had ebbed away from the realm of acoustic music in which he had been operating for the bulk of his career. Also revealing is the fact that Davis really emphasizes the word *deep* – he uses it three times in the two sentences – as the keystone of his thinking, and in the process frames Hendrix in the most instructive of terms, for when you listen to 'Voodoo Chile', 'Machine Gun' or 'Bleeding Heart' it is precisely that sense of elemental, fundamental sound, something that goes right to the core of black cultural history, that really comes to define the performance.

The related term would be *heavy*, which is a function of how loud Hendrix could be but it is also about the sheer force and punch of the playing and the kind of imperious character of both the improvising and the lyric writing, the daring nature of his whole aesthetic. Hendrix, the exemplar of all that is *deep and heavy*, thus becomes a pivotal reference for those who are interested in the evolution of both art music and popular music, for if Miles Davis's heady electric adventures are part of the guitarist's corollary then there is obviously a whole new chapter of hard rock and heavy metal that would not have been written without a similar acknowledgement of the ground that was covered by The Experience and Band of Gypsys. It is not just the iconic Brits, such as Led Zeppelin, Deep Purple and Black Sabbath, who are obvious beneficiaries; it is also the many American artists, such as ZZ Top, who had fine musicianship as well as melodic skills that still nodded to the place of the blues in rock and pop.

The number of soloists and composers who would go on to cover Hendrix songs from the 1970s to the present day further anchors the idea of him as a creative force whose work captured the imagination of musicians who had the formal training and art music credentials that he himself lacked. Given the fact that he was due to be involved in the Hendrix–Davis collaboration, Gil Evans remains one of the key Jimiphiles and his 1974 set *Plays The Music of Jimi Hendrix* is a compelling statement both on the melodic riches of the guitarist's songbook and the range of possibilities it presents for detailed orchestration. Following his pivotal contribution to the art of arranging in jazz history, both with Davis and as a bandleader in his own right, Evans was an entirely appropriate figure to take on the job of setting Hendrix to a palette of brass and reeds. His scores for 'Voodoo Child', 'Gypsy Eyes' and 'Crosstown Traffic/Little Miss Lover', among other pieces, really show how well the phrases and motifs originally heard on voice and guitar translate to horn and rhythm sections cleverly deployed to bring out the finer points of the original compositions.

Furthermore, there are nods to the rootedness of Hendrix in a deep heritage of black music and the futurism that branched out from it. The jaunty, breezy walking bassline and piping horns of 'Up From The Skies' recall the full-blooded swing of which Hendrix was capable while Evans's analogue keyboards create bubbling, gurgling sounds that evoke the guitarist's ingenuity with pedals but also unleash some of the stark funk and shower of colours that might have come from an inter-generational electric jam session between the trusted lieutenants of Ellington and James Brown.

Interestingly, Evans had already written and conducted for Kenny Burrell, a guitarist Hendrix was known to greatly admire, but the interpretation of the Hendrix songbook saw him broaden the tonal palette as well as raise the overall energy levels of his band, which features two skilled guitarists, Ryo Kawasaki and John Abercrombie, as well as the brilliant saxophonists, Billy Harper (tenor) and David Sanborn (alto).

Perhaps Evans's greatest achievement was to harness and convey both the finesse and aggression of Hendrix's music, or maybe show that the muscularity and fortissimo playing had been key elements of several schools in the history of jazz, from swing to avant-garde, and that the advent of an artist who saw loudness as a pivotal part of his aesthetic rather than a by-product brought a legitimacy to moves in a similar direction. To a certain extent that is also borne out by the roaring version of 'Purple Haze' that Art Ensemble of Chicago recorded in 1987, which has a robust attack of the horns that speaks of the passion, if not combustion and explosion, that Hendrix was able to convey in his work. Here was a reprise of a timeless pop masterpiece that fitted coherently into the AEC aesthetic of "great black music ancient to future".

Chopping down the mountain … running like a coon[7] ahead of the pack

Some of the elements that enabled Hendrix to become Hendrix – imagination, flair, daring, a desire for originality, the blues – provided the building blocks for other innovators who are not readily associated with him. Nonetheless there are interesting connections to be made. Alto saxophonist-violinist-trumpeter-composer Ornette Coleman had exhibited pronounced blues tendencies in his music since his debut in the late 1950s, and although the conceptual leap forward he made in the 1960s with regard to the fluidity of meter and harmony resulted in him being tagged a champion of the avant-garde, the bedrock of black folk music remained a part of his aesthetic.

Use of wiry counterpoint and polytonality in Coleman's work do not dim a strong country blues sensibility at times, and that is a common denominator with Hendrix, who was also able to create that kind of rural, back of the woods ambiance in his blues epics even though he could equally evoke a tense urban jungle elsewhere.

Like Miles Davis, Coleman went electric in the 1970s, though in the middle rather than the beginning of the decade. Like Davis, Coleman made the guitar a major component of the new sound palette for his songs. Like Davis, Coleman used two players (Charles Ellerbie and Bern Nix) to create tonal density and polyrhythmic drive. Albums such as *Dancing In Your Head* and *Body Meta* have a pronounced element of dance, which is at times calypso-like in sway and swerve, and recast the guitar, not the "clean" jazz iteration but the "dirty" blues version, as a fulcrum of the music.

There is thus an exciting process of enquiry about how one of the oldest and most pervasive string instruments in black music, after the banjo, could be positioned as a vital force for original thinkers like Coleman, and if Hendrix facilitated that in any way then it is perhaps the emergence of another six-string hero who lends credence to the argument. He was born in South Carolina and his name is James "Blood" Ulmer.

His superlative 1979 album *Tales of Captain Black*[8] features Coleman, and unveils "Blood" as a strikingly refreshing new exponent of the guitar whose chordal invention, with its incendiary, brash character, inevitably begs the question of what would the musical outcome have been if the saxophonist had had the opportunity to play with other guitar pioneers? While the meeting of Miles and Jimi has become one of the great "What ifs?" of modern music then surely the same can be said of a possible encounter between Ornette and Jimi. To a certain extent it proved a fitting sequel to the celebrated jam that Hendrix enjoyed with Rahsaan Roland Kirk in the 1960s, given that Coleman also had a distinctive timbre, deeply vocal "cry" and mercurial phrasing that may have resonated with a player such as Hendrix.

Of all the jazz musicians who came of age in the 1970s and drew the greatest influence from Hendrix as a black cultural role model as well as a musical idol, none is more interesting than saxophonist David Murray. Hailing from Oakland, California he developed a style that drew extensively from trailblazers such as Ben Webster, John Coltrane and Albert Ayler, and went on to become an iconic horn player himself in the 1980s. But, in his youth, once he had fallen under Hendrix's influence, Murray took to wearing a bandana and playing guitar, intent on following in his idol's footsteps before being drawn towards the saxophone and the way of improvised acoustic music.

> I didn't want to play like Jimi. I wanted to *be* Jimi. The entire Bay Area hippie movement, my band The Notations of Soul – and everyone else – dug Jimi. He had a crossover appeal that black, white, brown and Asian adored.[9]

Murray's interest in rock, pop and funk never waned and when one of the seminal bands he co-led, World Saxophone Quartet, recorded *Experience* in

2004 it was the tribute to Hendrix that Murray had been destined to pay for most of his artistic life.

Important as the trend of "Jimi Jazz" is, some improvisers have wanted to do more than interpret the guitarist-vocalist's songs. They related to him in a profound way. When I spoke to Murray about Hendrix he was very forthcoming about how much pieces such as 'Little Wing' or 'Machine Gun' had impacted upon him in his formative years. He also stated that, way beyond Hendrix's music, it was really Hendrix as a personality, a cipher of black expression and all-round agent provocateur who had made him think more deeply about what a life-changing phenomenon such as the blues really means, and how an individual artist can find their own place within its inspiring musical and cultural continuum.

Blues as something to be felt as well as heard is an oft-quoted principle but it is clear that the likes of Hendrix brought intellect to bear on the idiom and he was also able to consolidate the wit and whimsy of his predecessors. Murray thus perceived his role model as much more than a guitarist, despite his technical gifts. He recognized all of the oldness of Hendrix's spirit, the deep melancholia of his themes, the outré mischief of his lyrics.

Hence *Political Blues*, the very beautiful album that Murray, once again with World Saxophone Quartet, recorded in 2006 stands coherently in the slipstream of *Experience*. This is music that is rhythmically lithe and funky but timbrally bulky, as a horn section comprising baritone, tenor, alto and soprano saxophone is augmented by trombone, trumpet and didgeridoo. Interestingly, the band also features players who made an invaluable contribution to Ornette Coleman's adventures in electric music that, as previously argued, indirectly resonated with Hendrix's own work: bass guitarist Jamaladeen Tacuma and guitarist James "Blood" Ulmer. The latter sings lead vocal on a scintillating cover of a song that was a building block for Hendrix: Muddy Waters' 'Mannish Boy'. In other words it is not just the history of artists from one generation but the links to those of another that come fully into view, and the importance of this continuum cannot be overstated, quite simply because the complexity of the ongoing relationship between past and present in black music, not to mention the ambiguity of "old" and "new", was something that was writ large in the work of Hendrix. Together, WSQ's *Experience* and *Political Blues* thus represent the explicit and implicit acknowledgement of the artist's legacy.

In fact, it could be argued that 'Machine Gun', which is featured on the first album, would not at all be out of place on the second. These recordings should also be seen in the wider context of an investigation of black music that WSQ, which was formed in the mid-1970s by Murray, Julius Hemphill, Oliver Lake and Hamiett Bluiett, had already flagged up on the superb 1989 album *Rhythm & Blues*,[10] where they reprised, among others, the songs of Hendrix's peers, for whom he had great admiration, namely James Brown and Otis Redding. The fact that WSQ showed how much rhythm and how much blues could be drawn from an acoustic band with no drums, bass, guitar or keys, was testament to their creative verve and audacity.

Yet it is also worth considering that Hemphill, the alto player in the quartet, was a brilliant thinker as well as a pithy composer who himself had a strikingly profound perspective on black culture that led him to satirize the minstrel tradition, experiment with spoken word and "audio drama", celebrate ancient African civilization and recast African-American folk aesthetics. In each case there was the same quality of *deep* character that Miles Davis talked of when discussing the impact of Hendrix on his music, and the most vivid sense of Hemphill broaching similar ground to Hendrix is the absolutely masterful 1975 composition, 'The Hard Blues'. Although an acoustic, horn-led piece it is devastating in its use of a basic shuffle to create a sense of the shuddering menace that defines a Hendrix song such as 'Who Knows'. What Hemphill has done is create something that approximates the Hendrix concept of the *freakish blues* without resorting to the expected means of production to do so. Indeed the relatively slender, spindly scrape of Abdul Wadud's cello is probably the last sound one might expect to hear in the context of music that has so much toughness and swagger, and such an overwhelming sense of heaviness. But it works.

Beyond its narrative ingenuity, 'The Hard Blues' is also a manifestation of linguistic prowess. Ascribing a precise meaning to it is not as straightforward as one might think. On one hand it can be interpreted as an indication of music that is anything but light, but the blues has sufficient metaphysical substance to accommodate many other scenarios. 'The Hard Blues' as in the roughest deal on the wrongest side of the tracks, from which there is little possibility of gettin' on let alone gettin' over, or 'The Hard Blues' as in so tough I'll get to whoop your mama's ass as well as your papa's, brother's and sister's too. 'The Hard Blues' that hits you more than any other blues.

'The Hard Blues' is a scream of anguish and excitation. It could be a manic depression or a frantic dance, like its younger musical ally 'The Hard Funk'. (One of James Brown's lesser-known offerings is 'Just Plain Funk', which is nothing other than a motherlode hard blues.) 'The Hard Blues' could be both physical vigour and psychological turmoil.

Hemphill's great achievement as an artist was to invest his compositions with a great amount of narrative layers as well as musical substance. Hearing the aforementioned song in isolation is gripping for the way it moves so coherently from a rigidly set pulse to a freer time, but this blurring of the boundary between folk and avant-garde sensibilities has to be cast against a hugely provocative political backdrop, namely that the album on which 'The Hard Blues' appears is *Coon Bid'ness*.[11] It evokes and subverts the racist caricature to which blacks were subjected by mainstream white society in the late nineteenth and early twentieth centuries. Hemphill was greatly interested in the written and spoken word as well as composed and improvised instrumental music.

These compositions highlight the breadth of imagination in the blues as a lyrical as well as musical phenomenon that reaches right back to its progenitors. The supernatural qualities stamped on Hemphill's text resonate with generations of African-American wordsmiths that came before, bringing into sharp focus the infinite resources of black folklore as a space for surrealist thought and imagery, and the dynamic, evolutionary relationship that exists between words and music. There is a range of meanings in all the types of language that have been conceived and deployed by generations of black artists: what is spoken, what is written, what is sung, what is played, what is danced. Hendrix the musician and poet was surely not the only innovator to empower Hemphill the musician and poet but the multi-layered, richly imagistic work of the former was relevant to the latter, just as it was to his WSQ colleague David Murray.

Without a doubt the blues is one of the great vessels of truth in the history of the world, and its capacity for straight talking is unparalleled. But as much as it conveys truth and reality it can also be laden with fantasy and ambiguity, or challenge understanding. There are things to know. There are things *not* to know. There are things to work out if you dare. The codes cannot be cracked without some kind of personal investment, and the emergence of a more sophisticated verbiage in both the popular and art music of the black Diaspora has simply opened up further space for this kind of imaginative thinking.

Hendrix talking metaphorically about all things carnal may be clear enough, but some of his greatest flights of fancy remain, decades after they were conceived, thoroughly enigmatic. They spark our imagination and lend themselves to myriad interpretations. When he talks of standing up "next to a mountain" so that he can proceed to "chop it down" with nothing other than "the edge of my hand" before making an island of all the pieces, he is taking us far beyond the confines of the material world as we know it.

In other words the *Voodoo Child* is not of humankind. He grows into a super being whose powers far exceed those of mortal man, to the extent that he can do nothing less than reconfigure the elements around him, destroying a mass of stone to then reshape it in water. On one hand this is an opaque reflection on nature. On the other it can be seen as an unfettered act of resistance to an oppressive force, for the mountain is in the mind, as in the tortured psyche of the disenfranchised, and stands as a symbol of authority, the government, the military, the police, or any agents of bigotry. It was what Dr. Martin Luther King Jr, James Baldwin and others sought to scale.

Hendrix has unparalleled powers. He boldly breaks the great rock into submission with nothing other than body and soul, doing something that is far beyond the capacity of mortal man. It is the revenge of the countless faceless brothers and sisters working in state-enforced servitude. The words convey a great blackness, a deep *négritude*.

The intellectual malleability of the language, combined with the intensity of the accompanying sound, courtesy of Hendrix's guitar, is tremendously instructive to any artists who are wont to explore profound emotion through a novel conjunction of lyrical and instrumental flourish. As Hemphill's horn screams incandescent we are invited to contemplate startling images that move from the terrestrial to the celestial.

In the sleeve notes of *Coon Bid'ness* there is poetry by Hemphill and Wilma Moses that riffs on race and metaphysics. It is the imagining of the ex-slave underclass as a dynamic force that spars with nature, subverts prevailing stereotypes and hails the grand ideal of community. We are told of a "coon running ahead of the pack" resplendent in "black gold, yellow gold". More intriguingly, the scene evokes "bodies and minds in planetary orbits". The words convey a great blackness, a deep *négritude*.

To say that Hendrix directly influenced Hemphill may not be entirely accurate, but the former opens up a challenging and empowering space within the realm of the blues and blues poetry that the latter, very possibly under the inspiration of the likes of Amiri Baraka, Ishmael Reed and Sun Ra, moved into under his own steam.

What is no less interesting is how Hendrix and Hemphill also worked with the same musicians, even though they did not record together. Hendrix had a memorable session with poet-rapper Jalal Mansur Nuriddin (of hip-hop trailblazers The Last Poets) that birthed the funk-rock-spoken word gem *Doriella Du Fontaine* while Hemphill appeared on Nuriddin's 1973 set *Hustler's Convention*, a wizardly album that also featured saxophonist-arranger King Curtis, who had employed Hendrix in the mid-1960s. These overlaps reflect the way several of the prime movers in black music were spinning in the same creative orbit.

Crossing the line between what was considered to be "street" and what passed as "serious" high art had been done long before Hendrix rose to prominence, but his co-existence with Jalal, Hemphill, Curtis and many others really exposed some of the organic conceptual allegiances and parallels between these disparate figures. It is as easy to imagine a Hendrix cameo on *Hustler's Convention* as it is Hemphill taking a solo on any of the guitarist's torrid jams where the players were pushing the sonic envelope without the slightest compromise. As far as we know Hemphill did not write 'The Hard Blues' for Hendrix, but he could have feasibly dedicated it to his memory, given how apt a descriptive term it is for any number of Hendrix's compositions.

Coalition sans compromise

Other musicians who extended Hendrix's legacy in the early 1970s by acknowledging the rich possibilities of noise, textural invention and abstract arrangement as well as the emotional edge of the blues would above all include the fabulous guitarist Sonny Sharrock whose work with his wife Linda on *Black Woman* is really quite exceptional. It offers some delicious food for thought on how Hendrix may have sounded had he pitted his guitar against a strong female voice.

If the likes of Sharrock kept challenging orthodoxy with regard to the use of the six string then an artist who represented a more complete embodiment and extension of Hendrix also made his debut in the middle of the decade, initially finding mainstream commercial success elusive, though he would go on to become an icon in the 1980s.

Prince carried the mantle well because he was able to channel spirits both directly and indirectly related to Hendrix. Most obviously, Prince captured the high camp and hyperactive energy of Little Richard, the febrile eroticism of James Brown and the sonic imagination and melodic flourish of The Beatles, Stevie Wonder and Curtis Mayfield, all the while presenting a multi-faceted character that levelled the ground between dangerous sexuality and deep spirituality. He also had a healthy dose of the cynicism, humour and tenderness of Hendrix's best tunes. In terms of touchingly confessional moods, one can draw a line from 'Little Wing' to 'Purple Rain'.

A Prince song such as 'Let's Pretend We're Married', where he berates holy matrimony as a flaky idea could well have brought a smile to Hendrix's face just as his 'Belly Button Window', the point of view of an unborn foetus, could have tickled the rib of Prince himself. Also noteworthy is the fact that, as the music industry became ever more stratified, certainly in America, the land of juvenile rock DJs engaging in ritual mass destruction of disco records and the pace-setting broadcaster MTV infamously closing the door to black artists, musicians of colour did not skirt around the twin grenades of race and genre that had once blown up around Hendrix.

Prince does it playfully on 'Rockhard In A Funky Place' whereas Funkadelic confront the whole issue of which ethnicity is allowed to lay claim to a specific musical style on 'Who Says A Funk Band Can't Play Rock?' It is a hugely important track insofar as it openly questions not what might be called black music but what is the legitimacy with which the boundary between any number of genres should be morally policed. There is no justifiable reason why "a jazz band can't play dance music", or a "rock band can't play funky", or a "funk band can't play rock". Players gotta be free to be.

Built on a blistering blues shuffle with a mammoth bottom end, 'Who Says A Funk Band Can't Play Rock?' is a showcase for some brilliant Eddie Hazel guitar but the stinging licks are reinforced by another lyric which is even more apposite for the aesthetic of Hendrix – the unabashed allegiance to music at high volume. It is the revenge of the amplifier as well as the instrumentalist, the conviction that things need to be turned up for people to get down. There will be no restraint at all on noise levels. *We're gonna play some funk so loud.*

No greater tribute could be paid to the ethos of Jimi Hendrix, and his central point of view that electricity and rising decibel counts were tantamount to a form of religion. Funkadelic's text can be seen as a significant moment of protest in twentieth-century pop insofar as Clinton and his crew of polychrome and surreal subversives take down a myopic music industry, narrow-minded cultural establishment and divisive arbiters of good taste in one fell swoop, but they thrillingly up the ante with a postscript on the essential question of the intensity of performance and the sensation it generates. How hard can you rock? How heavy can you groove? How much can the band give as well as the audience take? The answer is unequivocal. *We're gonna play some funk so loud.*

This statement was made in 1978, just eight years after the death of Hendrix, and, as much as it honours him, it can equally be seen as a kind of empowering open letter to artists in all areas of black music – blues, jazz, rock, soul, funk – to cast off any constraints and refuse to compromise on creativity and stylistic versatility. Loud is both ally and agent of constructive change, an extension of Hendrix's thought-provoking remark that cranking up could be a way of doubling down on the forces of oppression embodied by the advent of slavery: "I wish they'd had electric guitars in the cotton fields back in the good old days. A whole lot of things would have been straightened out. Not just only for the black and white, but I mean for the cause."[12]

A Stratocaster's high-voltage scream is thus a politically charged action. For the most part it is not something that shocks in the context of the strains of pop, such as heavy metal, that Hendrix, among others helped to usher in. But the eruption of that sound within a song that is classified as soul, funk, jazz, fusion or avant-garde, remains exciting because, to a large extent, it is not readily associated with the aforementioned. One of the great gifts Hendrix gave to the world is the licence to make uncommon noise burst into any place, often where it was not expected, and to create a mandate for both sonic invention amid daring improvisation.

The late 1970s and early '80s saw that happen in abundance as excellent guitarists rocked inspiring bands doing soul-funk-jazz-blues-rock on their own terms. Think Blackbird McKnight with Headhunters; Kelvyn Bell with Defunkt; Donald Kinsey with The Kinsey Report; Ronnie Drayton with anybody from James Blood Ulmer to Material; Vernon Reid with Ronald Shannon Jackson & The Decoding Society. All the figures in this list are substantial talents, but it was Reid who went on to acquire the greatest cultural significance through Living Colour, the band he founded in the early 1980s and that made a major commercial breakthrough later in the decade with the album *Vivid*, featuring the memorable single 'Cult of Personality'. This was music that was as lyrically thought-provoking as it was intelligently composed and performed, with the presence of a charismatic and commanding vocalist.

Corey Glover, alongside Reid's expressive guitar and a superbly nailed-down drums and bass team of Muzz Skillings and Will Calhoun, made the band a hugely exciting arrival on the pop landscape in which the notion of black rock was an argument that needed to be won, despite the obvious wealth of documented evidence to the contrary.

First and foremost, there was an element of self-empowerment in Living Colour's modus operandi that spoke of free thinking, strong-minded individuals who were not cowed by partial or revisionist histories. Reflecting on his formative years Reid made this very telling statement: "I wasn't told that rock music was for white people, and that's something I give my parents a lot of credit for. I was listening to Yes and Zappa and Funkadelic and Morton Subotnick and Conlon Nancarrow and the myriad things I listened to. They may not have liked everything I was into, but the only thing they ever really told me was to turn it down because it was too loud."[13]

Like Hendrix and Funkadelic, Living Colour did not shy away from the decibel count. As with Hendrix and Funkadelic, Living Colour was not a stylistically limited band. Reid and co. drew on jazz, metal, funk, soul and punk to ensure that their version of rock was by no means reducible to a readymade formula, thus cogently upholding another key legacy of Hendrix and his scions. They showed a thorough understanding of Hendrix as a great eclectic, a maverick, a pathfinder willing to exercise creative freedom rather than freeze into any orthodoxy.

Most tellingly, Reid was astute enough to see the artistic totality of Hendrix. "I think that with him it was just *one* fluid thing; his songs, his playing, his whole vibe. People tend to get fixated on his playing but the thing about Hendrix is he created the *context* for his playing to exist", he told me in London in 2002. "That's the real genius."

Reid's musical interests are anything but narrow, and his subsequent career as a producer as well as player has seen him collaborate with anybody from American DJ Logic to Malian vocalist Salif Keita. In fact, the wide variety of situations in which he appears was mooted by the range of personnel featured in the early incarnations of Living Colour. Members included jazz musicians Jerome Harris and Geri Allen.

Such openness also framed a not-for-profit collective of which Reid was a founder member, along with journalist-musician Greg Tate, vocalist D.K. Dyson and producer Konda Mason: Black Rock Coalition. Its manifesto reads: "The BRC was created in New York in the fall of 1985 with the purpose of creating an atmosphere conducive to the maximum development, exposure and acceptance of Black Alternative Music".

The BRC mission statement is emphatically uncompromising: "Rock and roll, like practically every other form of popular music across the globe, is Black Music, and we are its heirs. We too claim the right of creative freedom and access to American and International airwaves, audiences, markets, resources, and compensations, irrespective of genre. The BRC embraces the total spectrum of Black Music."

Hence Black Rock in BRC signals more than blacks *doing rock*. Simply reducing the philosophy to a noun would be to sell short its depth and magnitude. It is also the possibility of rock as an active verb, as in *blacks rock*, which means that the supposed minority group is taking hold of its far-reaching history, or histories and truths, in order to negotiate a challenging future on its own terms rather than accept any of the partial definitions imposed by others. Black Rock is Black Eclecticism is Black Freedom.

As a guiding principle, nothing could be more relevant to Hendrix's times and what has happened since. The compartmentalization of gospel, blues, R&B, rock, soul, jazz and hip-hop by the music industry and media has been nothing but troublesome for artists who see the aforesaid genres as links in a long chain of evolutionary black cultural expression rather than distinctly separate entities that have no organic relationship.

This means understanding not just the continuum of Chuck Berry, Little Richard and Hendrix but the creative energies that bound Hendrix, James Brown, Sly Stone and Curtis Mayfield. Or understanding that Prince is a synthesis of all of the above who was also able to draw from the well of a superlative pop songwriter such as Elton John, who himself had ducked his head deep into the waters of black music during his formative years.

Living Colour's chart success and high profile gained through support slots for the likes of Guns 'n' Roses and the Rolling Stones were massively important. Yet there was a cornucopia of artists that emerged in the late 1980s and '90s to sustain the spirit of Hendrix both in his populist and experimental incarnations. Chief among them were Meshell Ndegeocello, Ben Harper, Michael Franti, Lenny Kravitz, Cody Chesnutt, Martin Luther, and Screaming Headless Torsos (SHT), a superb band that featured virtuoso guitarist David Fiuczynski, who, like Reid, is also a former Ronald Shannon Jackson sideman, and the commanding, charismatic vocalist Dean Bowman.

The albums SHT recorded between 1995 and the first decade of the millennium, such as its eponymous debut and *2005*, are thrilling examples of how the common rock set-up of vocals-guitar-bass-drums can benefit exponentially from the input of percussion to up the rhythmic ante on smart, often political songs that deal with anything from maddening urban mores ('S.U.V. S.O.B.') to industrial tragedies ('Chernobyl Firebirds') to ghastly conflict zones ('Wedding In Sarajevo'). SHT also impressively adapt Miles Davis under Hendrix's influence – 'Smile In A Wave (Theme From Jack Johnson)'.

Stone love for Lady T

If there is a contemporary band that stands as a more direct heir to Hendrix then it is Stone Raiders. Comprising guitarist-vocalist Jean-Paul Bourelly, bass guitarist Daryl Jones and drummer Will Calhoun, the group made an astounding debut in 2012 with *Truth To Power*, an album that pulled off the priceless feat of combining superlative musicianship with excellent melodies and thought-provoking lyrics. It honoured and extended the legacy of Hendrix as a songwriter as well as supremely gifted player.

Because they are three African-American musicians it is very tempting to see Stone Raiders as a millennial Band of Gypsys but Bourelly, whose 1995 album *Tribute To Jimi* is a notable Hendrix-themed set, chooses to draw on the entirety of Hendrix's aesthetic, which also includes the Experience songbook, the echoes of which are in his words as well as music. The strident anti-establishment strain of Stone Raiders is more explicit than Hendrix's yet Bourelly, a Chicago native whose varied career reaches back to the mid-1980s and has seen him work with unique musical minds such as Henry Threadgill, has developed his own complex relationship between voice, guitar and lyric that is in Hendrix's lineage and also reflects something of James "Blood" Ulmer's world-view.

In short, it is the weary blues for the twenty-first century. The artful blend of tenderness and disaffection evinced on an anthem such as 'Love's Parody' is deeply moving, above all because every verse and riff is granted a breathing space that makes it easier to process, and the low tempo enhances a real sense of meditative calm into which uncompromising sentiment is poured. The piece has a bruised cynicism. Its ambiance is not indistinct from one of the great heartaches Hendrix wrote, 'The Wind Cries Mary' and one of the wry contemplations he didn't live to hear, James "Blood" Ulmer's 'Are You Glad To Be In America?' Together these songs are a holy trinity of anguish and irony.

Bourelly and co. avail themselves of the latest in pedals and effects to fashion a pleasingly broad textural palette for Stone Raiders, enabling the group to fashion a ruggedly articulated, often deeply haunting proto-techno on occasion. Another trio that has similarly inventive soundscapes and great compositional ingenuity is Harriet Tubman, named after one of the icons of the slave resistance network, the "underground railroad". Active since 1998 the band comprises drummer J.T. Lewis, bass guitarist Melvin Gibbs and guitarist Brandon Ross, three musicians who, like the Stone Raiders, have had extensive experience in the field of jazz as well as soul, funk and progressive iterations of Afro-Brazilian pop. As one might expect, their musicianship has come well to the fore on their recordings to date but the band has found an excellent way of shifting the paradigm of the "power trio" that Hendrix, Cream and Tony Williams among others ushered in towards a form of vocabulary that coherently acknowledges the advent of breakbeat culture and the infinite new timbres of the laptop era without creating a stilted version of electro-jazz-rock in the process.

On albums such as *Prototype* and *I Am A Man*, Harriet Tubman performed material that operated effectively within the realm of theme-variation yet managed to avoid tried and tested strategies, sometimes wrapping a piece in discomfort blankets of noise, sometimes letting a guitar melody hover in the utmost melancholy while the drums and bass ebb and flow like waves on a jagged shoreline. The band achieves the feat of sounding inventive and disciplined. They push out and also skilfully rein in.

Recent releases *Ascension* and *Araminta* also indirectly revive the debate on what might have become of a Hendrix–Miles Davis encounter insofar as they feature two fine trumpeters, Ron Miles and Wada Leo Smith, respectively, who prove to be potent soloists and also well-integrated elements in the ensemble voice. Perhaps more importantly we also hear astute extrapolations of the electric vocabulary that Davis was happy to ascribe to Hendrix's impact upon him, namely the way that guitar and drums fostered a "deep African thing, a deep African-American groove".[14]

Harriet Tubman's 2018 offering *The Terror End Of Beauty* is one of its best to date and also nods to Hendrix insofar as the input of the personnel appointed to help sculpt the sound of the record is absolutely crucial. If Hendrix had Eddie Kramer engineering for him then Harriet Tubman has Scotty Hard, a respected figure who has worked across myriad genres.

Yet, amidst a sonic palette that is resoundingly contemporary the blues prevails: the tonal flourish; the depth of emotion encoded in mercurial patterns of notes; the need as well as desire to engage in both enlightening and *trickyfying* storytelling; the conviction that those who are darker than blue can shine the brightest light in society.

Harriet Tubman and Stone Raiders are seminal contemporary bands because they build on a range of legacies of which Hendrix is prominent, sans pastiche, and in the process they vindicate the Black Rock Coalition as a breeding ground for unshackled creativity and an empowering platform for politicized art of considerable gravitas. The musicians in these groups are part of a cohort who came of age in the early 1980s and either became members of the organization or collaborated with those who were. Most interestingly, BRC co-founder Vernon Reid remains a common denominator between Harriet Tubman and Stone Raiders insofar as the drummers in each trio, J.T. Lewis and Will Calhoun, respectively, are alumni of his much-loved Living Colour.

It would be hard to find a band more African-American and more New York than Living Colour because of their potent blend of musicianship, uncompromising attitude, powers of perception, artistic courage and visual flair; it is easy to forget that the sight of mohawked dreads was as much a shock to the system as people of colour out-rocking white rock and making black metal a term to be taken literally rather than figuratively.

Yet the band's history reaches beyond the Big Apple, and the clue to an international provenance is right there in its orthography. It is Living Colour, not *Color*. The choice of the British rather than American spelling is a quirk that chimes with Reid's own personal profile. He was born in Britain to West Indian parents. To call him an African-Caribbean-American might be ungainly, but it nonetheless serves as a reminder of the migration that for over a century has bound various beacon cities of the African Diaspora such as London, New York, Kingston and Port of Spain.

Hendrix travelled from North America to Europe to find success, and with a somewhat fateful symmetry, died in London after sojourning in New York. He left one home to return to a former one, his fire finally going out where it once burned bright. No greater symbol of this complex geo-cultural web came than in the shape of one of his last gigs. On 16 September 1970, Hendrix sat in with the English R&B singer Eric Burdon and multi-racial American funk band War (several African-Americans and one Dane) at Ronnie Scott's club in London. The guitarist did not renounce his key article of faith, "the jam". The ad hoc combo also presented the blues as an inextinguishable fire, especially on a smoking 'Tobacco Road'.

Last bastion of Englishness

Hendrix was a transatlantic artist. The pivotal role Britain played in the making of him as a commercial force to be reckoned with is not a historical novelty. The lineage of African-American musicians who decided to leave America for England reaches right back to the unknown fiddlers and drummers who were persuaded to fight for the British in the war of independence in exchange for freedom in the *mother country*.

The Victorian era saw minstrel troupes such as Haverly's Genuine Colored Minstrels entertain the masses while the gospel ensemble Fisk Jubilee Singers performed for the aristocracy, and they were followed by ragtime bands, from Louis Mitchell to Southern Syncopated Orchestra. Further down the line in the 1920s singer-actor-activist Paul Robeson ascended to icon status, particularly in Wales. These early U.S. invasions are wholly significant. They contributed to cultural change. They made Britain more interesting.

Among Hendrix's peers was a range of mighty soul sisters and brothers who worked in theatre as well as pop, such as Madeleine Bell, P.P. Arnold and Geno Washington, and who have stayed on in Britain to this day where they are all still working.

The fact that Washington and Hendrix also ended up on the same bill, at Barbecue '67 in Spalding, Lincolnshire, along with Zoot Money, Cream, Pink Floyd and The Move is testimony to the contiguity of psychedelic rock, pop and R&B acts at the time. Washington made a sizeable impact on the British soul scene through his high-energy performances with the Ram Jam band, but even more interestingly has spread his wings, penning children's stories, appearing as a rousing motivational speaker, and making occasional forays into the worlds of film and television.

Among his noted roles is a cameo in "The Axeman Cometh", a 2nd February 2007 episode of *Midsomer Murders*, the genteel crime drama whose unique selling point is that it shows that the way of the gun, knife or other gruesome means of destruction can be found as much on the splendidly manicured lawns of English rural havens as on the mean streets of urban hotspots. The torrid tales subsequently blew up into a race row when the show's (white) producer Brian True-May argued bluntly against any call for greater diversity in the casting. "Well, we just don't have ethnic minorities. We're the last bastion of Englishness and I want to keep it that way."[15]

How exactly Washington was viewed in his one-off appearance is an interesting topic for debate. He has been in the UK for over five decades but to listen to him make a stage announcement after a ripping version of 'Papa's Got A Brand New Bag', where he stretches the syllables of baby to bay-bee before he hollers "Now kick iiiit!", is to witness a black man born in America stay true to a fundamental part of his culture, namely a speech rhythm that brims with brio and confidence rather than diffidence.

What, then, are the most meaningful perceptions of people of colour from different parts of the African Diaspora? Did Washington make it on to the melanin-free set of *Midsomer* because he is still seen as an import rather than just a domestic product? Does the African-American enjoy a kudos denied the African-Caribbean? Does the ethnic minority actually become an exotic if not more palatable proposition because they are somehow *not* seen as part of the fabric of mainstream British society, and are therefore easier to abstract from the public imagination, posing less of a threat?

Numerous black British musicians have told me that they instinctively feel that "brothers" from America on tour in the UK are more accepted because they're due to board a plane the day after the gig, not to mention their added credibility as "the real thing" if they are playing jazz, blues or soul. As a rejoinder it is also worth noting the substantial difference between the treatment of black Africans, black Caribbeans and African-Americans in France, where artists of colour from the Big Apple have testified that they are likely to be dealt with way more leniently by the police in Paris if they exaggerate a yankee accent, even if they are able to speak French fluently.

Hendrix's 18-month sojourn in England has a timeless legacy. He irrevocably impacted British pop so that his name is now indelibly attached to British culture. Whosoever casts an eye on the blue plaque at 23 Brook Street, Mayfair would do well to contemplate not just the prestige of the accolade, and the quirk of fate that places Hendrix's badge of honour next to Handel's, but how we process his place in the national consciousness. By inducting him into the pantheon of white English heritage it is entirely possible that he is deducted from the no less illustrious Mecca of Black Britain, an entity still subject to great vulnerability vis-à-vis the "mother country". To be black in Britain does still not necessarily mean being British before black.

Windrush children who *thought* they were UK citizens were brutally told just that. The heartbreaking 2017 scandal of forced deportations of West Indians who had contributed substantially to British society only to be told they did not belong was the endgame of former Home Secretary Theresa

May's reprehensible policy of creating a *hostile environment* for immigration. It would have been interesting to hear Hendrix's view on it had he lived, for he made this quite prophetic statement in Berlin in 1967: "The race problem exists in Europe too, but they don't talk about it so much."[16] All this matters in Hendrix's story because he remains a complex and confusing phenomenon in terms of his notional identity even though his ethnicity may not be. Lest we forget, he was initially billed as a hot British import to American audiences.

Such is the prevailing narrative of Hendrix adopted by the white blues devotee, as embodied by the Jaggers and Joneses, it is often overlooked that he interacted with African-Caribbeans. Guyanese musician Eddy Grant was a visitor to Brook Street, Trinidadian promoter Wilf Walker booked some of his early gigs and Jamaican band Ossie Roberts & The Sweet Boys were the support act for one of his London shows.

Footage of Hendrix gigs in the UK show him as a black messiah to white audiences but Roberts pointed out that 'Hey Joe' was a heaven-sent "big tune" among West Indians in his adopted city of Manchester because they appreciated Hendrix as a balladeer, given the premium of romantic as well as rhythmic music for that particular audience. Furthermore, one might also speculate on how Hendrix, had he lived into the 1970s and spent more time in Britain or even sojourned in the Caribbean, would have related to the growth of innovative Jamaican sound system culture, which made a virtue of sky-high stacks of amps, tidal waves of volume, and showers of effects that strike a parallel with his own aesthetic. *King Jimis Meets Rockers Uptown*, if you will.

If a comprehensive definition of cultural black Britain can accommodate black America as well as Africa and the Caribbean then it makes sense to reframe Hendrix as an African-American *and* black Briton in the same way that his many predecessors and successors, the lineage running from the aforesaid Robeson in the 1920s to Carleen Anderson in the 1990s, can also be seen as superlative artists who straddle these borders with aplomb. They are symbols of dynamism within the black Diaspora.

With that in mind the artist who stands as one of the most valid of heirs to the Hendrix throne for his superlative writing skills is a black Irishman: Phil Lynott. His band Thin Lizzy became one of the biggest mainstream rock groups of the 1970s, and though the creative juices gradually dried up by the end of the decade, by which time they were becoming the cliché of the ubermacho spandex-wearing head bangers, the three albums the band cut between 1971 and 1973, *Thin Lizzy*, *Shades Of A Blue Orphanage* and *Vagabonds Of The Western World*, have many outstanding songs.

Sonically and texturally, these records may not have quite the breadth of Hendrix's work but the melodic and lyrical content of pieces such as 'Rise And Dear Demise Of The Funky Nomadic Tribes', 'The Friendly Ranger At Clontarf Castle' and 'Brought Down' are striking, above all for the way Lynott combines a storyteller's flourish with Irish folk influences to create an aesthetic that is deeply personal. He drew extensively on the musical vocabulary of mid-1960s rock, and the spirit of Hendrix, whose songs he regularly covered in a previous band Skid Row, remains strong. Lynott, like Hendrix, revealed poetic qualities, and had two books of verse published.

Sadly, the comparison with Hendrix extended to an early death, as Lynott passed away at the age of 36, and to a certain extent the very idea of a black British rocker ended with his demise. Furthermore, the general notion that a guitar band, whether an exponent of heavy metal or "jangly indie", was as confined to white musicians as a horn-led ensemble was to black, gained a significant amount of currency in the 1980s.

However, the mid-1990s saw a significant challenge to the status quo in the shape of Skunk Anansie, a band that shifted ages-old paradigms by replacing the expected voluminously coiffed male lead vocalist with a shaven-headed black front woman. Exuding volcanic charisma, Deborah "Skin" Dyer had a powerful set of pipes while the musicians alongside her – guitarist Ace, bassist Cass and drummer Mark Richardson – were highly skilled players who drew on a range of vocabularies from metal to dub to electronica. In many ways they built on the foundation of post-Hendrix performers such as Red Hot Chili Peppers, Bad Brains and Living Colour but Skin's bold black feminist leanings as well as the fierce political discourse of pieces like 'Little Baby Swastika' enabled the band to fashion a quite unique stylistic berth for itself.

If Skunk Anansie was an exciting outgrowth of the rock lexicon that Hendrix and others had a hand in shaping, then Jimi also acted as a source of inspiration to a number of important British jazz musicians in the millennium. In 2004 saxophonist-composer Pete Wareham made as clear a reference to Hendrix as possible by the very name of his band, Acoustic Ladyland, not to mention song titles such as 'Little Miss Wingate', which featured on *Camouflage*, an excellent album, full of plaintive, yearning themes that underlined Hendrix as a deeply sensitive soul as well as raging force of nature.

The use of the following quote from Hendrix on the sleeve emphasized the guitarist's ongoing importance to jazz, where individuality is sovereign and imagination nothing less than sacrosanct. "You just can't do everybody's songs, and if you're gonna do 'em, well you don't necessarily have to copy it like them. If you really dig the person and really, really dig the song, well then you do it your own way."

Therein remains part of the appeal and relevance of Hendrix to recent generations of improvising musicians. In the UK that includes horn players such as saxophonist Shabaka Hutchings, while highly accomplished guitarists such as Chris Sharkey and Chris Montague are providing thought-provoking clues on what Hendrix may have done had he lived to avail himself of the sonic possibilities of the digital age.

Another important guitarist who draws on Hendrix's influence is Tony Remy. His own solo work as well as his contribution (as producer and player) to major jazz and pop artists such as Jean Toussaint, Cleveland Watkiss and Annie Lennox, have given him an enviable C.V. but it is his unflagging commitment to the blues and the culture of jamming that was so important to Jimi – Remy has been leading a session at the iconic London jazz club Ronnie Scott's for over 12 years – as well as his virtuosity and embrace of new technology that make him an important keeper of the Hendrix flame.

Interestingly, Remy is also able to effectively place his role model in an instructive context during his live shows. In July 2019 he appeared at Ronnie's as a member of the band led by saxophonist Pee Wee Ellis, one of James Brown's revered horn players. On one scintillating solo, in which his tone conspired to brilliantly flicker and crackle as much as scream, he dropped in a seamless quote of The Beatles' 'Eleanor Rigby' and on another Miles Davis's 'Jean Pierre'. The musicians who inspired Hendrix and whom he subsequently inspired were presented as part of a coherent whole, a fitting snapshot of the artist's place beyond the borders of pop, rock and jazz.

A month later at London's Jazz Café there was a similar nod to Hendrix's ongoing relevance to both modern music amid the never-ending complexity of race relations. Lucky Peterson, former accompanist to R&B and blues royalty such as Etta James and Little Milton, played a storming set, which culminated in him standing up from behind the Hammond organ, strapping on a guitar, exiting the stage and wading into a hyperventilating crowd. On bended knee he struck up a medley: Hendrix's 'Voodoo Child (Slight Return)', Chuck Berry's 'Johnny B. Goode' and Stevie Wonder's 'Superstition'. In a not dissimilar way to Remy, Peterson was reframing Hendrix, revealing his key influence as well as one of his jamming partners. Most importantly the crucial musical connection between all three pieces was clear – the opening gambit of rock and the closing fanfare of soul both came from the bosom of the blues.

Yet in the middle of the sequence Peterson did something that knocked the audience sideways. He launched into Wild Cherry's 'Play That Funky Music White Boy'. For a black man to be quoting a song that was written by a white rock band as a response to it being told by black punters it was not serving up the beat the brothers and sisters wanted was a grand double irony that Hendrix, given his sense of humour, would have surely appreciated. Who was busting a move right in Peterson's face? The two most hip and happening dancers in the audience: a black man and a white woman, both of a certain age.

There were no announcements made during the medley. All the pieces were played as instrumentals. People sang the vocal choruses. Obviously. It would have been a redundancy bordering on an insult to the intelligence of the general public to announce any of the songs because their place in popular consciousness is so well established. The instant engagement of the audience with the material consolidated the idea that black music, in its many manifestations, from rock 'n' roll to rock to soul and funk, is an integral part of the cultural fabric of society that provides much more than superficial kudos to impress a discerning peer group. These genres really are meaningful soundtracks to our lives. They can greatly sublimate trial and tribulation.

Hearing Hendrix's songs in Peterson's live set alongside those of Berry and Wonder consolidates his place in an important cultural pantheon, but the significance is arguably more substantial than a moment of "Greatest hits" nostalgia. Both musicians and music lovers were being shown a wellspring from which new music is still drawn, a source of immense, infinite richness that continues to inspire songwriters to this day.

It is a reminder that Hendrix remains relevant to anybody who is sufficiently lucid to see beyond the putative genre boundaries, and realize that rock, loud guitars and all, can and does flow into soul, jazz and funk, and that, whether or not Hendrix is being specifically held up as a model, he has impacted dozens of artists *across* the stylistic spectrum. He stands as a pivotal, if not fundamental reference for all open minds.

Musicians who see him as a unique individual as well as part of a grand creative continuum are likely to reflect his influence at some point in their career. It thus makes perfect sense for Aaron Mills, the brilliant bassist with funk legends Cameo, to hold a jam in a studio where the walls are adorned with posters of Red Hot Chili Peppers, Ben Harper, and Hendrix supersized into the Statue of Liberty. You'd be right to think of Cameo as synth and horns heroes who don't care much for the decibel assault of electric six strings, but listen to 'Talkin' Out Of The Side Of Your Neck' and you'll hear how well they channel the spirits of Hendrix and Parliament-Funkadelic *entre autres.*

Trainin' in

Hendrix's place in contemporary pop culture is conspicuous to say the least. If it comes as no surprise to see him on the cover of mainstream rock journals such as *Mojo* then the sight of Hendrix's portrait in any number of music venues in Britain makes it clear how deeply embedded he is in the national psyche. This means that he is liable to float around, like a tricksy spirit, in the orbit of any bands who enter pop's ever-busy field of dreams. Hence Hendrix, resplendent in his hussar's jacket, brings a touch of magnetism to ska-lite hopefuls Chainska Brassika's promo for their 2020 single 'Simple Things', shot at The Fox and Firkin, a lively pub in Lewisham, South London. Yet this is nothing other than a sign of the permanency of Seattle's fire-starter mould-breaker son, as he has come to represent a timeless and universal value. When the camera flashes on his face there is no need for a caption underneath to explain who has come into view.

More importantly his repertoire still proves irresistible to many artists with very different aesthetics. For example, three covers of 'The Wind Cries Mary' in the past two decades have come from Guyanese flautist Keith Waithe; Belgian duo, vocalist David Linx and bass guitarist Michael Hatzigeorgiou; and British vocalist-pianist Jamie Cullum. The song stood as the most played cut on Cullum's 2003 album *Twenty Something*. It was also one of the favourite tunes of the mother of best-selling British crime writer Martina Cole.[17] Hendrix's appeal spans several generations, social classes and cultures. It is particularly enlightening to hear how some of the biggest names in rock and pop name-check him. For example, Jean-Jacques Burnel, bassist of punk legends The Stranglers, stated proudly that he was born in the hospital, St. Mary Abbot's in Kensington, west London, where Hendrix was declared dead,[18] and Robert Smith of goth rock pioneers The Cure once confided that he regarded Hendrix and David Bowie as role models because they were "rogue characters ... people who lived a life that was really like wild and colourful".[19] Stewart Copeland of The Police calls 'Spanish Castle Magic' one of his "Inheritance tracks", a song that changed his life and that he would pass on to others.[20]

Of the very recent Hendrix covers, the version of 'Little Wing' by the international trio Gilfema – Beninois guitarist Lionel Loueke, Hungarian drummer Ferenc Nemeth and Italian bassist Massimo Biolcati – is outstanding for the way it highlights the absolute beauty of the melody and the springboard it provides for improvisation. Hendrix remains a great gift for artists who both like to play themes and take solos.

Against the certainty of Hendrix's stature we have the uncertainty of his potential evolution had he not died so young. The most tantalizing question is how he would have responded to the substantial technological advances in music making that have occurred between the 1970s and the millennium. As argued in Part 2, Hendrix was a sonic adventurer of the highest order, and many of his songs have the breakbeat appeal that is crucial to hip-hop. He may have been able to achieve a great deal had he lived to collaborate with producers adept at the science of sampling and sequencing.

It is easy to imagine him equalling if not exceeding the funk-rock energy of Aerosmith alongside the ballsy rapping of Run DMC had he been asked to cut 'Walk This Way' in 1985. Furthermore, the collaboration between "live hip-hop" legends The Roots, singer Cody Chesnutt and guitarist Vernon Reid has provided a clue as to what Hendrix may have produced had he lived to see the flowering of spoken word and street poetry into the modern-day MC. Then again, if he'd been drawn into the world of beats and rhymes, would Hendrix have felt alienated by the replacement of a drummer by a drum machine and the erosion of his beloved jam culture that the praxis of cut & paste can also jeopardize? It is impossible to say. He may have stagnated and in the worst-case scenario even ended up as a stale stadium-filling pastiche of himself.

Beyond his rich musical legacy Hendrix leaves us with many delightful and enduring provocations. He questions what we understand by the blues, whether we see it as a static or dynamic force, a purely referential tradition or an experiential discourse of much complexity and subtlety, from which untold stories can be spun over and over. His genius was to see himself *of and beyond* the blues, to realize its restorative power and mutative energy, its position as a launching pad for what has not yet been named.

To reach the future he surfed the past, deep into ancestral waters, into early blues, to evoke not just the Johnsons and the Pattons but the blues musician sans nom who is invaluably documented in the accounts of W.C. Handy at the dawn of the twentieth century. We're talking about the "lean, loose-jointed Negro" making the *weirdest* music the composer had ever heard, startling him with a series of previously unknown sounds.

Handy encountered the itinerant guitarist at a train station, the place that has far-reaching psychological and socio-cultural resonance for African-Americans, be they musicians or not, insofar as it represents a viable means of escape from oppression, particularly in the south, and conduit to freedom, mostly in the north. No better example of the pivotal role of public transport for rural blacks who found themselves in quite perilous situations is the story told by the extraordinary writer Toni Morrison of her upbringing in Alabama. With her father being an itinerant musician who was often away from their small farm, her mother took the pivotal decision to move the family to Ohio because the young girls were seen to be in grave danger. The train was a real way out. In a most chilling letter to her husband she stated, "White boys are circling".[21]

As for the astounding Elizabeth Cotten, who, like Hendrix, was a left-handed guitarist-vocalist, she also wrote about the experience of having to leave town. On 'Freight Train' Cotten invested the iron horse with a quality of salvation, presumably from the real adversity she experienced as a black woman raised in North Carolina in the early twentieth century. She puts her faith in the train that "*run so fast*" and implores any fellow passengers not to tell "what train I'm on", or "what road I'm gone".[22]

The train is also a central backdrop against which class conflict plays out. Gospel legend Sister Rosetta Tharpe sang of "this train bound for glory" which engaged all believers in a covenant of righteousness, so they could find a seat on a "clean train ... everybody ride it in Jesus' name". However, the loafer-wanderer-backslider-hobo of no fixed abode is of a mind to jump one freight car after another, much to the dismay of all god-fearing folk, because he has to be resourceful to reach any destination. The hand of the good lord is not as apt as a set of quick wits.

Guitarist-vocalist Jesse Fuller gave a compelling account of this peripatetic lifestyle on his 1958 song 'Leaving Memphis, Frisco Bound'. In the introduction he makes it clear that he "took a lot of different roads", and that his instrument was one of the few constants in his world. "I wanted to leave Memphis, I got tired of living in that town. I got my old guitar, walked down the track waiting for that Frisco to come pulling down the line. Once I got all set I climbed on the top like hobos always liked to do!"[23]

Hendrix also saw the train as a theme for song and the station a scene for storytelling. In the sleeve notes he wrote for Buddy Miles's *Expressway To Your Skull* Hendrix evoked railroad tracks rumbling to the sound of the band The Express, loaded up with goodness – "Shaking steady ... shaking FUNK ...

shaking FEELING, shaking LIFE" – en route to the blessed Electric Church. And on the live version of one of his most affecting blues, 'Hear My Train A Comin'', Hendrix deigns to create his own rousing mythology, presenting a character borne of a fertile fantasy that nonetheless harbours a deep reality. It is the tale of the free thinker, the outsider, the original, and it rings dramatically true. He narrates a succinct but nonetheless compelling adventure.

> Here's a story that a lot of us have been through at one time or another, one way or another, about a cat he's running around town his old lady thinks she don't want him around, and a whole lot of people from across the tracks are putting him down. Nobody wants to face up to it ... the cat has something, probably everybody's against him because the cat might be a little bit different. So he goes on the road to be a voodoo child ... come back and be a magic boy. Right now, we're waiting for a train.[24]

He signs off by seamlessly moving from the personal to the collective. His story becomes our story. Or at least, a speech on behalf of anybody who cares something for happiness beyond the purely material. You don't have to be a voodoo chile to know what it's like to be put down, or to be "a little bit different" to end up on the receiving end of hard knocks. You don't have to be a magic boy to see a way out.

But when Jimi Hendix sings 'Hear My Train A Comin'' you do have to stop and think what you gon' do. You can let the locomotive pass you by. Or you can get on board.

Notes

Introduction

1. 'Jimi Hendrix Cleared of Blame for UK Parakeet Release', *BBC News*, https://www.bbc.co.uk/news/uk-england-50755015.

Part 1: The Song and Jimi Hendrix

1. 'Shotgun' [L1126], http://earlyhendrix.com/buddymen (YouTube), 5 September 2014 (accessed September 2018).
2. Hal Neely, sleeve notes for James Brown's *It's A Mother* (Polydor, 1967).
3. Tony Brown, *Jimi Hendrix Talking* (London: Omnibus, 1994), p. 12.
4. Al Hendrix, Rock n Roll Hall of Fame 2012, http://www.rockhall.com/exhibits/featured-collections/jimi-hendrix/ (accessed September 2018).
5. *A Film About Jimi Hendrix*, dir. Joe Boyd, Warner bros, 1973.
6. Brown, *Jimi Hendrix Talking*, p. 23.
7. Brown, *Jimi Hendrix Talking*, p. 21.
8. Ernie and Ronald Isley, 30 July 2017. CBS Sunday Morning Channel, http://bit.ly/20gXwJT.
9. Brown, *Jimi Hendrix Talking*, p. 20.
10. Sleeve notes of Otis Blackwell's *These Are My Songs!* (Inner City, 1977).
11. McHugh penned over 500 songs between the 1920s and 1950s and collaborated with the likes of Frank Loesser, Johnny Mercer and Dorothy Fields.
12. Ernie Isley, Hilton Teper, 4 May 2007.
13. Interview with the author, London, May 1999.
14. Brown, *Jimi Hendrix Talking*, p. 23.
15. Ronald Isley, Hilton Teper, 4 May 2007.
16. Little Stevie Wonder, 'Fingertips', featured on *The Jazz Soul of Little Stevie* (Motown, 1962).
17. Bobby Hutcherson, interviewed by the author, London, 2007.
18. Richard Houghton, *Jimi Hendrix: The Day I Was There* (Prestatyn: This Day In Music, 2018), p. 106.
19. *A Film About Jimi Hendrix*, dir. Joe Boyd, 1973.
20. Jimi Hendrix, *Live At Fillmore East* [DVD], Universal Island, 2001.
21. Austin John Marshall, *The Observer* magazine, 3 December 1967.

22. John McDermott with Eddie Kramer, *Hendrix: Setting the Record Straight* (London: Little Brown & Company, 1992), p. 115.
23. *A Film About Jimi Hendrix*, dir. Joe Boyd, 1973.
24. Houghton, *Jimi Hendrix: The Day I Was There*, p. 52.

Part 2: The Songs of Jimi Hendrix

1. Morgan Neville's *20 Feet From Stardom* (2014) is an invaluable documentary both on the largely hidden talents in the music industry – mostly black women – and the exploitation they have suffered. It shines a light on the likes of Darlene Love, Tata Vega, Merry Clayton and Lisa Fischer, among others.
2. John McDermott with Eddie Kramer, *Hendrix: Setting the Record Straight* (London: Little Brown & Company, 1992), p. 125.
3. McDermott with Kramer, *Hendrix: Setting the Record Straight*, p. 126.
4. *Los Angeles Times*, 24 December, 1967. Quoted by John McDermott on page 17 of *You Can't Use My Name*, RSVP/PPX sessions, Curtis Knight & The Squires (Sony, 2015).
5. McDermott, *Hendrix: Setting the Record Straight*, p. 435.
6. Booklet of Jimi Hendrix *People, Hell And Angels* (Sony, 2013), p. 19.
7. Harry Shapiro, *Alexis Korner: The Biography* (London: Bloomsbury, 1997), p. 158.
8. Shapiro, *Alexis Korner*, p. 114.
9. Tony Brown, *Jimi Hendrix Talking* (London: Omnibus, 1994), p. 39.
10. Early BBC live broadcasts are particularly rich in black music.
11. For an excellent overview of the material recorded for 'Auntie', see The Jimi Hendrix Experience, *BBC Sessions* (MCA, 1998).
12. According to producer Stanley Dorfman he was so pleased with what they got he kept the cameras rolling, but then the show literally ran out of time. There was another act (and a reappearance by Lulu) that didn't happen owing to the overrun.
13. Shapiro, *Alexis Korner*, p. 158.
14. Mostly likely a Hagstrom H-8.
15. Shapiro, *Alexis Korner*, p. 106.
16. Mezz Mezzrow and Bernard Wolfe, *Really the Blues* (Edinburgh: Payback, 1998), p. 148.
17. Alyn Shipton, *A New History of Jazz* (New York: Continuum, 2001), p. 462.
18. Booklet of *Jimi Hendrix BBC Sessions* (MCA, 1998).
19. Behind The Scenes, Crosstown Traffic, *Electric Ladyland* (Sony, 2010).
20. Ibid.
21. Ibid.
22. YouTube, Q1043 FM, New York, 3 December 2018.
23. Ibid.
24. Brown, *Jimi Hendrix Talking*, p. 61.
25. McDermott, *Hendrix: Setting the Record Straight*, p. 29.
26. Brown, *Jimi Hendrix Talking*, p. 62.
27. Behind The Scenes, Crosstown Traffic, *Electric Ladyland* (Sony, 2010).
28. Interview with Terry David Mulligan, Vancouver, 7 September 1968.
29. Ibid.
30. Solomon Burke, *Rock 'N' Soul* (Atlantic, 1964).
31. Mystikal, 'I Rock. I Roll', featured on *Let's Get Ready* (Jive, 2001).
32. Brown, *Jimi Hendrix Talking*, p. 23.
33. Brown, *Jimi Hendrix Talking*, p. 61.
34. McDermott, *Hendrix: Setting the Record Straight*, p. 82.
35. Henry Talbert, 'Shake It Baby', featured on Various artists, *Bayou Drive* (Chess, 1989).
36. Otis Taylor, interview with the author, London, June 2005.

37. Richard Houghton, *Jimi Hendrix: The Day I Was There* (Prestatyn: This Day In Music, 2018), p. 103.
38. Youtube.com/bbcnews, 22 February 2014.
39. Taj Mahal with Stephen Foehr, *The Autobiography of a Bluesman* (London: Sanctuary, 1992), p. 102.
40. Brown, *Jimi Hendrix Talking*, p. 13.
41. Brown, *Jimi Hendrix Talking*, p. 125.
42. W. C. Handy, *Father of the Blues: An Autobiography* (Boston, MA: Da Capo, 1941), p. 77.
43. Handy, *Father of the Blues*, p. 74.
44. By no means a definitive list; see also Paul Jackson Jr, Cornell Dupree, Eric Gale.
45. Interview with the author, London, June 2019.
46. Interview with the author (phone), September 2019.
47. *Guitar World*, 19 April 2019.
48. Interview with the author (email), March 2020.
49. Behind The Scenes, *Machine Gun. Band of Gypsys* DVD (Sony, 2010).
50. Niels Olaf Gudme, YouTube channel, Alabaster Jones, 1969.
51. Interview with the author, June 2019.
52. Behind The Scenes, *Little Wing, Axis: Bold As Love* DVD (Sony, 2010).
53. Interview with Terry David Mulligan, Vancouver, 7 September 1968.
54. *The Dick Cavett Show*, ABC, 9 September 1969.
55. Ringgold's *The People's Flag Show* at the Judson Memorial Church in Manhattan's West village in 1970 led to her arrest, along with that of John Hendricks and Jean Tuche. They were charged with desecration of the flag and ordered to pay $100 each or spend 30 days in jail. They were successfully defended by the American Civil Liberties Union.
56. Interview with the author, June 2019.
57. Interview with the author (phone), September 2019.
58. Keith Shadwick, *Jimi Hendrix Musician* (London: Backbeat, 2003), p. 109.
59. Interview with the author (phone), September 2019.
60. Interview with the author, London, June 2019.
61. Ibid.
62. For Terminator X in full effect see Public Enemy's *It Takes A Nation of Millions To Hold Us Back* (Def Jam, 1988).
63. Interview with the author, London, June 2019.
64. Behind The Scenes, *Crosstown Traffic, Electric Ladyland* (Sony, 2010).
65. Ibid.
66. Ibid.
67. Behind The Scenes, *Axis: Bold As Love* (Sony, 2010).
68. Behind The Scenes, 'Are You Experienced?' (Sony, 2010).
69. Brown, *Jimi Hendrix Talking*, p. 68.
70. The music of Motown records, one of the dominant commercial forces of black pop in the 1960s, was well known to Hendrix, who had also jammed with one of the label's stars, Stevie Wonder, in London.
71. Brown, *Jimi Hendrix Talking*, p. 102.
72. Behind The Scenes, *All Along The Watchtower, Electric Ladyland* (Sony, 2010).
73. Otis Redding, 'Fa-Fa-Fa-Fa-Fa [Sad Song]' (Stax, 1966). This is a great example of the precedence of the sound of the voice over the meaning of words, or rather the way an apparently nonsensical utterance such as Fa can acquire immense emotional substance through the richness of a singer's performance.
74. 'Belly Button Window', featured on *The First Rays of The New Rising Sun* (Sony, 2010).
75. Houghton, *Jimi Hendrix: The Day I Was There*, p. 176.
76. Brown, *Jimi Hendrix Talking*, p. 66.

77. Brown, *Jimi Hendrix Talking*, p. 10.
78. Ibid.
79. Sam Greenlee, *The Spook Who Sat by the Door* (London: Allison & Busby, 1969).
80. Brown, *Jimi Hendrix Talking*, p. 62.
81. Ibid.
82. Billie Holiday, 'My Man', featured on *Billie Holiday* (Vogue, 1973).
83. *The Dick Cavett Show*, 9 September 1969.
84. Langston Hughes, *The Weary Blues* (New York: Knopf, 2015).
85. Brown, *Jimi Hendrix Talking*, p. 96.
86. *Brown, Jimi Hendrix Talking*, p. 96.
87. James Brown, 'Soul Power' (King, 1971).
88. Funkadelic, 'What Is Soul', featured on *Funkadelic* (Westbound, 1970).
89. Brown, *Jimi Hendrix Talking*, p. 112.
90. Brown, *Jimi Hendrix Talking*, p. 100.
91. Justice Through Music, www.jtmp.org, 2 December 2012.
92. Brown, *Jimi Hendrix Talking*, p. 99.
93. *Band Of Gypsys: Live At The Filmore East* DVD (Sony, 2011).
94. Interview with the author (phone), 2004, discussing her album *The Life Of A Song*, issued in the same year by Telarc.
95. Houghton, *Jimi Hendrix: The Day I Was There*, p. 97.

Part 3: The Songs from Jimi Hendrix

1. Isely Brothers, 'That Lady', featured on *3+3* (T-Neck, 1973).
2. Bar-Kays, *Black Rock* (Volt, 1971).
3. Fresh Start, *What America Needs* (ABC, 1974).
4. Betty Davis, 'Anti Love Song', featured on *Betty Davis* (Epic, 1973).
5. W. C. Handy, *Father of the Blues: An Autobiography* (Boston, MA: Da Capo, 1941), p. 77.
6. Miles Davis with Quincy Troupe, *The Autobiography* (London: Picador, 1990), p. 319.
7. Julius Hemphill, *Coon Bid'ness* (Arista Freedom, 1975).
8. James Blood Ulmer, *Tales of Captain Black* (Artists House, 1979).
9. Booklet for World Saxophone Quartet, *Experience* (Justintime, 2004).
10. World Saxophone Quartet, *Rhythm & Blues* (Eletktra Musician, 1989).
11. Julius Hemphill, *Coon Bid'ness* (Arista Freedom, 1975).
12. Tony Brown, *Jimi Hendrix Talking* (London: Omnibus, 1994), p. 96.
13. John Wenzel, "Living Colour's Vernon Reid on the band's formulation, Mick Jagger and reaching audiences through 'Grand Theft Auto'", *Denver Post*, 24 October 2013.
14. Miles Davis with Quincy Troupe, *The Autobiography*, p. 319.
15. Anthony Barnes, "Midsomer Murders Producer True-May Suspended over Minorities Comment," *The Independent*, 15 March 2011. Following his remarks True-May was suspended by production company All3Media as an internal investigation was launched.
16. Brown, *Jimi Hendrix Talking*, p. 96.
17. *Saturday Live*, BBC Radio 4, 21 March 2020.
18. Tv5 Monde, November 2017.
19. Telerama.fr, July 2012.
20. *Saturday Live*, BBC Radio 4, 15 May 2020.
21. *Toni Morrison: The Pieces I Am*. Dir. Timothy Greenfield-Sanders, 2019.
22. Elizabeth Cotten, *Freight Train and Other North Carolina Folk Songs* (Washington DC: Smithsonian Folkways, 1957–58).
23. Jesse Fuller, *Frisco Bound* (Arhoolie Records, 1991).
24. Jimi Hendrix, *Blues* (Polydor, 1991).

Bibliography

Brown, Tony, *Jimi Hendrix Talking*. London: Omnibus, 1994.
Cotten, Elizabeth, *Freight Train and Other North Carolina Folk Songs*. Washington DC: Smithsonian Folkways, 1957–58.
Davis, Miles with Quincy Troupe, *The Autobiography*. London: Picador, 1990.
Greenlee, Sam, *The Spook Who Sat by the Door*. London: Allison & Busby, 1969.
Handy, W. C., *Father of the Blues: An Autobiography*. Boston, MA: Da Capo, 1941.
Houghton, Richard, *Jimi Hendrix: The Day I Was There*. Prestatyn: This Day In Music, 2018.
Hughes, Langston, *The Weary Blues*. New York: Knopf, 2015.
Mahal, Taj with Stephen Foehr, *Taj Mahal: The Autobiography of a Bluesman*. London: Sanctuary, 1992.
McDermott, John with Eddie Kramer, *Hendrix: Setting the Record Straight*. London: Little Brown & Company, 1992.
Mezzrow, Mezz and Bernard Wolfe, *Really the Blues*. Edinburgh: Payback, 1998.
Shaar Murray, Charles, *Crosstown Traffic: Jimi Hendrix and Post-War Pop*. London: Faber & Faber, 1989.
Shadwick, Keith, *Jimi Hendrix: Musician*. London: Backbeat, 2003.
Shapiro, Harry, *Alexis Korner: The Biography*. London: Bloomsbury, 1997.
Shipton, Alyn, *A New History of Jazz*. New York: Continuum, 2001.
Tate, Greg, *Midnight Lightning: Jimi Hendrix and the Black Experience*. New York: Lawrence Hill, 2003.

Index

3+3 (album) 189
'1983 (A Merman I Should Turn To Be)' 151, 153, 164
2005 (album) 203

Abercrombie, John 194
Ace (Skunk Anansie) 209
Acoustic Ladyland 209
Adderley, Cannonball 84
Advision studio 149
Aerosmith 212
A Film About Jimi Hendrix 33, 36
'A Hard Day's Night' 75
'Ain't Nobody Here But Us Chickens' 34
'Ain't No Telling' 76, 86, 106, 164
Akotché, Noel 148
'All Shook Up' 21
Allen, Geri 185, 202
Allen twins (Albert & Arthur aka Ghetto Fighters) 32, 47, 48, 178
'All Along The Watchtower' 119–122, 132, 145, 154, 156, 189
Almoctar, Goumar "Bombino" 148
'Alphabet Street' 98
'Am I My Brother's Keeper' 53
'And The Gods Made Love' 73
'Andalucia' (*Suite Espanola*) 130
Anderson, Carleen 208
'Angel' 102, 137, 157, 173
Animals, The 49, 65
'Anti-Love Song' 190
'Anything You Can Do I Can Do Better' 132
Araminta 205
Are You Experienced? (album) 46, 49, 71, 76, 82, 111, 152–153
'Are You Experienced?' (song) 152–153, 172
'Are You Glad To Be In America?' 204
Armstrong, Louis 86, 96, 148
Arnold, P.P. 206
Art Ensemble of Chicago 194
Ascension 205
Association, The 105
Atlanta Pop Festival 130, 140
Autry, Gene 21
"The Axeman Cometh" (*Midsomer Murders*) 206
Axis: Bold As Love 46, 49, 71, 76, 102, 150, 153, 169
Ayler, Albert 195

'Baby Please Don't Go' 117
Bach 108
Bad Benson 130
Bad Brains 209
Bag O'Nails (club) 49
Baker, Ginger 54, 190
Ball, Kenny 57
Baldwin, James 198
Band of Gypsys (group) 28, 46, 76, 104, 113–114, 174, 183, 187, 189, 191, 193, 204
Band Of Gypsys (album) 119, 129, 155, 181

Barber, Chris 53, 63
Bar-Kays 189
Basie, Count 1, 9
BBC 56, 68, 140
'Beale Street Blues' 109
Beatles, The 1, 3, 21–22, 33, 49, 59, 75, 100, 103–104, 149, 156, 163, 170, 185, 200, 210
Bechet, Sidney 66, 148
Beethoven 74
Bell, Kelvyn 201
Bell, Madeleine 206
'Belly Button Window' 73, 158, 200
Below The Fold 100
Benson, George 128–130, 155
Bernstein, Leonard 39
Berry, Chuck 12, 15, 22, 60, 62, 74–75, 103, 107–108, 156, 202, 210–211
Big Mama Thornton 126
Billboard 21
'Billie's Blues' 172
Biolcati, Massimo 212
Birth Of The Cool 191
Bishop Elvin 71
Black Elvis 28
Black Panther Party 178
Black Rock 189
Black Rock Coalition 202, 205
Black Sabbath 193
Black Woman 200
Blackwell, Otis 21
'Bleeding Heart' 162, 193
Bloomfield, Mike 105, 143
Blossoms, The 40–41
'Blue Suede Shoes' 107
blues
  cultural and conceptual importance 176–177
  Delta 116, 125
  epic performance 111–113
  formula and feeling 185
  Hendrix discussing meaning on Dick Cavett Show 175
  Hendrix's use in song titles 174
  musical history 108–109
  tradition of talkin' blues 157–158
Blues Incorporated 51
blues rock (genre) 90
'Blues Rock' (song) 90
Bluiett, Hamiett 196
Bob & Earl 9
Body Meta 195
'Bold As Love' 169–170
Booker, James 47
Booker T & The MGs 81, 137
Boosty's Rubber Band 188
Bourelly, Jean-Paul 203
Bowie, David 212
Bowman, Dean 203
'The Breeze And I' 130–132
British invasion 21
'Brought Down' 208
Brown, James 11–12, 23, 29–30, 32, 34, 75, 92, 97, 108, 179–180, 194, 196–197, 200, 210
Bruce, Jack 135, 190
Buddy & Stacy (Travis & Jonson) 9–10, 12, 16–17, 30
Burdon, Eric 65, 206
Burke, Solomon 89
Burnel, Jean-Jacques 212
'Burning Of The Midnight Lamp' 104, 133, 144–145, 159–160
Burrell, Kenny 87, 128, 194
Butterfield, Paul [Blues Band] 105
Byrds, The 32

Café Wha? 19
'Caldonia' 34
Calhoun, Will 201, 205
calypso 181
Cameo 211
Camouflage 209
'Can You See Me' 76, 93
Captain Sky 60
Carnaby Street 4, 166
Carr, Vicki 41
Carter, Benny 54
Caruso, Paul 18, 150
Casady, Jack 71, 73, 113
Cass (Skunk Anansie) 209
'Castles Made Of Sand' 164, 178
Castor, Jimmy 189
Cavett, Dick (Show) 174–175
Cetshwayo 3
Chainska Brassika 211

Chalpin, Ed 43–44
Chambers Brothers 188
Chandler, Chas 39, 65, 71, 73, 78–79, 81, 94, 101, 137, 149–151, 153, 168, 187
'The Changeling' 106
Charles, Ray 26, 41, 100, 103, 106
Checker, Chubby 24
'Chernobyl Firebirds' 203
Chesnutt, Cody 202, 212
chitlin' circuit 17, 54
Christian, Charlie 128, 148
civil rights 182
Clapton, Eric 28, 125, 160, 172, 190
Clinton, George 181, 191, 200
Clowes, Trish 124
CND 182
Coasters, The 16
Cochrane, Eddie 57
'Cold Sweat' 92, 97
Cole, Martina 212
Coleman, Ornette 194–196
Collins, Albert 123
Collins, Boosty 188
Coltrane, John 86, 120, 195
Colyer, Ken 53, 57
'Come On In My Kitchen' 116, 176
'Come On Let The Good Times Roll' 104
Cooke, Sam 129, 155
cool jerk (dance) 11
Coon 'Bidness 197
Copeland, Stewart 211
Coronation Street (television programme)101
Cosey, Pete 192
Cotten, Elizabeth 213
Cousins (venue) 52
Covay, Don 155
Cox, Billy 6, 12, 28, 102, 114–115, 182, 184
'Crawling King Snake' 62, 106
Cream 32, 51, 58–59, 90, 100, 103, 135, 140, 156, 163, 170, 190, 204
Cromwellian, The (club) 49
Cropper, Steve 81, 133
Crosby, David 35
'Crosstown Traffic' 82–88, 156–157, 171, 193
Crudup, Arthur "Big Boy" 170
The Cry Of Love 47
Crystals, The 40–42
Cugat, Xavier 130
Cullum, Jamie 211
'Cult Of Personality' 201
Cure, The 212
Curtis, King 17, 20, 199

'Daddy Rollin' Stone' 21
dance
  central place in African-American culture 12
  inspired by animal kingdom 30
  inspired by automation and machines 30–31
  variety of steps in African-American culture 11
Dancing In Your Head 195
D'Apres Le Livre Des Morts Tibetain 34
Davies, Cyril 51–52
Davis, Betty 190
Davis, Miles 29, 40, 190–193, 195, 197, 203, 210
Davis, Spencer 33
'Daytripper' 102
Dee, Joey & The Starliters 24
Defunkt 201
Deep Purple 193
Definition Of A Circle 100
Diddley, Bo 12, 57
Dillards, The 105
'Dirty Mind' 99
Dixon, Willie 190
Dizzee (Rascal) 1
Dobells 104
'Dolly Dagger' 48, 87
Domino, Fats 24, 107
Donegan, Lonnie 57
Donovan 169
'Don't Be Cruel' 21
Doors, The 106
'Doriella Du Fontaine' 47, 199
Down On Stovall's Plantation 32
'Downtown' 51
'The Dragon From Carlisle' 102
Dragon, The (pub) 103
Drake, Nick 53
Drayton, Ronnie 201
'Drifter's Escape' 164

'Drifting' 157
'Drivin' South' 65
duckwalk (dance) 12
Ducret, Marc 148
Dupree, Cornell 102
Dunbar, Aynsley 50
Durham, Eddie 148
Dylan, Bob 34, 70, 104, 116, 120, 144, 146, 156, 170, 172
Dyson, D.K. 202

"Eager" Beaver, Fitzgerald 14
Earth Abides 168
Earth Blues (album) 33
'Earth Blues' 47, 174
'Easy Blues' 174
Edwards, Jimmy 54
Elbert, Donnie 91
'Eleanor Rigby' 201
Electric Flag, The 104, 188
Electric Lady studios 72, 102
Electric Ladyland 46, 71, 76, 82, 87, 104, 153, 155, 177
Electric Mud 188
Ellerbie, Charles 195
Ellington, Duke 1, 9, 89, 146, 191, 194
Ellis, Pee Wee 210
Emerick, Geoff 103
Eno, Brian 141
E.S.P. 191
Etchingham, Kathy 2, 5, 101, 126, 161
Evans, Gil 193
Experience (World Saxophone Quartet album) 195–196
Experience, The 22, 27, 29, 36, 49, 56–57, 61, 73, 79, 85–86, 103, 113–114, 140, 165, 182, 185, 189, 191, 193, 204
'EXP' 102, 150
Expressway To Your Skull 174, 213
'Eyes And Imagination' 169
'Ezy Rider' 47

Fab Four 21, 23
Faithfull, Marianne 171
Fame, Georgie & The Blue Flames 84
Fat Mattress 103
Father of the Blues (W.C. Handy) 121
feedback
  concise use 77, 142, 144
  early experiments 20
Fender Stratocaster 126, 141, 201
'Fight For Your Mind' 146
Filles De Kilimanjaro 191
'Fingertips' 26–27
Finlayson, Don 56
Finnigan, Mike 87
'Fire' 32, 73, 88, 93, 171, 173
Fisk Jubilee Singers 206
Fiuczynski, David 203
Four Tops 11
Fox & Firkin 211
'Fox Chase' 146
'Foxy Lady' 73, 76, 97–98, 143, 171
Frank, Paul 189–190
Franklin, Aretha 47
Franti, Michael 203
Freak Out! 104
Fredericks, Harry St. Clair 105
'Freedom' 48
'Freight Train' 213
Fresh Start 189
'The Friendly Ranger At Clontarf Castle' 208
Fuller, Jesse 213
Funkadelic 181, 188, 200, 202
fuzzface (guitar pedal) 144

Gaumount, Dominique 192
Gaye, Marvin 166
Generation (club) 71–72
Gentlemen Prefer Blondes 39
'Georgia Blues' 174
Ghetto Fighters, The 47
ghosting (film and music industry) 37
Gibbs, Melvin 204
Gilfema 212
'Give Me The Night' 130
Glover, Corey 201
'God Bless The Child' 157
'God Save The Queen' 138
Goldmark, Goldy 21
Goodman, Benny 54
Gordy, Berry 75
Grant, Eddy 207

Grateful Dead 55
Greek mythology 167, 170–171
'Green Onions' 81
Green, Grant 128
Green, Peter 125
Greenlee, Sam 166
Griffin, Jeff 63
Gudme, Niels Olaf 132
Guns 'n' Roses 203
Guy, Buddy 71, 123
'Gypsy Eyes' 87, 92, 118, 164, 171, 193
Gypsy, Sun & Rainbows 114

Hall, Rick 47
Hallyday, Johnny 56
Handel, George Frideric 3, 101
Handy, W.C. 109–110, 112–113, 121, 191, 213
'The Hard Blues' 197
Hard, Scotty 205
Harper, Ben 146–147, 211
Harper, Billy 194
Harriet Tubman (band) 204–205
Harris, Jerome 202
Hatzigeorgiou, David 211
Havens, Richie 71
Haverly's Genuine Colored Minstrels 206
'Have You Ever Been (To Electric Ladyland)' 168, 173
Hawkins, Coleman 54
Haynes, Roy 85
Hazell, Eddie 188
Head Over Heels 190
'Hear My Train A Comin' 47, 118–119, 158–159, 214
heckling 160
Hemphill, Julius 196–198
Henderson, Fletcher 9
Hendrix, Al (father of Jimi) 15
Hendrix, Margie 41
Henry, Pierre 34
'He's A Rebel' 40–41
'He's Sure The Boy I Love' 42
'Hey Joe', 43, 58, 79, 91, 140
hippies, 131
'Hold On I'm Coming' 75
Holiday, Billie 157, 172
hoodoo 170
Hooker, John Lee 62, 106, 158, 170
Hopkins, Lightnin' 33, 117
'Hound Dog' 126
Houston, Cissy (Sweet Inspirations) 71
Howlin' Wolf 28, 62, 156, 170
Hoyt Axton 105
Hughes, Langston 177
Humperdinck, Englebert 55
Hunt, William Holden 3
'Hush Now/Flashing' 43–44
Hustler's Convention 199
Hutchings, Shabaka 209

I Am A Man 204
'(I Can't Get No) Satisfaction' 75
Iceberg Slim 172
'I Don't Live Today' 73
'I Got You (I Feel Good)' 75, 97
'I Got My Mojo Working' 51
'If 6 Was 9' 73, 93–96, 118, 151, 156, 158, 166–167, 180
Ikettes, The 91
'(I'm Your) Hoochie Coochie Man' 62–65, 68, 95
Irwin, Suzie & Big Dee 91
Isle of Wight festival 32, 182, 192
Isley Brothers, 17–19, 22, 26, 30, 40, 53, 74, 92
Isley, Ernie 189
Isley, Kelly 22
Isley, Ronald 17, 23–26, 155
'It's All Over Now' 24
'It's Your Thing' 92
'I Was Made To Love Her' 70
'Izabella' 47, 92, 120

Jackson Jr, Al 87
Jackson, Michael 13
Jackson, Ronald Shannon & The Decoding Society 201, 203
Jagger, Mick 22, 41, 163, 171, 208
James, Elmore 33, 123, 162
James, Etta 47, 210
'Jammin' 70
jam session 65, 68
Jazz Café (London) 210
'Jean-Pierre' 210
Jeffrey, Michael 43, 72

'Jimmy's Blues' 174
'Johnny B. Goode' 15, 210
Johnson, Robert 116, 125, 170, 176, 213
Jones, Brian 71, 208
Jones, Daryl 203
Jones, Elvin 85
Jones, Quincy 100
Jones, Ronnie 53
Joplin, Janis 55, 105, 187
Jordan, Louis 34
'Just Plain Funk' 197

Karismaki brothers 2
Kawasaki, Ryo 194
'Keep Your Hands Off Her' 51
Keita, Salif 202
Kern & Hammerstein 162
Kerr, Deborah 39
Kerr, John 39
Kessel, Barney 128
'Killing Floor' 62, 68
Kind Of Blue 191
The King And I 39
King, Albert 123, 128
King, B.B. 71, 123–124, 155
King, Ben E. 180–181
King, Freddie 20, 123
King Casuals 13
King, Dr Martin Luther Jr 71, 177, 198
Kinsey, Donald (Kinsey Report) 201
Kirk, Rahsaan Roland 108, 195
Knight, Curtis 17, 43, 45–46, 48, 64–65, 68
Kool Herc 147
Kooper, Al 71
Korner, Alexis 50–54, 62–64
Kramer, Eddie 6, 47, 72–73, 78, 82, 94, 114, 129, 136–137, 149–154, 205
Kravitz, Lenny 203
KRS-One 140

Lake, Oliver 196
'Land Of A 1000 Dances' 12, 79, 85
Last Poets, The 47, 199
'Laundromat Blues' 31
Leadbelly 33, 50, 89, 158
'Leaving Memphis, Frisco Bound' 213
Lecuona, Ernesto 130–131, 140
Led Zeppelin 190, 193
Lee, Arthur & Love 105
Lee, Bill 39
Lee, Jerry 114
Leeds, Gary (Walker Brothers) 94
Lennox, Annie 135, 209
'Let Me Have Some' 11
'Let's Pretend We're Married' 200
Lewis, J.T. 204–205
'Like A King' 146
Linx, David 211
'Little Baby Swastika' 209
Little Milton 210
'Little Miss Lover' 73, 87, 92, 120, 171, 189, 193
'Little Miss Strange' 104, 155
'Little Miss Wingate' 209
Little Richard 9, 12, 17–18, 30–32, 53, 74, 90, 155, 165, 200
Little Stevie Wonder 26–27, 69
'Little Wing' 120, 133–138, 153, 157, 179, 196, 200, 212
Living Colour 201–202, 205, 209
Logic, DJ 202
Lonely Ones 85
'Long Hot Summer Night' 104
'Look Over Yonder' 174
Loueke, Lionel 212
Love, Darlene 40, 44
'Love Or Confusion' 57
'Love's Parody' 204
'Loverman' 164
Loving Kind, The 85
Lovin' Spoonful, The 105
Lucas, Reggie 192
Lulu 58, 103, 140
Luther, Martin 203
Lynott, Phil 208–209
Lyttleton, Humphrey 57

Mabley, Moms 29
'Machine Gun' 113–115, 129, 183–184, 193, 196
Magic Mountain festival 90
Magic Sam 123
Magical Mystery Tour 103
'Manic Depression' 164
Mann, Manfred 59

'Mannish Boy' 196
Marquee, The (club) 51–52
Martin, George 103, 149
mashed potato (dance) 11
Mason, Dave 71, 84
Mason, Konda 202
Material 201
Matthews, Brian 59
Mattox, Matt 39
'Maybellene' 15
May, Theresa 207–208
'May This Be Love' 78–79, 93, 173
Mayer, Roger 127, 144
Mayfield, Curtis 133, 137, 200, 203
McCartney, Paul 101
McClain, Marlon "The Magician" 122
McDaniels, Eugene 188
McDermott, John 46
McDuff, "Brother" Jack 128–130
McGhee, Brownie 170
McHugh, Jimmy 21
McLaughlin, John 190–192
'Mellow Yellow' 169
Melly, George 57
'Memphis Blues' 109
'Mess Around' 106
'Message Of Love' 73
Mezzrow, Mezz 66
Miami Pop Festival 143
Midsomer Murders (television series) 206
Miles, Buddy 47, 71, 76, 104, 114–115, 155, 174, 213
Miles, Ron 205
Milestones 40, 191
Miley, Bubber 146
Mills, Aaron 211
Mitchell, Joni 71, 172
Mitchell, Louis 206
Mitchell, Mitch 6, 36, 49, 61, 63, 69, 71, 73, 78, 83–85, 88, 102, 112, 114, 134, 136, 139, 149, 152, 182
'Mojo Man' 47–48
'Money In The Pocket' 84
Monk, Thelonious 24
Monkees, The 56
Monroe, Marilyn 39
Montague, Chris 124, 141–142, 145, 147, 209
Monterrey festival 32, 90, 190
Montgomery, Wes 87, 128
Morris, Sarah Jane 135
Morrison, Toni 213
Moses, Leonard 13
Moses, Wilma 198–199
'Moses Smote The Water' 62, 158
'Mother Popcorn' (song and dance) 12
Mothers of Invention 104–105
Motown 11, 75, 154
Mountain 190
MTV 200
Muddy Waters 53, 62, 95, 103, 106, 117, 156, 170–171, 188, 196
Mulligan, Terry David 85, 107
Murray, David 195–196, 198
Muscle Shoals studio 47
'My Favourite Things' 120

Nancarrow, Conlon 202
Nanton, Joe "Tricky Sam" 146
Native American heritage (Hendrix) 131, 134, 164–165, 178
Ndegeocello, Meshell 203
needle time 57
négritude 198–199
Nelson, Tracy 105
Nemeth, Ferenc 212
Neville, Morgan 42
'Night Bird Flying' 133
Night Train (television show) 10
Nix, Bern 195
Nixon, Marni 39–40
'No Particular Place To Go' 15
Notations of Soul 195
Nuriddin, Jalal Mansur 47, 199

octavia (guitar pedal) 144
Odetta 172
'Ol' Man River' 162
Olympic studio 94, 102, 149, 153
'One On Eight' 128–129

Page, Jimmy 125
Pair Extraordinaire, The 105
'Papa's Got A Brand New Bag' 97, 207
The Parable Of Arable Land 104
Parker, Charlie 132

Parliament (band) 60, 188, 211
Peterson, Lucky 210–211
Pickett, Wilson 17, 79, 85, 155
'Pinetop's Boogie Woogie' 95
Pink Floyd 206
Pitney, Gene 41
'Play That Funky Music White Boy' 210
Plummer, Christopher 39
'Poison Ivy' 16
Political Blues 196
'Politician' 190
politics (Hendrix's general view) 183
pony ride (dance) 17
popcorn (dance) 11
'Power Of Soul' 92, 178, 180–181
power trio 183, 191
PPX 43
'Preachin' The Blues' 51
Presley, Elvis 14, 21
Pretty Things 84
Prince 98–99, 200
Prince Philip, His Royal Highness 54
'Private Joy' 99
Procol Harum 82
Prototype 204
psychedelic music 106
'Psychedelic Sally' 84
'Purple Haze' 43, 73, 79, 81, 97–98, 136, 151, 156, 167, 189, 194
'Purple Rain' 200
Pye studio 149

Quality Street (confectionery) 101

Rachmaninoff 24
Radio Caroline 58
Radio Luxembourg 58
Radio One
  jingle 59, 62
  station 59
Raelettes, The 41
Rainbow Bridge 47
'Rainy Tuesday' 51
R&B From The Marquee 51
Record Plant 72, 113
Red Hot Chili Peppers 209, 211
'Red House' 111–12, 115, 177
Redding, Noel 6, 36, 49, 61, 63, 69, 71, 73, 85, 104, 112, 136, 151, 155–156
Redding, Otis 32, 47, 87,137, 156, 189, 196
'Red Rooster' 190
Reeves, Martha & The Vandellas 11
Reid, Vernon 148, 201–202, 205, 212
Remy, Tony 135, 145, 209–210
reprise/remix/return 192
'Return To Sender' 21
Revolver 103
Rhythm & Blues (album by World Saxophone Quartet) 196
rhythm & blues
  audiences 53
  character of the beat 16
  genre 60
  indignities suffered by musicians 54
  song (Hendrix at BBC) 62
  term coined 20
Ringgold, Faith 141
'Rise And Dear Demise Of The Funky Nomadic Tribes' 208
Roberts, Billy 79
Roberts, Ossie & The Sweet Boys 208
Robeson, Paul 206, 208
Robinson, Smokey & The Miracles 11, 69
rock
  Black Rock Coalition manifesto 202
  DJs discriminating against black music 200
  in the history of black music 89–90
'Rock Hard In A Funky Place' 200
'Rockin' In Rhythm' 89
Rock & Rhythm, King Of (Little Richard) 18, 89–90
Rocking Teens, The 15
Rodgers, Nile 122
Roller Trio 125
'Roll Over Beethoven' 60, 74–75
Rolling Stones 1, 22, 24, 51, 75, 90, 105, 149, 163, 203
Rollins, Sonny 132
Ronnie Scott's club, London 206, 210
'Room Full Of Mirrors' 158
Roots, The 212
Ross, Brandon 148, 204
Rotschild, Baron 54

Rovers Return (pub) 101
Royal Albert Hall 52
Run DMC 212
Rush, Otis 123

'Sad Song (Fa-Fa-Fa-Fa-Fa)' 156
Sam & Dave 9, 75, 180
Sanborn, David 194
Saturday Club 57
Saturday Skiffle Club 57–58
Scene, The (club) 72, 113
Screaming Headless Torsos 203
'Searchin' 16
Seattle 14–15
Seven Brides For Seven Brothers 39
Sgt. Pepper's Lonely Hearts Club Band 103, 149
Shades Of A Blue Orphanage 208
Shankar, Ravi 34, 55
Shapiro, Harry 50
'Shake It Baby' 95
Sharkey, Chris 125, 128, 142–44, 209
Sharp, Martin 170
Sharrock, Sonny & Linda 200
'She's Long, She's Tall, She Weeps Like A Willow Tree' 170
'She's So Fine' 155
Shepherd's Bush Empire 146
Shipton, Alyn 67
Shocking Blue 81
'Shotgun' 86, 106
Short, J.D. 170
'Shout' 75
Showtime 30, 34
Sill, Lester 41
Silver, Horace 84
Simon & Garfunkel 32
'Sing A Simple Song' 106
'Sittin' On The Dock Of The Bay' 137
Sister Rosetta Tharpe 213
Six Five Special 57
Sketches Of Spain 191
Skid Row (band) 209
skiffle 57
Skillings, Muzz 201
Skin aka Deborah Dyer 209
Skunk Anansie 209
Sly & The Family Stone 55, 92, 104, 106, 108, 188, 190, 203
Smash Hits 46
'Smile In A Wave' (Theme From Jack Johnson) 203
Smith, Clara 31
Smith, Clarence "Pinetop" 95, 106
Smith, Fred 87
Smith, Jimmy 62, 87
Smith, Norman "Hurricane" 103
Smith, Wadada Leo 205
Soho, central London 51–52
Son House 51, 109
soul (music/culture) 178–181
Soul Deuce 9
'Soul Man' 180
Soul Party 91
'Soul Power' 179
South Pacific 39
Southern Syncopated Orchestra 206
'Spanish Castle Magic' 73, 88, 130–131, 149, 168, 179, 191, 212
Speakeasy, The (club) 49
Spector, Phil 40, 44–45, 56
Spider Sam 170
The Spook Who Sat By The Door 166
Squarepusher 124
Starr, Edwin, 91
Starr, Ringo 101
'Star-Spangled Banner' 138–142, 151, 183
Stax records 180, 189
'Stepping Stone' 173–174
Stevens, Cat 55
Stewart, George R. 168
Stickells, Gerry 29
'St. Louis Blues' 109
'Stone Free' 78, 91, 156, 163, 171
Stone Raiders 203
'Stormy Monday' 51
Stranglers, The 212
Subotnick, Morton 202
Suite Espanola 130–131, 140
Sullivan, Ed 21, 49
Sultan, Juma 114, 139
Summerise, Bob 14
'Sunshine Of Your Love' 58, 103, 140
'Superstition' 210

Supremes, The 10
'S.U.V. S.O.B' 203
'Sweet Angel' 102
Sweet Inspirations 71, 104

Tacuma, Jamaladeen 196
Taj Mahal 105–106, 188
Talbert, Henry 95
Tales Of Captain Black 195
'Talkin' Out The Side Of Your Neck' 211
Tate, Greg 202
Taylor, Otis 100
Tchaikovsky 74
Temple, Johnnie 170
Temptations, The 11
Terminator X 147
The Terror End Of Beauty 205
Terry, Sonny 146
'That Lady' 188–189
'Them Changes' 76–77, 155
Thin Lizzy (album) 208
Thin Lizzy (band) 208
'Third Stone From The Sun' 73, 82, 132, 168
Thomas, Carla 87
Thomas, Fred & The Tomcats 15
Thomas, Irma 24
Threadgill, Henry 204
'Time Is On My Side' 24
'Tobacco Road' 206
'Tomorrow Never Knows' 103
Tony Williams Lifetime 191, 204
Top Gear 69
Top Notes, The 40
Toussaint, Allen 24
Toussaint, Jean 209
Townshend, Pete 2
'The Tracks Of My Tears' 11
Traffic 84, 149
'Tramp' 87
tremolo arm 140
Trio VD 125
The Trip 104
Troika 124
Troutman, Roger 122
True-May, Brian 206
Truth To Power 203
Turner, Ike & The Ikettes 41, 172
Turner, Ike & Tina 16–17
Turner, Tina 23, 31, 172
Turrentine, Stanley 87
Turtles, The 105
Twenty Something 211
twist (dance) 12, 24
'Twist And Shout' (song and dance) 22, 25–26, 40

Ulmer, James "Blood" 195–196, 201, 204
underground railroad 204
'Up From The Skies' 88, 168, 194

Vagabonds Of The Western World 208
Valente Catarina 130
Velez, Jerry 114
Velvetones, The 15
'Venus' 82
Vietnam 138, 182
'Villanova Junction Blues' 174
Vincent Gene 57
Vivid 201
'Voodoo Child (Slight Return)' 82, 117, 127, 145–147, 170, 193, 198, 210
'Voodoo Chile' 73, 113, 115, 118–119, 125, 171, 179, 193

Wailers (Tacoma) 15
Waithe, Keith 211
'Walk This Way' 212
Walker Brothers 55, 94
Walker, Junior 10, 20, 86, 106
Walker, T-Bone 20, 90, 123, 155
Walker, Wilf 208
wammy bar 142
War (band) 206
War Heroes 47
Wareham, Pete 209
Washington, Geno 206–207
Watkiss, Cleveland 209
The Weary Blues 177
Webster, Ben 195
'Wedding In Sarajevo' 203
'We Gotta Live Together' 106
Welcome To The Cruel World 146
West Side Story 39–40
What America Needs 190
'What Is Soul?' 181
'What's Going On' 166

'When My Sugar Walks Down The Street' 21
'Whipping Boy' 146
White African 100
White Rabbit 130
'A Whiter Shade Of Pale' 82
Who, The 59
'Who's That Lady' 189
'Who Knows' 197
'Who Says A Funk Band Can't Play Rock' 200
Wild Cherry 210
Wiley 1
The Will To Live 146
Williams, Big Joe 117
Williamson, Sonny Boy 33
Wilson, Jackie 155
'The Wind Cries Mary' 43, 133, 137, 157, 161, 186, 204, 211
Windrush scandal 207
Winwood, Steve 71, 113, 118
Womack, Bobby 24
Wonder, Stevie 200, 210–211
Wood, Chris 71
Wood, Natalie 39–40
Woodstock 55, 90, 111, 138, 143
World Saxophone Quartet 195–198

'Yakety Yak' 16
Yardbirds, The 51, 90
Yes 202
Yesterday, Today, Tomorrow 41
'Young Blood' 16
Young, Larry 191

Zappa, Frank 202
Zoot Money 206
ZZ Top 193

Lightning Source UK Ltd.
Milton Keynes UK
UKHW021956130521
383680UK00003B/68